TO TAME A DUKE

She is Lily Hawthorne—the only daughter of a Boston tavern owner, a delicate, raven-haired beauty with sapphire eyes and a daring spirit. But as the war of 1812 rages on, few know that she is also the Gilded Lily, Boston's most notorious spy-catcher . . . a patriotic young woman who daily risks her life to aid her country's cause.

He is James Armstrong, the fourteenth Duke of Kinross—a rakishly handsome British nobleman determined to avenge his older brother's death at the hands of the Americans. He vows he will not rest until he has tracked down the one most responsible. But when James finally corners the Gilded Lily, he receives a huge shock, for his quarry is no rough-hewn soldier but a foolhardy young woman who refuses to be cowed. Now, lovely Lily is his prisoner to do with as he wishes. Yet when James sweeps her off to his gilded English estate, captor and captive alike will find themselves battling a blazing temptation . . . one that could endanger their lives, even as it joins their warring hearts. . . .

BOOK YOUR PLACE ON OUR WEBSITE AND MAKE THE READING CONNECTION!

We've created a customized website just for our very special readers, where you can get the inside scoop on everything that's going on with Zebra, Pinnacle and Kensington books.

When you come online, you'll have the exciting opportunity to:

- View covers of upcoming books
- Read sample chapters
- Learn about our future publishing schedule (listed by publication month *and author*)
- Find out when your favorite authors will be visiting a city near you
- Search for and order backlist books from our online catalog
- Check out author bios and background information
- Send e-mail to your favorite authors
- Meet the Kensington staff online
- Join us in weekly chats with authors, readers and other guests
- Get writing guidelines
- AND MUCH MORE!

Visit our website at
http://www.zebrabooks.com

TO TAME A DUKE

Patricia Grasso

ZEBRA BOOKS
Kensington Publishing Corp.
http://www.zebrabooks.com

ZEBRA BOOKS are published by

Kensington Publishing Corp.
850 Third Avenue
New York, NY 10022

All Kensington titles, imprints and distributed lines are available at special quantity discounts for bulk purchases for sales promotion, premiums, fund-raising, educational or institutional use.

Special book excerpts or customized printings can also be created to fit specific needs. For details, write or phone the office of the Kensington Special Sales Manager: Kensington Publishing Corp., 850 Third Avenue, New York, NY 10022. Attn. Special Sales Department. Phone: 1-800-221-2647.

First Printing: July 2001
10 9 8 7 6 5 4 3 2 1

Printed in the United States of America

Prologue

Boston, September 1804

"Great guardian angel, please intercede with the Father to help my mother recover from this difficult birth."

Ten-year-old Lily Hawthorne stood in the kitchen doorway of her father's tavern, the Four Winds. She took two steps forward onto the bayside of Howell's Wharf and inhaled deeply, savoring the scent of saltwater and the warmth of the sun upon her face.

Brushing several wisps of ebony hair away from her face, Lily gazed at one of her favorite sights, Boston Harbor, and tried to banish the hopelessness settling in the pit of her stomach. Billowy puffs of white clouds dotted the blue horizon, ending only where the sky and the water became one. She heard the shrieking cries of seagulls and shifted her gaze to watch them diving to the top of the water and then flying off again. Overhead, a large squadron of Canadian geese were migrating south in military formation.

Worry troubled Lily's delicate features and an aching sadness filled her chest, making breathing almost painful. Hopeless desperation weighed heavily upon her, and she struggled against the tears threatening to spill.

Weeping would only worry her mother. Though she wanted to throw herself down and cry forever, Lily refused to succumb to instinct. Her appearing with tearstained cheeks in her mother's chamber would only add to her mother's worries.

Her wonderful mother was dying.

Lily sighed raggedly. Her heart railed against what her mind knew to be true. Her mother was dying, bleeding to death from delivering her second child, a son.

She already had an older half brother, Lily thought. So why had her parents needed another child? Her mother's life for her baby brother's didn't seem like an even exchange. But there was nothing to be done for it now, only await the end.

Lily closed her sapphire blue eyes and whispered fervently, "Great guardian angel, hear my prayer and save my mother from death's snare. I'll do anything if you intercede with the Father on her behalf."

Would God be offended by her trying to bargain with Him? Lily wondered, a sudden chill of apprehension running down her spine. What if He punished her by taking away her father and half brother, too?

"God, I'm terribly sorry for trying to bargain with You," Lily whispered, unwilling to take chances with her loved ones' lives. "I only meant for you to save my mother. That is, if doing so wouldn't upset Your grand scheme."

"I heard your mother was dying," said a voice behind her.

Lily whirled around to see Hortensia MacDugal, her personal nemesis, standing there. The only daughter of a tavern owner on the next wharf and the woman who was acting as her mother's midwife, Hortensia was much taller than Lily even though they were the same age. Lily had always envied the other girl's blond hair and cornflower blue eyes, but now she envied the fact that Hortensia's mother was in no danger of dying. Compared to losing her mother, being born with black hair seemed insignificant.

Lily stared at the other girl. She supposed the blackest day in her life wouldn't have been complete without Hortensia showing up.

"What do you want?" Lily asked.

"I'm waiting for my mother," Hortensia answered.

"She'll be delayed a while longer," Lily told her, glancing toward the kitchen door. "You might as well go home."

Hortensia wore a mulish expression. "I'll wait."

Suspicious about the other girl's reason for loitering, Lily narrowed her gaze on her and remarked, "I've never known you to cling to your mother like this."

Hortensia gave her a knowing smile. "I heard that Bradley Howell is inside with Seth."

So that was it. Hortensia had a fondness for her brother's well-to-do friend, the only son of the owner of Howell's Wharf.

Lily rolled her eyes. "I should have known there was another reason."

"Bradley is so handsome," Hortensia gushed. "I'm going to marry him someday."

"Go away, Hortensia, and bother someone else."

"Are you jealous?"

Lily lifted her nose into the air and said, "I could

never be jealous of a tart like you who, as everyone knows, smells like low tide."

"Why, you . . ." Hortensia stepped forward with her hands clenched at her sides.

"Lily!"

Turning around, Lily saw her brother standing in the kitchen doorway with Bradley Howell. "Is it time?" she asked.

Fifteen-year-old Seth nodded, a grim expression on his face. With a heavy heart and leaden feet, Lily walked toward the kitchen door.

As she neared him, Bradley stepped out of her way and whispered, "Be brave, Lily."

She nodded, acknowledging his words.

From behind her, she heard Hortensia say, "Oh, Bradley, could you possibly walk me back to my own wharf?"

"I'd be honored," he answered.

"May the saints forgive me," Lily muttered, brushing past her brother, "but I do despise that girl."

Lily and her brother walked through the kitchen into the tavern's common room. The silence in the usually bustling chamber weighed oppressively on her, reminding her that her mother was dying.

Feeling as though she was living in a nightmare, Lily slowed her pace as they started up the stairs. If she didn't go inside the bedchamber to bid farewell to her mother, perhaps her mother wouldn't die. No, she knew that wasn't true.

"I don't want to go inside," Lily said, hesitating outside her parents' bedchamber.

"Are you afraid?" Seth asked, crouching down to be at eye level with her.

"You know better than that," Lily replied. "I'm not afraid of anything."

"You are afraid of the dark," he reminded her.

Lily shook her head. "No, the dark merely worries me."

"Are you worried now?" Seth asked.

"Yes."

Her truthful admission brought the hint of a smile to his lips. "Your mother has something to give you before she—"

Knowing what he'd been about to say, Lily bit her bottom lip.

"Are you going to cry?"

Lily shook her head, not daring to speak lest she start weeping.

"Crying will only upset her," Seth told her. "Can you be brave for her sake?"

Lily squared her shoulders, lifted her chin a notch, and nodded. "I will do anything to ease her passing."

"That's a good girl," Seth said, touching her shoulder. He stood then and opened the door for her.

Lily stepped inside. With the shutters closed, the room was dark. Mrs. MacDugal, Hortensia's mother, stood in one corner of the chamber and held the infant. Her father sat on the edge of the bed beside her mother.

"Emmett, she's here," her mother said, glancing toward where Lily stood near the door.

"Very well, Sarah," her father said, rising from his perch on the edge of the bed. He looked at Lily and said, "Sit here. Mother has been waiting for you."

Lily crossed the chamber and sat in her father's place. Tears welled up in her sapphire eyes as she looked at her mother. Hopelessness and desperation filled her until she felt that she was drowning in those emotions.

"Please don't cry," her mother said, and gave her a wan smile. "None of us really dies. Our spirits move to a better place, and our memory lingers on in the hearts of our loved ones."

Her mother's gentle tone and words conspired against Lily. Momentarily losing control, she grabbed her mother's hand and cried, "Don't leave me, Mama."

"God is calling me home," came the simple reply.

"Tell Him to wait!"

Her words brought a smile to her mother's lips. "No one can order the Almighty. Besides, I'm so very tired."

Lily studied her mother's face, consigning it to memory. Her mother did appear as if she needed a long rest. That realization made Lily feel guilty about trying to keep her mother with her. She knew it was selfish, but how could she live without seeing her mother's face or feeling her embrace? How could she get along without her mother's loving guidance?

"My only regret is not seeing you grow into womanhood," her mother said, as if she knew her daughter's thoughts. Then, "I have a gift for you."

Lily watched her mother remove the necklace she always wore, a necklace passed down to her from her own mother, and her mother before her. On a delicate gold chain hung an unusual cross of gold adorned with the Greek letters *alpha* and *omega*.

Beckoning her closer, her mother set the chain of gold over her head, and it fell into place around her neck. Almost reverently, Lily reached up to touch the cross, her mother's legacy to her.

"*Alpha* and *omega* mean the beginning and the end-ing," her mother told her. "That which is, which was, and which is yet to be."

"I don't understand," Lily said, puzzled by her mother's words.

Sarah Hawthorne smiled lovingly at her daughter. "You do not need to understand," she told her. "Only remember that your own true love will be the first and the last for you. *Alpha* and *omega.*"

Lily fingered the cross and announced with all the confidence of youth, "That will be Bradley Howell, of course."

"I want you to name your new brother," her mother said, turning the subject away from true love. "Then I'll let you hold him."

"Today is the feast of Saint Michael," Lily said with-out hesitation. "He must be named Michael in honor of Michael the Archangel."

After glancing at her husband, who nodded in agreement, Sarah Hawthorne turned a somber expres-sion on her daughter. "I need you to take my place with him. Will you do that for me?"

"I'll guard him with my life," Lily promised, proud to be chosen for such a trusted position. Raw, aching emotion caught in her voice when she added, "I'll tell him about you, Mama. I won't let him forget his mother."

"You're a good girl." She looked at Mrs. MacDugal, who gingerly placed the infant into Lily's arms, saying, "Hold his head steady."

With the baby cradled in her arms, Lily studied his face for a long moment and then looked at her mother in surprised confusion, exclaiming, "His eyes are slanted."

"Your brother is a special gift from God," her mother said, confusing her even more.

Lily looked from her mother to her brother. She failed to see anything different about him except his slightly slanted eyes. "Why is he special?" she asked.

Her mother was silent for a long moment and then answered, "Children like Michael make God smile. . . ."

One

Boston, November 1812

"Monkey, monkey. Drooling, slant-eyed monkey!"

Those faint words floated through the air like a whisper on the breeze to Lily, who had paused in the kitchen doorway of her father's tavern to enjoy the unusual November warmth. She stepped forward onto the bayside of Howell's Wharf and turned her face to the sun.

Indian summer, she thought with a smile. Her favorite moments in the year's cycle. God had certainly given her a wonderful birthday gift.

Cocking her head to one side, Lily listened for the all-too-familiar chanting but heard only silence. She relaxed against the door frame, her favorite place to daydream, and conjured in her mind's eye the handsome image of Bradley Howell, the man she intended to marry once the war ended. Too bad the war had interrupted her plans.

Lily fingered her necklace, her mother's legacy to her. On a delicate gold chain hung the cross of gold adorned with Greek letters. *Alpha* and *omega* meant the beginning and the ending. That was what her mother had told her. The man who was the first and the last would be her own true love. She didn't know how her mother could possibly have known that, but she never questioned the veracity of those words.

"Great guardian angel, please make Bradley Howell the first and the last for me," Lily whispered a prayer. After a moment, she added, "And, if it isn't too much trouble, let him remember that today is my birthday."

Brushing several wisps of ebony hair away from her face, Lily gazed at the familiar sight of Boston Harbor. A singsong chanting reached her ears.

Lily lifted her head, as if sensing danger. And then she heard it again, louder this time, a half-dozen children's voices in front of the tavern.

"Monkey, monkey. Drooling, slant-eyed monkey!"

Lily ran down the alley behind the wharf's various businesses. Reaching the end, she raced around the corner in time to hear Hortensia MacDugal say, "The devil touched you, Michael Hawthorne. You are the devil's spawn."

Several of the children started chanting, "Devil's spawn . . . devil's spawn . . . devil's spawn!"

Lily burst upon the scene just as one of the boys picked up a stone and raised his arm to throw it at her brother. She grabbed the boy's wrist, forced him to drop the stone, and then whirled him around.

"You're hurting me," the boy cried.

"You're lucky you didn't throw that stone, Douglas MacDugal," Lily told the twelve-year-old. "I would have been forced to break both of your wrists." She pushed him away, ordering, "Get back to your own wharf or you'll be sorry."

The group of children scattered. Only Hortensia MacDugal stood her ground.

"Don't ever touch my brother again," Hortensia ordered.

Lily wasn't frightened by the other girl. She gave her a look of contempt and said, "You horse-faced—"

Without warning, Hortensia slapped Lily hard and pushed her to the ground. In one swift movement, Lily leaped to her feet and drew the small dagger she kept in a leather garter strapped to her leg.

Hortensia MacDugal looked at the dagger and then ran off the wharf, screaming to anyone who would listen, "Lily Hawthorne is going to murder me."

"I only wish that witch would stand still long enough for me to carve her up," Lily muttered, returning her dagger to its sheath.

She heard her eight-year-old brother laughing and turned to him with a smile. "How did you like the entertainment?" she asked, making him laugh louder.

"I liked when you pulled your dagger," Michael answered. "Boy, was she ever surprised."

"Wipe your chin," Lily said, closing the distance between them. "Keep your tongue inside your mouth, and remember to keep your mouth closed when you're not talking."

Michael wiped the bit of drool from his chin on the sleeve of his shirt. Lily put her arm around him and drew him toward a pile of lobster traps.

When the two of them sat down, Michael patted her arm. "Sister, why don't the others play with me?" he asked, looking at her through sapphire blue eyes that resembled her own.

Lily gazed at her brother's open mouth and slightly slanted blue eyes. *They don't want to play with you because you're different,* she wanted to say but remained silent. Most of the children mirrored their parents' ignorance about her brother's impediment. Others, like Hortensia MacDugal, enjoyed being cruel. A few might even believe he'd been touched by the devil at birth. How could she explain such meaningless hatred to her brother?

"Don't you know the answer?" Michael asked.

"I know the answers to every question, even the ones that haven't been asked yet," Lily told him in a lofty tone of voice, making him smile.

"Then what is the answer?" he asked.

Lily realized he wasn't going to let her sidestep his question this time and decided that her brother was smarter than everyone assumed. "The others don't play with you because their parents are afraid," she began, searching for words that wouldn't hurt his feelings. "They can see that you are different from them and don't understand you."

A puzzled look appeared on his face. "How am I different?"

"Something happened when you were born," Lily told him. "That makes you special."

"I don't want to be special," he whined. "I want to be the same."

"I know you do," Lily said, pulling him against the side of her body. "We'll always be together, though, won't we? Wipe your chin."

Michael nodded and wiped the drool from his chin. "Tell me the story, Sister."

"I named you Michael because you were born on Saint Michael's Day," Lily said, relieved to change the subject. "Saint Michael is an archangel. Do you remember what he did?"

Michael grinned. "He fought Lucifer and threw

him out of heaven. I wish I could remember every word of the story like you do."

"Remembering what I read is a special gift," Lily told him. "Very few people have that ability."

"I wish I could," her brother repeated. "Then the others would like me."

"You have your own special gift," Lily said.

"What is it?"

"You make God smile," she answered, echoing her mother's dying words. "Your joy for life makes everyone smile."

Lily felt an insistent tugging on her heartstrings when her brother looked in the direction the children had run and said, "Not the others."

Lily opened her mouth to reply but stopped when she heard a voice say, "And here's my little wharf rat."

With a smile lighting her whole expression, Lily turned to see twenty-three-year-old Bradley Howell, leading his horse onto the wharf, and her half brother Seth. "Gentlemen should never refer to ladies as rats," she chided him.

"Then how about Lady Rodent?" Seth teased. He winked at her and added, "Come with me, Michael."

Lily blushed when Bradley sat beside her on the vacated lobster trap. Lord, but she suffered from hot goose bumps whenever he was near.

Is this love? Lily wondered, casting him a sidelong glance. With his sandy brown hair and warm brown eyes, Bradley Howell was irresistibly attractive. She knew there were other young women who gazed at him longingly, like she did.

"I hear you've been practicing with your last-resort dagger," Bradley said with an amused smile. "I knew you'd be an apt student."

Lily smiled jauntily. "I do believe you saw Hortensia recently." She lost her smile when she added, "I wish those children would stop taunting Michael."

"Children can be cruel," Bradley agreed. "I have no doubt that Michael will survive as long as you champion his cause."

Lily watched the people walking past the wharf. She sighed and said, "I wish we could escape these people."

"You will escape when the war ends and we marry," Bradley told her. He stared down at her for a long moment and then said, "Seth told me about your special gift." He pulled a parchment from inside his waistcoat, passed it to her, and ordered, "Read this."

Lily felt like screaming in frustration. Her brother had promised never to tell Bradley about this special gift of hers. Demonstrating her ability made her feel freakish.

Opening the parchment, Lily saw a copy of the Declaration of Independence. "I've seen this before," she said, handing it back to him without bothering to read it. Then she recited, " 'When in the course of human events it becomes necessary for one people to dissolve the political bands which have—' "

"Oh, no you don't," Bradley interrupted her. "Everyone knows the beginning. Tell me what sentence six says."

" 'But when a long train of abuses and usurpations, pursuing invariably the same object evinces a design to reduce—' "

"The second paragraph, please," Bradley said, interrupting her again.

Lily sighed. " 'We, therefore, the representatives of the United States—' "

"Who signed it?"

Lily smiled at him. "John Hancock, Button Gwinnett, Lyman Hall, George Walton, William Hooper—"

Bradley burst out laughing. "I believe your brother's boasting. That talent of yours could prove useful."

"I fail to see how remembering words on a page can be useful," Lily replied.

"Would you consider using your gift for the cause?" Bradley asked.

His question confused her. "What cause?"

"I meant for the war effort."

Helping the war effort meant spending more time with Bradley, she thought. "What would be required of me?" Lily asked.

"Seth and I would accompany you to rendezvous with our agents, who would give you coded messages to consign to memory," Bradley told her. "Then we'd deliver the message to another agent who, in turn, would pass it along to someone else. The important thing is that once you've received the message, nothing is in writing. No secrets could fall into the wrong hands."

"What about the agents who give me messages or receive them?" she asked. "How is their security guarded?"

"You are not the only one in the universe with the gift of a perfect memory," Bradley answered. "Though a woman with such a gift is rather unusual, which makes you the best choice for passing secrets within the city."

"Women are just as smart as men," Lily told him, annoyance tingeing her voice.

Bradley smiled at her. "What would you like for your birthday?" he asked.

"You remembered my birthday?" she exclaimed in pleased surprise.

"I could never forget such a momentous occasion as your eighteenth birthday," he teased her. "What would you like?"

"A kiss," Lily answered, and promptly closed her eyes.

"Ladies never ask for kisses," Bradley told her.

Lily opened her sapphire blue eyes and said, "I thought I was a wharf rat."

Bradley tapped the tip of her upturned nose playfully. "I have something for you," he said, rising from the lobster trap. He searched the satchel slung across his horse and pulled out a package.

Too large for a betrothal ring, she thought.

Bradley sat down beside her again and passed her the package, saying, "For you."

Lily gazed at him through adoring eyes. She didn't want to open the package. She wanted to freeze this moment in time and make it last forever.

"Open it," he said.

Lily untied the red ribbon fastened around it. She gasped in delight when she saw the red woolen shawl, embroidered with a gleaming metallic gold border and scattered star motif.

"I will cherish it always," Lily said, wrapping it around her shoulders. "Thank you, Bradley."

"How about that kiss?" he asked.

Needing no second invitation, Lily snapped her eyes shut and puckered her lips. She sensed him inching closer and inhaled his fresh scent. A bolt of disappointment shot through her when she felt his lips touch her cheek. Then she heard his chuckle and opened her eyes.

Bradley stood and held out his hand to help her up. He gazed down at her, and Lily felt hot goose bumps rising on her arms.

"I'll see you soon, my little wharf rat," Bradley said, and then walked away.

Lily watched him lead his horse back down the wharf to Blackstone Street. When he disappeared from sight, she retraced her steps down the alley behind the wharf's businesses. She wanted to be alone to replay the last few minutes over and over in her mind. With her new red shawl wrapped around her shoulders, Lily fingered her *alpha* and *omega* cross.

The beginning and the ending, she thought, a warm feeling coursing through her body. The first and the last.

Indeed, Bradley Howell was her own true love. He would marry her and take her away from the wharf. And Michael would come, too.

London, March 1813

"A thousand pounds a month for pocket money seems awfully meager," the woman complained in a velvety soft voice.

James Armstrong, the second son of the late Duke of Kinross, turned his dark eyes to the beautiful blonde who stood beside him. Valentina St. Leger, the twenty-year-old sister of the Earl of Bovingdon, fidgeted but returned his gaze unflinchingly. Like all beautiful women, she was greedy and shallow. These less-than-noble qualities came as no surprise to James. He knew exactly what he was getting in a wife.

"A thousand pounds is better than nothing," James told her flatly.

When she opened her mouth to argue, James held his hand up in a gesture for silence. He had no intention of arguing about money or anything else in front of an audience consisting of his mother, his two aunts, and his intended's brother, the Earl of Bovingdon.

"Please excuse us," James said, glancing at the others. "We'll return in a moment."

He grasped his betrothed's wrist in a firm but gentle grip and forced her to walk toward the salon door. If they were going to have their first argument, they would have it in the privacy of the dining room.

Behind him, James heard his mother saying, "Oh, dear. I wanted to host a ball in their honor and invite absolutely everybody. What will I do if he cancels their engagement?"

"Tess, darling, there's no chance of that happening," replied Aunt Donna. "He's burning for her. The stupid chit could have anything she wanted if she used her charms wisely."

"Don't be too sure of that," Aunt Nora disagreed. "I feel trouble brewing. Their stars are not in harmony, you know."

The Earl of Bovingdon chuckled. "Everything will be harmonious once my sister learns to keep her mouth shut," Reggie St. Leger told them. "Would any of you care to place a small wager on the outcome of their conference?"

Only silence greeted the earl's question.

James felt relieved to escape the scrutiny of the others. How insulting to be spoken of as if one couldn't hear what they were saying. He led Valentina down the length of the corridor and steered her into the dining room.

James closed the door behind them and turned to face his betrothed, ordering, "Sit down."

Valentina surveyed the enormous dining room with its forty-foot mahogany table, matching mahogany chairs, and two gigantic crystal chandeliers looming overhead. James stopped her when she moved to sit in the armchair at the head of the table.

"Over there," he ordered, pointing to one of the side chairs, determined to show her who would be the boss in their family. Without waiting for her to sit down, he sat in the chair at the head of the table.

Valentina said nothing. She wasted several minutes settling herself in the chair and then looked up at him through her fabulous green eyes.

James paused a moment before speaking, long enough to admire the alluring curve of her bosom. Was Aunt Donna correct about his feelings for Valentina? Was he burning for her? No, he had never burned for anyone in his life and didn't intend to start now. This marriage was a simple business affair, nothing more and nothing less.

Determined never to let any woman gain the upper hand with him, James refused to budge on the question of pocket money. Valentina would make do with a thousand pounds a month. The amount was non-negotiable.

Why was he even bothering to marry her? James wondered. He didn't love her. She didn't love him.

Valentina St. Leger, like most females of his acquaintance, was interested in what he could give her. As the owner of one of England's most successful shipping lines, he could afford to give her anything she wanted. But he refused to let her dictate to him.

He wanted to bed her. That much was true.

James decided that he'd proposed to Valentina because the time for marriage had arrived and she appeared to meet all his qualifications. With an impeccable bloodline, Valentina St. Leger was an exceptionally beautiful woman. Too bad she was shallow. But then, most women were painted dolls who walked and talked. Did the weaker sex ever think about anything besides gowns, jewels, money, and titles? Women had no honor, no loyalty, no brains.

Valentina pouted prettily. "A thousand pounds won't cover the cost of gowns, furs, and jewels," she complained.

"Heaven forbid you should pay for life's necessities out of your allowance," James said dryly, and then realized his sarcasm was lost on her. "Of course I will purchase whatever is needed for your continued survival."

"Oh, James, you should have told me," Valentina cried, visibly brightening. "I feel like such a fool."

James smiled indulgently at her. "A very pretty fool, though."

Valentina blushed as if on cue. James wondered how she always managed to blush or to weep at just the right moment.

When they returned to the salon, James announced, "The problem has been solved."

"A silly misunderstanding on my part," Valentina agreed.

Lady Donna looked at Lady Nora and drawled, "I thought their stars weren't in harmony."

"They aren't married yet," Lady Nora reminded her.

"I've been anticipating a large wedding," the dowager duchess said, giving her sister a censorious glare.

She looked at Valentina and asked, "You will allow us to help, won't you?"

"Of course, your grace."

Standing beside a table, James lifted the quill and handed it to Valentina, saying, "Sign first, my dear."

Valentina quickly signed the betrothal contract. She started to pass James the quill, but he stopped her.

"As your guardian, your brother should sign next," James said, delaying his own signing. He wasn't exactly looking forward to wedded bliss.

Reggie St. Leger lifted the quill out of his sister's hand and signed the document even more quickly than his sister had. Then he passed it to his future brother-in-law.

With quill in hand, James leaned over the table to sign the betrothal agreement. The door burst open, startling him. He whirled around, as did everyone else.

Twenty-five-year-old Sloane Armstrong, James's cousin, hurried into the study. After nodding curtly at the others, Sloane fixed his gaze on James. Anguish shone from his eyes and his usual smile had vanished.

"What are you doing here?" James asked. "Have you returned from the States already? Where is Hugh?"

"He's dead," Sloane said without preamble, his expression grim.

James heard his mother's cry of horror and turned to help her. His aunts gestured him away as they helped their sister to the chair in front of the hearth.

"I came directly from the ship as fast as I could," Sloane said. "Christ, I wish I wasn't the one to deliver such bad news."

"Was it an accident?" James demanded. "I want to know what happened."

"The Americans hanged his grace as a spy," Sloane burst out, his voice rising with outraged indignation.

James heard his mother's moan behind him and exploded, "I knew he shouldn't have gone. I tried to dissuade him from going. Those unscrupulous bastards extended an invitation to send a peace emissary and then hanged him!"

"I'm sorry," Sloane said, his voice choked with raw emotion. "They hanged him on Boston Common. *Death to British spies* had been written on parchment and attached to his jacket. Retrieving his body was too dangerous."

"The Americans did this to strike a blow against the English aristocracy," James said, flicking a concerned glance at his mother, who'd begun to weep quietly. "Bloody Christ! What better way to demoralize us than by executing the thirteenth Duke of Kinross, one of the oldest titles in England."

"I never liked the number thirteen," Aunt Nora spoke her thoughts.

"James, you are now the fourteenth Duke of Kinross," Valentina said, drawing everyone's attention.

"She's correct, your grace," his mother spoke for the first time.

"God's balls—" James looked at the ladies and apologized, "Pardon my language." He ran a hand through his black hair and said, "How could this have happened?"

"Boston boasts the Americans' most successful agent, the Gilded Lily, who has caused the deaths of more than a few of our agents," Sloane told him.

James fixed his black gaze on his cousin. "Why are you still living? Where were you when this happened?"

he asked. "You were supposed to guard his back. At least that's what you offered to do."

"James, how can you speak so cruelly to family?" his mother rebuked him. "I'm certain Sloane feels bad enough."

"I do blame myself," Sloane said in an aching voice. "I let Hugh go out alone and will never forgive myself."

"Hugh's death is not your fault," James relented, reaching out to touch his cousin's shoulder. "You and I are the only Armstrongs left, Sloane. This Gilded Lily is another matter."

"What are you going to do?" his cousin asked.

James could not allow his brother's death to remain unavenged. He'd get even with that colonial devil if it took a thousand years.

"I am going to roast his heart and feed it to my dogs," James answered. He turned to the others and said, "I am sailing for America to set this matter right. Only then can I continue with my own life. The Gilded Lily's days are numbered, I can promise you that."

James glanced in his mother's direction. Protest had etched itself across her face, but she knew him well enough to hold her silence.

"I'm going with you," Sloane said. "I'd like a piece of the bastard too."

"I need you here to look after my affairs," James said.

"I am partially to blame for what happened," Sloane argued. "You stay in England and I'll return to—"

James's forbidding look ended his cousin's words abruptly.

"What about me?" Valentina cried. "What about our betrothal?" She turned to her brother, ordering, "Do something."

"Be reasonable, Val. The man has lost his brother," Reggie St. Leger said. "Even if he remained in London, his grace would be in mourning."

"Delaying our betrothal won't bring his brother back from the dead," Valentina whined like a spoiled child. "Besides, his signing the contract is the only thing left to do." At that, she burst into tears.

Insensitive witch, James thought, turning his black gaze on her. He swore without apology and signed the betrothal contract. Then he flung the quill down in disgust.

"If you'll excuse me," James said to the others, "I need to prepare for my journey." Turning away, he headed for the door.

"Is it legal?" he heard Valentina ask between sobs.

"Yes, Val," Reggie St. Leger answered in a long-suffering voice.

With any luck, she'd fall in love with Sloane, James thought as he climbed the stairs to his third-floor bedchamber. The first order of business would be to settle with the Gilded Lily, and then he'd let Valentina down. He could never be content married to a woman who placed her own interests before the people she supposedly cared about. Breaking their betrothal would not be difficult. He would offer her brother a generous monetary settlement.

And then James dismissed Valentina from his thoughts and focused on the Gilded Lily. What kind of code name was that for an agent? Well, he knew one thing for certain: The Gilded Lily was a walking dead man.

Two

Boston, May 1813

"A thousand pounds seems like a piddling sum to catch me," Lily said, staring at the pamphlet that had been passed to her.

"Not you," Seth corrected her. "The Gilded Lily."

"Always guard your tongue," Bradley Howell told her. "You never know who is listening."

Lily scanned the empty kitchen of the Four Winds Tavern. "The hour is late," she said, sweeping the two men an amused look from beneath the fringe of her ebony lashes. "We three are alone."

"Breaking cover is unwise," Bradley admonished her. "No matter the circumstance."

"Brad is correct," Seth said, drawing her attention. "Remaining anonymous needs to be as natural as breathing."

"I defer to your combined wisdom," Lily said, giving them a jaunty smile. "Still, I am insulted that the lobster-backs have offered so little for Boston's notorious agent. Why, the Gilded Lily is worth ten times that. How many agents have the gift of a perfect memory?"

Her brother chuckled. "Careful, Sister. 'Pride goeth before a fall.' "

"That pamphlet is no joking matter," Bradley said, looking at her.

"Speaking within the security of the Four Winds kitchen is fine, but danger lurks outside the door," Seth said, becoming serious.

"Several people know who the Gilded Lily is," Bradley added. "I never saw such a badly kept secret."

"No faithful American would ever betray me," Lily argued.

"Tell me, little one, how can you tell the difference between a faithful American and an unfaithful one?" Bradley countered.

Lily stared into his brown eyes and shrugged. No man walked through the streets of Boston wearing a sign that proclaimed him a traitor. She knew she'd been bested in their debate. For the moment, at least.

Seth cleared his throat. "Brad and I believe the Gilded Lily should retire for a while."

"We're supposed to meet a contact tomorrow night at the Salty Dog," Lily reminded him. "The MacDugals are loyal Americans and would never betray me."

"Would you place your trust in Hortensia Mac-Dugal?" her brother teased her. "The road to marriage with Bradley would be cleared for her if you were out of the way."

Lily blushed and flicked a sidelong glance at Bradley, who appeared disgusted by the thought of marriage to Hortensia. She giggled at the sight of one of Boston's most eligible bachelors feigning a cringe.

"I'll disguise myself," she argued. "Besides, no one really knows when they've been visited by the Gilded Lily."

"The Gilded Lily will not meet that contact tomorrow night," Bradley said emphatically, the tone of his voice precluding further argument.

"She'll disappear until we return," Seth added.

"Return?" Lily echoed in surprise.

Bradley nodded. "Seth and I leave Boston tonight on an errand."

"An errand?"

"An errand for the cause," her brother explained.

"Where are you going?"

"We aren't at liberty to say," Bradley told her.

"You don't trust me?" Lily asked, surprised anger etching itself across her sweet features.

"Of course we trust you," he said. "We are sworn to silence."

Lily could accept that as long as the errand was completed quickly. After all, the war effort against the British needed the talents of the Gilded Lily. American agents were depending on her.

"When do you think you'll return?" she asked.

Bradley shrugged.

"We could be gone for several months," Seth admitted.

Lily looked in surprise from her brother to his friend. How could they leave her so abruptly? Especially Bradley, who'd professed his love for her. Did they really expect her to retire the Gilded Lily for so long a period of time?

"Take no risks," Bradley warned, as if he knew her thoughts. "Do nothing foolish while I'm gone."

Lily gave him a reluctant smile. "I promise to take no risks."

Bradley gave her a smile that made her feel weak all over. He leaned close and gave her a chaste kiss on the cheek. Then he stood and turned to her brother, asking, "Are you ready?"

Seth nodded and rose from his chair.

"You're leaving now?" she cried.

"Bolt the door behind us," Bradley ordered.

Lily stood and walked with them to the kitchen door. She felt tears welling up in her eyes.

Bradley smiled at her upturned face. "Thank you in advance for missing me," he said in a husky whisper, raising her hands to his lips. "Until we return, my love."

"Each day will seem like a hundred years," she told him.

"I hope so." With that he pulled her into his arms, but instead of kissing her said, "Lock the door."

Lily closed the door and bolted it. She longed to watch until they'd vanished from sight but knew they wouldn't leave until she'd locked the door.

Leaning back against the weathered wood, Lily wondered how she would survive all those long, lonely days and nights. She decided to wrap herself in the red shawl Bradley had given her. Whenever she felt melancholy, wrapping herself in the shawl made her feel better.

Too bad she hadn't accepted his last marriage proposal, she thought, fingering her *alpha* and *omega* cross. If she'd accepted his offer before the war began, she would have been ensconced in his house on Beacon Hill. Michael would have—

There was the rub and the reason she hadn't accepted his proposal of marriage but the war also precluded planning a wedding. What would Bradley do if she delivered a child like her impaired younger brother? Yes, he liked Michael, but her brother was not his son.

With those troubling thoughts swirling around in her mind, Lily climbed the narrow stairs to her chamber above the tavern. Touching her cross, she knew that Bradley was the man who matched it. *Alpha* and *omega*. The beginning and the ending. The first and the last for her.

Lily knew she needed to stop worrying about things she couldn't control. She needed something to occupy her time while Bradley and her brother were away. What she really needed was to bring the Gilded Lily back from early retirement.

The following day dragged slower than a crippled snail. How many days would she pass like this? By late afternoon, Lily was beside herself with boredom. The days of May, growing longer until the middle of June, loomed like a monstrous beast in front of her.

Lily stood in the kitchen doorway of the Four Winds Tavern and inhaled deeply of the warm evening air. She stared across the water in the direction of the Salty Dog Tavern. The agent would be waiting in vain for the Gilded Lily.

Feeling a presence near her, Lily glanced to the left. Her eight-year-old brother stood beside her and stared in the same direction. He looked as bored as she felt.

Lily opened her mouth to tell him to wipe his chin. As if he knew what she was about to say, Michael reached up and wiped his chin on the sleeve of his shirt.

"What are you looking at?" she asked, still staring straight ahead.

"What are *you* looking at?" he returned.

"I asked first," she answered.

"I asked second," he replied.

Lily burst out laughing. Michael grinned broadly at her.

"Do you know what today is?" Lily asked, putting her arm around his shoulder.

"Friday?"

"Friday the thirteenth," she qualified.

Her brother stared at her blankly.

"Friday the thirteenth is the unluckiest day of the whole year," Lily explained. "Thirteen is an unlucky number, and Jesus died on a Friday."

"How do you know what day Jesus died?" Michael asked. "You weren't there."

Lily laughed. "Good Friday commemorates his death."

"Oh. Should we go inside and hide from the bad luck?"

"That won't be necessary." And then an outrageous idea popped into her mind. Leaning close to his ear, she whispered, "Would you like to have an adventure?"

Her brother's blue eyes, so much like her own, sparkled with excitement. "What kind of adventure?"

"A *secret* adventure," she whispered.

Michael nodded his head vigorously and placed a finger across his lips. Then he said in a loud whisper, "No one can know."

"Go upstairs," Lily told him. "Bring me a pair of Seth's oldest breeches, a shirt, and a jerkin. Don't forget a belt and a cap."

Michael raced up the narrow staircase to the second floor. While she waited, Lily looked out the kitchen door again. Colors ranging from mauve to indigo slashed across the horizon as twilight faded into evening. The first sprinkling of stars were visible in the eastern sky.

"Here," her brother said.

Lifting the clothing out of his hands, Lily ordered, "Turn your back."

Once he'd turned away, Lily discarded her gown and chemise. She pulled on the black breeches and fastened the belt around her waist to keep them from falling. Next she donned the shirt, the jerkin, and the cap, which she pulled down low in front to cover her forehead and hide her eyes.

"You look like a boy," Michael said.

"We're going to the Salty Dog," Lily told him, leading the way to the kitchen door. "Wipe your chin."

Michael wiped his chin on the sleeve of his shirt and said, "I'm ready."

Together, they left the safety of Howell's Wharf and walked south when they reached Blackstone Street. They passed Rowe's Wharf first, but then slowed their pace as they approached Hancock's Wharf.

"This is serious business," Lily told him. "Do not call me by name. Understand?"

Michael narrowed his gaze on her. "I'm not stupid."

"I only want to be certain you'll maintain our secrecy," she replied.

"What is *maintain?*"

"Maintain means keep, keep our secret," she explained.

Pulling the cap lower on her forehead, Lily led the way down Hancock's Wharf and into the Salty Dog. She crossed the tavern and sat down at a table across the room from the hearth.

Lily let out a soft sigh of relief when Michael sat

down opposite her without calling any undue attention to them. She froze in dismay when he lifted his arm to wipe his chin. If anyone saw that familiar gesture . . .

Lily scanned the large common room. No one seemed to be paying any attention. Thanks to her guardian angel, Hortensia MacDugal was not in attendance that night.

While she was worrying that someone they knew would enter, the tavern keeper approached their table. Colin MacDugal, a giant of a man and father of her nemesis, stood beside their table. With his massive frame shielding them from view of the tavern's patrons, he dropped a slip of paper onto the table in front of her.

Lily snapped her gaze from the slip of paper to the tavern keeper, who winked at her conspiratorially. Sweet lamb of God, did MacDugal know the Gilded Lily's identity? Not only that, but he'd recognized her in spite of her disguise.

She looked at the slip of paper and sucked in her breath at its message. *Beware the British bull.*

Lily looked up and then tried to see past him to the other patrons of the tavern. He moved when she moved, effectively blocking her from sight.

"Leave by the kitchen door," MacDugal whispered. *"Now."*

Lily nodded. She rose from her chair as soon as the man moved away and said, "Follow me, Brother."

Michael wiped the drool from his chin and asked, "Aren't we going to—?"

Lily gave him a warning look. He would have had to be dead to misunderstand what she meant.

Leading the way, Lily crossed the tavern to the

kitchen. She ignored the startled looks from the kitchen help and headed straight for the tavern's rear door.

The door clicked shut behind them. Lily and her brother stood in the alley behind the Salty Dog.

Night shrouded them, lending a feeling of security. Lily looked up to see hundreds of stars dotting the sky, but no moon shone. She inhaled deeply and recognized the familiar scent that tickled her nostrils. The reassuring smell of low tide.

"Why did we leave?" Michael asked in a loud whisper.

"British agents are watching for me," she answered. "Come on."

Taking his hand in hers, Lily started to lead him in the direction of Blackstone Street. They hadn't gone more than ten paces when someone grabbed her from behind.

Struggling against her assailant, Lily opened her mouth to scream for her brother, but a massive hand covered her nose and mouth. She struggled frantically for breath, finally finding refuge in a faint.

Several moments later, Lily regained consciousness and realized she'd been wrapped in a blanket and was now being carried like a sack of grain over someone's shoulder. Bobbing against her captor's back, Lily fought the nausea that threatened.

Michael was the only thing she could think about. Had he escaped? How could she live with herself if her brother had been injured because of her stupidity? She'd promised her mother to protect Michael and now she'd failed.

Oh, why hadn't she listened to Seth and Bradley? She should have trusted their judgment.

Lily knew she was being carried down a flight of stairs when the bobbing increased and then decreased as abruptly as it had started. She felt herself being lowered to the floor, and then a door closed somewhere behind her. Suddenly, someone whipped the blanket off her.

Lily opened her eyes slowly and stared at a pair of black boots. Were they American boots or British?

Uncertain, Lily lifted her gaze to well-muscled legs clad in tight black breeches. Higher she raised her gaze to the man's tapered waist, his chest, and then . . .

Summoning her courage, Lily shifted her gaze to his face. The man's hair and eyes were blacker than mortal sin and, though uncommonly handsome, the uncompromising set to his jaw shouted his arrogance.

Sweet lamb of God, Lily thought in a panic as she stared into his black eyes. *The devil is a gentleman*. . . .

God's balls! The devil is a woman, James thought, staring into the most disarming sapphire blue eyes he'd ever seen.

James flicked a quick glance at the boy. Shifting his gaze back to the woman, he cocked a dark brow at her and said, "The Gilded Lily, I presume?"

"No, Lady MacBeth," she answered, staring him straight in the eye.

"Indeed, your hands are covered with the blood of Englishmen," James said. "I am—"

"The British bull, I presume?" she interrupted him.

James smiled without humor. "Those fortunate ladies who have shared my bed sometimes refer to me in those terms."

No sooner had the last word slipped from his lips when her fair complexion began darkening, coloring into a vibrant scarlet. When was the last time he'd seen a sincere blush staining a woman's cheeks? Still, he couldn't credit that the notorious American agent would blush because of a sexual innuendo.

"Where is my brother?" she demanded. "If you harm him in any way—"

"I am here," the boy answered.

James watched his captive glance over her shoulder to verify that the boy was safe. He noted the softening of her expression when she looked at him, but it hardened when she turned back to James.

"I don't know why you have abducted us," she said in a reasonable tone of voice that was obviously costing her a lot in self-control. "Our father is not a rich man and won't pay a penny for us. I suggest you release us at once."

James stared at her for a long moment, trying to unnerve her. "As I was saying, I am the Duke of Kinross."

"A real duke?" the boy piped up.

"Michael, be quiet and let me handle this," the woman ordered. Flicking a glance at the boy, she added, as if it were a habit, "Put your tongue in your mouth. Wipe your chin."

James watched the boy wipe his chin on the sleeve of his shirt. It was then he realized the boy was impaired.

The girl loved her brother; that much was obvious. Had she been forced to work for the Americans in order to support him? Well, that mattered little. His own brother was dead, and she would pay the price for her part in the deed.

"Michael is your name?" James asked the boy in a friendly tone of voice.

"Don't tell him anything," the girl ordered.

The boy shot his sister a worried glance and then looked at him, saying, "I'm Michael Hawthorne."

"How old are you?" James asked.

"Eight, but I'll be nine on September twenty-ninth," the boy told him. "That's Saint Michael's Day, and—and Lily named me in honor of him." He glanced at his sister for confirmation, saying, "Didn't you, Lily?" Without waiting for her verification, he asked, "Do you know what Saint Michael did?"

James smiled. "What did he do?"

"He threw Lucifer out of heaven."

"Ah, yes," James said. "I do recall that story." He gestured to the girl, asking, "How old is Lily?"

"She's eighteen years old," Michael answered. "We have—"

"Be quiet," Lily said.

The boy shut his mouth abruptly.

"What do you have?" James prodded.

The boy gazed at him through sapphire blue eyes that resembled his sister's. Then he gave him an engaging smile and answered, "Should I call you Duke?"

James's first thought was that the boy was trying to outsmart him by answering a question with a question, but he dismissed that as ridiculous. He was about to correct the boy's misuse of his title but decided against it. Now was not the time to give a lesson on protocol.

"Duke would be fine," James said.

Standing by the door, his man chuckled. Michael and Lily turned to look at him.

"Who's that?" Michael asked, pointing at the giant.

"That man is Duncan MacGregor," James answered. "He works for me."

James glanced at the girl, who appeared ready to

explode. Then he asked the boy, "Have you ever sailed across the ocean?"

"We're not going anywhere with you," Lily cried.

"Keep your mouth shut," James said sternly. "You are my prisoner now and will follow orders."

"Don't speak like that to Lily," Michael said, drawing his attention. "You'll make her angry, and then she'll make you sorry."

"Is that so?" James replied, flicking a glance at the girl who looked like a strong wind could blow her over. "Does she frighten you?"

"I'm not afraid of anything," the boy bragged, puffing his chest out. "Are you taking us for a ride in your boat?"

"This is a ship," the girl informed her brother.

"Lily, Duke said to be quiet," Michael replied. "I think he must be more frightening when he's angry than you."

"I'm taking Lily and you on a trip to England," James told the boy.

"M-Merry olde England?"

James nodded. "That's correct."

"Do you know Robin Hood?"

"Who?"

"Robin Hood and his band of Merry Men," Michael explained. "Lily told me a story about them. Robin and his Merry Men live in Sherwood Forest, and the Sheriff of Nottingham is always trying to catch them. Maid Marian spies for them."

The word *spies* wiped all amusement from James's expression. The boy and his sister were so entertaining, so unexpectedly naive that he'd almost forgotten his brother and his revenge.

"I've never met the man," James said gruffly.

"Oh." The boy sounded disappointed. Did he actually believe there was such a person as Robin Hood living in England?

"I want to speak privately with Lily," James told the boy. "Go along with Duncan and he'll give you something to drink and let you sleep in his quarters. Tomorrow will be here before you know it."

"You cannot mean to separate us," Lily cried, drawing his attention. "You can see that he needs me."

"Duncan will take good care of him." James walked to the door and opened it for them. "Watch over the boy," he instructed his man. "I want him kept safe."

"Yes, your grace."

"His name is Grace?" Michael asked loudly, walking out the door with the big Scotsman. "He told me to call him Duke."

James managed to squelch the urge to laugh. He closed the door slowly and prepared to confront his brother's murderer. It was then he felt the cold tip of steel touching the back of his neck.

The little bitch had a dagger.

He'd assumed his man had confiscated any weapons she'd carried. Well, he would need to reprimand Duncan for being so negligent. That is, as soon as he'd disarmed his guest.

"Move, and I'll skewer your neck like a sausage on a stick," Lily threatened him.

"No decent lady draws a dagger on her host," James told her in a pleasant tone of voice. The longer he kept her talking, the better the chance he had of disarming her without doing injury to either of them.

"You're not my host," she snapped.

"I stand corrected," he replied, his amusement apparent in his voice. "What would you call me?"

"Satan's son," Lily answered, her voice filled with contempt. "Please, do not tempt me to insult you further."

"Surely the devil is not so black as he is painted," James said.

"Certainly not," she agreed, surprising him. "He has the power to assume a pleasing shape."

"I'm flattered that you find me so attractive," James said, with laughter lurking in his voice. "What will you do now that you have me at your mercy?"

"I-I don't know," Lily answered honestly, surprising him again. "I need to think."

"We cannot stand here like this forever," he told her.

"Be quiet," she ordered, desperation tingeing her voice.

James stared at the door and waited. He didn't want to frighten her into stabbing him by accident. He'd already judged her incapable of murdering a man by design, only causing his death as she'd done to his brother.

She stood so close he caught her soft, delicate scent, which held a sensuous trace of musk. She smelled like lilies in a forest; the fragrance wrapped itself around him seductively, enticing him to kiss every inch of her, starting with the valley between her breasts.

God's balls, James thought, mentally giving himself a shake. His brother's murderer held a dagger to his neck and he'd responded with a hardening in his groin. He must be insane.

"If I held something out to you, would you take it in your right hand?" Lily asked abruptly.

James couldn't credit what he was hearing. The chit was even more stupid than Valentina.

"Well?"

"Yes, of course."

"When I tell you and not before, slowly move to the right until you are facing me," Lily said.

And then James realized the witch was more intelligent than he'd thought. What she wanted to do was prevent him from attacking her with his strong hand.

"Move now," she ordered. "Slowly."

James turned toward the right. As he faced her, he struck out with his left hand, catching her on the right cheek.

She screamed as the force of his slap sent her crashing to the floor. The dagger slipped out of her hand and fell a few feet away.

"You should have skewered me while you had the chance," James said, picking up her dagger. "Nothing is so perilous as procrastination."

"I'll remember that for the next time," Lily said, holding her throbbing cheek. "You lied to me. You're left-handed."

"Ambidextrous," James said. He reached down and yanked her boots off. Strapped to her left calf was a leather garter holding the dagger's sheath. "No decent lady walks around with a last-resort dagger strapped to her leg."

"No decent gentleman abducts a lady," she shot back.

"Surely, you haven't mistaken me for a gentleman?" James asked. "Are you carrying any other weapons? Answer me truthfully. If I need to disarm you again, I'll take you across my knee and spank you."

"H-How d-dare you," she sputtered in anger.

"Damn it, do you have any other weapons?"

"No."

"How can I be sure you aren't lying to me?" he asked, staring down at her.

"You are the liar, not I," she told him in a superior tone of voice.

In an instant, James dropped to his knees and grabbed her wrists in one hand. He pinned them over her head and proceeded to pat every inch of her body. Starting with the spot he'd wanted to kiss, the valley between her breasts, James began a slow caress of her body.

"No!" Lily squirmed beneath his touch and struggled in vain to free herself.

"Be still or it will go worse for you," he threatened.

When she stopped moving, his hand continued its search. He moved the palm of his hand across each breast and wished she hadn't been wearing any clothing. He slid his hand beneath her arms and then dipped lower to the juncture of her thighs.

Staring into the most disarming sapphire eyes he'd ever seen, James caressed the soft valley between her legs. He could feel her heat through the breeches she wore.

Her body trembled beneath his touch, yet she remained still lest he do worse. He gazed into her eyes and saw confusion mingling with the fright he'd expected.

Finding no bulge of a weapon, James stood and said, "For once a woman has spoken truthfully."

"Anglo-Saxon swill," Lily cried, sitting up and scurrying backward away from him. "How dare you touch my person."

If she hadn't been insulting him, James would have applauded her queenlike attitude. "Be careful," he warned. "I could strip you naked and search in earnest."

And then she did what he least expected her to do. She burst into tears.

James hated the contrived tears of women. But this girl lying at his feet was weeping in all sincerity.

Too bad, he thought. He'd begun to have a grudging respect for her foolhardy bravery. She'd ruined the effect by dissolving into tears.

"Damn this jackassery," he muttered.

James marched across the cabin, yanked the door open, and stepped outside. Letting her know his displeasure, he slammed the door behind himself and locked it. Then he started down the narrow passageway, intending to go on deck to clear her scent from his senses. The sound of furious banging reached him. He looked down the passageway toward his cabin.

"Release me at once, you lobster-backed bastard," his prisoner demanded, kicking the cabin's door. "Do you hear me, Lord Beef-witted Bore?"

More banging. And then, "Owww . . ."

James threw back his head and shouted with laughter. His captive had just redeemed herself.

By the time he stepped onto the quarterdeck, James was in a different frame of mind. Even dressed like a boy, the chit was lovely and as amusing as hell, but she had caused his brother's death and would pay for it.

James looked up at the night sky. Darkness shrouded the ship, but overhead the stars glowed. Orion's army of jewels sparkled in the western sky. To the north lay the Big Dipper and Polaris, the North Star, but the most beautiful jewel of all at this time of year lay in the eastern sky. Solitary Arcturus, a yellow-orange giant, the second brightest star in the sky, perched in the eastern horizon. Only Sirius, the Dog Star, bested it for brilliance.

Calmed by the night's beauty, James inhaled deeply of the crisp air. The natural lights from above, the pungent smell of the sea, and the motion of the ship soothed his senses.

Killing a woman, even in the name of justice, was beyond his capability. So what was he to do with her? Keeping her out of play for the duration of the war seemed to be the only course of action. Where was the punishment in that?

Why, in God's name, had the Americans placed their trust in her? Women were such flighty creatures. With her disarming sapphire eyes and ebony hair as black as his own, the woman in his cabin was unlike any female he'd ever met.

The hint of a smile touched his lips. Imagine, the delicate creature belowdeck had dared to draw a dagger on him. The journey to England would certainly be interesting.

Abruptly, James left the quarterdeck and returned below. The boy would tell him everything about his sister, and then he would know how to handle her.

Without knocking, James walked into the cabin one door down from his own. Duncan MacGregor was more than a retainer. He was a valued and trusted friend who had proven his loyalty and worth a hundred times over. So, whenever they traveled on one of his ships, James insisted Duncan receive special treatment, as befitting an officer.

Walking into the cabin, James grinned at the sight of the eight-year-old swaying back and forth on the hammock that Duncan had strung up. The big Scotsman was just beginning a story about his famous ancestor, the legendary Rob Roy MacGregor.

"Bring the boy something to eat and drink," James ordered his man.

Duncan nodded and left the cabin.

"You've had an exciting evening, haven't you?" James said to open the conversation, staring into the boy's slightly slanted sapphire eyes.

"I never got snatched before," Michael said. "Are you going to make Lily and me walk the plank?"

"We forgot all of our planks in England," James said. The boy's disappointed look made him smile. "Tell me about your life in Boston."

"What do you want to know?"

"Where and how do you live?"

"My father owns the Four Winds Tavern on Howell's Wharf," Michael told him. "We live upstairs."

So the girl was a wharf rat, James thought. That explained the dagger.

"Do you like living there?" James asked.

Surprisingly, the boy shook his head.

"Why not?"

"The others don't like me," he answered. "They always tease me."

"What others?"

"The children."

"Why don't they like you?" James asked.

Michael stared at him through disarming sapphire blue eyes, so much like his sister's. He leaned close, as if divulging a secret, and answered, "I'm different."

James felt sorry for him. All boys needed at least one friend.

"What makes you so different?" he asked, already knowing the answer.

Michael shrugged. "I was born different. Lily says I'm special, but I want to be the same."

James reached out and touched the boy's shoulder. Apparently, he was impaired enough to be different but smart enough to know that he was.

"You aren't going to hurt Lily?" Michael asked, changing the subject. "She's only a girl, you know."

"I would never hurt a girl," James assured him.

Michael leaned close again and said in a loud whisper, "Lily thinks she protects me, but I really protect her. Don't tell her, though."

"I won't."

"Do you have a sister?"

Who was questioning whom? The boy was turning the conversation on him. Perhaps he wasn't as impaired as he looked.

"I had an older brother once," James said. "He died recently."

"My mother died," Michael replied. Then, "Is dying part of living?"

James nodded. "I'm wondering why the Americans would use a girl as an agent. What does your sister do for the war effort?"

"She remembers."

What was the boy talking about? Before he could question him, the boy went on.

"Lily reads and remembers," Michael bragged, his chest puffing out with pride. "No one else does that better than Lily. I wish I could read like she reads."

James nodded, but the boy's words puzzled him. He realized he'd get no better explanation out of him and would need to investigate this on his own.

"Duncan will return shortly," James said, walking

toward the door. "He'll finish his story of Rob Roy MacGregor."

"Good night, Duke."

James winked at him. "Good night, Michael."

What did the boy mean about remembering? James wondered, pausing outside his cabin. Even more important at this moment, how would the little witch react to sharing his cabin and his bed?

Perhaps he should lock her in—

James gave himself a mental shake. Why deprive himself of an interesting journey home?

Stepping inside the cabin, James saw his captive sitting on the floor. With her eyes closed in sleep, she rested her head against the side of the bed. She looked damned uncomfortable, too.

She's only pretending to sleep, he realized with an inward smile. Oh, this really was becoming fun. What should he do to shock her into alertness?

James stood there silently and watched her trying to keep her expression placid, as if in sleep. He knew the curiosity about what he was doing had to be killing her.

Struggling against laughter, James moved forward. The sound of his boots on the wood seemed unusually loud in the cabin's silence as he walked closer and closer to her. The bed creaked, protesting his weight, when he sat down to await her reaction.

Still, his captive sat motionless with her head resting against the bed.

Was she just going to sit there like a blinking idiot?

Three

Was he just going to sit there like a blinking idiot? Lily wondered, beginning to panic at the prolonged silence. She opened her eyes a crack to catch a peek and nearly swooned. His leg was so close, she could have bitten it. Great guardian angel, what should she do? Run or stay where she was?

The duke pulled off one boot and then the other, tossing both aside.

Lily raised her gaze. Her captor was unbuttoning his shirt.

"Do not touch another button," she cried, leaping up and running to the other side of the cabin.

The duke smiled, as if amused by her outburst.

Lily felt her cheeks growing hot with embarrassment. She could just imagine how red they were.

"Do you expect me to sleep with my clothes on?" he asked.

"I expect you to sleep elsewhere," she answered.

James looked her up and down. "I think not."

"You, sir, are a scoundrel."

"The proper way to address me is *your grace,*" he informed her. "I suppose one cannot expect correct manners from a colonial."

"I am no colonial," Lily told him. "We Americans

won that war. Remember? Furthermore, I'll address you however I see fit."

The duke narrowed his black gaze on her and started to rise from his perch on the edge of the bed.

"Your grace," she added hastily.

"Your brother is much pleasanter than you," he said.

"Where is he?" Lily demanded. "I want to see him."

"Tomorrow, perhaps. If you behave yourself."

The duke sat down on the bed again. Leaning back, he folded his arms across his chest and studied her. Finally he asked, "Are you afraid of me?"

"Certainly not."

"Just a little?"

Lily gave him a look of contempt and stood proudly erect, knowing her petite height wouldn't frighten a flea. " 'Cowards die many times before their deaths,' " she announced in a lofty tone of voice. " 'The valiant never taste of death but once.' "

"A wharf rat who quotes Shakespeare?" James shook his head, apparently amused by an educated commoner. "That was *Julius Caesar*, wasn't it?"

Insulted by his words and his notion that she was incapable of reading Shakespeare, Lily stared him straight in the eye and said in a voice that held a note of challenge, "Act Two, Scene Two, line thirty-two."

James said nothing for a long moment and then, apparently deciding to call her bluff, slid off the bed. He crossed the cabin to a small bookcase built into the wall. Finding the volume, he sat at the table and flipped through its pages. He stopped at one page and, using his index finger, traced the words down the column.

Suddenly he snapped his head up to stare at her in surprise.

Lily felt like crawling beneath a rock. His expression said she was freakish. Sweet lamb of God, why had she needed to show off her talent? Not only did he know why she served as an agent but he also knew what a freak she was.

To belong was the only thing she'd ever really wanted. Why couldn't she have been born a good cook or a nimble seamstress? She was as different from the women of her acquaintance as her brother was from the other children.

"How did you do that?" James asked.

Lily shrugged and dragged her gaze away from his face.

"I will know how you did that before we reach England," he told her.

Lily sighed wearily. "Well, you won't be hearing it from me."

Closing the book, James yawned and stretched. "The hour is late. Get into bed."

"I am not sleeping with you," Lily told him.

"Would you prefer the company of my crew?" he countered.

Lily refused to dignify that with an answer. She shifted her gaze to the bed and argued, "There's only room for one."

A boyishly infuriating smile stole across his features. "We'll cuddle."

"I'd rather sidle up to a serpent," Lily snapped, shocked by his suggestion.

"Guard your tongue, lady. That is, if you want to see your brother tomorrow."

"I'll sleep here," Lily said, plopping down on the floor. "Give me a blanket."

"You'll get sick, and I won't have your death on my conscience," James told her. "Trust me, lady. You have nothing I want."

Lily didn't know if she should be insulted or relieved. " 'Things are often spoke and seldom meant,' " she said without thinking. *"Henry VI,* Part Two, Act Three, Scene One, line two-sixty-eight."

The duke dropped his mouth open in surprise. He didn't bother to verify if she was correct or not. Within mere seconds, he had assumed a sober expression.

"Very nice. Now get into bed."

Lily opened her mouth to refuse, but he seemed to know her intention.

"Get in the damned bed," James ordered in a voice that brooked no disobedience.

Angering him was a little like poking a panther, Lily thought. She rose from the floor and crossed the cabin to the bed. "Very well, as long as you remain dressed."

James inclined his head.

Fully clothed, Lily slid into bed and yanked the blanket up. Turning her back on him, she faced the wall. The bed creaked when he slid in beside her.

"Your dubious virtue is safe with me," she heard him say.

Dubious? Lily bolted up in the bed and looked down on him. Even in the dark she could see his infuriating smile.

"How dare you insinuate that I am less than pure?" she said. "You—you defiler of maidens."

"I assure you that I have no need to ravish the unwilling," James replied.

"Self-praise is no recommendation," she shot back.

Instead of reacting with anger, the duke said, "Go to sleep." Then he rolled over and turned his back on her.

Lily lay down on the bed. Again, she turned her back on him.

What terrible sin had she committed that required this punishment? What would Bradley and Seth do when they returned to Boston and discovered her missing? Would Bradley still want to marry her? If not, how could she protect Michael?

"Lily?" The duke's voice broke the silence in the cabin.

"Yes?"

"This is the only night I'm wearing my clothes to bed."

Lily was too tired to argue. Eighteen hours lay between now and then.

"We'll discuss it tomorrow," she told him.

"There's nothing to discuss," he told her.

"I said we'd discuss it tomorrow." *Whether you like it or not* remained unspoken.

He made no reply.

Several silent moments passed.

"Lily?"

"What now?" She couldn't keep the irritation out of her voice.

"Call me *James*," he said. "That's my name."

"No, thank you, your grace."

"I order you to call me *James*."

"Good night, James."

"That's better."

"Do you always need to have the last word?" she asked.

"Yes, I do."

Lily smiled in spite of her predicament. She listened to his breathing until it evened and sensed when he dropped into sleep.

Falling asleep proved more difficult for Lily. Since there was little room in the bed, she tossed and turned mentally.

Escape popped into her mind. Where could she go? They were surrounded by water.

Besides, there was her brother to consider. She couldn't risk endangering him.

Escape was out of the question. She would need to persuade the duke to turn the ship around. How could she do that? And why, for God's sake, had he abducted her?

The duke smells like mountain heather, Lily thought as her eyelids closed in sleep. And she liked it. . . .

"Oh, God, you're real," Lily moaned when she opened her eyes the next morning. "I thought I was having a bad dream."

The duke sat at the table. He looked more handsome than any man should.

Lifting her gaze, Lily saw that he was watching her. Embarrassment stained her cheeks. His stare made her feel feverishly hot right down to her toes.

He smiled at her.

She curled her upper lip at him in a gesture of angry disdain.

"I wish you wouldn't do that," James said in a pleasant voice. "Your life would be ruined if that expression froze on your face."

"My life *is* ruined," Lily told him, staring him

straight in the eye. "You destroyed it when you abducted me."

"Your future cannot be so terribly bleak," James replied. "A woman of your considerable talents and breeding will be successful at any venture."

Was he insulting her or not? Lily suspected the worse, but no one—especially not Hortensia MacDugal—had ever insulted her so pleasantly. The residents of Boston's waterfront hurled insults at each other instead of daggers. Insincerely civil must be the aristocratic British way.

"No reply?" he asked, rising from his chair.

Lily shrank back on the bed.

"Don't be a twit," James said. "I'm not coming near you."

He pulled out his pocket watch and stared at it for a moment. After placing it on the table, he started walking toward the door, saying, "I'll give you fifteen minutes. The commode is over there."

Lily couldn't swallow her gasp of embarrassment, but he ignored it. "Fifteen minutes," he reminded her before closing the door.

As soon as the door shut behind him, Lily threw the blanket off and leaped out of bed. She headed for the door but came to an abrupt halt in the middle of the cabin.

Torn between a certain physical need and her desire to escape, Lily looked from the door to the commode and then back again. Her physical need won the battle.

A few minutes later, Lily hurried across the cabin. She pressed her ear to the door but heard no telltale noises in the passageway outside. She reached for the doorknob but stopped, realizing she needed a plan before stepping outside.

Escape was the ultimate goal. In the middle of the damned Atlantic Ocean? Not the middle, she corrected herself. Only about twelve hours out, which really wasn't too far. Too far for a swim, she reminded herself.

Lily stood there motionless while a plan formulated in her mind. She needed to find Michael and hide somewhere on board, a place safe from detection. Then she would sneak from their hiding place and steal a weapon. A gun would be most effective, but she didn't know how to use one. A sharp dagger would do nicely, though.

Once armed, Lily would capture the duke. She nearly laughed out loud at the thought of holding him captive.

Do unto others as they would do unto you, Lily thought. That was the wharf's Golden Rule.

Holding the duke at dagger point, Lily would force him to return the ship to Boston. Then he could sit out the duration of the war.

With determination stamped across her features, Lily yanked the door open and cried out in surprise.

There stood the duke, wearing that infuriating smile of his, his six-foot-and-two-inch frame blocking her path to freedom. "Ten minutes," he said.

Son of a bitch, Lily thought, and slammed the door shut. She leaned back against it to catch her breath and slow her heartbeat. The duke's laughter from the other side of the door did nothing to calm her.

"Nine more minutes," she heard him call.

"Your soul is blacker than your hair and eyes," Lily shouted in frustrated fury. "Go hang yourself."

The duke was silent. When he spoke, his voice had lost its amusement, "Yes, my lady. There is a hanging between us."

Lily heard his footsteps as he walked away. Why did he sound so personally affronted by the thought of a few British spies getting their just punishment?

Apparently the duke suffered from seizures of nastiness. Too much inbreeding in the English aristocracy, no doubt.

Her anger vanished, leaving her depleted. She washed her face and sat down at the table to wait.

Lily inspected the cabin for the first time since she'd entered the previous night. The table had been made in heavy oak, as were the matching armchairs, and permanently fastened to the floor. On one side of the cabin near the portholes was a desk, also made of oak. Bookshelves had been built into the wall and were filled to capacity with books, except for *The Complete Works of Shakespeare*, which lay on the table in front of her. Lamps had been permanently affixed to the table, desk, and walls. To the left of the door stood the commode and, behind that, a privacy screen. At the foot of the bed was an enormous sea chest.

Lily had never been onboard a ship before, but the cabin seemed luxurious to her, much more comfortable than her tiny room at the Four Winds Tavern. Obviously, the Duke of Kinross was a very wealthy man.

The door opened, drawing her attention, and the duke walked in. His retainer, carrying a tray of food, followed him. She knew he'd recovered from his seizure of nastiness when he sat opposite her and smiled.

Duncan placed the tray down on the table. When

the giant set her plate in front of her, Lily gifted the man with a sweet smile.

"Thank you, sir," she said.

The gruff-looking giant actually blushed.

"That will be all for now," the duke said to his retainer.

"I want to see my brother," Lily said as soon as the big man had gone.

"We'll discuss it after breakfast," James said pleasantly.

"When will we be released?"

"You are free to leave whenever you wish." He gave her that infuriating smile of his. "Unfortunately, there's no place to go."

"I despise men who gloat," Lily sneered.

"And I despise women who sneer," James countered.

"I wasn't sneering," she told him.

He cocked a dark brow at her. "What were you doing?"

"I was expressing my displeasure."

The duke laughed and said, "Eat your breakfast, little girl. You'll need all your strength to fight me."

Lily knew that further conversation would be useless. The man wanted to torment her. She lifted her fork off the table and began to eat the scrambled eggs, griddle cakes, and sausage.

"You eat very well."

Lily shifted her sapphire gaze from her plate to her captor's dark eyes. "What do you mean?" she asked, suspicious.

"Most women of my acquaintance eat very little," he told her.

Lily blushed, feeling conspicuous. Apparently she'd

broken some rule of etiquette of which she'd been unaware. Only God knew how odd these British were with their strange notions of what was proper.

"Your wife must be smaller than a—"

"I'm not married."

"Then your fiancée . . ."

"I'm not engaged."

Lily blushed again and dropped her gaze to her plate. Feigning a nonchalance she didn't feel, she lifted her fork and began to eat. She wondered briefly why she'd blushed more in the past twelve hours than she had during the previous twelve months.

From beneath her lashes Lily stole a peek at the duke. If the truth be told, he was a handsome man, his black eyes and hair lending him an aura of dangerousness. Hortensia MacDugal would take after him in less than two seconds.

The duke had been relatively kind to her and her brother. That is, if one overlooked the fact that he'd abducted them and was afflicted by bouts of nastiness. On the other hand, if he'd wanted to murder or ravish her, he would have done so last night.

"What's your full name again?" James asked conversationally, drawing her away from her thoughts.

"What's yours?" Lily asked.

"I asked first."

She inclined her head. "Lily Hawthorne."

"I am James Armstrong, the fourteenth Duke of Kinross," he introduced himself.

"I would say how pleased I am to make your acquaintance but I never lie," Lily said.

"How refreshing."

"I beg you to turn this ship around and return me

to my home," she said, urgency making her lean forward.

"Your sleeve is in the scrambled eggs," he told her, and smiled when she quickly leaned back in her chair. "Returning to Boston is impossible because you, Lily Hawthorne, are too dangerous to be let loose. . . . By the way, do you always dress in boy's clothing?"

"Certainly not," Lily answered. "I was in disguise last night."

"You can't wear the same clothing for a month," James told her. "Later, I'll find other clothes for you and your brother."

"When may I visit my brother?" Lily asked.

"When I allow it and not a moment earlier," he answered.

"When will that be?" she asked, her frustration apparent in her voice.

"I haven't decided." James relaxed in his chair and gave her a long look. "Tell me about yourself and your life in Boston."

"Social conversation is not required with captives, only guests," she replied.

"Humor me." His tone of voice brooked no disobedience.

"I was born in Boston eighteen years ago and have lived there my whole life," Lily told him. "My father owns a tavern, and we live upstairs."

"Who is 'we'?"

"My father, my older half brother, Michael, and me."

"Your mother?"

"She died birthing Michael," she answered.

James nodded. "So, you've been a mother and a sister to the boy."

"I suppose so." Lily wondered why he was asking so many questions. Why would a peer of King George's realm be interested in her boring, plebeian life?

"How did you become the Gilded Lily?" he asked.

"I don't know what you mean," Lily replied, unwilling to confess to anything. "I believe you've made a horrible mistake, but I'll forgive you if you return me to Boston."

"Give over, little girl."

Lily sighed in resignation. "My fiancé recruited me."

Surprise registered on his face. "You have a fiancé?"

"Yes, and he'll murder you once he catches up to us," she told him. "He'll tear you limb from limb with his bare hands and hold your innards up for you to see."

"Stop, you'll give me nightmares," James said, holding his hand up. "What's his name?"

Lily looked away and silently refused to answer.

James rose from his chair. "My man will return shortly to remove the tray. No more tricks."

"How am I supposed to occupy myself?" Lily asked.

"Read *The Complete Works of Shakespeare*," he suggested, pushing the thick book toward her.

"I've already read it."

James snapped his dark brows together and then turned away to retrieve another thick volume from the bookcase. He placed it on the table in front of her and said, "How about the Bible?"

Lily met his gaze. "I've read that, too."

"Both testaments?"

She nodded once. "Shall I recite them?"

"Is that what Michael meant by remembering?" James asked.

Lily shrugged. "I won't forget you any time soon."

James smiled, and this time it seemed less infuriating than before. "Am I unforgettable?"

"About as much as my last toothache," she answered sweetly.

He perched against the side of the table.

Lily looked from his dark eyes to his thigh, clad in tight-fitting breeches. He was much too close for her peace of mind. She rose from the chair and crossed the cabin to look out the porthole.

"I'm waiting to know if I'm unforgettable."

Lily whirled around and said, "English born and English bred, strong in the arm and weak in the head."

James burst out laughing. "How am I weak in the head?" he asked.

"You have sudden seizures of nastiness," she told him. "Of course, I haven't known you very long, so I'm sure you possess other quirks."

"If I had known that Yankee Doodles were so amusing, I would have abducted one sooner," James said, and headed for the door. Before leaving, he called over his shoulder, "Read any book you like." And then he was gone.

The cabin seemed empty without his presence, and the hours dragged by slowly.

First, Lily crossed the chamber and looked behind the privacy screen. It was as she'd thought: A tub, large enough for a man, stood there.

Without bothering to try the door, Lily walked to the porthole and stared out at the endless horizon of water and sky. She wondered where Michael was and what he was doing. She didn't believe anyone would hurt him. Her brother had merely been in the wrong place at the wrong time with the wrong companion.

Where were Bradley and Seth? What would they do when they returned to Boston and discovered her missing? Of course, they would have no idea of where Michael and she had gone. Entertaining the notion of Bradley and Seth rescuing them was absurd. They could not rescue them, and that was the truth of the matter.

She had better become accustomed to those obnoxious British accents, Lily decided. She would be listening to them until peace broke out.

British accents reminded Lily of her captor, and the faintest of smiles touched her lips as she conjured his image in her mind's eye. Broad shouldered and lean but muscularly built, the duke cut an imposing figure in those tight-fitting breeches of his. Framed by that black hair, his face was handsomely chiseled without being pretty. What attracted her the most were his eyes, black and gleaming.

Shakespeare had said that eyes were the mirror to the soul, but the duke's black eyes were fathomless. She felt as if he could see her darkest secrets and her worst insecurities.

A knock on the door drew her attention. Then it opened to admit Duncan with her lunch.

"Where is my brother?" Lily asked, crossing the cabin. "When will I be allowed to see him?"

"Your brother is on deck with his grace," Duncan told her. "He's having fun."

"His grace or my brother?" she asked dryly.

Duncan gave her a stern look and said, "Enjoy your meal." Then he left her alone.

Knowing Michael was safe, Lily ate her lunch of broth with pieces of meat swimming in it. Then she lifted the Bible off the table, dragged a chair to the porthole, and sat down. Opening the Holy Book to the first page, Lily started to read, hoping that God would send her a solution to her intolerable situation.

A door slammed. Lily opened her eyes and realized that she'd dozed off just as Noah was building the ark. The dim light in the cabin told her that afternoon was racing toward twilight.

Footsteps crossing the cabin sounded on the floor behind her. Lily turned to see the duke and said, "I would like to see my brother."

"So would I." James dropped a pile of garments into her lap, ordering, "Change into these. I'll return shortly."

"Where are you going?" she asked, still drowsy.

"I answer to no one, Mistress Hawthorne," the duke said. "However, I will make this one exception. I am going to bring your brother a change of clothing, compliments of the captain's cabin boy." And then he was gone.

Lily inspected the garments he'd dropped on her lap. There were a boy's black breeches, a white shirt, and a black leather jerkin. Apparently her new outfit was compliments of the cabin boy, too. Did the poor child have any clothing left?

Rising from the chair, Lily changed behind the privacy screen in case she was interrupted. The boy's breeches fit her like a second skin but not uncomfortably so. The shirt was altogether too flimsy to suit her, but the leather jerkin covered the indecent display of her breasts.

Lily rolled up the sleeves and walked around the

screen just as the door opened. "Michael," she cried, and flew into his arms.

"Duke brought me new clothes," Michael said, giving her a hug, "but I'm saving them for tomorrow."

"How thoughtful of him," Lily said. Then, out of habit, "Wipe your chin, brother."

Michael wiped the drool off his chin with the sleeve of his shirt. "What a Goddamned good time I'm having," he told her.

Lily stared at him in surprise. "Never let me hear you curse again," she reprimanded him.

"My crew curses," Michael told her. "Cook has a little white pig with pink eyes. I'm going to play with it again tomorrow."

"That sounds like wonderful fun," Lily said, "Sit down and we'll eat supper together."

"No way, Sister. I'm eating with my crew." At that, Michael turned and marched out of the cabin.

Lily stared after him, surprised by the sudden change in his demeanor. She'd never seen him so animated and happy. While she was enduring the most miserable time of her life, her brother was having fun.

"Your men won't tease him because of his . . . condition?" Lily asked, shifting her gaze to the duke.

"They haven't yet," James answered. "The first mate was teaching him rope knots this afternoon."

Duncan walked into the cabin and set their supper down on the table. Without sparing them a glance, he left and closed the door behind him.

"Shall we?" James asked, gesturing to the table.

Lily sat down. On the table before her were a pork pie, a loaf of crusty bread, and a pitcher of ale.

While she watched, James cut her a portion of the pie and placed it in her dish. "Pork is one of my favorite meals," he said conversationally. "I especially like it roasted."

Lily lifted her gaze from her plate to his dark eyes. She couldn't imagine why he was being so bloody pleasant, but she might as well take advantage of his mood.

"Why did you abduct my brother and me?" she asked. "You sometimes sound as if the war was a personal situation between us."

"We'll discuss it later," James answered. "You do realize that if you were a man you would already be dead?"

"We'll discuss it now," Lily insisted, becoming irritated. "And if I were a man, *you* would be dead, not I."

His infuriating smile returned. He gestured to the plate as if she hadn't spoken. "Are you going to eat that food or play with it?"

"I'm going to play with it," Lily told him, a challenge in her voice. "Perhaps I'll get a leash and take it wherever I go."

At that, she stood and crossed the cabin to stare out the porthole at complete blackness. The night was as black as her tormentor's eyes. *And soul.*

"Your emotional outbursts are quite entertaining," James said in an amused voice. "And your derriere looks delightful in those breeches."

Lily whirled around, too appalled to speak. He stood only inches from her, so close she needed to tilt her head back to look him square in the face.

"You killed my brother," he said in a quiet voice.

His accusation shocked her. "This whole abduction has been a terrible mistake," Lily said when she found her voice. "I am not the person you want. I've never met your brother."

"Are you the Gilded Lily?" he asked.

Lily nodded.

"Then you caused my brother's death."

"I never caused anyone's death," she cried.

James moved closer until she felt herself pinned to the wall behind her. "If that fiancé of yours loved you," he taunted her, "the man would have protected you and kept you out of men's affairs."

"Men's affairs?"

"War, subterfuge, and politics."

"My fiancé loves me dearly and has faith in my abilities," Lily told him, summoning angry righteousness from deep within her. "Why, he's loved me for years. We'll be married as soon as the war ends, and then Michael will live with us on Beacon Hill. The three of us will live happily ever after."

James smiled without humor. "Real life has no happily ever afters, little girl," he told her. "Besides, why would you want to live with your brother? Most people who profess to be in love want to be alone together."

Slant-eyed monkey. Slant-eyed monkey.

Lily recalled the hurtful names hurled at her brother and her anger rose like a winter's gale. "The other children are cruel to him," she burst out. Gaining control of herself, she said in a calmer voice, "My fiancé is financially secure. Michael will never hear those horrible children taunt him again."

"Do you want to marry this paragon of manhood because you love him?" James asked, staring her straight in the eye. "Or do you love him because he can afford to protect your brother?"

His probing question surprised her, and Lily looked

away uncomfortably. She didn't know if she could answer that question. How much of her love for Bradley was real and how much was a desire to protect Michael? And then there was the troubling matter of any child of hers being born with Michael's affliction.

"Has the man no pride?" James spoke, drawing her back from her thoughts. "I wouldn't want you to marry me in order to protect your brother."

"I wouldn't marry you to save my life," Lily told him. "So you need have no fear of that."

His smile was lazy, amused, and oh so infuriating. And then he spoke, his words even more infuriating than his smile.

"I could make you love me," James boasted. "Oh, yes, I could make you love me *just . . . like . . . that.*" He snapped his fingers in front of her face.

Lily rolled her eyes. "Please, spare me the—"

Before she could utter a protest, James pulled her against his unyielding body. His strong arms encircled her and his clean scent of mountain heather teased her senses.

Lily stared unwaveringly into his dark eyes. His face inched closer and closer until his mouth covered hers—touching, tasting, exploring her sweetness.

His lips are warm, she thought.

Closing her eyes, Lily surrendered to his slow, persuasive kiss. His tongue flicked across the crease in her lips, which parted for him like flower petals opening to the warmth of the sun. Mesmerized by his languorous kiss, she succumbed to instinct and entwined her arms around his neck, pressing her body against his.

Lily trembled with these new, exquisite sensations.

She returned his kiss ardently, demandingly, and met his thrusting tongue with her own.

Her young body was on fire. The secret place between her thighs throbbed with desire, and she felt her nipples hardening into peaks, aching for his touch. And then he slid his hand inside her shirt to tease her aroused nipples.

Lily became lost in the rioting desire that overwhelmed her. She heard a woman's low moan of pleasure as if from a great distance. And sanity returned with the realization that she was the woman.

Lily pushed his hand away and stared dazedly into his gleaming black eyes. She raised her hand and slapped him with all her strength.

With his body, James pressed her against the wall. "Just . . . like . . . that," he repeated, nose to nose with her. Then he snapped his fingers.

"My fiancé will kill you for daring to touch me," Lily said.

Placing the palms of his hands on the wall on either side of her head, James asked, "Is that before or after you fall in love with me?"

"I believe I'll enjoy killing you myself," Lily said, summoning a bravado she didn't feel. "I intend to do that at the first opportunity."

"Do you plan to threaten me to death?" James asked. Abruptly, he turned and crossed the cabin to his sea chest. Digging inside, he produced one of his shirts and tossed it on the bed, saying, "Sleep in that. You have fifteen minutes for your private needs." He headed for the door, stopping only to take his plate of pork pie with him.

Lily's simmering anger became boiling rage, which she was unable to control. Not only had the English devil abducted her, but now he was laughing at her expense.

Without thinking, Lily pulled her boot off and threw it in his direction. The boot hit him hard between his shoulder blades.

Lily doubted her own sanity when he whirled around and she saw the forbidding expression on his face. He took two steps toward her.

"I'm sorry," Lily cried, holding her arm out as if to ward him off. "I would never want to hurt anyone, not even you."

"We'll discuss your behavior when I return," James said in a menacing tone. "In fifteen minutes." And then he walked out the door.

Four

The impertinent minx had struck him.

In angry disbelief, James marched down the narrow passageway and went above deck. The murderous little wharf rat had dared what no man ever had. A frown from him usually sent his clerks into near-incontinence, yet here was this slip of a girl challenging him at every turn. Where did she get the gall?

Or bravery, he thought, the hint of a smile touching his lips. The girl was a fool who would fight to the death for a cause. If she hadn't been challenging *him,* he would have patted her on the back for a job well done.

James stepped on deck and looked up at the night sky. Like the previous evening, God's jewels winked at him from the perfect setting of a black velvet sky—Orion in the west, Polaris in the north, Arcturus in the east, and Betelgeuse in the south. No moon shone overhead, but this was the time of year when the crescent moon would lay on its back and smile down upon the earth and its fools.

Judging that fifteen minutes had elapsed, James breathed deeply of the night air and fortified himself for the next battle. He hadn't had this much fun in a long, long time. Certainly, Valentina held no challenge for him.

James knew that the girl from Boston's wharves would prove no match for him in the end. He had to admit, though, that she was giving him a pretty good fight.

Pausing in the passageway outside his cabin, James wondered what she was doing on the other side of the door. What was she thinking? Did she fear his return to the cabin?

That thought brought a rueful smile to his lips. His intrepid captive appeared to fear nothing. At least his little wharf rat assumed a courageous front.

His little wharf rat? When had he started to think of her as his possession? The girl in his cabin belonged to him only temporarily. Forgetting that fact would lead to trouble.

James opened the door, stepped inside the cabin, and smiled at what he saw. Wearing one of his shirts that dropped to her knees and a pair of hose, Lily sat at the table and read the Bible. She kept her gaze fixed on the book even though he knew that she knew he had returned.

Without saying a word, James walked to his desk to get a bottle of whiskey and two glasses. Then he sat down in the chair opposite hers.

Still, Lily refused to acknowledge his presence.

James filled a shot glass with whiskey and downed it in one gulp. Then he poured whiskey into the second glass and pushed it toward her.

Lily looked up at him then. Her disarming sapphire eyes fixed on his gaze. "No, thank you," she said, and returned her attention to the book.

"Brandy, perhaps?" James said, playing the gracious host.

"I don't care for spirits," she said without looking up.

"My spirits or all spirits?"

Lily looked at him. "I never acquired a taste for spirits."

James cocked a dark brow at her. "Your father owns a tavern."

"I don't need to drink spirits in order to serve them," she replied.

"I understand."

Lily dropped her gaze to the Bible again and resumed reading. James drank her glass of whiskey and then relaxed back in his chair to stare at her.

Several long moments passed in silence.

James watched in amazement as she scanned two pages and turned to the next two pages in less time than he would need to read one column. When she glanced up at him as if feeling his gaze on her, he gave her a broad smile. She did not return his smile but dropped her gaze to the book again.

With amused satisfaction, James watched her begin to fidget because his attention was fixed on her. He reached for the bottle of whiskey, filled his glass, and then downed it. The liquor burned a trail to his stomach. He was just beginning to pour himself another drink when she spoke.

"Are you planning on getting drunk?"

"That's none of your damned business, sweetheart," James answered.

Lily arched an ebony brow at him. "Cursing demonstrates a definite lack of vocabulary, James."

"And lecturing one's abductor demonstrates a lack of common sense," he returned.

"Spare me your threats, your grace. You don't frighten me."

"What are you reading?" James asked, letting her words pass unanswered.

"I'm reading about God's destruction of Sodom and Gomorrah," Lily answered. Staring him straight in the eye, she added, "Their road to oblivion began when they indulged in drinking spirits."

James burst out laughing, which earned him a grudging smile from his lovely captive. "I knew I could make you smile," he said. "I hope you don't give the same lecture to your father's patrons."

"Certainly not," Lily said, her smile growing. "I've grown fond of eating regularly and sleeping with a roof over my head, which I would be forced to forgo if my father lost his business."

"I see your point."

Lily rested her elbow on the table and raised her hand to her chin. She gave him a long look and asked, "And what does a duke actually do to earn his keep?"

James smiled, enchanted by her flirtatious demeanor. "Most dukes do nothing but attend social events, spend their family's inheritance, and raise their monocles to their eyes to exclaim *egads* and *tally ho*," he told her.

"Do not forget *jolly good*," she said. "What do *you* do?"

"I cannot claim even one monocle to my name," he teased her. "However, I do own one of England's largest shipping lines."

Lily nodded and then asked, "What do these other dukes do when they run out of money?"

"They marry rich merchants' daughters," James answered.

"And taint the ancestral bloodlines?"

James shrugged. "Even dukes like to eat regularly and sleep with roofs over their heads." He leaned across the table and said in a loud whisper, "Never divulge this to anyone. Those sacred bloodlines usually began with an invader stealing land or a rogue stealing money from someone."

Lily laughed, a sweet, melodious sound that completely enchanted him. Those sapphire eyes of hers could make a man forget his own name.

"Are you certain you won't join me?" James asked, pouring himself another whiskey.

Lily shook her head.

James gulped his drink and then leaned back in his chair. Making himself more comfortable, he lifted his legs and rested them upon the table. "You love your brother very much," he said without preamble.

Her placid expression instantly registered suspicion. "What do you mean by that?"

"What about your other brother?" James asked, ignoring her question. "Do you think he's looking for you?"

"He doesn't know I've been . . . I've left," she answered. "He was away at the time, but when he discovers me missing, your days will be numbered."

James smiled at her threat. "Where did he go?"

"He had a lengthy errand to—" Lily broke off.

"What kind of errand?" he asked, determined to find out all that she knew. "Something for the war effort, I assume."

"You may as well save your breath," she told him. "I don't know anything."

"Your brother doesn't trust you?" James baited her.

Lily slammed the Bible shut and snapped, "Yes, of course he trusts me."

"My brother trusted me, too," James said, his voice deceptively mild, though he felt his anger at his brother's untimely death welling up in his chest. Suddenly he dropped his legs to the floor and leaned across the table.

"They hanged him," he told her, holding her gaze captive. "Have you ever seen a hanging?"

Again, Lily shook her head.

"Shall I tell you about it?"

"I am sincerely sorry for your brother's death and would make amends if—"

"Death has no remedy," James interrupted her. "My brother hanged because of you."

"Only indirectly because of me," Lily defended herself. She bolted out of the chair and crossed the cabin to stare out the porthole.

James followed her. She jumped when he placed his hands on her shoulders and forced her to face him.

"I do not want to listen to this," she told his chest.

With one hand, he lifted her chin and waited until she raised her gaze to his. "The rope would have caused an inverted *V* shaped bruise on his neck. Tighter and tighter the rope compresses the veins, but the blood continues to flow until the pressure inside the head causes small bleeding sites in the lips, the mouth, the eyelids. The face and neck become congested and dark red—"

"I thought the neck was broken," Lily interrupted him. "I thought that death was quick. You're trying to upset me."

"A broken neck and instant death happen only rarely," James told her, feeling grim satisfaction as her complexion began to pale. "The man thrashes at the end of the rope, wheezing as he struggles for air. Then there's a terrible stench as the man loses control of his bodily—"

"I don't want to hear this," Lily cried, holding her hand up as if to ward off his words. "Please, stop!"

Grabbing her hands, James forced them to her sides and kept talking. "The rope dances until there is one final jerk and all motion ceases. That could take fifteen minutes."

Lily was white. Her whole body shook with violent tremors, but her gaze remained fixed on his, as if she couldn't tear them away.

"If they left him hanging there after death as a warning to the British, his skin would become bluish gray and his lips would pale within three minutes," James went on, determined to make her understand the enormity of what she'd done. "Five hours later his body would be cool to the touch and his neck and jaw stiff. Twelve hours later his body would be totally frozen, the look of horror fixed on his face. His skin would become greenish red within one day. Three days later his body would swell, his skin blister, and his orifices leak fluid. The skin begins to burst open within—"

Her eyelids fluttered and she dropped away in a dead faint. He caught her before she hit the floor.

"Shit," James swore, and crossed the cabin to lay her on the bed. Staring down at her, James felt the stirrings of guilt and some other emotion he couldn't identify. Turning away, he filled a glass with brandy and returned to the bed.

Lily was moaning softly. Her eyes opened and fixed on his concerned expression.

"I shouldn't have done that," James said. "I apologize."

The duke was apologizing to her? Lily thought in disoriented surprise.

"Sip this," he ordered, helping her to sit up.

"What is it?" she asked weakly.

"Cold tea."

Lily swallowed a large gulp of the tea. In the next instant her eyes widened in surprise as the liquid burned a path to her stomach. She coughed and wheezed and then accused, "This isn't tea."

"Cold tea is brandy," James told her. "You've had a slight shock. Slide beneath the coverlet and go to sleep. It's bedtime anyway."

Lily nodded and passed him the glass. She touched his hand and said in an urgent tone of voice, "If I had known my work would cause another's death, I wouldn't have done it. You must believe me."

James stared at her for a long moment. "We cannot change the past," he said noncommittally. He set the glass on the table and began to undress. First he removed his shirt, but when he reached for his belt, Lily stopped him.

"Please, leave your pants on," she said.

James turned around and looked at her. Finally, as if he'd decided she'd had enough surprises for one day, he nodded at her. He returned to sit on the edge of the bed and pulled his boots off.

Lily watched as he turned around to slide beneath the coverlet. A gold chain around his neck caught her attention. Attached to the heavy gold chain was a cross, its center medallion depicting the Lamb of God, flanked by the Greek letters *alpha* and *omega*.

Lily dropped her mouth open in surprise. *Alpha* and *omega*, the first and the last. Her dying mother had told her that her true love would be the first and the last for her. How could this English duke, her sworn enemy, be her own true love? Bradley Howell was the man meant for her. This had to be pure coincidence. She could never love her enemy, and he could never love the woman who'd caused his brother's death.

"What's wrong?" James asked.

Lily reached out to touch his chest. "Your *alpha* and *omega* cross." She reached inside her shirt and withdrew her own cross. "See, I have one, too."

James looked from her face to the gold cross and then lifted his gaze to hers again. "I fail to see the significance in both of us wearing crosses."

He lay back on the bed and pulled her down. With his arm around her shoulders, he drew her close against his body.

Lily tried to ease away from him. That proved impossible in the tiny bed.

"Don't struggle," he said sternly, "or it will go worse for you."

An empty threat, Lily thought, a smile touching her lips.

"Lily?"

"Yes?"

"This is absolutely the last time I'm wearing my breeches to bed," James told her.

"We'll debate that point tomorrow," she replied.

"These breeches are too constricting," he insisted. "I'm dropping my breeches tomorrow night whether you like it or not."

Lily felt her cheeks grow warm with his words. She had no intention of letting him drop his breeches and then climb into bed with her. That would lead to disaster.

"Lily?"

"We'll see . . ."

There was no significance in the duke wearing the *alpha* and *omega* symbol, Lily told herself. Merely an unsettling coincidence.

That was Lily's first drowsy thought when she awakened the next morning. Rolling over, she discovered the cabin was empty.

Lily rose from the bed, washed hurriedly, and then sat at the table where Duncan had left her bread and cheese. She wondered briefly what Michael was doing, though she had no fear for his safety with Duncan watching over him. The big Scotsman would never let anything happen to her brother. She was certain of that.

Sunlight streamed through the porthole into the cabin, and Lily smiled at the motes of light dancing in the air. She remembered that, as a child, she'd always tried to catch them. Once she nearly drowned when she tried to grab the sunbeams glinting off the harbor's water.

How could such a happy child come to this? Poor choices, Lily answered her own question.

Oh, why hadn't she married Bradley Howell the first time he'd asked? She and Michael would be safe at home on Beacon Hill instead of sailing across the Atlantic Ocean.

Lily already knew the answer to that question, too. She had delayed accepting Bradley's offer because she feared giving birth to an impaired child like her brother.

Banishing that disturbing thought, Lily closed her eyes to conjure her beloved's image. Unfortunately, the duke's handsome face and black eyes appeared before her.

Raising the devil was easier than laying him, she decided.

Lily turned around when the door opened. Looking indecently handsome, the duke walked in and smiled at her.

"Would you like a bath?" James asked.

She smiled at him.

The duke turned and gestured to someone outside. Ten crewmen, each carrying two buckets of steaming water, marched inside and emptied their buckets into the tub behind the screen. With eyes averted, they left without sparing her a glance.

James produced a bar of soap and then held up the garment he carried slung across his arm, a blue muslin walking dress embroidered up the front. Accompanying the gown was a matching shawl.

Lily could not suppress her delight. "Where did you—?"

"Compliments of the captain," James told her. "Or rather, the captain's wife, who won't be receiving these gifts when her husband returns to England."

"I couldn't accept a gift meant for another," Lily said, unable to hide the disappointment in her voice.

"You had better accept them," James told her. "I paid the man double what they're worth."

Lily smiled and rose from her seat at the table. "I certainly wouldn't want you to waste your money," she said, touching the shawl. "Cashmere? I've never worn anything so luxurious. I can only pray to be worthy of such extravagance. I wouldn't want all of your ancestors' plundering to be for nothing."

James grinned and handed the garments to her. "I'll leave these with you and return when you're finished. We'll go above deck for some air."

Lily nodded, eager to be out in the sun again. She waited until the door closed behind him and then stripped her clothes off. Soaking in steaming water was good for the soul, she decided, easing herself into the tub. After a leisurely bath, she toweled herself dry, brushed her hair, and donned the blue gown. Grabbing the shawl off the bed, she artfully wrapped it around her shoulders and waited for the duke's return.

Great guardian angel, she felt like a real lady, not a wharf rat. Excitement built within her and made her restless. She hadn't felt this wonderful since her birthday, when Bradley had given her the red shawl.

Hearing a knock on the door, Lily called, "Come in."

James walked inside and looked her up and down as he crossed the cabin. Without giving her a chance to retreat, he grasped her hand and raised it to her lips. "The gown is lovely," he murmured, "but its loveliness pales when compared to yours."

Lily felt as if they were two different people. She was a real lady and the duke was an admirer who sought to woo her into marriage. And she felt young again, something she hadn't felt since the day her mother died and protecting her brother became one of her duties.

"Shall we, my lady?" the duke said, and escorted her to the door.

Stepping on deck, Lily breathed deeply of the fresh sea air and sighed when she felt the warmth of the sun caressing her face. Freedom and sunlight were two of God's most wonderful creations.

"You remind me of a cat basking in the sun," James said.

Lily gave him a sidelong glance and looked around, saying, "Where is the captain? I'd like to thank him for the gown and shawl."

"Captain Roberts is a busy man and cannot stop his duties to socialize with us," the duke told her.

"Are you certain you didn't order him to stay away from me?" Lily asked. "I noticed how the crew avoided looking at me this morning. Are you afraid I might make a friend to help me escape?"

"The only thing you will accomplish by escaping is drowning yourself and your brother," James told her.

"Speaking of my brother, where is—?"

"Sister!"

Lily heard her brother's call and looked around. He was nowhere.

"Up here, Sister!"

Lily raised her gaze and nearly swooned at what she saw. Her sapphire eyes widened and her body trembled at the sight of her brother in the lookout perch.

"Get him down before he falls," she said, grabbing the duke's arm for support.

"You underestimate his ability," James replied. "Michael climbs with the agility of a monkey."

"Sister," Michael called again.

Lily forced herself to smile and wave at her brother. "Get him down," she insisted.

The duke cupped his mouth with his hands and

shouted, "Come down now." He followed that with a beckoning gesture.

Michael climbed out of the perch and started down the mast. Lily closed her eyes at the sight lest he lose his footing and fall to the deck. She could face most things bravely but not her brother's death.

"You can open your eyes," James said in an amused tone of voice. "Michael is down."

Lily looked at the duke and blushed at her own cowardly behavior. Everyone had a weak spot, and now he knew hers.

"Did you see me, Sister?" Michael asked, advancing on them.

Lily suffered the urge to scold him but knew that wasn't the correct approach. Instead, she smiled and said, "I'm so proud of you, Brother. You did marvelously well, but seeing you up there frightens me. I wish you wouldn't do that again."

Michael nodded in understanding. "I'll only climb up when you're belowdeck," he told her.

Lily ignored the duke's chuckle. "That makes me feel much better," she forced herself to say.

"Come on," Michael said, grabbing her hand. "I want to show you Cook's little white pig."

Lily sent the duke a sidelong glance and let her brother lead her away. James followed two steps behind. The three of them went below deck to the galley, where the cook and his assistant were already preparing that evening's meal.

"Good afternoon," James said, gaining their attention.

The two men whirled around from the table, where they were kneading dough for bread. "Good afternoon, your grace," the cook spoke for the two of them. "Do you have any special requests, your grace?"

"Michael tells us you have a piglet on board," James said. "We'd like to see it."

The cook crossed the galley to an open-topped box and lifted a squirming, squealing piglet. He handed it to the duke who held it up for Lily's inspection.

The piglet was tiny and pure white. Its only color was the pink tip of its snout, pink trotters, pink irises, and deep red pupils.

"What a strange little creature," Lily said, scooping it out of the duke's hands and cuddling it against her chest.

"I heard your grace liked pork," the cook said by way of an explanation, "but the darned pig won't grow."

"You can't cook him," Lily cried.

"That's my pet," Michael shouted.

"Please don't kill the poor thing," Lily implored the duke. "Pigs are known to bring good luck to business ventures."

"Are they now?" James said, amused by their protection of a pig. He looked from her to the boy to the cook and said, "The pig won't grow. It's an albino dwarf."

"What's *albino?*" Michael asked.

"The pig has no color," the duke explained.

"Can we keep it?" Lily asked.

"I didn't say that."

"Duke, I love that pig," Michael announced.

James looked at the cook and said, "Keep the pig safe until I decide." At that, he gave Lily a broad grin that told her that she'd better behave herself or the pig would suffer.

Lily realized this was something else he could hold over her head like a sword—the pig's life and her brother's happiness. The duke was an incorrigible opportunist.

"Shall we go?" James asked.

"I'm staying to play with—what should we name him, Lily?"

"How about Prince?"

James smiled and told them, "The pig is a female."

"We'll call her Princess," Lily said. "Prinny for short." She smiled at the duke, who inclined his head, acknowledging her clever insult to England's Prince Regent. Before he could say anything, she handed the pig to her brother and said, "Wipe your chin."

Michael wiped his chin on the sleeve of his shirt and then kissed the top of the pig's head. "Thank you, Sister."

"Take care of the boy until Duncan comes for him," James ordered the cook.

Instead of returning above deck, James escorted her to their cabin. When he opened the door, she said, "Couldn't we go above deck for just a while longer?"

"I have ledgers waiting for my attention," James told her. "We'll go above deck after supper and stargaze."

Already bored, Lily sat down with the Bible at the table. She opened to the section where Noah builds his ark and stared at the page without seeing. She shifted her gaze to the duke, sitting with his back to her at his desk.

Without thinking, Lily admired his black hair, slightly scraggy on his neck. His broad shoulders looked magnificent in his black waistcoat.

"Have you decided?" she asked abruptly.

James looked around at her. "I beg your pardon?"

"Have you decided Prinny's fate?"

He stared at her for a long moment and then said, "Read your book."

Lily closed the book silently and stared at him for a long time. James looked around, as if he felt her gaze on him, and asked, "What are you doing?"

Lily smiled sweetly. "I'm bothering you."

"Read your book," he said.

"I'm tired of the damned Bible," she complained.

"That's blasphemy."

Lily narrowed her gaze on him. Was the devil now tutoring her about religion?

"God will send you straight to hell for murdering Princess," she told him.

James smiled at her. "In that event, we will finish this conversation there."

"Perhaps if I had something to occupy my hands . . ." Lily said, ignoring his comment.

"I can think of a few things for you to do with your hands," he said.

Lily noted the gleam in his black eyes and frowned. "I meant needlework."

"You are the only woman on a ship of men," James told her, his tone of voice implying that she was an idiot. "There is no needlework here. I have a hundred books in that case. Pick one."

"You simply do not understand," Lily told him. "I need to pace my reading. If not, I'll finish those books in a few days."

His expression told her that he didn't believe her. She couldn't blame him either. Total recall was a rare gift. *Curse*, she corrected herself.

"A pet might occupy my time," Lily told him.

"Write a book," he suggested.

"It would never be published," she replied.

James tossed the quill down in disgust and said, "*I'll* publish the damned thing."

"I suppose I could write about a little lost pig," she said. "A white one, I think."

Rising from her chair, Lily crossed the cabin to sit on the bed. Relaxing back, she announced, "I need a plot for the pig's story."

"Write about a kidnapped girl who gets spanked," James suggested.

"That really is too bad of you," Lily said.

"Madam, silence is a woman's best garment," James told her. "Wear it."

Lily gestured as if she were buttoning her lips together. The duke returned to his work.

Intending to focus on Bradley, Lily closed her eyes to conjure him in her mind's eye, but it was the duke's image that appeared. She truly wanted to think about Bradley, Lily thought, suffering a twinge of guilt. She was unable to picture his face in her mind. What did that mean?

"I could make you love me just like that. . . ."

Lily recalled the duke's boast of the previous evening.

"James?"

"What now?" He didn't bother to turn around.

"I could never love a man who murdered a helpless creature," she announced.

"Thank you for the warning," James said, turning around, a smile flirting with his lips. "I'll keep that in mind."

Five

"Supper awaits your pleasure, my lady."

Lily opened her eyes and focused on the duke, who was smiling down at her. Without thinking, she returned his smile and accepted his hand like a queen accepting a dance with a courtier. He escorted her to the table and assisted in seating her.

Lily wondered why he'd been so pleasant all day, and then she knew. "Your ploy will not work," she announced, giving him an unamused look.

James cocked a dark brow at her. "To what are you referring?"

"Your kindness will not win my love," she told him.

"Oh, drat," he replied, obviously feigning disappointment. "I thought I was being discreet."

"I doubt you possess even one ounce of discretion," Lily told him. "I could never love an Englishman."

"You make us sound like lepers," James said.

Lily smiled as sweetly as she could. "I mean no insult."

"The hell you don't," he said.

Ignoring that, Lily looked over the evening's fare. There was cabbage and potato soup, haddock fried in batter, greens in vinaigrette, and a crusty loaf of bread.

"What a relief! I thought we'd be dining on pork," Lily said. Then she asked, "How do you manage to keep these vegetables for so long a period of time?"

"We made a side trip to Bermuda before we sailed for Boston," he told her.

"Even your revenge wasn't enough to forgo your pleasures," Lily baited him.

"My dear, I'd already decided you were a dead man," James replied, his tone arrogant. "Why rush the funeral? Unfortunately, you turned out to be a woman."

"I suppose the best-laid plans of men often go astray," Lily said, lifting her spoon and beginning to eat.

" 'The best-laid plans,' " James said. "What an appropriate phrase."

Lily frowned, which only made him smile. He seemed to be in such a good mood that she wanted to beg for the piglet's life. Her brother was attached to the pig, and no one was going to harm it if she could do anything to stop him.

Lily opened her mouth to plead for the pig but raised a piece of haddock to her lips instead. Begging for the piglet's life would have the opposite effect on the duke, who would delay his decision in order to torment her.

They ate in silence. Each time Lily raised her gaze to steal a peek at the duke, he was looking at her. She began to feel uncomfortable, so she stared at his hands on his glass and noticed how long his fingers were, recalling how they'd felt caressing her breasts.

"Tell me about your codes," James said, breaking the silence between them.

Startled by his voice, Lily coughed as a bit of broth

slipped down her windpipe. Recovering herself, she stared into his gleaming black eyes. Did the blinking idiot believe his good looks would incite her to spill all she knew?

"My codes?"

His expression told her that he knew she was stalling. "Your American codes."

"If you think to break the American codes, forget it," Lily told him pertly. "Whatever I passed on was meaningless to me."

"Tell me what you know about codes in general," he said.

He was trying to trip her up, Lily decided. Too bad; he was destined for disappointment. She really hadn't any idea about the messages she passed on.

"I know there are several types of codes," Lily told him. "There are the simple columnar transposition, the true double transposition, the bilateral-monoalphabetic substitution, and the multiple alphabet substitution. The double transposition is especially secure because the enemy must break the code twice, sometimes using two key words."

"And what would you tell your contacts?" James asked.

"Well, after reading the cryptograms, I would destroy them," she replied. "Then, I would dictate them to a contact who knew the key."

James cocked a dark brow at her. "So, you had absolutely no idea what message you were delivering?"

Lily shook her head. "My fiancé and brother believed that I would be safer that way." She gave him a rueful grin and added, "I suppose they were wrong."

"If they'd wanted to keep you safe, they should never have involved you in this business," James said.

Ignoring his statement, Lily leaned slightly forward, her sapphire eyes sparkling. "Would you like to know a secret?" she asked.

James inclined his head.

"We Americans won the last war because of the code we used. The messages were sent using Indian words and then translated a second time into English," Lily told him. "Quite clever of us, don't you think?"

"Quite so," James agreed, smiling at her.

Lily couldn't imagine what he found so amusing about losing a war, but she'd already concluded that these English were an odd lot.

"That is what's meant by Yankee ingenuity," she boasted. "Now, tell me about yourself."

"There's not much to tell," he said.

"I cannot credit those words coming from a duke," Lily replied. "False modesty is unbecoming to you."

James stared her straight in the eye and informed her, "Unlike some people, I never go about divulging my life story to every person I meet."

Lily wasn't sure if he was insulting her or simply making a general statement. She decided to give him the benefit of the doubt. *This time.*

"How do you fill your days?" she asked. "I'm certain you don't make a habit of sailing around the world abducting young ladies."

"Since I was born the second son, I hadn't planned on inheriting and needed to make my fortune in business," James told her. "I own several shipping lines and travel all over the world. Working relaxes me, and when I need to escape civilization, I retreat to my ancestral home in Scotland, Kinross Castle."

"Oh, that must be the reason you're unlike other

Englishmen," Lily replied, feeling as though she were giving him high praise.

"And how many Englishmen have you actually met?" he asked, a smile flirting with the corners of his lips.

"Counting you?"

James inclined his head. "If you like."

"I've met two Englishmen," Lily told him.

James snapped his brows together. "Who is the other one?"

"Duncan."

"Do I detect in your words the notion that I might have a redeeming quality?" he asked.

"I wouldn't go that far," Lily answered honestly.

James grinned.

"Have you ever met the king?" she asked.

"The last time I saw him, George was debating an elm tree," James told her. "The tree was winning."

Lily burst out laughing, charmed by him. The duke wasn't such a bad man after all.

"Tell me about your life in Boston," he said.

Lily shrugged. "I help my father in the tavern and protect my brother."

"That cannot be your whole life," he replied. "What about friends?"

I don't have any friends, Lily thought. She had no female accomplishments to her credit. She couldn't cook very well, and her sewing was even worse than her cooking. Her only talent was her ability to recite all that she read. The only young woman with whom she had any relationship was Hortensia MacDugal, and no one would ever mistake them for friends.

"I don't have any friends," Lily answered, shifting

her gaze away from him. "I'm different from the other young women of my acquaintance."

"In what way are you different?" he asked quietly.

"For one thing, I know how to read and—" She broke off, uncertain of what else there was to say.

"And?"

"And I spend a lot of time with my brother," she added. "Michael needs constant stimulation and supervision."

Was that pity in his eyes? Lily wondered. She hoped not. She despised that emotion and all it implied— that she and her brother were pathetic creatures.

"I do have an enemy, though," she said for good measure. Having an enemy was an ordinary occurrence, and ordinary was what she'd always longed to be.

"I cannot imagine anyone not liking you," the duke remarked, obviously feigning surprise.

"You never met Hortensia MacDugal," Lily informed him, the hint of a smile touching her lips.

James smiled. "And what is wrong with Hortensia?"

"She dislikes me because I never followed her lead," Lily answered. "Jealousy consumes her because of my fiancé."

"So, Hortensia had an interest in this paragon, too?"

Lily nodded.

"I see that all females have certain traits in common," James said, shaking his head. "Their circumstances in life matter little when set against their instincts."

Lily arched a perfectly shaped ebony brow at him. "Is that a compliment or an insult?"

"Take it as you like it."

"I know one thing for sure," Lily said. "Hortensia would take after you in a minute."

"Why do you say that?"

"Because Hortensia—she just would."

Lily had no intention of praising the duke for his handsomeness or anything else. He was the monster who had abducted her and her brother and deserved her contempt, which she would resume giving him the first thing in the morning. Tonight had been so pleasant, she didn't want to mar it with arguments.

"You did promise me to go above deck after supper," Lily reminded him.

"So I did." James inclined his head and rose from his chair.

Lily had never seen anything as black as the night on the ocean. She felt as though she were falling through space. If the stars hadn't been shining above, she would have lost all sense of direction.

The ship glided through the calmest of seas. Only the crispness of the night air kept Lily from believing that she was in a dream.

"High in the northern sky is the Big Dipper," James told her, pointing in that direction.

Lily followed the direction in which he pointed but couldn't see any definite shape. "I don't see what you're looking at," she said.

James stepped closer and, putting his right arm around her shoulders, pointed toward the heavens with his left hand. "Over there," he said. "Do you see it?"

His hand on her shoulder and his closeness to her body prevented Lily from seeing anything. Sweet lamb of God, she couldn't hold on to a thought with his body so close and his warm breath upon her cheek.

"Yes, I see it now," she lied, and moved one step away from him.

The man seemed to enjoy tormenting her because he put both hands on her shoulders and turned her in another direction, saying, "The brightest star in the eastern sky is Arcturus. The Big Dipper's handle curves in its direction."

"I can see that, too," Lily lied again. All of her being was centered on the two strong hands touching her shoulders. The stars were merely bright dots in the sky.

"Arcturus means 'guardian of the bear' because it's so close to Ursa Major," James told her.

" 'It is the stars, the stars above us govern our condition,' " Lily murmured, quoting Shakespeare.

"And where does that Shakespearean line appear?"

"Look it up," she replied.

"I will one day when I'm bored and have nothing to occupy my time," James said. He gently drew her back against the warmth of his body and whispered against her ear, "I am proud of you for not mentioning the pig even once."

A rueful smile touched her lips. Lily turned her head to the side and told him, "I knew you would only torment me more if I did."

"I'm not that much of a monster."

"Have you listened to your own conversations lately?"

"That really is too bad of you," James chided her. "How could you live with yourself if your insults angered me and I killed the pig in revenge? You know, a kiss could go a long way in saving its life."

"Is this extortion?" Lily asked, whirling around to face him, regretting her action when he stepped closer to her. "Kissing the enemy is unacceptable," she announced, stepping back two paces.

"We aren't enemies."

"What are we?"

"We are two ordinary people caught in extraordinary circumstances," James answered.

"I would never call you ordinary," Lily said.

"Thank you."

"I meant to insult you."

"In that case, how dare you?" James replied.

Lily burst out laughing.

"All cats are gray in the dark," he said. "If you close your eyes, you'll never know I am the enemy."

"Oh, very well," Lily agreed with a long-suffering sigh. She closed her eyes and waited, but nothing happened. She opened her eyes and saw the duke smiling at her. "Well, your grace, let's get this over with."

Again, Lily closed her eyes. Again, nothing happened. Yet again, she opened her eyes.

"I want *you* to kiss *me,*" he told her.

"I don't know how," she said. "I have never been the one who kisses, merely the recipient."

"Kissing is easier than falling out of a tree," James said with a smile. "Much, much easier than remembering words on a page. Step closer and put your arms around my neck."

Lily took a step forward. Hesitantly, she reached up and placed her arms around his neck. That action brought her body in contact with his, and his clean, masculine scent assailed her senses. If she hadn't been blessed with inner strength, she knew she would have swooned dead away.

"Draw my head down," the duke said in a husky whisper.

Slowly, Lily drew his head down to hers. His face was a mere touch away.

"Now press your lips against mine," he said in a choked voice.

Tentatively, Lily pressed her lips against his mouth. His lips felt warm and firm and oh-so-inviting.

Lily melted into the kiss when she felt one of his hands go around her back and pull her body against his. He cradled the back of her neck with his other hand, making escape impossible. She relaxed against him, feeling as though she belonged in his arms.

And then the tempo of the kiss changed. His lips became demanding, stealing her breath away, persuading her lips to part for him. When they did, he dipped his tongue inside and explored the warmth of her mouth.

Great guardian angel, Lily thought, drawing back to stare dazedly into his eyes. *Bradley Howell had never kissed her like that.*

"Shall we go belowdeck?" James asked in a husky whisper.

Lily stared at him in confusion. Sweet lamb of God, the duke sounded as though he were asking to bed her. Was he as affected by their kiss as she was?

"I would like to say good night to my brother," Lily said, struggling to regain her composure.

James gestured toward the stairs. "After you, my lady."

Uncomfortably feeling his eyes upon her, Lily walked down the stairs to the passageway. She paused when she reached Duncan's cabin, and heard her brother's exclamation, "Holy hell, I won again."

Lily looked at the duke in displeasure. James shrugged his shoulders and knocked on the door.

"The lady wants to say good night to her brother," he called.

"Come in," Duncan said.

Followed by the duke, Lily marched inside the cabin. She placed her hands on her hips and confronted her brother, saying, "What did I tell you about cursing?"

"*Hell* isn't a curse," Michael defended himself. "*Hell* is a place. Isn't that right, Duncan?"

"What is that on the floor between you?" she demanded, without giving the big Scotsman a chance to answer.

"Duncan is teaching me to dice," Michael told her. "It's fun."

The Scotsman looked away. Lily glanced at the duke, who wore a sober expression, but laughter shone in his eyes.

"Dicing is the devil's own game," Lily said. Then, "Would you like me to tell you the story?"

Michael nodded.

Lily sat on the edge of the bed, and Michael sat beside her. She put her arm around his shoulders and began, "War broke out in heaven. Michael and his angels fought Satan, that ancient serpent, and his followers. The devil and his black angels were cast down out of heaven." Lily smiled at her brother's rapt attention and gave him a hug. "And so I named you Michael in honor of God's greatest angel because you were born on his feast day. When I held you in my arms, our mother said that you would make God smile."

"I like that part of the story," Michael told her. "Where did Satan go?"

"England."

"That isn't what you told me before," Michael said.

"The devil lives in hell because he can never again enter the gates of Paradise to be in the presence of God," Lily answered. "And the road to his damnation began with cursing and dicing."

"I won't do those things anymore," Michael promised. "Especially when you are around."

The duke chuckled, earning himself a censorious stare from Lily. She shifted her gaze to Duncan, who'd begun to cough. Her lips twitched with the urge to laugh, but she didn't want to encourage her brother's mutiny. Michael was smart enough to find a way around her discipline and innocent enough to give voice to it.

"Good night, Lily," she heard her brother say as she turned to leave. "Good night, Duke Grace."

Lily bit her bottom lip to keep from laughing and left the Scotsman's cabin. James's voice stopped her as she reached for the door of his cabin.

"Take a few minutes for yourself," James said.

Lily nodded without looking at him and walked inside the cabin. The door clicked shut behind her.

After changing into her nightshift, one of the duke's shirts, Lily completed her evening ablutions. Then she sauntered around the privacy screen. While they'd been above deck, someone had filled the wooden tub with steaming water. She'd already taken a bath that afternoon so the water could only mean the duke was planning on bathing.

Did he actually believe that she would allow him to strip naked and bathe in their cabin? Lily thought in irritation. On the other hand, how could she stop him?

Lily plopped down on the chair at the table and

waited, her irritation simmering, ready to boil over into full-bodied anger at the least provocation. She whirled around when the door swung open and started to rise, but the duke gestured at her to sit.

Suspicious about his intentions, Lily watched him sit opposite her and pour whiskey into two glasses. He drank one and gently shoved the other across the table toward her. In answer, she lifted the glass to her lips and gulped the whiskey.

James cocked a dark eyebrow at her.

Mimicking him, Lily arched a dark brow at him.

James smiled, apparently expecting her to return his smile.

Instead, Lily said in a voice rising with her agitation, "If you think I will allow you to strip naked and bathe while I'm in this cabin, then you had better think again, your grace."

Without saying a word, James stood and removed his belt, letting it drop to the floor. He reached for the top button on his shirt.

"Do not remove your shirt," she ordered.

James held her gaze captive and, ever so slowly, unfastened each button on the shirt. He hung the shirt neatly across the back of his chair.

Lily dropped her gaze from his black eyes to the *alpha* and *omega* cross he wore, its gleaming gold seeming to taunt her. "I mean it," she cried. "Do not remove anything else."

"What's a little flesh between friends?" James asked, sitting on the chair to remove his boots.

"Do not dare drop those breeches," Lily warned, her voice rising.

In answer, James stood and reached for the top button.

"Did you hear what I said?" Lily shouted.

"I believe every man on this ship heard your words," James replied without raising his voice. He dropped his breeches, revealing that he wore nothing beneath them.

"Sweet lamb of God," Lily gasped, and turned her back. She felt her face flush hotly. Making matters worse, he laughed at her embarrassment.

Great guardian angel, protect me from the man's audacity, Lily thought. She refused to look at him or even dignify his behavior with a blandishment. It would do no good anyway. And yet she suffered the unexpected regret that she had turned away so quickly.

Finally, Lily heard the sloshing of water as he climbed into the tub. To calm her nerves, she poured herself another shot of whiskey and downed it in one gulp. The amber liquid created a burning sensation from her lips into her stomach and relaxed her.

When she heard him begin humming a spritely tune, Lily cast an irritated glance in the direction of the privacy screen. If she went to sleep, she could escape him until morning and, with that in mind, stood to cross the cabin to the bed.

"Oh," she heard him exclaim in a disappointed voice. "Lily?"

What now? she wondered. "Yes?"

"I can't reach my back," James said.

"Should I fetch Duncan for you?" Lily asked.

"I wouldn't want to disturb him," he said. "Could you—"

"No."

"Please?"

"No!"

"Oh, that poor little porker," James drawled.

"Bastard," Lily muttered, sliding off the bed.

"Did you say something?" he called.

"I said I'm coming," she snapped.

Lily marched across the cabin. Unprepared for the sight of him in the tub, she sucked in her breath when she rounded the privacy screen.

Holding up the soap, James sat with his back toward her. He appeared even bigger in the small tub. By candlelight, the duke was an English Adonis.

Lily gave herself a mental shake and grabbed the soap out of his hand. She began lathering him. The muscles in his back relaxed beneath her touch, and she admired their sinewy strength.

"What are you thinking?" James asked.

"Nothing."

"Come now, my lady," he said. "You can share your innermost thoughts with me."

"I never imagined my station in life would be reduced to playing lady's maid to an English duke," Lily told him. She sensed his smile rather than saw it.

"Life does have its interesting twists and turns," James agreed. "Could you possibly go a little lower?"

He was taunting her. Anger swelled in Lily. She reached up and tossed the soap into the water in front of him.

"A slab of bacon with my breakfast sounds delicious," she announced.

Lily left him there and marched back across the cabin. The irritating sound of his husky laughter followed her. She slid into the bed and faced the wall.

The man was a monster sent to earth to torment her. He threatened the only two valuables she had—her brother's happiness and her innocence.

Lily heard the water sloshing as he climbed out of

the tub and then toweled himself dry. Unbidden, the image of the duke in all his naked magnificence paraded across her mind's eye. Surprised by her own thoughts, Lily softly recited the Twenty-third Psalm. When that didn't help, she began whispering the Lord's Prayer, " 'Our Father, Who art in heaven, hallowed be thy name . . . and deliver us from evil—' "

The bed creaked as the duke slid in beside her.

Lily had a mind to tell him exactly what a foul demon he was. She turned over, only to find him leaning over her. Again, his *alpha* and *omega* cross gleamed, as if taunting her with its presence.

"Good night, sweetheart," James whispered in a husky voice.

Lily opened her mouth to inform him that she was most definitely not his sweetheart. Her gaze dropped from his face to his naked chest and then lower.

Her sapphire eyes widened and she gasped, "Sweet lamb of God, you're still naked."

Six

"Making love requires no clothing," James said in a quiet voice.

"If you think that—" Lily stopped speaking as the realization of what he'd said seeped into her conscious. Staring him straight in the eye, she asked, "Are you going to rape me?"

"Certainly not." James fixed an affronted look on his face. "Your question offends me."

"You crawl naked into my bed and then find my suspicions offensive?" Lily asked in disbelief.

"I climbed into *my* bed," he corrected her, a smile touching the corners of his lips. His expression softened when he added, "I would never force you to do anything."

"You are forcing me to travel to England," she reminded him.

"I would never force you to do anything *except for that*," James amended.

Lily opened her mouth to reply, but he lightly brushed one long finger across her lips. "I have wanted to lay here like this and kiss you since the first moment I saw your beautiful face," he told her.

His compliment surprised her, and his gesture was

unexpectedly intimate. "I have a beautiful face?" she asked.

"Your loveliness will haunt me for all the days of my life," James answered.

Lily stared up at him, his black, fathomless gaze holding hers captive, oblivious to the effect her gaze was having on him. She ignored the rational voice that urged her to flee. Instead, she enjoyed the feel of his finger tracing the outline of her lips.

He's going to kiss me, Lily thought, but made no move to push him away.

James dipped his head. His face moved closer and closer until his mouth covered hers—touching and tasting in a gently persuasive kiss.

With a sigh of pleasure, Lily fell under his spell as a languorous feeling overwhelmed her senses. She entwined her arms around his neck and pressed herself against him.

The tempo of the kiss changed with her surrender, becoming more ardent and demanding. Lily trembled when he flicked his tongue along the crease of her lips.

His slow, soul-stealing kiss lasted almost forever. His lips left hers and sprinkled dozens of feathery-light kisses on her temples, eyelids, and throat.

"You are rarer than a forest lily, sensuous and innocent, unaware of your siren's allure," James murmured, his breath mingling with hers.

He stroked her cheek and the column of her throat. When his hand dropped to her breasts, Lily jerked back in surprise.

"Let me touch you," he whispered. "I promise to stop whenever you want."

Staring into his eyes, Lily felt powerless to resist. She wanted to feel his hands caressing her bare skin.

James kissed her while he unbuttoned her shirt and pushed it aside, baring her breasts. "You are exquisite," he whispered, staring into her disarming sapphire eyes.

James dipped his head to kiss her lingeringly, pouring his passion into that stirring kiss. He slid his tongue past her lips to explore the sweetness beyond them and then glided his fingertips across her sensitive nipples to tease them into aroused hardness.

And Lily knew desire. Overwhelmed by his touch, she surrendered to passion and returned his kiss in kind.

An unexpected jolt of sensation shot through James when he felt her tongue flicking between his lips to explore his mouth. "Touch me, lady," he whispered, his lips hovering above hers.

"Touch you?"

She sounded surprised and frightened. The innocence in her tone and question was an aphrodisiac to James. "Glide your hand across my chest," he coaxed.

James knew she wanted to touch him and feel his muscles ripple beneath her fingertips. He guided her hand to his chest, and she traced her fingertips through his mat of dark hair to touch his *alpha* and *omega* cross. Becoming bolder, she flicked her thumb across his nipple and lifted her gaze to his when it hardened.

James moaned in pleasure at her touch. Her fingers were silken threads sliding seductively across his skin.

"You see, darling," he whispered. "You affect me as I do you."

Holding the back of her head in one hand, James covered her mouth with his lips. "Now I am going to touch you the same way," he whispered in a husky voice. "Will you allow it?"

"Yes," she breathed against his lips.

James dropped his heated gaze to her bared breasts. With their pink-tipped peaks, her breasts were flawless and perfectly formed. He kissed her again and, when she sighed against his lips, glided his hand down her body to tease her sensitive nipples, igniting a throbbing heat between her thighs.

Her breath caught raggedly in her throat. She leaned into his caress, silently asking for more.

"Kiss me, lady," he whispered thickly.

Lily needed no second invitation. She looped her arms around his neck, pressed her mouth to his, and kissed him for an eternity.

Gone was the unsophisticated girl of the previous days. The essence of innocence remained, yet fiery passion had transformed her into the aroused woman in his arms.

James drew back to look down at her and became mesmerized by her ripe breasts and tiny waist. Her thighs had been created to wrap tightly around him, and her rounded hips were suited for nurturing his seed.

"Lady, you are so very beautiful," James murmured against her lips as one of his hands stroked the curve of her hip.

"You are beautiful, too," Lily said on a sigh.

James kissed her lingeringly, as if time had ceased and they had an eternity to do whatever they wished. He intended to coax her slowly into doing his bidding, savor her exquisite flesh. His kiss became possessive and demanding, stealing her breath away.

Responding instinctively to his passionate kiss, Lily pressed her nakedness against him. For the first time in her young life, she experienced the incredible sensation of masculine hardness touching her female softness. And she liked it.

"I want to love you," he whispered.

"Yes, love me," she said in a breathless voice.

Caressing her flushed cheek, James claimed her lips again in a kiss that lasted forever. Lily returned his kiss with equal ardor, and then some. He flicked his tongue across the crease between her lips and then explored the sweetness beyond them. Their tongues touched almost tentatively and then grew bolder, swirling together in a mating dance as old as time itself.

Lily sighed with pleasure as James sprinkled dozens of kisses across her temples, eyelids, nose, and throat. His mouth returned to cover hers, and he caressed her silken body from the delicate column of her throat to her thrusting breasts with their engorged nipples.

James moved his lips slowly down her throat and then beyond. His tongue swirled seductively around her nipples. Capturing one nipple between his lips, he suckled upon it, and her throaty moan of pleasure excited him and encouraged his seduction.

"Spread your legs for me," James whispered.

Without hesitation, Lily did as she was told. James covered her mouth with his own while he inserted one long finger inside her.

That startled her into alertness. Lily opened her eyes and tried to skitter away from his probing finger.

"Be easy, lady," James soothed, keeping her imprisoned within his embrace. "Trust me . . . *please.*"

James knew she was as skittish as a young mare about to experience her first covering. He wanted her hot, wet, and willing to receive him into her tight virgin's body. He wanted to mount her like a stallion, control her body and soul, make her his completely and forever.

"Trust me," he whispered again, his voice cracking with the aching need to possess her. *"Trust me, love."*

Lily answered by spreading her legs wider. Her invitation was unmistakable; she yearned to be possessed as much as he yearned to possess her.

James dipped his head to her breasts to suckle upon her nipples and then inserted a second finger inside her. Judging her accustomed to the feel of it, he began to move his fingers rhythmically, seducing her to his will.

And then his fingers were gone. James knelt between her thighs. The knob of his manhood teased the dewy pearl of her womanhood, making her moan low in her throat.

With one powerful thrust, James pushed himself inside her, breaking her virgin's barrier, and buried himself deep within her trembling body. Lily cried out in surprised pain and clutched him tightly. He lay perfectly still for a moment to let her become accustomed to the feel of him inside her, and then he began to move, enticing her to move with him.

Lily wrapped her legs around his waist and met each of his powerful thrusts with her own. Suddenly, unexpectedly, she exploded as wave after wave of throbbing sensation carried her to paradise and beyond.

Only then did James release his need. He groaned

and shuddered and poured his hot seed deep within her.

They lay still for several long moments, their labored breathing the only sound within the cabin. James rolled to one side, pulling her with him, and planted a kiss on her forehead.

Lily hid her face against his chest and wept quietly.

Of all the things she could have done, her weeping was the furthest from his expectation. James could have handled her anger, but her tears were different. He held her close and waited for her weeping to subside.

"Did I hurt you?" he asked.

Lily shook her head.

"Then why are you weeping?"

"I'm not crying anymore," she answered.

"I beg your pardon," James said. "Why *were* you weeping?"

Clutching the coverlet to cover her breasts, Lily rose up on one elbow and met his gaze. Her sapphire eyes, glistening with tears, reminded him of the Highland's blue lochs in summer.

"I was weeping for what I've lost," Lily told him.

"Why not smile for what you have gained?" he countered.

"What have I gained?"

James grinned. *"Me."*

Lily smiled in spite of herself, but her smile vanished as quickly as it had come. "Witty remarks slip easily from the lips of a wealthy English duke," she said in a soft voice.

"What does that mean?" he asked.

Lily met his gaze unwaveringly, but embarrassment stained her cheeks. "A wealthy woman has many valuable gifts to bring a potential husband, but a poor girl like me has none of that," she told him. "I've given away my virtue, which was the only thing of value I had to offer."

"You are wrong," James said, holding her close and tracing a finger down her cheek. "You are uncommonly lovely and highly intelligent."

"Beauty fades with age," Lily disagreed, "and intelligence is not a quality most men seek in a wife."

"Stupidity is not prized by men," James told her. "A man needs to converse with his wife. Besides, you possess other admirable qualities."

"I do?" She sounded surprised.

Unconsciously, James fingered her *alpha* and *omega* cross. "Shall I expound upon them?"

Lily smiled softly. "Please do."

"You are very brave," he told her. "Most men quake when I frown at them."

"I don't believe you," she scoffed.

James snapped his dark brows together and grimaced with great exaggeration. "Doesn't that frighten you?" he asked.

"No."

"The sight of that expression always sends my clerks scurrying away," he told her.

Lily laughed. "What a bully."

"I am that," James agreed. "Now, shall we return to your finer points of character?"

She inclined her head.

"You are uncommonly steadfast and loyal. Your devotion to your brother is the crowning jewel in your character," he said. "You always champion the underdog, too."

"Thank you for your kind words," Lily replied.

"However, I do not understand how you can possibly know all that about me in a few days."

"I am an excellent judge of character," James said. "Besides, I never give praise lightly." He touched her *alpha* and *omega* cross, saying, "How strange that both of us wear the same symbol, *alpha* and *omega.*"

"The first and the last, the beginning and the ending," Lily whispered.

"Quite so."

"Be careful, your grace," she teased him. "You are beginning to sound like an Englishman."

James smiled at that. "I suppose I should tell you about my family before we reach England."

"You have a family?" She sounded surprised again. "I never imagined villains as having families."

"I have three meddling witches in my life," James told her, ignoring her teasing insult. "My mother is a social butterfly, my Aunt Donna is a self-proclaimed expert on men, and my Aunt Nora is possessed with the sixth sense. I have a cousin Sloane who is not related to either of my aunts, and I have one friend whom I trust completely, Adam St. Aubyn."

James looked down. Her eyelids had closed in sleep and her breathing had evened.

Guilty remorse for seducing her coiled around his heart. He was an experienced man of the world, and she had been an innocent who never stood a chance against his superior expertise.

The girl was wrong about possessing nothing of value, though. Compared to the ladies he knew, Lily Hawthorne was a queen, and as beautiful within as she was on the outside. Too bad she hadn't been born into the English aristocracy. He would have proposed marriage the moment he saw her . . .

God's balls, James thought when he realized the bent of his thoughts. Was he falling in love with his brother's murderer?

When she opened her eyes the next morning, Lily gasped in drowsy surprise. The duke sat beside her on the edge of the bed and watched her.

How long had he been sitting there? The thought of him watching her sleep was disconcerting.

"Good morning, sweetness," James said, smiling.

"Good morning," Lily mumbled without raising her gaze.

"Are you greeting me or my legs?" he asked, laughter lurking in his voice.

Lily lifted her gaze to his and managed a smile.

In turn, James lifted her hand to his lips and kissed it. "I want to thank you for last night," he said. "I've never had a more wonderful evening."

Lily felt her cheeks warm with his words. How could he mention what they had done last night? What she wanted most was to forget her immodest behavior, but he sounded as if he'd actually enjoyed it. Didn't his own reckless action embarrass him?

"Maidenly blushes suit you," he said, making her even more uncomfortable.

"Having someone watch me while I sleep is disturbing," Lily complained, ignoring the real reason for her embarrassment.

James raised her hand to his lips again and said, "I only stayed here because I knew you'd worry about seeing me after the night of passion we shared. I did not want to prolong your misery."

Lily yanked her hand out of his. "How much practice have you had?"

"Practice?"

"You seemed to know what my reaction would be. I can only assume you've had a great deal of practice—" Her face reddened. "You've had a great deal of practice deflowering virgins."

"You have done nothing to be ashamed of," James told her, ignoring her comment. "Take care of your private needs while I bring breakfast."

Lily arched an ebony brow at him. "A British duke serving a colonial wharf rat? My, my, the world must be coming to a bad end."

" 'There are more things in heaven and earth,' my darling, 'than are dreamt of in your philosophy,' " James quoted Shakespeare.

"*Hamlet,* Act One, Scene Five, line one-sixty-six," Lily said without forethought.

"I'll take your word on that."

"A British duke *trusting* a colonial wharf rat?" she exclaimed, her hands flying to her chest as if she were shocked. "I'll live on tenterhooks awaiting your next revelation."

"My next revelation could be undressing and laying down beside you," James replied with a wicked grin.

Lily felt her cheeks warming with his words. "Oh, but I am so very weak from hunger."

"I'll return shortly." James rose from the edge of the bed and left the cabin.

Lily stared at the door for a long moment. The duke could be charming when he chose. Dozens of aristocratic ladies must be attracted to him. She supposed hundreds of beautiful women ached to be his wife.

Realizing that moments were passing, Lily rose from the bed. She washed hurriedly and then donned the cabin boy's clothing. She would save her one gown for the evening.

Lily sat at the table when she finished with her toilet and waited. Yes, she'd already faced the duke, but shame for her wanton behavior washed over her in waves. She hoped the duke wouldn't expect lovemaking to be a nightly occurrence. He needed to understand that.

And then she thought of Bradley. How could she ever face him again? He expected her to be a virgin.

Lily sighed. She would need to tell him the truth. Marrying him under false pretenses would be unfair.

Steeling herself against the duke's charm, Lily told herself how much she loved Bradley and wanted to be his wife. She and Michael belonged with him in Boston.

Lily leaned back in the chair and closed her eyes. She tried valiantly to conjure Bradley's image in her mind's eye, but the only face that appeared belonged to the duke. His black eyes gleamed with passion; his infuriating smile taunted her; and his magnificent hands caressed her breasts, her thighs, her . . .

The cabin door opened, startling her out of her sensuous reverie. Remembered passion flushed her cheeks a becoming pink.

"You cannot still be blushing about last night," James said, setting the tray on the table.

Lily refused to rise to the bait. His commenting about the previous night was ungentlemanly.

James sat opposite her at the table. "Or perhaps you are remembering our lovemaking?"

Lily felt her cheeks grow even hotter. She knew she must be a vibrant scarlet. Bradley never made her blush. What kind of power did this Englishman have over her?

Without further comment, James lifted a covered dish from the tray and set it in front of her. Lily only had eyes for his magnificent hands.

"Are you going to eat?"

Lily raised her gaze from his hands to his eyes and then realized what he'd said. She lifted the silver cover off the plate and then stared in surprise at what she saw.

On her plate was a brooch shaped like a salamander. Its four legs and feet were solid gold; its head, body, and tail were made completely of diamonds. Two emerald eyes gleamed at her.

Lily had never seen anything like it in her life. She stared at it in confusion and then lifted her gaze to his. "Is this payment for services rendered?" she asked in an offended voice.

"How dare you even suggest such a thing?" he replied in an equally offended voice. "I have never paid nor will I pay for a woman's body."

Lily calmed. "Then what is it?"

"A gift for a beautiful woman," James answered smoothly.

"Where did you get it?"

"I purchased it in Bermuda."

"Was it meant for some other woman in particular?" she asked, suspicious. There was no way she would accept a gift meant for another woman.

"While in Bermuda I purchased several pieces that appealed to me," he answered.

"Truly?"

James inclined his head. He reached across the table and covered her hand with his own. "An unseen force must have guided me, because deep within my heart I felt you about to enter my life."

"Of course you felt me about to enter your life," Lily said, her lips turning up in a smile. "You were hoping to kill me."

James grinned and shrugged. "The salamander reminded me of you."

"I look like this?"

James laughed. "No, sweetness. In mythology, the salamander is an elemental being with the power to endure fire without harm. If I am the fire, then you are the salamander."

"You certainly have a high opinion of yourself," Lily replied.

"What do you mean?"

"Fire was mankind's greatest discovery."

"Am I not womankind's greatest discovery?" James teased her.

Lily rolled her eyes. The man was incorrigible.

"Are you going to starve me into agreeing," she asked, "or were you planning on serving me breakfast?"

James lifted the silver covers off their plates. There was oatmeal porridge, hot cinnamon biscuits, and strawberry jam.

"You are quiet this morning," James remarked as they ate. "What troubles you?"

"What troubles me?" Lily echoed, her voice dripping with sarcasm. "Do you mean besides the fact that you abducted my brother and me? That my father, brother, and fiancé must be frantic with worry? That you are given to sudden bouts of nastiness?"

"I asked a simple question," James said. "What else bothers you?"

Lily looked him straight in the eye and told him, "We must pretend that last night never happened. No good can come from it. And—"

She stopped speaking when James rose from his chair and sauntered around the table to stand behind her. He placed his hands on her shoulders and leaned close to whisper in her ear, "You are tense, love."

Lily couldn't think straight with his warm breath tickling her ear.

"What were you saying?" he asked.

"Last night was a mistake," she answered.

James slid his hands forward and slipped them inside her shirt to cup her breasts. He caressed her nipples into aroused hardness.

Lily's breath caught raggedly in her throat. She felt herself go hot and cold all over and shivered from the heat he was creating inside her.

"We will not repeat our behavior from last night," Lily managed to say in a breathless voice. "Do you understand?"

"Completely." James nuzzled her neck and then whispered, "Come back to bed with me, love."

Lily sighed. "Yes."

James helped her rise from the chair and turned her to face him. He drew her close, and she entwined her arms around his neck. He lowered his head to claim her lips.

Bang! Bang! Bang!

A knock on the door startled them. Lily leaped back a pace.

"Who is it?" James called.

"It's me." The voice belonged to Michael Hawthorne.

"Come in," Lily called.

Carrying the white piglet, Michael burst into the cabin. Duncan stood discreetly outside the cabin's door and sent the duke an apologetic look.

Michael pointed to the piglet, which wore a bright red leather collar. "Duke Grace said I could keep her."

Lily sent James a grateful look and then said, "Princess looks beautiful. I do believe red is her color."

"I'm keeping her in my cabin," Michael told her. "I don't want Princess to fall overboard."

"That's a good idea," she said.

"Oops," Michael exclaimed. "Look what she's doing."

A stream of water fell from the piglet and formed a puddle on the floor.

"I'll clean it," Lily said quickly, grabbing a napkin off the table. She crouched down to wipe the puddle, saying, "Take Princess back to your cabin."

"Once we reach England, we'll house train Princess," James said. "Pigs are intelligent creatures that can do whatever dogs can."

Michael left the cabin. Duncan closed the door behind them.

"The salamander brooch doesn't match your boyish garb," James said. "Change into the gown I gave you."

"I was saving it for this evening," Lily told him. "I only have the one and don't want to wear it out."

James stared at her for a long moment. "Change into the gown," he ordered. "I'll return in a few minutes."

When the door shut behind him, Lily donned the blue muslin walking dress and shawl. Then she fastened the brooch to the left side of the gown's bodice just above her heart. She loved the gown, but wearing it every day would ruin it.

James walked in then, carrying an armload of clothing. He placed six gowns, one cloak, and several shawls on the bed.

He turned to her, smiling, and said, "Now you have a gown for each day of the week."

Lily stared at the gowns, day dresses in a variety of colors from midnight blue to pale pink to white. "I don't know what to say."

"Say 'Thank you.' "

"I cannot accept them."

"You had better accept them," James told her with a rueful smile. "Captain Roberts is forever indebted to you, since your presence on this ship has made him a great deal of money. I fear he may purchase his own ship and leave my employ."

Lily smiled softly. "Thank you, James. I see that you are a generous man despite your many flaws."

"Thank you for the praise," James said dryly. "If I had known how expensive keeping a captive would be, I might have left you alone. Would you care to join me on deck? I need to confer with the captain about something."

Lily nodded, eager as a young girl. She accepted his offered arm and, together, they left the cabin.

Reaching the quarterdeck, Lily sent Captain Roberts a grateful smile and stood by the railing. She watched the duke speaking to his man but didn't bother to follow their conversation. While the duke's attention was on his captain, Lily took the opportunity to study him. She admired his rugged handsomeness and black hair and then dropped her gaze to his body. That brought back memories of the previous evening, so she lifted her gaze and turned away.

"I could make you love me just like that."

Lily recalled his words to her, and the awful truth hit her like an avalanche of bricks. She was in danger of falling in love with her abductor.

Seven

"Do you believe in love at first sight?"

Lily raised her gaze from the book she'd been reading and looked at the duke, who sat at his desk. What kind of a stupid question was that? she wondered, shifting her gaze to her book again. Why would a sophisticated man of the world ask such a silly question?

"Well, do you?"

"No. Do you believe in it?" she asked without looking up.

" 'Who ever loved that loved not at first sight,' " James quoted Shakespeare.

"*As You Like It*, Act Three, Scene Five, line eighty-two," Lily said without thinking.

"Look at me when I speak to you," he ordered.

"You order me to read and then tell me to look up?" Lily said, irritated. "What madness is this?"

"I've finished this ledger and have time to talk before dinner," James told her.

"I am busy now," Lily said.

"You need to pace yourself. What are you reading?"

"Jane Austen's *Pride and Prejudice*," Lily answered, surrendering to the inevitable by closing the book. "What a wonderful story. Do you think Elizabeth really loves Mr. Darcy, or does she just want to live in that mansion?"

James shrugged. His smile told her that he knew the answer.

"Won't you give me a hint?" she asked.

"Read on, and you will find out for yourself."

Lily dropped her gaze to the book.

"I meant for you to read later," he amended himself.

Lily looked up and gave him a jaunty smile.

"So, you really don't believe in love at first sight," James said. "How unromantic of you."

"I have never experienced love at first sight," Lily told him.

James joined her at the table. "At your age, sweetness, you haven't experienced much."

"I have experienced a villain's abduction," Lily said, arching an ebony brow at him.

"Someday this adventure will be an interesting tale for your grandchildren," James said. "Though I hardly think our activities of last night would be a proper story for them."

The duke was a wicked man, Lily decided. She opened her mouth to tell him so, but he spoke first.

"You look lovely tonight," he said.

Lily wore the midnight blue gown because its color emphasized the brilliance of her diamond salamander brooch. The only other adornment was her *alpha* and *omega* cross.

"That color gown accentuates your sapphire eyes," James said.

"I thought it would show off the brooch," Lily told him.

James leaned forward and said in a husky whisper, "Your eyes are far lovelier than the brooch."

Lily felt herself blushing not only at his words but also at his tone. The huskiness in his voice reminded her of their lovemaking.

Breaking the mood, a knock on the door drew their attention. James rose from the chair and opened the door for his man, who carried a tray with their dinner. Lifting the tray out of the man's hands, he shut the door with his foot and walked back to the table. There were red pottage soup, stewed carrots and celery, fried whitings garnished with parsley and lemon, and baked apple with cinnamon. A bottle of red wine completed the meal.

"There's no cider," Lily said, looking over the fare.

"May I pour you a glass of wine, my lady?" James asked.

Lily inclined her head. She sipped the wine and said, "This doesn't taste too bad."

"I'm relieved that it meets with your approval," James said dryly.

Lily began to eat in silence. Each time she glanced at the duke, she noted him watching her. This, in turn, made her reach for her goblet of wine. Slowly, the wine warmed and soothed her, and she held her goblet out for a refill.

"Where is Michael?" Lily asked, already knowing the answer.

"He's eating with his crew."

"Would you consider ordering him to eat supper with us?" she asked.

James smiled. "Then I wouldn't be alone with you."

"Are you trying to make me fall in love with you?" Lily asked flirtatiously, the wine making her bolder.

"Why would I do that?"

Lily stared at him from beneath the fringe of her ebony lashes, little realizing the effect it would have on him. "I'm certain you have nefarious ends in mind."

"Sweetness, your cynicism wounds me," James said, wearing a feigned expression of disappointment.

"My heart belongs to another man," she warned him.

"Or so you keep telling me, my love."

"Are these terms of endearment devised to seduce me to your will?" Lily asked.

"I am planning to seduce you," James told her. "Shall I tell you what I am going to do to you?"

"No, thank you."

James grinned and then started speaking. "I am going to kiss you so deeply that I'll steal your breath. Then I will place hundreds of kisses on your lovely face and nuzzle your neck."

Lily felt herself flushing. "I told you—"

"Next, I'll caress your beautiful breasts with their pink-tipped nipples," James said in a husky voice. "They darken delightfully when you're aroused."

Lily covered her ears with her hands. It did no good. His voice seeped into her brain.

"I'll glide my hands along the curve of your hips and inner thighs," he continued. "Then I'll run my tongue and lips down each of your legs and nibble upon each of your toes and nip at your inner thighs. After that, I'll give you a real surprise."

"What?" Lily asked, her hands still covering her ears.

"You'll see," he said with an infuriating smile.

Lily thought she would die from the heat. "Could we possibly go up on deck for a little while?"

James inclined his head, but that infuriating smile of his never left his face. "Of course, sweetness."

They stood on the quarterdeck together. James slipped his arm around her waist and pulled her close against his body.

"Tell me what to expect in England," Lily said in an effort to keep her mind off the arm he had wrapped around her.

"You'll live in luxury at my country estate, Kinross Park," James told her, "which should not be confused with my Scottish hideaway, Kinross Castle."

"How will I pass all of those days until the war ends?" she asked.

"We'll ride together in the morning," he answered.

"I don't know how."

"I'll teach you," he said. "We'll play chess in the afternoon."

"I don't know how."

"I'll teach you."

Lily smiled. "And what else will you teach me?"

"Some things come naturally," James said. "You'll find the English an odd lot of people."

"How so?"

"We walk around all day saying things like *egads, tally ho,* and *jolly good.*"

"The first time anyone says one of those things to me, I'll burst out laughing," she said.

They stood in silence for a time. "The night on the ocean is one of the most beautiful sights I've ever seen," Lily remarked, breaking their silence.

"How can you see anything in the darkness?" he asked.

"I feel its beauty."

"The world is bigger than Boston's wharves and possesses many incredible sights," James told her.

Caught by the faraway tone in his voice, Lily turned to look up at his profile. He was as handsome from the side as he was from the front.

James dropped his gaze to her upturned face. "Do you believe in magic?" he asked.

"What do you mean?"

"You, sweetness, are far lovelier than a handful of starlight strung on a moonbeam and embellished with a thousand tiny golden suns," James said.

"I never realized how poetical a duke could be," Lily said dryly.

"Being poetical comes easy," he told her. "We dukes have all that leisure time for practice."

"You mean, when you're not marrying rich merchants' daughters or stealing land from the unsuspecting?"

"Precisely."

James turned her to face him and traced a finger down the side of her face. "Any man who sees your hauntingly lovely face will fall under your spell forever," he whispered.

James lowered his head to hers and claimed her lips. He kissed her lingeringly, and Lily savored every moment.

"What new torture do you have planned for me?" she asked in a hushed voice.

"Darling, you have an adventurous soul," he replied, a smile in his voice. "I guarantee you will enjoy whatever I have planned in my devious British mind."

Without another word, they left the quarterdeck

and returned belowdeck. As usual, James left her at the cabin door, allowing her a few moments of privacy.

Lily undressed and donned her usual nighttime attire, one of the duke's shirts that fell below her hips. She poured herself a small glass of brandy, sat down at the table, and began to read her book.

James returned ten minutes later. She turned her head and smiled at him but then gave her attention to the book.

Sitting opposite her at the table, James removed his boots and jacket. Then he poured himself a glass of brandy.

"Are you back to reading that book again?" James asked needlessly.

"Yes," she answered without looking up.

"You must like the story."

"I do."

"I thought you didn't like spirits," he remarked.

Lily looked up at him and then glanced at her glass of brandy. "I was in the mood."

"What else are you in the mood for?" James asked suggestively.

Lily felt her cheeks grow warm with a blush. "Reading," she answered, and then dropped her gaze to the book. Though, this time her awareness of him blinded her to the words on the page.

James rose from his chair and walked around her. She heard him rummaging in his sea chest and then the sound of him disrobing.

Stealing a peek in his direction, Lily saw him lift his black silk robe off the bed. She enjoyed a good, long look at his naked backside before he shrugged into the robe.

Sweet lamb of God, Lily thought. The duke was a

perfect specimen of manhood—all hard, muscular planes and rippling muscles.

And then Lily felt him lift her black mane of hair and drop a kiss on the nape of her neck. A chill danced down her spine. She felt him flicking his tongue, making a path of sensation from her neck to her ear.

"Elizabeth Bennett loves Mr. Darcy," James whispered in her ear. "Eventually they marry and live happily ever after."

Lily jerked her head around to look at him. "Now that you've revealed the story's ending, why should I even finish the book?"

"Finishing the book would be a waste of time," James said, plucking the book out of her hands and tossing it on the floor. Gently but firmly, he grasped her wrist and drew her out of the chair. He pulled her close and said, "Now you can give me your undivided attention."

Thoroughly exasperated, Lily suffered the urge to stomp on his bare feet. Apparently men were the same the world over. Only their own desires mattered.

"Your behavior was childish," she admonished him. He didn't look the least bit contrite.

"All men are childish when their desires are being thwarted," he told her, as if he'd read her thoughts.

Lily smiled in spite of her anger. She placed the back of her hand against his cheek and then his forehead. When he looked puzzled, she said, "I thought you might be feverish because you just admitted to being flawed."

"One tiny flaw," James corrected her. He scooped her into his arms, carried her across the cabin to the bed, and gently set her down. Then he lay down beside her.

With practiced ease, James unfastened her shirt and slid it off her shoulders. Then he rolled her onto her back and rose from the bed to remove his robe.

Lily lay exposed to his admiring gaze. She only wore a pair of hose that reached to her thighs and the golden *alpha* and *omega* cross.

God's balls, James thought, staring at her. She was lovely enough to play courtesan to a king, and no royal cock would ever tire of her.

James felt his manhood stirring to life, hardening exquisitely at the very sight of her. "You are a goddess, my love," he whispered hoarsely.

Without any trace of shyness, Lily held her arms out to him. James fell upon her and kissed her until she gasped for breath.

James left her lips and rained tiny wet kisses down the column of her throat. Lower and lower slid his lips, until he was suckling upon her aroused nipples.

When she moaned at the incredible sensation he was creating, James knelt on the floor between her thighs. With his tongue, he slashed her moist female's crevice. He knew he'd shocked her when she tried to pull away, but he held her hips and kept her captive to his exploring tongue.

"I want to taste each delicious part of your sweet flesh," he whispered against her cleft, his words making her squirm.

Up and down, James flicked his tongue in a gentle assault on her womanhood. He licked and nipped her tiny female button while his fingers taunted her hardened nipples.

And then she melted against his tongue.

He heard her cry out as wave after wave of throbbing pleasure washed over her. He felt her whole body trembling in ecstasy.

"Get on your knees," James whispered thickly, rising from the floor.

Holding her steady, James mounted her from behind and rode her hard until she shrieked with pleasure. Then he surrendered to her, shuddering and spilling his seed deep within her.

When their breathing evened, James lay down on the bed and pulled her into his arms. He planted a kiss on top of her head.

"What are you thinking?" James asked.

Lily raised herself up and looked down at him. A smile touched the corners of her lips when she said, "I was thinking that you were supposed to seduce me."

James grinned boyishly. "I did, but you cooperated."

Lily raised her hand to strike him, but he grabbed it and yanked her down on top of him.

"Sweetness, your beauty seduced *me*," James told her. "Inspired by your uncommon beauty, I performed heroic persuasion."

Lily planted a chaste kiss on his lips. "That's better."

Silence.

"Darling, do you think you could manage to resist for a few minutes next time?" James asked. "I enjoy being challenged."

Lily rolled off him and turned her back, saying, "I never promised there would be a next time."

"Are you married?"

At the sound of her brother's voice, Lily moaned

softly and opened her eyes. Naked beneath the coverlet, she lay cuddled in the duke's arms. Thanks be to her guardian angel, the blanket covered her more interesting endowments.

"Did you get married?" her brother repeated.

"We did in a manner of speaking," the duke said.

"I didn't know," Michael said brightly. "Lily, why didn't you tell me you fell in love?"

"We fell in love last night after you'd gone to sleep," James answered for her.

"Will you be making babies?" Michael asked.

Lily felt her cheeks grow warm. At that moment, she could cheerfully have throttled her brother.

"I'll let you answer that one, darling," James said, giving her a sidelong smile.

Lily curled her lip at him and then looked at her brother. "No babies," she said simply.

"Not even one?" James said in a teasing voice.

Lily refused to acknowledge that he'd even spoken. "Now, Michael—"

The cabin door opened. "Are you in there, Michael?" Duncan called softly.

"Come here," her brother ordered.

The Scotsman stepped inside the cabin. He smiled when he spied the two of them in bed.

Embarrassed, Lily hid her face against the duke's chest. Why didn't they just invite the whole damned crew inside?

"What time is it?" the duke asked his man.

"Six o'clock."

"Rise and shine," her brother said in an overly loud voice. "Shake a leg there, mates."

Lily felt the duke's deep chuckle.

"The hour is a little too early for us," James told the boy. "Go with Duncan, and we'll see you later."

"Aye, aye, Duke."

Lily watched her brother turn to leave. A smile flirted with the corners of her mouth when she heard him grumbling, "Holy hell, I never thought Dukie would want to lie in bed with a girl."

"I'll bolt the door tonight," James promised after their visitors had gone.

"That will be unnecessary," Lily told him. "We won't be sleeping together again."

James ignored her pronouncement. Instead, he gave her one of his infuriating smiles and asked, "Now that we're awake, what would you like to do?"

"Go back to sleep." Lily rolled over and faced the wall.

"A delightful idea." James rolled over and pressed himself against her. His arm went around her body and he cupped her breast in his hand. "Pleasant dreams, sweetness."

Cuddling against his warmth, Lily glanced down and looked at his hand cupping her breast. A sudden surge of guilt for her actions welled up inside her. How could she give herself so completely to the duke, her enemy? She loved Bradley Howell, didn't she?

Her head ached from this whole sordid situation. She needed to postpone those guilty feelings until later, when she would be strong enough to deal with them.

Lily closed her eyes and let the duke's breathing lull her to sleep. She did not dream.

Awakening two hours later, Lily yawned and stretched and rolled over. The bed was empty. She opened her eyes to see the duke shrugging into his shirt.

"Good morning," James greeted her with a smile. He sauntered across the cabin and planted a kiss on her forehead. "And were all of your dreams pleasant?"

"No."

James snapped his dark brows together. "Unpleasant?"

"I had no dreams."

"I'm going to fetch us breakfast," he said. "Use this time—"

"—for my private needs," Lily finished.

James inclined his head and left the cabin. Lily rose from the bed and began her daily toilet. She chose to wear the pale pink gown with matching shawl.

Wrapping the shawl loosely around her shoulders, Lily recalled another shawl given to her by another man. A red shawl with gold embroidery.

Another surge of guilt shot through her, weakening her enough into sitting at the table. Not only had she behaved wantonly, but now her brother had witnessed her shameful morals.

The door opened. Carrying a tray with covered dishes, James crossed the cabin and sat opposite her at the table.

"Breakfast smells delicious," Lily said, banishing all disturbing thoughts from her mind. She could dwell on them later. After all, the war wasn't going to end anytime soon.

"No food could taste more delicious than you," James said.

Lily blushed at the reminder of what they'd shared the previous night. Talking about such things in the light of day seemed obscene.

James set a dish in front of her. Lily lifted its silver cover and gasped at what she saw.

A brooch shaped like a bird on a rock lay upon the plate. Set in platinum, the bird was made of diamonds. Its eye was a ruby; its plume, feet, and beak were gold. The bird stood on top of a large amethyst.

The sight of the expensive jewel angered Lily. "What is this?" she demanded.

"Another gift for a beautiful woman," James answered, mirroring his words of the previous morning.

"Another piece from Bermuda that you couldn't resist?"

James inclined his head.

"This smells of payment for services," Lily said, pushing the plate with the jewel toward him. "I don't want it."

"How amazing," James said. "You, my darling, are the only woman who ever refused the gift of a priceless jewel. Unless you're madder than King George."

"I will not accept this brooch," Lily said emphatically.

James inclined his head. "Then walk over to that porthole and toss it into the sea."

"You cannot mean to throw money out the window," Lily gasped in surprise.

"I've given you the brooch and will never give it to another woman," James told her.

"Gifts are meant for guests, not prisoners," she argued.

"Consider yourself my guest," he replied.

"I cannot do that."

"Then you'll earn your keep," James said, cocking a dark brow at her. "My socks need mending."

"You're a wealthy man," Lily said in refusal. "Buy yourself another pair. Besides, I don't know how to sew."

James gave her a skeptical look. "Very well, you'll cook my lunch."

"I am a prisoner of war," Lily announced in a haughty tone of voice, too proud to admit she knew nothing about cooking. "Not your slave."

James burst out laughing. "Sweetness, you'd have a bright future in Drury Lane if you decided to remain in England after the war."

Lily curled her lip at him.

"You wouldn't need to waste any time memorizing your lines," he added.

"Go to hell, your grace," she said.

James rose from his chair, walked toward the door, and said, "I'll see you there."

"Where are you going?" Lily asked when he reached for the doorknob.

"To hell," James answered with an infuriating grin and then walked out the door.

Lily grabbed the bird-on-a-rock brooch and marched across the cabin to the porthole. She'd show that insufferable lout what she thought of him. She reached to open the porthole but then dropped her hand to her side.

Perhaps the duke was sincere, Lily thought. Perhaps he did care for her. Or perhaps his irresistibility made rational thinking impossible.

Lily kept the brooch.

Four hours later Lily stood outside the cabin door. Behind her stood Duncan. Both carried trays laden with covered dishes.

"Please open the door," Lily said, stepping aside. "I can't manage both."

Duncan opened the door and then waited for her to enter. Lily saw James leaning back in his chair with his boots propped up against the table. He grinned, as if the sight of her serving him gave him infinite pleasure.

"I see that my slave has been busy in the galley," James said.

Lily ignored him. "Set your tray on the desk," she ordered Duncan. "I'll serve this first."

Lily placed her tray on the table, sat down across from the duke, and waited for the Scotsman to leave. Then she set one of the covered dishes in front of the duke.

"You're not eating?" James asked.

"No."

He looked suspicious. "Why?"

Lily shrugged. "I suppose the cooking stole my appetite."

James looked from her face to the covered dish. He lifted the cover and stared in apparent surprise at his lunch.

Lily suppressed the bubble of laughter rising in her throat. The bloater looked positively poisonous, burned on the outside and raw on the inside.

The blinking idiot is actually going to eat it? Lily thought, watching him cut a piece.

"I learned there are various ways to cook bloaters," Lily said before the piece of fish disappeared into his mouth. "Cut off its head and tail, open the bloater down the back, and bone it. Of course, you may also cook it without removing its backbone."

"Its gills are still moving," James said, pushing his dish away. "Are you trying to kill me?"

"What a lovely idea," Lily said. "However, Duncan would toss me overboard if anything happened to you."

Lily deposited the dish of bloater on the desk and returned with another covered dish. She set that one down in front of him.

"What's this?" James lifted the cover and smiled at the bowl of Cook's stew.

They ate in silence for a time.

"Tell me why a tavern owner's daughter never learned to cook," James said finally.

"I've been too busy."

James laughed. "Doing what?"

"I promised my mother I would watch over Michael," Lily answered. "That task requires my full attention."

James nodded, as if he understood the heavy burden of responsibility she'd borne all those years. He rose from his chair and walked around the table, saying, "I'd like dessert now."

"I'll need to return to the galley," Lily said, rising from her chair.

James scooped her into his arms, saying, "I want you for dessert."

Lily smiled when he carried her across the cabin to their bed. She raised her arms in a silent invitation, and he lay down beside her and gathered her into his arms.

Lily sighed with pleasure and, for a time, forgot that she and the duke were enemies.

Eight

I love him, Lily thought, listening to the sounds of James's humming emanating from behind the privacy screen where he was bathing. Wearing only the white shirt she'd been using as a nightshift, Lily lounged on the bed and waited for him to finish.

June twenty-third, she thought, *the night before St. John's Day. Midsummer's Night.*

It was hard to believe that more than a month of days had passed, and their ship would be docking in London in the morning. Time passed much too quickly when she lay under the covers with James.

Guilt welled up inside her at the thought of Bradley Howell, but she took a deep breath and banished his image from her mind. She'd always believed that she loved Bradley, but now she knew what real love was. She couldn't help what she felt any more than she could change her duty to her younger brother.

Besides, Bradley Howell was a proud man who wouldn't want to marry her if she loved another. He would be hurt, but, in the end, would give her his blessing to marry James.

The wharf rat who became a duchess, Lily thought, a smile touching her lips. Perhaps Jane Austen would write a story about her.

"Are you ready?" James's voice brought her back to reality.

Lily rose from the bed and unbuttoned her shirt. Lifting it off her shoulders, she let it drop to the floor at her feet. All she wore was her *alpha* and *omega* cross.

Keeping his dark gaze fixed on hers, James crossed the cabin, and they met near the table. Lily entwined her arms around his neck and pressed her body against his. Drawing his head down, she kissed him lingeringly.

James wrapped his arms around her and then dropped his hand to her buttocks. He slid his fingers between her thighs and then whispered against her lips, "You are wet for me."

"I love you," Lily whispered. She rained feathery-light kisses all over his face, and then her lips traveled down the column of his throat. Pushing the black robe off his shoulders, she rubbed her face against the dark mat of hair covering his chest.

Licking and nipping, Lily suckled upon his nipples. She heard his sharp intake of breath and moaned low in her throat. Her power over him was a heady experience, a natural aphrodisiac.

Lily dropped to her knees and pressed her face against his groin. Desperate with wanting, she took his manhood into her mouth and sucked until it grew too big. Licking the long length of it, she flicked her tongue this way and that and then swirled it around his ruby knob.

James moaned with the exquisite pleasure. He pulled her to her feet and kissed her slowly, wetly, lingeringly.

"Touch me," Lily said on a sigh.

James reached out and pushed the books off the

table, letting Shakespeare and Jane Austen fall to the floor together. Then he lifted Lily onto the table and stared down at her. He stroked every inch of her sweet flesh and then dropped his head to suckle upon her aroused nipples while his fingers teased the sensitive pearl of her womanhood.

Lily moaned low in her throat and gazed at him through sapphire eyes glazed with passion. "Take me," she urged.

James gave her what she craved. Pulling her to the edge of the table, he mounted and rode her in a wild frenzy until she cried out with ecstasy. Only then did James explode, shuddering as his seed flooded the deepest part of her.

Recovering first from their tempest of love, James lifted her off the table and carried her to bed. He lay down beside her and pulled her into his embrace.

Lily had never felt happier in her life. Lying within his embrace made her feel secure, loved, and cherished. She suffered a tiny twinge of regret for what might have been with Bradley but knew she could never marry him now. She and Michael would remain in England, and she would give her handsome duke a dozen strong sons and beautiful daughters. Together, they would make England their paradise.

"A shilling for your thoughts," James said, planting a kiss on the top of her head.

Lily smiled. "I was thinking how only a few weeks have changed my opinion about the British."

"Dare I hope it's a change for the better?"

Lily kissed his chest and vowed, "I love you."

Silence met her declaration. Was she too bold? Nothing could be too bold after the intimacies they'd shared.

Without knowing why, Lily was suddenly apprehensive. "When will we marry?" she asked.

"Excuse me for one moment," James said, setting her aside to rise from the bed.

Confused by his behavior, Lily watched him don his black silk bedrobe. He poured a generous amount of whiskey into a glass and then took a healthy swig of it. Finally he turned around to face her.

Clutching the coverlet to cover her nakedness, Lily sat up. The coldness in his expression made her heart pound with fear. Anxiety closed her throat, making her breathing shallow.

"I have no intention of marrying my brother's murderer," James told her bluntly. "I have had my revenge."

Lily couldn't move or find her voice. Her face drained of color. Their affair had been a ploy to hurt her?

"I could make you love me just . . . like . . . that." His boast slammed into her with the impact of an avalanche.

" 'Tis the strumpet's plague to beguile many and be beguiled by one,' " James said, quoting Shakespeare.

Lily flinched, as if he'd reached out and struck her. The duke was naming her a whore?

Without regard for her nakedness, Lily rose from the bed. She stood as proudly as a queen and advanced on him. Merely inches away, she stared into his dark eyes for a long moment.

Suddenly, Lily slapped him hard. The force of it jerked his head to the right. When he looked at her again, she saw the angry twitch in his right cheek.

"Shall we turn in for the night, my lady?" James asked in a voice heavy with sarcasm.

Lily tried to slap him again, but he caught her wrist and warned, "You are pressing your luck, my dear."

"What will you do, your grace?" Lily challenged, undaunted by the tight grip he had on her wrist. "Abduct and seduce me?"

"How refreshing that you used the correct word *seduce* instead of flinging the word *rape* at me," James said, cocking a dark brow at her. "I duped you and must applaud your acceptance of my victory."

"Keep the applause for your own skilled performance," Lily said, yanking her wrist out of his grasp. She smiled without humor and added, "How hard could it have been for a sophisticated aristocrat to fool an unsuspecting wharf rat? Surely your victory is a hollow one."

For one excruciatingly long moment they stared into each other's eyes. The duke had developed an angry twitch in his left cheek.

"Leave me alone to lick my wounds," Lily said, depleted of energy.

James seemed to hesitate. "This is my—"

"I said *get out,*" Lily shouted, cutting his words off.

Without taking his gaze from hers, James grabbed his clothing and boots. He paused at the door for a parting shot. "I had assumed you'd be a better loser than this," he drawled. "Egads, what a disappointment."

Trembling with rage and shame, Lily donned the nighshift and sat on the edge of the bed. She held her head in her hands and willed herself not to cry.

It did no good.

A teardrop rolled down her cheek and dropped onto her lap. Another followed it. And then another.

Surrendering to the inevitable, Lily gave herself over to her tears. She didn't bother to look up when she felt the light touch on her shoulder.

"Did Duke hurt you?" Michael asked.

Lily shook her head and sobbed, "I h-hurt m-myself."

"Where?" he asked.

Lily smiled in spite of her pain. She placed her hand over her left breast and said, "Here. My heart is broken."

Michael patted her back soothingly. "We'll always be together, won't we?"

"Always," she agreed. "Will you stay here with me tonight?"

"Duke sent me to take care of you," Michael told her, and then pointed to the piglet sitting on his lap. "Princess came along to help."

Lily lifted the piglet out of her brother's arms, saying, "Good evening, Princess. She's wearing a diaper."

"Duncan doesn't like her fouling the cabin," Michael told her.

"Let's sleep, Brother." Lily drew back the coverlet and gestured Michael into the bed. Then she slipped beneath the coverlet, and the piglet lay at the foot of the bed like a dog.

Lily felt her eyes growing heavy. Suddenly, a loud thump came from the cabin next door.

Both Lily and Michael bolted up in bed. They heard a second thump. And then a third.

"What was that?" Michael whispered.

"Something heavy fell," Lily said. "When the ship

docks tomorrow morning, we are going to escape. Are you with me, Brother?"

"I'm with you. *Always.*"

The duke is a coward, Lily decided when the Scotsman walked into the cabin the next morning to serve them breakfast.

"The fare is light this morning as there won't be any cooking done while in port," Duncan told her. He set biscuits, jam, and tea on the table between her and Michael.

"Where is his grace this morning?" Lily asked.

"He's busy at the moment," Duncan answered, averting his gaze. "You'll remain in the cabin until he returns for you."

"And when will that be?"

"Who can say?" the man said with a shrug, and gave her brother a wink before leaving.

Lily poured tea for her brother and herself. Then she took a biscuit and wandered to the porthole to get her first glimpse of England.

Spring had ripened into early summer. Hazy sunshine shone on the river, congested by a crush of ships and barges. Scents of spices, grain, and lumber wafted through the air.

All waterfronts are similar, Lily thought. London's docks could easily have been Boston's, except that she knew she was on the opposite side of the Atlantic Ocean.

Surviving outside the duke's protection wouldn't be a problem unless the war lingered on for several years. She had the two brooches to sell, as well as a purse of gold coins she'd taken from the bottom of the duke's sea chest that morning.

What she needed to do was get off the ship without being seen. How best to make their escape?

Lily glanced over her shoulder at her brother. He would never agree to leave the piglet behind. So be it.

Returning to her place at the table, Lily sat across from her brother and said, "We need to plan our escape."

"What are we going to do?" he asked.

"We need a place to hide while the others are busy above deck," she told him. "Then we'll sneak off the ship under cover of darkness and ask directions to the American embassy."

"What's *embassy*?"

"An embassy is where representatives of a foreign country live and work," Lily explained. "I have some money to keep us for a while. Since you've been all over the ship, tell me a good place to hide."

"Under the bed?"

Lily smiled. "No, Brother. We need a deserted storage area."

"There's a pantry off the galley," Michael told her.

"That's a good idea," Lily said. "Do you need to relieve yourself?"

Michael shook his head.

Lily arched an ebony brow at him. "You won't be able to go later, Michael."

Lily changed the piglet's diaper while her brother went behind the privacy screen to use the chamber pot. Then she grabbed one of the shawls the duke had given her and made a sling to carry the pig.

"I'll carry Princess," Michael said, walking around the screen.

"I'll carry Princess," Lily replied. "You wrap those biscuits in a napkin and bring them."

Michael did as ordered and then crossed the cabin to the door where she waited.

"Are you ready?" Lily asked.

Michael nodded.

"No talking once we've left the cabin," she reminded him.

"Holy hell, I'm not stupid," Michael said in apparent exasperation.

Lily narrowed her eyes on him to express her displeasure with his vulgar language. The British had been a bad influence on both of them.

Michael cocked his head to one side and asked, "Are we escaping now?"

Lily placed one finger across her lip for silence, and Michael imitated her gesture. Pressing her ear to the door, she listened for footsteps outside.

Noiselessly, Lily opened the door a crack and peered outside. The passageway was deserted.

Lily beckoned her brother to follow and, on tiptoes, the two of them started down the passage. They heard a cacophony of sounds above deck—men's voices and the offloading of the cargo.

The galley was located on the same level but at the opposite end of the ship. Stopping outside the galley, Lily motioned her brother to stay behind her. Then she peeked inside. It was empty.

"Where's the pantry?" she whispered.

"That door on the other side of the galley stacks," he whispered back.

Followed by her brother, Lily tiptoed across the galley and disappeared into the pantry, being careful to close the door behind them. The room was small, and crates were stacked along three walls. More had been piled in the middle of the room.

"We'll sit behind that pile of crates in the middle of the room," Lily said. "We can't be seen if anyone enters."

Sitting down behind the crates with her brother, Lily lulled Princess into sleep by stroking her snout. She only wished she could do the same with her brother until it was time for them to escape.

As long as they remained silent, they had a good chance of escaping. Once the alarm had been sounded, anyone who opened the pantry door would think the room was empty.

An hour passed slowly. And then another.

Lily felt as if she had been sitting there for an eternity. She had never thought about how hard a wooden floor was. And then her brother began to fidget.

"How long do we sit here?" Michael whispered.

"We can't leave until dark," Lily told him.

"I'm thirsty," he complained.

"Don't think about it," she said.

"No one is in the galley. Can't I—?"

"No. Then you'll need to use the chamberpot." Lily lifted her finger to her lips, saying, "Shhh." She heard the sound of footsteps in the galley.

"No one is here," she heard Duncan say.

"Check the pantry," came the duke's reply.

Heavy footsteps on the wooden floor came closer. Lily held her breath.

Silence. Then the footsteps moved away, and she heard the Scotsman say, "The pantry is empty."

"God's balls, where could they be?" the duke said. "I'm certain they're hiding somewhere on the ship."

"I'll look in the bosun's storeroom," Duncan said.

Ahhchew! Princess sneezed.

Great guardian angel, protect us from the devil's snare, Lily thought. She heard the sound of the footsteps returning to the pantry.

"The game is up," the duke said in a stern voice. "Show yourself."

Resigned to being caught, Lily stood up and passed the piglet to her brother. She didn't know what the duke would do, but she wanted her hands free for defense.

Lily stood protectively between the duke and her brother. Facing him, she noted the duke's two bruised eyes and momentarily forgot her anger. "Does it hurt?" she asked, concerned. "How did it happen?"

"I walked into something," the duke said in a grim voice.

Lily shifted her gaze to the Scotsman and caught his grin. That a retainer would strike his employer surprised her, but that would explain the thumps in the night. What would cause a rift between them?

Marching across the pantry, the duke towered over her and said, "You should thank that pig for saving your life."

"What do you mean?" Lily asked.

"Danger lies outside my protection."

"I am familiar with dockside dangers," Lily told him in a haughty voice. "Besides, who is protecting me from *you*?"

James flicked a sour glance at his man, and Lily realized the two had fought about her. Had she made an ally in Duncan? Could the Scotsman be persuaded to help her escape?

"My lady Blockhead, you have no money," James said, his voice rising in anger. "How would you live?"

Lily smiled with feigned sweetness. "I planned to sell those two brooches, my lord Beef-wit."

"And we have the money Lily borrowed from the sea chest," Michael added.

Son of a bitch, Lily thought. She closed her eyes against her brother's gaff and hoped the duke wouldn't press criminal charges.

"That wasn't very wise," James said. "Dukes have long arms."

"And tiny brains," Lily said sarcastically.

Without warning, James grabbed Princess out of her brother's arms and threatened, "If you try to escape again, I'll eat the pig."

Two things happened simultaneously. First, Michael burst into tears. At the same moment, Lily lunged for the pig.

James pushed her away, and she crashed to the floor, hitting her right temple on the side of a crate. He tried to help her, but she slapped his hand away.

"Don't touch me," Lily cried.

James stood there and watched as she slowly got to her feet. He winced visibly when he saw the blood on her temple.

"Duke, I'll kill you for that," Michael threatened.

"God save me from these mad Americans," James exclaimed. He passed the piglet to Duncan, ordering, "Get them into the coach." He stormed out of the pantry.

Five minutes later, Lily sat inside the ducal coach. On the seat opposite her sat her brother.

Softer than a lady's lap, Lily thought, sliding her hand across the coach's leather seat.

Unexpectedly, the door opened, and the duke

climbed inside. He gestured to Michael to sit beside Lily and took the opposite seat for himself.

"You're riding with us?" Lily asked in surprise.

James inclined his head. "Tormenting you for the next two hours held a certain appeal to me." He held out his handkerchief and added, "For your injury."

"I prefer bleeding," Lily said, lifting her gaze from the handkerchief to his eyes.

"God's balls," James muttered. He leaned forward and grasped her chin in one hand while he wiped the blood off her temple.

"I never meant to injure you," he told her.

"I find that difficult to believe," she said.

"Believe whatever you like." James leaned back against his seat and folded his arms across his chest.

Lily decided to ignore his existence. She turned her head and gazed out the window as the coach began to move.

Full-bodied summer landscaped the view outside the coach. Rich, robust scents wafted through the air, and lush greenery was everywhere she looked.

"Kinross Park lies two hours from London on the northern outskirts of St. Albans," James said conversationally. "St. Albans is a cathedral city, a market town with a tremendous history. It's been in existence since eight hundred A.D."

Lily looked at him and yawned. Her unspoken insult made him smile.

"Where's Sherwood Forest?" Michael asked.

"Sherwood Forest is much farther north," James answered. "Kinross Park covers twenty-five acres that is set in two hundred and fifty acres of deer park with an enchanted forest."

"Did a witch cast a spell on the forest?" her brother asked.

"Merlin the Magician enchanted this forest," the duke replied. "I'll give you a tour through it."

"I think I like m-merry olde England," Michael said.

James smiled and looked at her. Lily kept her face an expressionless mask. The duke might fool her brother, but *she* never made the same mistake twice.

"A shilling for your thoughts," the duke said.

" 'Sweet are the uses of adversity,' " Lily quoted Shakespeare. "Beware, your grace. Two can play the revenge game."

James looked her up and down and then smiled, as if she were as inconsequential as a gnat. Lily closed her eyes and relaxed back against her seat. She wouldn't give him the satisfaction of knowing how angry he made her.

"Lily?" The duke's voice seemed to come from a far distance. "Lily, wake up. We are nearly there."

She opened her eyes and realized that she'd fallen asleep. Her brother also slept with his head against her arm. Princess snored on the duke's lap.

"I thought you might like to see the approach to my home," he said.

"Where's the enchanted forest?" Michael asked, awakening.

"Be patient," James told him. "You'll see it later."

Lily sat up straight and stared out the window. The only thing she saw was trees.

"Kinross Park has been in my family for two hundred years," James said. "Originally a red-brick Tudor manor house, it's been enlarged and renovated by various of my ancestors through the centuries. My great-grandfather added turrets, griffins, and gargoyles."

"How long before we arrive?" she asked.

James smiled. "We have arrived already. We've been riding on Armstrong land for the past fifteen minutes."

And then Kinross Park came into view.

Lily gasped. Kinross Park looked more like a palace than a house. How could anyone afford to live in such a place? Apparently, the duke was as wealthy as a king.

"Kinross Park has two hundred rooms, twenty staircases, and several courtyards," James told them.

"And one enchanted forest," her brother added.

Lily looked in surprise from the mansion to the duke and then back at the mansion again. Who really was this lobster-back? The bloody King of England?

Their coach came to a halt inside the main courtyard. Duncan was there in an instant. The Scotsman opened the door and pulled down the steps. James climbed down first and then turned to assist Lily and Michael.

A host of retainers had formed several lines inside the foyer in order to welcome their master. A tall, formally dressed older man stepped forward and said, "On behalf of the entire staff, I wish to welcome you home, your grace."

"Thank you, Pennick," the duke replied.

Lily scanned the three-story marble hall with its soaring, fluted columns and grand staircase. It seemed more like a rotunda than an entry hall and was a thousand times larger than her father's tavern. She felt the curious gazes fixed on her and her brother. She could bear their insults, but if anyone teased her brother, she would make that person regret it.

"I've brought guests from America," James was saying to his majordomo in a voice loud enough for all to hear. "Please make both of them comfortable and give them the same respect you give me."

"Yes, your grace," the man replied. "Perhaps your guests would like to rest after their long journey."

James inclined his head. "A good idea."

With a flick of his wrist, the majordomo dismissed all but three servants. The housekeeper, a maid, and a footman were the only retainers left in the hall.

"Mrs. Bea, see that my guests are made comfortable," the duke said to the housekeeper. "Peggy can assist the lady, and Digby will assist her brother."

Without acknowledging that he'd spoken, Lily and Michael followed the three servants across the foyer to the grand staircase. They started up the stairs. Mrs. Bea led the way and was followed by Lily and Michael. Then came the maid and the footman.

"Lily?"

She hadn't climbed more than eight steps when she heard him call her.

Lily turned around. "Yes?"

James made a sweeping gesture at the marble hall and asked, "Have you nothing to say?"

Lily stared directly into his eyes and said in a loud voice, "I hate you."

Nine

James snapped his brows together. Her profession of hate elicited audible gasps of shock from the three servants remaining in the foyer, but he ignored it.

"That slip of a girl is the infamous Gilded Lily," James told his majordomo, lowering his voice.

Pennick looked surprised. "The villain is a woman?"

James inclined his head and shifted his gaze to his lovely prisoner, who was nearing the top of the staircase. The hint of a smile touched his lips when he noted how her back had stiffened, as if she felt his gaze upon her.

When Lily vanished from sight, James climbed the stairs and went directly to his office, located in one end of the Long Library. His favorite room, the Long Library was fifty-four feet long and eighteen feet wide and occupied the entire west front of one wing. Its walls were decorated with books, its floors covered with thick red Persian carpets, and its furniture oversized and comfortable. Above the main fireplace hung a mosaic of a lion and a leopard made from thousands of different colored tesserae.

James walked the entire length of the library to his desk, situated near the window. He poured himself a whiskey and gazed out the window at the waterpool's grand fountains, sculpted figures portraying the legend of St. George and the Dragon.

Lily had been correct, James thought. *His was a hollow victory.*

He should never have abducted her and her brother. She had been a simple girl with a remarkable gift; he was a sophisticated man of the world, a master in the art of seduction.

James had no doubt that if she had known her gift was costing men their lives, she would never have agreed to use it. Damn the chit's fiancé and her brother for getting her involved in this mess.

What was he to do with her now? Her existence needed to be kept a secret from his mother and meddling aunts, not to mention Valentina and her brother. Society could be kept at bay, but he wasn't too sure of his relations.

"Excuse me, your grace."

James turned away from the window at the sound of his majordomo's voice.

"Her grace instructed me to move your personal belongings into the state bedchamber," Pennick said.

"And?"

"I've settled your guests into the two bedchambers at the opposite end of the corridor," his man told him. "Is that acceptable?"

"I want Mistress Hawthorne installed in the chamber next to mine," James said.

The majordomo looked surprised but remained silent on the subject. "And the boy?"

"Leave Michael where he is," James answered. "Tell Duncan I want him to sleep in the chamber with the boy, and I want Digby to follow him wherever he goes. As you probably have noticed, Michael is impaired."

"And the lady?" Pennick said. "Shall I tell Peggy to—"

"Mistress Hawthorne is free to roam without supervision," James interrupted his man.

"You know best, your grace, but how dangerous—?"

"The lady is not dangerous and is singularly devoted to her brother," James said, holding his hand up in a gesture for silence. "She would never escape without her brother."

Pennick inclined his head and asked, "Will there be anything else, your grace?"

"Give me an hour and then return," James replied. "I'll need couriers to deliver messages to Sloane, St. Aubyn, and Madame Janette."

"Madame Janette?" Pennick echoed in confusion.

James gave his majordomo a lopsided grin. "Madame Janette is London's most sought-after dressmaker," he informed his man. "Why, she's all the rage just now."

Pennick looked at him blankly.

"I cannot allow the lady to walk naked around Kinross Park."

Pennick retained a bland expression, but the hint of a blush colored his cheeks. "As you wish, your grace."

"I want Mistress Hawthorne brought here an hour before dinner," James added.

Pennick inclined his head and left the library.

At five o'clock that afternoon Lily sat in front of the darkened hearth in her bedchamber. She felt tired, both physically and emotionally. Briefly, she wondered why her bedchamber had been moved from one end of the long corridor to the opposite one.

The duke must have feared she'd escape and knew she'd never leave her brother.

Lily had never seen such an enormous house. She smiled at her own poor choice of words. This was no house; this was a palace.

This bedchamber was larger than her father's entire tavern. The room had been decorated in ivory, gold, and blues of every shade. Even the Chippendale furniture had been painted ivory and gold to match the textiles. The canopied tent bed was supported at the back by a bedhead and at the front by fluted, carved columns. The bed's canopy, curtains, and counterpane matched. Other furniture in the chamber included a toilet table with recesses for toilet articles, a washstand on a tripod with a porcelain bowl above small drawers, and special soap. A chaise, a dressing table, a cheval mirror, and a tallboy completed the furnishings, along with several small tables.

A blue printed silk hung on the walls to the dado. A blue Persian carpet fitted the wooden floors.

Peggy, who insisted she was her maid, floated around the chamber. She was keeping herself busy by pampering the few gowns the duke had bought her.

"Peggy?"

"Yes, my lady?"

"I am Lily," she told the girl. "Please address me as such."

Peggy shook her head as her hands flew to her breast. "I couldn't do that, my lady."

Lily rolled her eyes and then pointed to a door at the opposite end of the bedchamber. "Where does that door go?" she asked.

The girl blushed. "That is his grace's chamber."

Lily snapped her head around to look at the girl.

"Inform that lecherous jackass that I won't sleep in the chamber next to his."

Peggy looked like she was about to faint. She shook her head and backed away several paces, saying, "Oh, no. I couldn't do that."

"Then, I'll tell him myself," Lily said, her determination apparent in her voice.

A knock on the door drew their attention. The maid hurried across the chamber and opened the door a crack. She spoke in a low voice to someone and then opened the door wider to allow the footman entrance.

"Excuse me, mistress."

Lily stared at him.

"His grace requests your presence in the library," the man said, fidgeting as if nervous. "You are to come with me."

"What's your name?" Lily asked, giving the man a sweet smile.

Recovering from his surprise at her question, the man answered, "Digby."

"Mr. Digby, inform his grace that I'm not hungry and won't be down for dinner," Lily said.

"His grace said that if you're not downstairs in ten minutes, he'll come up here and cram the food down your throat," Digby said, dropping his gaze to the carpet.

Lily slid her gaze to the girl, who quickly averted her eyes. Clearly, the maid disapproved of her, but that didn't matter. Disapproval from others was an old friend of hers.

"Tell his grace I'll be down promptly," Lily acquiesced, looking at the footman. "Peggy will show me the way."

The footman nodded and left the chamber. The maid shut the door behind him.

Lily sighed and rose from her chair, her gaze fixed on the door connecting their chambers. Apparently, the duke was bent on making her visit a difficult one. If he dared to walk through that door and climb into her bed, she would send him to visit his deceased brother.

Stepping in front of the cheval glass, Lily studied her appearance. She wore the high-waisted sapphire gown with matching shawl that the duke had given her, but she refused to wear either of the brooches. The *alpha* and *omega* cross was her only ornament.

She wouldn't win any prizes for beauty, Lily thought, but she would do.

"You look lovely, my lady," the maid said.

"Thank you, Peggy," Lily replied. "I believe his grace doesn't deserve any more than neat and clean."

Downstairs, they walked the length of a long, carpeted corridor. Peggy stopped outside a door and said, "Have a nice dinner, my lady."

Before she could remind the girl to call her Lily, a footman opened the door for her. She stepped inside the enormous chamber and saw the duke at the far end. He sat at his desk and wrote.

On silent feet, Lily stepped forward and made her way through the library. A smile stole across her face as she saw the thousands of books covering the walls from floor to ceiling.

"I knew you would like it," the duke said, drawing her attention.

"I never realized how many books existed," she said, shifting her gaze back to the walls of books. Great guardian angel, she could spend her whole life here and never finish reading.

"My collection should keep you busy for the next few months," he said.

"I won't be here that long."

"Do you know something about the war's ending?"

Lily smiled. "I am escaping at first opportunity."

"I'll eat the pig," the duke threatened.

"I'll take the pig with me," she returned.

James cocked a brow at her. "And leave your brother?"

"What do you mean?" Lily asked.

"You are free to roam wherever you wish," James told her. "Michael is being guarded, though."

"Bastard," she muttered.

Instead of becoming angry, as she would have expected, James smiled and said, "I assure you that my mother married my father."

"That doesn't mean you aren't someone's bastard," she shot back.

"Be careful, Mistress Hawthorne," James warned, narrowing his gaze on her. "I could send you to the dungeon." Then, "Shall we go down to dinner?"

"Where's my brother?"

"He'll join us in the dining room."

James grasped her arm and led her out of the library and down the stairs to the ground level. A footman opened the door for them.

"I never realized how indolent aristocrats are," Lily remarked.

"What do you mean?"

"You can't even open your own doors for yourself."

"If the man didn't open the door for me, his family

would starve because he would be out of work," James told her.

The dining room was enormous. Three place settings lay at one end of the forty-foot dining table. Overhead hung two chandeliers. On the table with the place settings were a candelabra centerpiece, a soup tureen, ashets, and cover dishes. The knives, forks, and spoons were fashioned in silver with ivory handles.

Lily had never seen a room or dining table like this. She was about to ask why they were eating in such a big room when her brother walked in with Princess in his arms.

"I will not share my table with a pig unless it has been cooked," James said, ordering the piglet from the room.

Digby lifted the piglet out of her brother's arms and left the chamber.

James sat at the head of the table. On either side of him sat Lily and Michael.

"Holy hell, look at all the knives and forks," Michael exclaimed. "Which one do I use?"

Lily felt her face grow hot with embarrassment. The duke had done this on purpose to demonstrate how ignorant she was. Only the wealthy used more than one of each utensil at a time. She had no idea which to use either.

Stalling for time, Lily scolded her brother. "Michael, I told you not to use vulgarities."

"Well, which fork do I use?"

"Start with the outside utensils and work your way toward your plate," James said.

"I could have told him that, your grace," Lily lied.

"You needn't instruct my brother about table manners. Or me, for that matter."

"I apologize," James said.

His voice was condescending, and Lily felt as if he knew she was lying.She greeted his apology with silence and lifted her spoon off the table.

Lily had never eaten a more delicious meal. Dinner began with tomato soup, enriched with a swirl of cream, topped with chopped basil. Next came ribbons of cool raw cucumbers with cayenne pepper in a sharp dressing that was served with light, crusty rolls. Cold asparagus dressed with hollandaise arrived with plump, moist chunks of haddock, poached in milk and generously dotted with sweet butter. Lemon sponge cake with a dollop of whipped cream was their dessert.

"Duke, I saw fire from my window," Michael said.

"Those would be the St. John's Day bonfires on St. Stephen's Hill," James told him. "Would you like to walk outside after dinner and see them?"

"Michael and I are tired from the journey," Lily announced. "We are going directly to bed."

"I'm not tired," Michael protested.

"I am," Lily replied.

"It's settled, then," James said before she could speak. "You will go upstairs, and Michael will walk with me outside."

Lily didn't want her brother alone with the duke but didn't know how to refuse. Instead, she announced, "I would like another chamber, if you don't mind."

"Is there something wrong with the one you have been given?" James asked.

Lily stared him straight in the eye and answered, "I dislike its neighbor."

"You'll need to make do," James said with an infuriating smile. "Prisoners, after all, do not choose where they would like to sleep." He turned to her brother without giving her a chance to reply and said, "Perhaps tomorrow I'll take you on a tour of the enchanted forest."

"Can Lily come with us?" Michael asked, glancing at her.

"Of course Lily is welcome," the duke told him. "That is, if she isn't too tired from the trip."

Lily didn't know why the duke was being so damned pleasant and solicitous of her brother. No doubt he had some dark scheme in mind. She could handle emotional pain, but she would kill him if he hurt her brother's feelings.

Immediately after dinner, Lily climbed the stairs while the duke and her brother walked outside the mansion. Gaining her chamber, she found the maid waiting for her.

"What are you doing here?" Lily demanded, surprised to see the other girl.

"I'm supposed to help you dress and undress, my lady," Peggy replied.

"I've been dressing and undressing myself for eighteen years," Lily said, crossing the chamber to inspect the connecting door. "My name is Lily. Use it."

"Aunt Bea would scold me if I did that," Peggy told her.

"You may call me *my lady* if you help me move the tallboy in front of the connecting door," Lily said.

"Why do you want to do that?"

"The door has no lock."

With the girl's help, Lily moved the tallboy inch by inch across the chamber until it stood in front of the connecting door. Both were panting and sweating by the time they finished.

Alone in her chamber, Lily removed her gown and carefully hung it in the amoire. In spite of her dislike of the duke, she didn't want to ruin the gowns he'd given her. She had never owned anything so fine. She donned her nightshift and climbed into a bed as big as Boston Common.

How absurd of her to have thought she would marry the duke and become mistress of all this, Lily thought. Great guardian angel, she wasn't one of Jane Austen's heroines and hadn't even known which eating utensil to use.

The enormous bed in the great chamber made her think about how far she was from home. Even Hortensia MacDugal would be a welcome sight.

Lily knew she would never be able to fall asleep in this bed in this chamber in this enemy country. And that was her last thought before she fell into a deep, dreamless sleep.

Before dawn, Lily awakened and tossed the coverlet aside. In spite of its enormous size, the chamber held the heat from the summer's night. She glanced toward the closed window and then rose from the bed.

Sweet lamb of God, Lily thought, these English were pea-brains. Who was so stupid as to leave the windows closed in the middle of summer?

Lily padded on bare feet across the chamber and opened the window. She inhaled deeply of the garden's intoxicatingly sensuous scent and let the night's air cool her skin.

Her mind traveled down the stairs to the Long Library, with all of those books. Lord, but she could hardly wait to get her hands on them. And why should she wait? If she went now, she'd certainly miss seeing the duke.

Turning away from the window, Lily grabbed a shawl for modesty's sake in case she met a servant along the way. She wrapped it around her shoulders and left the chamber.

Lily glided like an apparition down the corridor to the stairs. When she reached the Long Library and stepped inside, she realized she wasn't alone. The duke slept in one of the chairs in front of the hearth.

Determined not to leave empty-handed, Lily tiptoed to the nearest bookcase and grabbed the thickest book. Then she slipped out of the library's door and flew up the stairs to her chamber.

After lighting a candle, Lily looked at her selection and smiled. In her hands was *The Complete Works of William Shakespeare*. She glided the palm of her hand across the book's leather cover as if greeting one of her dearest friends.

Lily decided that her choice had been fortuitous. After all, she would never have been able to concentrate on anything new until she accustomed herself to England. Reading Shakespeare was as comforting as a visit from a loved one.

Placing the book aside for later, Lily dragged a chair across the chamber to the window and sat down. A gentle breeze blew into the room and caressed her skin, seeming to assure her that all would be well in the end.

Hours later, after she'd dressed, Lily sat in the same chair with the book. She had no intention of going downstairs. Confronting the duke could wait until afternoon. With any luck, he would have taken her brother to see the enchanted forest by the time she left her chamber.

A knock on the door drew her attention. Before she could call out, her brother marched into the chamber.

"Sister, will you go outside with me?" Michael asked, wiping the drool from his chin with one hand while he held the piglet in the other.

"I thought the duke was taking you to see the enchanted forest," Lily said.

"He's busy," Michael told her. "We can wade in the pool."

"That sounds delightful," Lily said, rising from her chair. She clutched the book in one hand and offered, "Shall I carry Princess?"

"I'll carry her."

Followed by Digby, Lily and Michael wandered outside to the grand pool with its fountains. Sparing a wary glance at the footman, Lily took off her shoes and hose and then hiked up the skirt of her white muslin gown while her brother took off his own shoes. Side by side, sister and brother sat on the edge of the pool and cooled their feet in the water.

The English devil lived in an earthly paradise, Lily thought.

The ducal grounds contained sweeping vistas and a glorious profusion of colors. There were green borders, shrubberies, and lawns, making avenues of flowers. On one side of the main courtyard clipped yews stood guard. Red roses clung to the patch of earth near a terrace while purple irises watched from a short distance away. Azaleas brought an exotic flourish of color, and the brilliant fuchsia peony opened its petals to reveal a yellow interior.

"I like merry olde England," Michael said.

"I suppose it will do until the war ends," Lily replied.

Michael wiped his chin and said, "Tell me the story, Sister."

"A war broke out in heaven," Lily said, putting her arm around his shoulder. "Michael and his angels fought the dragon. The dragon and his angels fought back, but they were defeated. There was no longer any place for them in heaven. . . . Satan, the deceiver of the world, was thrown down to earth, and his angels were thrown down with him."

"Did the dragon look like that?" Michael asked, pointing at the statues.

"The man on the horse is St. George, who fought and killed a dragon in a lake," Lily told him. "Whole armies had not been able to kill it. The only way to appease the monster was to give it two sheep to eat every day. When sheep became scarce, it demanded a maiden. The lot fell upon the king's daughter. After making the sign of the cross, George killed the dragon and saved the princess. The king and his people converted to the true religion, and St. George gave the reward money to the poor and went on his way."

"George was a brave man," Michael said, obviously impressed. "Are there any more dragons?"

"George killed the last one."

Lily stood up then but lost her balance. She saved Shakespeare from a soaking but ended up sitting in the pool.

Michael burst out laughing. Then he jumped into the pool to sit with her, and Princess began swimming around, which made both of them laugh. Digby stepped forward to help them, but Lily passed him the volume of Shakespeare and then gestured him away.

Lily stood up and inspected the damage to her gown but failed to notice what the wet muslin clinging to her curves revealed. She decided to enjoy the water, since the gown was already ruined.

"Come on, Brother," Lily said, wading across the pool. "Let's ride St. George's horse."

Michael grinned and splashed water at her, saying, "I want to ride the dragon."

While Lily and Michael were splashing around in the grand pool, James sat behind his desk in the Long Library. Across from him sat Adam St. Aubyn, the Marquess of Stonehurst, his most trusted friend. His cousin Sloane relaxed in the chair to the left of St. Aubyn's.

"And so the Gilded Lily was actually a beautiful woman with a startling gift," James was saying.

"A woman?" St. Aubyn echoed in surprise. "I cannot credit that."

"I swear it's true."

"You didn't kill the woman, did you?" Sloane asked.

"You know me better than that," James replied. "I snatched the girl and her young brother and brought them to England until the war ends. You'll meet them at lunch."

"You abducted the girl?" Adam laughed. "That must have been one bloody hell of a trip across the Atlantic."

"What's this gift of hers?" Sloane asked.

"The chit possesses a perfect memory," James told

them. "She can read a written page only once and then recite it back."

"You're joking," Adam said.

"I'd like to see that," Sloane said.

"I'll make her show it off later," James said. "Though I'll need to trick her into it."

Adam flicked a sidelong glance at Sloane and then said, "Because of the mourning period for your brother, the St. Legers haven't announced your engagement, but I hear that Reggie is running up some hefty gambling debts."

"He's been assuring his creditors that you intend to pay off his losses," Sloane added. "I've escorted Valentina to several social events in order to keep her entertained, but she's annoyed about being forbidden to tell the world she's about to become a duchess."

James lifted his glass of whiskey off his desk and sipped it. "And?"

"Valentina has been favoring a couple of rich Americans vying for her attention," Adam said.

"I guess I should return to London and smooth things over with her," James said.

Adam St. Aubyn rose from his chair and refilled his glass of whiskey. Then he wandered over to the window and looked outside. "You don't sound as if you missed your sweet betrothed."

"One wife is as good as another," James replied.

"You don't need to make connections," Adam said, over his shoulder. "Why marry a woman you don't love?"

"Who said that marriage had anything to do with love?" James asked, smiling at his friend's back.

"I still believe that Valentina St. Leger is a mistake," Adam said.

"I agree with Adam," Sloane spoke up. Then he changed the subject by asking, "When do we meet your prisoner?"

"I'll order her to luncheon with us," James said.

"Do she and her brother have black hair?" Adam asked without turning around. "And a pet pig that swims?"

James snapped his head around to stare at his friend. "Are they letting that pig swim in my pool?"

"All three of them are frolicking in your grand pool," Adam said, his voice filled with laughter. "I believe she's the one riding in front of St. George."

"God's balls," James muttered, rising from his chair.

Followed by Sloane, James marched across the library to look out the window. There she was, bigger than life itself, sitting astride St. George's horse. The girl was laughing and waving at her brother, who rode one of the dragons.

Sloane burst out laughing. Adam joined him.

James felt his anger heat from a simmer to a boil. Even from this distance, he could see that both were wet. God's balls, they'd been swimming in the ducal pool.

Without a word, James hurried out of the Long Library. He flew down the stairs and only slowed his pace when he reached the main courtyard. His guests were right behind him.

"Get out of there," James called, gesturing with a wave of his arm as he advanced on them.

"Hello, Duke," Michael called, returning his wave.

James heard the muffled chuckles behind him. His anger heated by several degrees.

"Get the bloody hell out of my pool," he shouted, his black gaze fixed on his prisoner.

Lily stared at him blankly for a moment, as if he were speaking a foreign language. Then she dismounted from St. George's horse, lifted the piglet into her arms, and waded across the pool to help her brother down from the dragon.

James stared hard at her as she and her brother crossed the grand pool and climbed out. He dropped his gaze to her wet body. The gown clung to her like a second skin, revealing her lush curves.

The wanton had the audacity to provoke him even more when she spoke. " 'Brother, it is the bright day that brings forth the adder and that craves wary walking,' " Lily said, quoting Shakespeare.

This time the chuckles behind James weren't quite so muffled.

Lily shifted her gaze from his face to his guests. With a smile that seemed to mock him, she asked, "Have you sent for reinforcements?"

Neither of his reinforcements bothered to hide his amusement. Adam and Sloane laughed out loud.

"Do *not* encourage her," James said, without looking at them. Holding her gaze captive, he accused, "You've ruined the gown."

"I saved Shakespeare from a drowning," she replied, gesturing to the book Digby held.

"The gown looks indecent," James said, ignoring her words. "Go inside and change."

"It covers my skin."

"That flimsy piece of material leaves nothing to the imagination."

"Englishmen have no imaginations," Lily drawled, flicking a glance at the others.

"Return to your chamber at once, Mistress Hawthorne," James ordered in a voice that brooked no disobedience. "We lunch in thirty minutes."

" 'There's small choice in rotten apples,' " Lily shot back, and then turned and walked in the direction of the mansion. Clutching the piglet in one arm, she turned around only once to point a finger at him and added, *"The Taming of the Shrew,* Act One, Scene One, line one-thirty-four."

"How appropriate to quote from *The Taming of the Shrew,"* James shouted back.

"Now you've done it, Duke," Michael called, following his sister. "You've made her angry."

Adam and Sloane roared with laughter, but James kept his gaze fixed on Lily. He was smiling as she disappeared into the mansion. Christ, she was glorious in her fury. Too bad she hadn't been born into the English aristocracy. Perhaps he could keep her as his mistress.

Sloane grabbed the book out of Digby's hand. He flipped through the pages and then exclaimed, "The girl is correct. How did she do that?"

"Forget the girl's memory," Adam said. "Look at your cousin's face. He loves her."

"I do *not* love her," James insisted. "She is my prisoner until the war ends and nothing more."

"How will you explain her to Valentina?" Sloane asked.

"I hadn't planned on explaining her presence to anyone," James informed them, and then began walking toward the mansion.

"His grace is a very great fool, indeed, if he thinks to keep her existence a secret from his mother and aunts," Adam said in a voice loud enough to carry across the courtyard.

The two men laughed loudly at that.

James knew they were correct. The only thing that would keep those three meddling witches away was his own absence from Kinross Park.

The two men laughed joyfully that
Joanna they were correct. The only thing that
would keep those three unrolling window area was
his own distance from Kansas Park.

Ten

The duke was a beef-witted bore, Lily thought, human pestilence with a Christian name. How dare he embarrass her in front of others?

Lily marched up the stairs in front of her brother, but her thoughts remained fixed on the man in the courtyard. She'd get even with him if it was her final earthly act.

And then an idea popped into her mind, its simplicity bringing a smile to her lips. She knew exactly what to do, and the punishment would fit the crime.

Lily touched her brother's shoulder as he moved to pass her chamber. "Come into my chamber," she said. "I want to speak with you." She glanced at the footman, adding, "Excuse us, Mr. Digby. Please take Princess to my brother's chamber."

"I have orders to remain with the young master," Digby told her.

"I would never wish to cause you trouble by trying to escape," Lily assured him.

"I believe you, miss." Digby lifted the piglet out of her brother's arms and continued down the corridor.

Lily pulled her brother into her chamber and closed the door behind them. Then she laughed out loud.

"I thought you were angry," Michael said, wiping drool from his chin.

"I *am* angry," Lily said with a smile. "However, we are going to get revenge on his grace."

"What's *revenge*?"

"Revenge is hitting back," Lily answered. "Duke embarrassed us in front of his friends, and we are going to do the same for him."

"How?"

"His grace believes that Americans are barbaric," Lily told him. "We are going to live up to his expectations."

"I don't understand," Michael said.

"When we join the men for lunch, we are going to use bad table manners," Lily said.

"What should I do?" Michael asked with a smile.

"Use the wrong utensils," Lily told him.

"That's easy."

"Burp a lot," Lily added, her lips curling up in a smile. "Even pick your nose if you want."

Michael laughed out loud. "Should I eat the pickings, too?" he asked excitedly.

Lily didn't know whether to laugh or to vomit. "Eating the pickings might make him suspicious," she said.

Michael nodded in understanding.

Thirty minutes later, Lily had changed into another gown. She and Michael descended the stairs to the dining room. James and his guests were already there.

"Allow me to introduce myself," one of the men said, hurrying forward to greet them when they appeared. "I am Sloane Armstrong, his grace's cousin."

"You seem much pleasanter than your cousin, sir," Lily replied, returning the young man's smile. "Perhaps not all of the Armstrong blood has gone bad."

Sloane laughed at her words. "I did inherit all of the finer Armstrong qualities of character."

"I am Adam St. Aubyn, his grace's friend," the second man said, crossing the chamber to greet her.

"I didn't realize his grace had any friends," Lily said, flicking a glance at the duke.

Both men smiled at that remark. The duke scowled.

"Adam is the Marquess of Stonehurst," Sloane said.

"Holy hell, what do we call him?" Michael asked.

Both men grinned. Even the duke smiled.

"Call him *my lord*," Sloane answered.

Michael shook his head. "My Lord is in heaven."

"This is a different lord," Sloane said.

"Lily told me there's only one," Michael replied.

"Call me Adam," the marquess said, clearing the matter up.

"Shall we sit down?" James said.

Lily smiled sweetly at him. "Your wish is our command, your grace."

"What are you planning?" he asked, his expression suspicious.

" 'The whirligig of time brings in his revenges,' " Lily quoted Shakespeare.

Ignoring her words, James sat at the head of the table. Lily and Michael sat opposite each other. Sloane took the chair on Lily's right, while Adam sat down beside Michael.

Luncheon consisted of mushrooms on toast in the French style, cucumber soup subtly flavored with sorrel and Gallic herb chervil and enriched with egg yolks and cream, and wild dandelion salad dressed with crisp morsels of fried bacon and a sharp vinaigrette. For dessert there was cold Pithivers cake with whipped cream. Lily and her brother drank lemon barley water while the men were served white wine.

"We hear all sorts of wild stories about America," Sloane said. "Tell me about your life there."

"My life in Boston is rather mundane," Lily answered. She flicked a glance at the duke. Then, instead of cutting a bit of the mushroom toast, she lifted the whole piece of bread and took a gigantic bite. With her mouth full of food, she asked her brother, "Do you like this?"

Michael lifted a handful of mushrooms off his toast and popped them into his mouth. "I like it," he said with a nod.

Lily glanced at the duke, who stared into her eyes. He dropped his gaze to her eating utensils and shifted it to her plate.

Laughter bubbled up in her throat. Ignoring his hint, she took another enormous bite of the toast.

"How do you live there?" Sloane asked.

"She's a wharf rat," James said flatly.

"My father owns a tavern on the wharf," Lily said.

"How interesting." Adam entered the conversation. "Boston is an important port."

"Boston is the cradle of liberty," Lily announced. "I'm only sorry we won't be home for the big celebration in a few days. Ooops, I shouldn't remind you of the first war you lost to us."

Lily lifted her spoon, glanced at the duke, and smiled inwardly. She proceeded to slurp away at her cucumber soup.

"Delicious," she pronounced when she'd slurped the last drop. "Try the soup, Brother. You'll like it, too."

Michael shook his head and pushed the bowl away. "The soup looks like snots," he announced.

James choked on his soup and coughed. Sloane and Adam chuckled.

"Are you trying to embarrass me?" James asked, regaining his breath.

Michael burst out laughing. "Oh, Duke. You're too smart for us."

Lily felt like throttling her brother. She refused to look at the duke. The others appeared hard-pressed to contain their mirth.

"Michael, go upstairs," James ordered. "The servants will bring you something more to your liking."

Lily nodded at her brother. Only then did he leave the dining room.

"Have you anything to say, Mistress Hawthorne?" the duke asked in a stern voice.

Lily remained silent for a moment and then offered, *"Egads?"*

Sloane and Adam burst out laughing, which made her smile. Lord, but she liked his friends. They, at least, had a sense of humor.

"You know, sweetness, I've missed you beside me at night," James said unexpectedly. His voice held a note of intimacy.

Lily snapped her head around to stare at him. She could feel her face heating into a blush while angry embarrassment welled up in her chest. How dare he refer to their previous relationship in front of others?

And then Lily recalled her earlier words to the duke. *The whirligigs of time bring in his revenges.* The duke was getting even with her for getting even with him.

Lily pushed her chair away from the table. She needed to get out of there.

"Tell me you've missed me, sweetness," James said, covering her hand with his own.

Lily yanked her hand away from his, saying in a choked voice, "Excuse me, please."

"What?" James mocked her. "No witty Shakespearean quote?"

"Give over," Sloane said.

"Have a care for your company," Adam warned.

"I do have a care for my company; I care that she isn't in my bed at night," James said. To Lily, he added, "Sweetness, allow me access to your bed again."

"Yes, of course, James," Lily said, giving him a warm smile, obviously surprising him.

He looked perplexed. "Tonight?"

"No."

"Tomorrow night?"

"Sorry."

"When?"

Lily bolted out of her chair so fast that it toppled over. "You may visit my bed when the devil hosts an ice-skating party in hell."

At that, Lily marched out of the dining room. Behind her, she heard his friends' protests: "That was uncalled for" and "If you love her, make peace with the girl and marry her."

"I do *not* love her," she heard the duke insisting.

Lily hurried upstairs. Alone in her chamber, she wept softly. The others were wrong; the duke did not love her. No man would so crassly insult the woman he loved. Well, she wasn't going to cry for the enemy anymore, and she certainly wasn't going to break bread with him.

Lily refused to leave her chamber for the remainder of the day. Peggy brought her a light supper that evening, but she had no appetite.

Feeling stronger the next morning, Lily decided she needn't starve herself. She didn't know if she felt relieved or disappointed when she strode battle-ready into the dining room and found only servants.

After breakfasting on hot Geneva rolls smothered in butter, Lily started to leave. She reached the doorway just as the duke filled it.

"Good morning, Mistress Hawthorne," James greeted her.

Lily dropped her gaze from his expressionless face to the evening clothing he wore. Apparently he was just arriving home.

"Civilized people greet each other no matter the circumstance," James chided her.

"Spare me your droll English customs," Lily said, brushing past him and out of the room.

How dare he tutor her on the habits of the civilized! He'd snatched her from the safety of her home, stolen her virginity, and then humiliated her. She had every right to be disagreeable.

Lily remained hidden in her chamber all day, her only visitors her brother and Peggy. Without knowing the reason, she felt nervous when she walked downstairs to the dining room that evening.

Lily ate her second lonely meal of the day. Even Michael had abandoned her, preferring the warm camaraderie in the kitchen.

The second day was a repetition of the previous one. Lily ate two lonely meals. She was beginning to wonder why the duke was leaving her alone and if escape was possible.

On the third morning Lily sat alone at the forty-foot dining table. She wished she had joined her brother in the kitchen, where even Princess was welcome.

Accustomed to the noisy bustle of tavern life, Lily felt lonely. She glanced to the left, where Pennick stood near the sideboard.

"I wonder where he goes," Lily spoke her thoughts out loud.

"I beg your pardon?" Pennick said.

"Where does his grace go?" she asked.

Pennick lifted a newspaper off the sideboard and passed it to her, saying, "Turn to page three."

Lily opened the *Times* to page three and began reading an article entitled "The Reluctant Valentine." James Armstrong, the Duke of Kinross, was vying for the affections of Valentina St. Leger, the Earl of Bovingdon's sister. Lady Valentina, irritated with his grace for some unknown reason, was definitely enjoying the competition. Did this lovely valentine care for the duke? Did she prefer his handsome cousin? Or would one of the two wealthy Americans win her hand in marriage?

Sudden tears welled up in Lily's eyes, but she managed to blink them back. How humiliating to be used and tossed aside. The duke was an evil man destined to rot in hell. Her only wish was to send him there sooner rather than later.

Without a word to Pennick, Lily rose from her chair and started to leave the room but found her way blocked when she reached the door. She looked up into the duke's dark eyes.

"Good morning, Mistress Hawthorne," James said in a cold voice.

Lily cocked an ebony brow at him. "Is it?"

"I beg your pardon?"

"Bastard," Lily muttered. And then she did the unthinkable. She slapped him hard.

Lily left the dining room and hurried up the stairs to her chamber. She felt no satisfaction at his stupid, shocked expression.

After locking her door, Lily threw herself down on the bed. Tears streamed down her face, and then she gave herself over to sobs.

Bang! Bang! Bang!

Lily raised herself up when she heard the pounding on her door. She knew who it was and refused to answer.

"Open the door," James called.

"Leave me alone," she said in a voice choked with tears.

"Open the damned door," he ordered.

Lily slid off the bed and crossed the chamber to the door. "What do you want?" she called.

"I want to know what's wrong with you."

"I'm unwell." That much was true. The wrenching realization of being tossed aside had turned her stomach queasy.

"Shall I send for a physician?" James asked after a moment's silence.

"That will be unnecessary," Lily said.

"Is there anything I can do?" he asked.

Love me, Lily thought. "Go away."

"As you wish," James called. "If you aren't better by this evening, though, I'm sending for my physician."

Lily didn't bother to answer. She listened at the door for several minutes and then, certain that he'd gone, dragged a chair across the room to sit in front of the window. She passed the remainder of the day reading Shakespeare.

Deeming the duke had left for London and his courtship of Lady Valentina St. Leger, Lily ventured downstairs just before dinner. She planned to borrow another book from the Long Library before going to dine.

Lily stopped short when she entered the library. The duke sat behind his desk at the far end of the chamber.

"What are you doing here?" Lily asked, before she could swallow the words and back out of the room.

James looked up from the papers he'd been reading. "I live here," he said. "Remember?"

Lily narrowed her sapphire gaze on him. She should have wagered money that he'd answer her with a sarcastic remark.

"Excuse me," she said, turning to leave.

"Wait," he called.

Lily took another step toward the doorway.

"Please."

Lily paused. She couldn't credit that his high-and-mighty grace had actually used the word *please*.

Lily turned around to see him advancing on her. Suffering the urge to step back several paces as he neared, she forced herself to hold her ground but mentally readied herself for the oncoming battle.

"I want to apologize for my behavior the other day," James said, his voice low and persuasive. "I hope you will forgive me."

Lily stared into his black eyes. He seemed sincere. And yet—

"I cannot accept your apology at this time," Lily

said, steeling herself against him and, more importantly, her feelings for him.

James snapped his brows together. "Why not?"

"If you criticize me in public," she told him, "then the apology must be given in public."

"I promise to treat you with respect henceforth," he replied. "I will give you a public apology at first opportunity."

"In that case, I accept your apology," Lily said. "However, I won't forget your transgressions until the public apology is given."

James nodded. "That sounds fair."

"I do realize how hard apologizing must be after all those years of autocratic conditioning," she added.

" 'A dog's obey'd in office,' " James replied, quoting Shakespeare.

Lily smiled. *"King Lear,* Act Four, Scene Six, line fifty-eight."

James grinned. "May I escort you to dinner?"

"I've already made plans to eat with my brother in the kitchen," she told him, turning to leave.

"Eat in the kitchen?" James echoed, his voice mirroring his surprise. "Why would you want to do that?"

"We like kitchens," Lily told him. "Eating in the kitchen feels like home."

"May I join you?" he asked.

Now it was her turn to be surprised. "Isn't that beneath your station?"

James gestured around him, saying, "The whole house belongs to me, even the kitchen."

"Why do you want to eat in the kitchen?" she asked.

"I want to eat with you," he said, lowering his voice.

Lily shrugged indifferently. "You own the kitchen and can dine there if you like."

"I'm glad that's settled," James said, offering his arm. "You may not believe this, but I've never eaten in my own kitchen."

"How shocking," Lily drawled. "You have led a rather parochial life in spite of your vast wealth."

"As a matter of fact, I have never eaten in any kitchen," he told her.

Lily burst out laughing. "Then, your grace, you are about to experience the bustle of supper in the kitchen. You may never return to the dining room again."

A large pine work table set out with the cook's essential equipment dominated the kitchen. Along one wall was an open range complete with drip pan, cauldron, and kettle. Hanging copper pots, pans, and molds covered another wall.

Several doors led out of the kitchen. One went to the kitchen gardens and orchards, others led to the butler's pantry, the store closet, and the servant's hall.

Everyone stopped talking when Lily and James walked into the kitchen. Only Michael seemed unaffected, calling out, "Good to see you, Duke."

All the servants gasped. Only Duncan wore a broad grin on his face.

Before two minutes had passed, the kitchen had cleared except for Duncan and Michael. Duncan gestured to the empty kitchen.

"Was it something I said?" James asked. "Duncan, tell Pennick to bring me the chess set and that book of rules and strategies."

Michael went with Duncan, leaving them alone.

"I never realized the effect I had on people," James said.

Lily shrugged, unwilling to voice any derogatory

thoughts on the subject. The duke was being pleasant, and she far preferred him that way.

"Something smells delicious," she said, walking over to the range.

Fisherman's soup, with its opulent broth and mussels and oysters, simmered over the flame. Potato bread, hot from the oven, sat on the counter beside a crock of creamy butter. A crisp salad of lettuce with dressing sat there, too.

Pennick entered on the run, saying with a nervous laugh, "Oh, your grace, you've given us a real surprise."

A squadron of footmen, armed with serving bowls and platters, walked in behind him. One footman set the chess set and pieces down on the table.

"What is the meaning of all this?" James asked, gesturing to the footmen.

Pennick stood straight and recited, "Tonight we have Dover sole with carrots and potato . . ."

"Take it away," James ordered.

"Take it away?" Pennick echoed, looking flabbergasted. "What will you eat?"

"The lady and I are eating whatever is in that cauldron," James informed him.

Lily smiled in agreement.

Pennick looked horrified. "What will the staff eat?"

" 'Let them eat cake,' " Lily chirped.

James burst out laughing. "Let the staff eat Dover sole," he said to Pennick.

"And where will they eat it?" the man asked, his exasperation becoming apparent in his voice.

"Serve them in the dining room," James suggested. "The lady and I wish to sup *alone* in the kitchen."

"In the kitchen?" Pennick echoed, as if he couldn't credit what he was hearing.

"The lady likes kitchens," James said. "I do believe I'm developing a fondness for them, too."

"This is highly irregular," the man complained.

"I apologize for upsetting you, Pennick, and promise we won't succumb to this urge every evening," James told the man.

Lily couldn't credit the fact that the duke was offering an apology to a retainer, his second apology of the day. Could there be a small glimmer of hope for him? Was he hiding a redeeming quality she hadn't noticed before?

Pennick looked astounded. Taking the Dover sole with him, he made a hasty exit from the kitchen.

"Fill the bowls with soup while I set the chessboard," James ordered.

The duke's behavior confused Lily. One day he acted colder than the north wind, and the next day he was warmer than a summer's land breeze.

The chessboard was made of polished wood. Handcrafted of resin and ground stone, the chess pieces depicted famous Elizabethans. Elizabeth Tudor and Mary Stuart were the queens, of course. Lord Burghley served as the English king, as did James VI for the Scots. The bishops, knights, and rooks were famous English and Scots figures like Dudley, Devereux, Raleigh, Darnley, and Bothwell. The pawns, famous English poets, readied for battle against the Scots pawns representing various Highland clans.

"The field appears to be a battle of the pen against the sword," Lily remarked, pushing his bowl of fisherman's soup toward him.

James inclined his head. "You are knowledgable and observant, my lady."

"I thought I was a wharf rat," Lily said, tossing his previous description of her back at him.

James winked at her and said, "A very pretty little rodent."

Lily began eating her soup. "Are there Armstrongs in the front lines?"

"No."

"Are the Armstrongs cowards?"

"Armstrongs are Lowlanders," James said, cocking a dark brow at her, clearly unamused. "By the way, why aren't you slurping your soup?"

Lily smiled. "Would you like me to slurp it while we play?"

"No, thank you." James drew her attention to the board, saying, "The board is set up so that each player has a white square on his right."

"Why?"

"That is rule number one."

"I don't understand what difference it makes," Lily remarked.

"Do you want to play or argue the point?" James returned. "The rooks stand in the corner, followed by the knights and then the bishops. The white queen stands on the white square and the black queen on the black square. Their kings stand beside them. The pawns are the front line of defense."

"We would never want the powerful to die first," Lily said dryly.

"The queen is the most powerful piece on the board," James continued, ignoring her editorial comment. "She combines all the moves of the bishop and the rooks."

Take **4 FREE** Books!

We created our convenient Home Subscription Service so you'll be sure to have the hottest new romances delivered each month right to your doorstep — usually before they are available in book stores. Just to show you how convenient Zebra Home Subscription Service is, we would like to send you 4 Kensington Choice Historical Romances as a FREE gift. You receive a gift worth up to $24.96 — absolutely FREE. There's no extra charge for shipping and handling. There's no obligation to buy anything - ever!

Save Up To 32% On Home Delivery!

Accept your FREE gift and each month we'll deliver 4 brand new titles as soon as they are published. They'll be yours to examine FREE for 10 days. Then if you decide to keep the books, you'll pay the preferred subscriber's price of just $4.20 per title. That's $16.80 for all 4 books for a savings of up to 32% off the cover price! Just add $1.50 to offset the cost of shipping and handling. Remember, you are under no obligation to buy any of these books at any time! If you are not delighted with them, simply return them and owe nothing. But if you enjoy Kensington Choice Historical Romances as much as we think you will, pay the special preferred subscriber rate of only $16.80 each month and save over $8.00 off the bookstore price!

we have 4 FREE BOOKS for you as
your introduction to
KENSINGTON CHOICE!

To get your FREE BOOKS,
worth up to $24.96, mail the card below
or call TOLL-FREE 1-888-345-BOOK
Visit our website at www.kensingtonbooks.com.

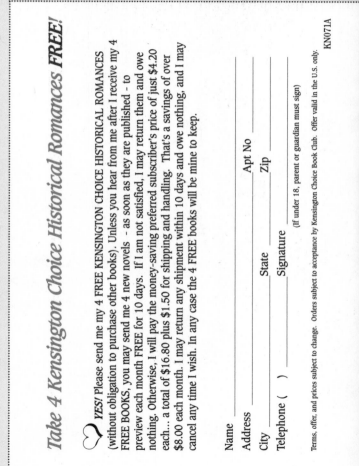

Take 4 Kensington Choice Historical Romances FREE!

♡ *YES!* Please send me my 4 FREE KENSINGTON CHOICE HISTORICAL ROMANCES (without obligation to purchase other books). Unless you hear from me after I receive my 4 FREE BOOKS, you may send me 4 new novels - as soon as they are published - to preview each month FREE for 10 days. If I am not satisfied, I may return them and owe nothing. Otherwise, I will pay the money-saving preferred subscriber's price of just $4.20 each... a total of $16.80 plus $1.50 for shipping and handling. That's a savings of over $8.00 each month. I may return any shipment within 10 days and owe nothing, and I may cancel any time I wish. In any case the 4 FREE books will be mine to keep.

KN071A

Name _____

Address _____ Apt No ____

City _____ State _____ Zip _____

Telephone ( ) _____ Signature _____

(If under 18, parent or guardian must sign)

Terms, offer, and prices subject to change. Orders subject to acceptance by Kensington Choice Book Club. Offer valid in the U.S. only.

llɪɪlɪɪllllɪɪɪlllllɪɪlɪlɪɪlɪɪllɪllɪɪllllɪɪll

KENSINGTON CHOICE
Zebra Home Subscription Service, Inc.
P.O. Box 5214
Clifton NJ 07015-5214

PLACE
STAMP
HERE

Lily looked up at him in confusion. "Why isn't the king the most powerful?"

"The king needs protection," James explained. "Once he's dead, the game is over."

"Why can't the queen take over?" Lily asked.

"She's a woman," James said in an exasperated voice. "That's why."

"Becoming upset will ruin your digestion," Lily said.

"You'd like that, wouldn't you?" James snapped. "Now, who do you want to be?"

"Elizabeth is my favorite historical figure," Lily told him.

"How nice to know you admire someone," James said dryly. "Let's play." He moved one of his pawns two squares forward.

"You're cheating," Lily said.

"A pawn may travel two squares forward on the first move," he told her. "That way the queen and bishop can jump into action."

Lily countered by bringing out her queen's-knight, who leaped over her pawns.

"You enjoy risks," James said in a seductive voice, gazing at her through black eyes that gleamed with renewed respect.

Lily felt a melting sensation in the pit of her stomach. "I like to win," she said softly.

The game continued. Fifteen moves later James announced, "Checkmate."

"What does that mean?"

"You lose."

"I want a rematch," Lily demanded.

"We'll play tomorrow after you've studied the book," James said, passing her the book of rules and strategies. "Perhaps you'll offer a bit of a challenge then."

Lily ignored his insult.

"What will you give me for winning the game?" he asked.

"What do you want?" It was the wrong thing to say. Lily knew that as soon as the smile spread across his handsome face.

"A kiss?"

Without a word, Lily leaned close, and her gaze became trapped by the dark intensity of his. His lips touched hers in a chaste kiss, and she closed her eyes, savoring the sensation.

"I have some paperwork to finish," James said, drawing back. "Would you care to read the book in the library while I work?"

Lily didn't trust herself to be in his presence. Any longer and she would be marching through the connecting bedroom door to demand her rights as his captive. In theory, at least, ravishment was beginning to appeal to her.

Lily shook her head. "Generals do not plan strategy in the enemy's camp."

James offered his hand. Together, they left the kitchens and walked up the stairs to the second floor.

"I'll escort you to your chamber," James said.

"I know the way," Lily refused. She hurried up the stairs to the third floor. She felt his dark eyes upon her but refused to turn around.

Gaining her chamber, Lily leaned back against the door. She didn't know what to expect from the duke anymore. He confused her. She could feel his heat, yet the reluctant valentine awaited him in London.

He's staying home tonight, Lily reminded herself. Was it because of her or for some other reason?

Lily crossed the chamber and set the rule book down on the table. She would read it in the morning. For tonight, she would sit in the chair in front of the window and conjure the incredible sensation of the duke's lips on hers.

Five days passed.

James never left Kinross Park.

Lily lost every game of chess and forfeited a kiss each time. She was beginning to cool toward the game of chess but warm to the duke.

The sixth day dawned rainy and cool enough to light fires in the hearths. That afternoon, Lily sat across from James at the chessboard in front of the library's fireplace. She was determined to win, though she didn't mind forfeiting a kiss when she lost. He'd already charmed the virtue out of her; she might as well enjoy an occasional kiss.

"Are you ready, sweetness?" James asked.

Lily nodded. "Are you ready to lose?"

"Feeling confident today, are we?" he asked. "Perhaps you'd like to risk more than a single kiss?"

"Forget about my bed, your grace," she said, narrowing her sapphire gaze on him.

"You misunderstand me," James said with a smile. "You must forfeit a kiss each time you lose a chess piece."

That sounded interesting. "And what will you forfeit?"

"Ten pounds a piece," James said. "When you've saved enough for passage across the Atlantic, I'll send you and your brother home."

That sounded really interesting. "You have a deal, your grace."

"Call me James."

"Call *me* the winner."

"You might win more by losing," James said.

"I doubt it."

James turned the chess set around so that Lily could be the black queen, Elizabeth. He took the white queen, Mary Stuart.

"You don't mind being Mary Stuart every game?" she asked.

"Mary Stuart is a sentimental favorite of mine," James told her.

"I should have known you'd be partial to a woman who allowed men to ruin her life," Lily remarked. "Such a waste."

"A tragic figure," James agreed. "Make your move."

"After you, James."

James started the game by moving his king's-pawn two squares forward. Lily countered by bringing out her queen's-knight, which leaped over the pawns, ready for further action.

"Still taking risks, my love?" James commented.

Lily froze for a brief moment. *My love?* Was he trying to break her concentration and thus win the game?

Keeping her face expressionless, Lily looked him in the eye and said, "Make your move."

James advanced his queen's-pawn two squares, unblocking his other bishop. Both of his bishops were now free to move.

Lily countered by moving a pawn two squares forward, attacking his queen's-pawn with both black knight and pawn.

"You have several choices," she said. "What will you do about that?"

"I could move my queen's-pawn one square forward to threaten your knight," James said with a smile. Instead, he moved his pawn to capture hers. "I'd rather have a kiss, though."

James and Lily leaned across the board toward each other. She gave him a chaste kiss on the lips and then drew back.

"That's a miserly reward for capturing your pawn," he complained.

"Perhaps you would have had better luck if you'd let my man live," she teased him. "Besides, you'll need to win the game if you want emotion."

Four moves later, James called, "Check."

"How did you maneuver me into that position?" she asked, surprised.

"Save your king, Lily," James said, ignoring her question. "Move your queen's-bishop one square."

"I don't need help," Lily told him, moving her bishop one square. "I would have figured it out myself."

Two moves later, James called, "Check."

"Sweet lamb of God," Lily cried in exasperation. "Are you cheating?"

James gifted her with an infuriating smile, folded his arms across his chest, and waited for her to save her king.

Lily moved her king out of check, away from a diagonal attack.

James countered by moving his knight, checking her king. Lily moved her king one square forward in order to get out of check again.

"Checkmate, darling," James said, moving his bishop's-pawn one square forward.

Lily stared hard at the chessboard. How had she managed to lose? She'd read the rules and strategies several times over.

"I suppose you want that kiss," she said, looking up at him.

"With emotion, please."

Lily started to lean forward, but James stopped her. "I'd like to stand for this one."

Lily placed her hand in his and rose from the chair. She stepped closer and tilted her head back to gaze into his incredibly dark eyes.

Without warning, James yanked her into his powerful embrace. He captured her lips in a demanding kiss that made her senses reel. His lips slashed across hers, parting them, and his tongue ravished the sweetness of her mouth, sending ripples of desire dancing down her spine.

Lily moaned throatily. She entwined her arms around his neck and returned his kiss in kind.

"So it *is* true," said a voice from the doorway.

Eleven

"God's balls," James muttered in a low voice, setting her aside.

Lily whirled around to see three middle-aged women crossing the Long Library toward them. A blonde marched in front of a brunette and an auburn-haired woman. Behind them walked Sloane Armstrong and Adam St. Aubyn.

The duke's mother and aunts, Lily thought, beginning to panic. Advancing on them, the three women only had eyes for Lily. She felt excruciatingly awkward and could feel the heated blush rising on her cheeks.

Lily glanced at the duke's cousin and friend. Both men were smiling. James, however, wore one of the blackest scowls she'd ever seen.

"She's lovely," the auburn-haired woman said in a loud voice. "I bet he's hot for her."

The brunette nodded in agreement. "The vibrations in this chamber positively scream a harmonious pairing."

"What do you have to say for yourself, James?" the blonde asked, halting in front of the duke.

"Go back to London, Mother," he said, staring her straight in the eye.

The dowager arched a brow at her son, assumed a

disapproving expression, and said, "I have no intention of returning to London and allowing you to continue to dishonor this child."

"With all due respect, Mother, mind your own business," the duke said.

"Certainly, James," the dowager replied in a pleasant voice. "I'll mind my own business as soon as you've married the girl."

Her remark shocked Lily. She gasped and stared openmouthed at the older woman.

James looked as startled as Lily felt.

"You heard correctly, Son." The dowager seemed ready for battle.

Sloane Armstrong chuckled, earning a censorious glare from James. Lily sent the marquess a pleading look for help.

"Let's have tea and make the proper introductions before the arguing begins," Adam St. Aubyn said, insinuating himself into the conversation. "Shall we?" Without waiting for a reply, the marquess called, "Pennick!"

The majordomo rushed into the library so quickly that Lily knew he'd been eavesdropping outside the door. A scintillating tidbit to gossip about in the kitchen, no doubt.

"Serve tea, please," Adam instructed.

The dowager and her auburn-haired sister sat on one of the settees near the hearth. The brunette sat on the settee opposite them and motioned for Lily to sit beside her. Sloane sat in the high-backed chair while James, still scowling, and Adam remained standing.

"Your grace and my ladies, I present Mistress Hawthorne," Adam made the introductions. "Lily, this is

James's mother, the dowager duchess, and beside her is Lady Donna. Lady Nora sits beside you."

"How do you do?" the dowager asked in a cultured voice.

"Well, thank you, your grace," Lily answered.

"Tell us about yourself," Lady Nora prodded her.

"Don't you already know?" Lady Donna challenged her sister. "You always claim the ability to know things without being told."

"I do not find your skepticism amusing," Lady Nora replied.

Ignoring her sisters, the dowager caught Lily's eye and said, "Tell us about yourself, dear."

Lily glanced nervously at James, who appeared distinctly unhappy. She dropped her gaze to the carpet and said, "There's very little to tell."

"Come now, my dear," the dowager coaxed. "Don't be shy."

Lily took a deep breath and raised her gaze. "I live in Boston with my two brothers and my father, a tavern owner," she said. "Most of my time is spent caring for my younger brother, who is slightly impaired.

"What is his problem?" Lady Donna asked.

"Michael is slow," Lily answered, squaring her shoulders and sitting a little straighter. "Your son abducted him, too."

"You abducted an innocent girl and her impaired brother?" the dowager said to her son, shaking her head with disapproval. "You sailed to America to find this Gilded Lily. How could you take such dastardly action against two innocents?"

Lily froze inwardly at the mention of the Gilded Lily. The dowager would probably order her hanged if she knew the truth about the Gilded Lily.

"Fate brought them together," Lady Nora announced.

"Actually, Duncan's stupidity brought us together," James spoke up. "I sent Duncan ashore to discover what he could about the Gilded Lily. When he heard Lily called by name, Duncan assumed he had his man."

Lily stared in surprise at the duke. She couldn't understand why he would lie for her, though she was thankful for it. She would have expected him to tell the whole sordid truth.

Fearing the other two men would tell the truth, Lily looked at Adam. He and Sloane were grinning at each other.

"Anyone can tell she's a girl," Lady Donna scoffed.

"Lily was dressed in boys' clothing," James explained. "In the darkness of night, she appeared to be a small man."

"Why were you dressed in boys' clothing?" the dowager asked, fixing her gaze on Lily.

"It was a joke," James spoke up.

"Let the girl speak for herself," the dowager said.

Pennick saved Lily from answering by bringing their tea. After serving them, the man left the library.

"Well?" the dowager said.

"I was playing a joke on a friend who lives nearby," Lily said, thankful that the duke had thought of the lie for her.

"What kind of joke?" Lady Donna asked.

"What does that matter?" Lady Nora said. "Fate brought them together, and marriage will keep them together."

Lily peeked at James, who looked uncomfortable at

the mention of marriage. She couldn't blame him; she didn't want to marry him either.

"I could kill you," James said to his cousin. Then he looked at Adam and said, "Or was this *your* idea?"

"Never mind whose idea it was," the dowager said. "You will marry the girl."

"I will *not* marry her," James said emphatically.

Lily felt like crawling into a hole. She'd nearly succumbed to the duke's charm again. Perhaps this visit from his relatives was fortuitous. After all, their arrival was keeping her out of the duke's bed.

"Never mind him," Lady Donna said in an obvious effort to console. " 'The course of true love never did run smooth.' "

"*A Midsummer Night's Dream,*" Lily said without thinking. "Act One, Scene One, line thirty-four."

When Adam and Sloane burst out laughing, Lily realized what a blunder she'd made. All three women were staring in surprise at her.

" 'Wiving goes by destiny,' " Sloane said, quoting Shakespeare.

The Merchant of Venice, Lily thought. She felt grateful to the duke's cousin for deleting the section of the quote that began with the word *hanging.*

"You compromised her," the dowager announced. "Now you will marry her."

"For Christ's sake, Mother, the chit is a wharf rat," James said in a disgusted tone of voice.

Lily understood that the duke did not want to marry her, but he needn't be so insultingly cruel. Lily rose from her chair and said, "I have heard enough from ill-mannered aristocrats. Please excuse me."

"Sit down," James barked at her.

"And be quiet," the dowager ordered.

Lily plopped down in the chair. "Don't *I* have a say in my future?"

"No!" both mother and son said simultaneously.

Adam and Sloane burst out laughing. The duke's aunts smiled at each other and nodded.

"You will become betrothed," the dowager said to her son. "After we educate her for a lady, you will marry her."

"I'll host her come-out ball," Adam said.

"What a wonderful idea," the dowager gushed. "I do love balls."

"I insist on a long betrothal," James said.

The dowager inclined her head, generous in her victory over her son. "As you wish, your grace."

"You can't be serious," Lily cried. "I will not betroth myself to this—this—*Englishman.*" The word *Englishman* sounded like the vilest of insults.

"Don't be absurd," the dowager dismissed her.

"You'll become a duchess," Lady Donna told her.

"I don't want to be a duchess," Lily wailed.

The women looked at her as if she'd suddenly grown another head. Apparently, they couldn't imagine any woman not wanting to marry James Armstrong.

Lily felt trapped. Her stomach rolled, and she felt queasy. Resting her head against the settee, she closed her eyes and fought back the nausea.

"Are you ill?" James asked in a concerned voice.

Lily opened her eyes. "I need to go upstairs now." Shrugging off his helping hand, she rose from the chair and said, "We will continue this debate later."

Lily walked to the door slowly. Behind her, she heard the dowager say, "I hope she's not sickly." Then one of the aunts asked, "Could she be with child?"

The question startled Lily, but she pretended deafness and walked out the door. Gaining her chamber, Lily lay down on the bed. Could she be with child? The thought was too absurd. These infuriating British had sickened her, and nothing more.

Lily worried herself to sleep.

When she opened her eyes an hour later, Lily was staring into red eyes. She lay perfectly still and tried to figure out whether she was dreaming. Then she heard a snorting grunt and a tongue licked her face.

Lily sat up in the bed. The red eyes and the grunt belonged to Princess.

"What's wrong?" Michael asked. "You never sleep in the afternoon unless you're sick."

Lily patted the edge of the bed in invitation. When he and the pig joined her there, she told him, "I needed the rest after my interview with the duke's mother."

"I didn't know Duke had a mother," Michael said. "Is she mean?"

"No, she's obstinate."

"What's *obstinate?*"

"She's stubborn," Lily explained. "She insists I marry the duke."

"What about Bradley?" her brother asked.

Fingering her *alpha* and *omega* cross, Lily worried her bottom lip with her teeth. Where was Bradley? Was he thinking of her? Had he and her brother discovered them missing?

Lily knew she couldn't marry Bradley Howell. She'd lost that option when she gave herself to the duke.

"Are you worried about Duke's mother?" Michael asked.

"Nothing worries me," Lily told him.

"Can we live in merry olde England when you marry Duke?" he asked. "Nobody calls me names."

"I'm glad you are enjoying yourself," Lily said, her heart wrenching at his words. Nobody should ever call her brother a derogatory name. He was closer to God than anyone she'd ever met.

"Did you ask Cook to bake the special cake?" she asked.

Michael nodded. "Cook laughed and said yes."

Someone knocked on the door, and then they heard Duncan's voice, calling, "Michael, are you ready?"

"I'm coming," Michael shouted. He lifted Princess off the bed and said, "Duncan is teaching me chess."

Alone again, Lily leaned back against the headboard and sighed. Too bad the duke didn't love her. Then Michael could live where people accepted him. Or did they accept him because the duke was his protector?

Her indiscretions had doomed Michael to a life on Boston's waterfront, Lily thought, guilt swelling up in her chest. For the rest of his life, her brother would bear the brunt of other people's ignorance.

Another knock on the door drew her attention.

"Yes?" she called, sliding off the bed and smoothing the skirt of her gown.

"Lily, are you feeling better?" James called through the door.

Lily crossed the chamber and said, "Yes, your grace."

"May I come in?" he asked.

"Why?" she asked in return, unable to hide her suspicion.

"I need to speak privately with you," he answered.

Lily opened the door and stepped back to allow him entrance. "Leave the door open," she ordered.

James inclined his head. "I want to apologize for— What is the highboy doing against the door?"

"I moved it there so you couldn't sneak into my bed at night," Lily said, a challenge in her voice.

James grinned. "You don't trust me?" he asked in an offended tone of voice.

"You do not inspire trust, your grace."

"I am wounded by your distrust."

"Better to be wounded by my distrust than my dagger," Lily said pleasantly. "What is it you want?"

"If I answered that question with the word *you*, would you strike me?"

"Yes, with great pleasure."

"In that case, I came here to apologize for my behavior downstairs," James said. "I never meant to hurt your feelings."

"You didn't," Lily lied. "Is there anything else?"

"Will you be down for dinner?" he asked.

Lily never wanted to go downstairs or see the dowager duchess and her sisters again, but she knew that was impossible. She might as well get the inevitable over with as quickly as possible.

"I plan to set your mother straight about her ridiculous plans," Lily told him.

"Please don't do that," James said, his expression becoming serious. "Mother is getting on in years and my brother's death was a shock. Could you—would you humor her by pretending to agree with her plans for us? Betrothals can always be broken."

"How will your mother feel when she learns that I am the Gilded Lily?" Lily asked.

"She won't," James assured her. "Adam and Sloane have agreed to remain silent on the subject."

"Very well. I'll go along with the pretense," Lily said reluctantly.

"Thank you," James said, and leaned close as if to kiss her.

Lily stepped back a pace, out of his reach.

"I'll see you at dinner," he said, and then left the chamber.

Lily closed the door behind him. How ridiculous her position was. Now she was going to pretend to become betrothed as well as pretend she didn't love him.

Loving the duke was futile, Lily knew, but she could no longer deny her feelings for him. Her intention to marry Bradley Howell seemed like a lifetime ago.

Three hours later, Lily walked down the carpeted hallway to the stairs. She wore a midnight blue gown with a high waist, scooped neck, and short puffy sleeves. She had considered wearing one of the brooches the duke had given her but decided against it. He had given her the brooches as payment for bedding him, not because he cared for her.

Lily felt nervous as she walked down the stairs to the first-floor dining hall. She wished she hadn't agreed to pretend a betrothal. She should have begged the dowager to send her home to Boston.

And then you would never see the duke again, Lily told herself. Would that be so bad? She would forget him in time. Or would she?

James sat at the head of the table. On either side of him were Lily and the dowager. Beside them sat Lady Donna and Lady Nora, and then Adam and Sloane.

Lily felt uncomfortably out of place. She hoped she wouldn't disgrace herself by using the wrong utensil. Relief that her brother preferred the kitchen made her ache with guilt.

Pennick served them from the sideboard. The first course was tomato soup, enriched and colored with a swirl of cream and chopped parsley. A salad of wild dandelions dressed with crisp morsels of bacon and sharp vinaigrette arrived next, followed by steamed mussels cooked in light stock, wine, and herbs. Deviled rump steaks flavored by a marinade of olive oil, vinegar, cayenne, and mustard was the main course.

"Where is your brother?" the dowager asked her.

"Michael prefers the kitchen," Lily answered. "If the truth be told, I prefer the kitchen myself. He will be up to meet you when dessert arrives."

"You prefer the kitchen?" Lady Donna asked in surprise.

"I ate with Lily in the kitchen one night," James said. "I thoroughly enjoyed myself, although Pennick wasn't thrilled."

"Perhaps, the company was what you enjoyed," Lady Donna said.

"I would enjoy dining with my guest anywhere," James said with a smile.

His statement surprised Lily. She blushed and dropped her gaze to her plate.

"Apparently, Lily is a good influence on you," Adam remarked.

James smiled at her again. "Why aren't you wearing one of the brooches I gave you?"

"This is the only jewel I value," Lily said, fingering her *alpha* and *omega* cross. Then she quoted Shakespeare, saying, " 'Rich gifts wax poor when givers prove unkind.' "

"You are an educated young lady," the dowager remarked. "Are you a bluestocking?"

"No, I am a Bostonian," Lily replied, wondering what a bluestocking was.

The three men burst out laughing, which only made things worse. Embarrassed, Lily felt a hot blush rising on her cheeks and dropped her sapphire gaze to her plate again.

"You must be a brave lady," Lady Donna said, changing the subject. "I know I would swoon dead away if anyone abducted me and dragged me across an ocean."

"There's little chance of that happening," Lady Nora told her sister. "Only a blind man would abduct a middle-aged woman. In your case, he'd also need to be deaf."

Lady Donna looked like she itched to slap her sister.

" 'A heart unspotted is not easily daunted,' " Lily quoted Shakespeare again.

"From which play does that come?" the dowager asked.

"Henry V, Act Five, Scene Two, line sixty-two," Lily answered without thinking.

The dowager gave her a knowing smile.

"Is she correct?" Lady Donna asked.

"Of course she's correct," Lady Nora said.

"How do you know?" Lady Donna asked. "You aren't partial to Shakespeare."

"I know because I know," Lady Nora said emphatically.

The men chuckled. Even Lily managed a smile.

"Lily likes Shakespeare and Queen Elizabeth," James told them.

"Lily *was* Queen Elizabeth in a past life," Lady Nora said.

"Spare us your nonsense," Lady Donna drawled.

"Lily wouldn't be caught dead being English," James said. "She speaks about us as if we were lepers."

Everyone stared at her. Lily felt like crawling beneath a rock. The duke had no right to tell the others of the dislike she harbored for the English.

"The girl needs clothing," the dowager said to her son.

"I've taken care of that," James assured his mother. "Madame Janette will be arriving in a few days."

Lady Donna gushed with excitement, "We'll teach you to walk, talk, dance, flirt with a fan, who to sit next to whom—"

"All of the really important things in life," Lady Nora said, and then winked at her.

"Lily already knows how to swim," Sloane told them. "We caught her swimming in the grand pool. She was riding St. George's horse."

Lily blushed when the dowager frowned at her.

"That unseemly behavior will cease immediately," the dowager ordered.

"Ladies do not swim," Lady Donna added.

"I thought it was charming," Adam said.

"So did I," Sloane agreed.

"I thought so, too," James said, covering her hand with his own.

"As I recall, you didn't say that at the time," Lily said, freeing her hand from his grasp. She didn't want the duke touching her; she didn't think she had the strength to resist him.

"Shall we adjourn to the library for our surprise dessert?" James said, ignoring her comment.

"You know about that?" Lily asked.

"I know everything that goes on in my own household," James told her.

Once they were seated in the library, Pennick arrived with Michael, who carried a cake with a lit candle. "I'm sorry, your grace," the majordomo said. "Michael insisted upon carrying the cake."

"I never let him carry the cake at home," Lily said, reaching to help her brother.

Together, they set the cake on the table and stepped back so that everyone could admire it. Michael wiped his chin on his sleeve and then blew the candle out.

Lily placed her hand over her heart, and Michael did the same. "Happy birthday to America," Michael said.

"And may she win this war," Lily added just to be perverse.

The others refused to rise to her bait.

"You must be Michael," the dowager said.

Michael nodded. "Lily named me in honor of Michael the Archangel."

"Is that so?" the dowager remarked. "Do you like England?"

"I love merry olde England," Michael told her. "I want to live here forever and ever."

"Too bad your sister doesn't feel the same way," the dowager said. "She'll settle in, though. What's this I hear about a pig?"

"Her name is Princess," Michael said. "I have to

go now. Duncan is teaching me chess." At that, he raced out of the library.

"Your brother is very nice," the dowager said to Lily. She turned to James, saying, "You must become betrothed tonight."

"That's impossible," James said. "We have no contract. When I go to London in a few days—"

"I took the liberty of having a contract drawn," Sloane spoke up, drawing a parchment from inside his jacket. "I am only missing a few bits of information."

"I have no ring," James countered.

"I took the liberty of purchasing one I thought you would like," Adam said, reaching into his pocket and passing it to him.

Why was the duke delaying? Lily wondered. Their betrothal was only a pretense. What did it matter if they signed the contract today or next week? Signing it today would be more believable to the others.

"There is another gift I promised Lily," James said, turning to her. "My behavior a week ago was insensitive. I publicly apologize for my bad behavior."

"I accept your apology," Lily said with a smile, her heart soaring. He hadn't forgotten.

James placed the ring on the third finger of her left hand. Lily looked at it and nearly swooned. Set in platinum, an enormous emerald-cut yellow diamond sat between two white emerald-cut diamonds.

James kissed her hand and said in a low voice, "The rain stopped. Would you care to walk outside?"

Seeing a chance to escape his relatives, Lily nodded and said, "I'd love to walk outside."

"I need to know Lily's date of birth for the contract," Sloane called as they walked toward the door.

"November sixth," Lily called over her shoulder.

"What year?"

"Every year."

James burst out laughing and escorted her out of the library. When they reached the grand foyer, Lily extricated her hand from his and said, "Actually, I feel rather tired. I think I'll pass on the walk outside."

James stepped closer. "Thank you for being agreeable to my mother."

"I am always agreeable," Lily said with a jaunty smile.

James moved to kiss her, but she stepped back.

"There's no need to pretend when we're alone," Lily said, enjoying the sight of his disappointed surprise. She left him standing there and never looked back.

Twelve

"I know you love her."

Relaxing in the leather seat inside his coach, James turned his gaze away from the passing scenery and fixed it on his friend. He gave Adam his blackest scowl and returned his attention to the scenery, saying, "We've reached London."

"Can you deny you care for her?" Adam asked.

"I care for my hounds but do not intend to marry any of them," James said dryly.

"That really is too bad of you," Adam replied, the hint of a smile touching his lips. He stretched his long legs out, folded his arms across his chest, and added, "Thankfully, Sloane doesn't feel as you do."

"What do you mean by that?" James asked, instantly alert, sitting up a little straighter.

"Sloane remained at Kinross Park because he has a fondness for Lily," Adam told him.

"Perhaps my cousin feared being alone with me in London," James said. "You know, Sloane wouldn't have the nerve to set my mother and aunts on me. I should have let those boys beat you to death when we were at Eton."

"You don't mean that," Adam said, a disappointed

look on his face. "Saving my life could save your own one day."

"I doubt it," James said with a grin. "You've been my cross to bear since the day I saved you."

The carriage came to an abrupt halt in front of the St. Aubyn mansion on Park Lane. Without waiting for the coachman, Adam opened the door.

"Are you going to Upper Brook Street first?" he asked.

"Berkeley Square," James answered. "I don't relish this interview with St. Leger and want it over as soon as possible."

Adam nodded in understanding. "I'll see you at White's?"

"I'll be there."

Alone in his carriage, James tried to plot in his mind what he would say to Reggie St. Leger about begging off the betrothal with Valentina. His thoughts, however, were fixed on Lily.

Was it true what Adam said about his loving her? She had none of qualities he expected in a wife—no breeding, no money, no shallowness. She was loyal and caring, as her relationship with her brother proved.

The little wharf rat would never be accepted into the ton. This come-out ball was going to be a disaster. Then his mother and aunts would forget about their plans to marry him off.

He smiled inwardly. When he left Kinross Park, Lily was tormenting his mother and aunts with her pianoforte playing. A few hours of dance lessons would probably put them into their graves.

James looked up when the coach stopped in front of the St. Leger town house in Berkeley Square. The short ride from Park Lane had scarcely given him a chance to think.

He supposed that honesty was the best policy. How humiliating to explain to an inferior that his mother had demanded he marry the young American he'd abducted.

No one can force you to marry her, an inner voice told him.

James banished that voice to the nether regions of his mind. Believing his mother was forcing him to marry the girl was easier than admitting he loved her.

Alighting from the coach, James paused a moment to look up at the town house. This action was going to cost him a great deal of money. He'd never realized how expensive abducting someone could be. He'd be damned if he ever did that again.

James knocked on the door. He waited several moments and then knocked again.

No one answered.

Perplexed, James stared at the door. Even if Reggie and Valentina were absent, one of the footmen should have answered.

He was turning away when the door opened. St. Leger's majordomo stood there.

"The earl is not at home, your grace," the man said. "He didn't say when he would return."

"Please tell the earl that I want to see him at the earliest possibility," James said.

"I will give him the message, your grace." The man closed the door in his face.

Surprised by the man's rudeness, James stared at the door for a moment and then walked back to his carriage. He would also need to speak with Reggie about his man's behavior.

James paused before climbing into his carriage and looked back at the St. Leger town house. A movement in an upper window caught his attention. Reggie St. Leger was peeking out the second-floor window.

What the bloody hell was the man doing? James wondered, irritated that a man of Reggie's station would insult a superior. He marched back up the stairs and knocked on the door again.

The majordomo opened the door. "Your grace, I—"

"I saw the earl peeking out the second-floor window," James cut off his words, brushing past him into the foyer.

"Your grace, I'm sorry." St. Leger appeared at the head of the stairs and raced down them. "I thought you were one of my creditors."

James smiled inwardly. A bankrupt St. Leger would be more amenable to a financial settlement, especially a generous one.

"Financial troubles, Reggie?" James asked, cocking a dark brow at the man.

"A temporary problem," St. Leger said, dismissing the idea with a wave of his hand. "Valentina isn't here at the moment."

"I haven't come to see Valentina," James told him. "I have an important matter to discuss with you."

St. Leger smiled ingratiatingly. "Please come into the drawing room, your grace."

"The foyer will suffice," James said, not wanting to stay any longer than necessary. "Only privacy is required."

With a flick of his wrist, St. Leger dismissed his majordomo. James waited until the man had vanished from sight.

"There is no easy way to say this so I will be direct,"

James said. "I am breaking my engagement to Valentina."

"You can't do that," St. Leger cried, looking panicked. "Valentina will be crushed. What is the problem? Perhaps, I can—"

James held up his hand and the other man shut his mouth. "I have become betrothed to another woman whom I met in America."

"You are betrothed to two women at the same time?" St. Leger exclaimed in obvious shock.

"A slight overlapping," James said, having the good grace to smile sheepishly. "Valentina need not lose face. I will slip a word to a friend at the *Times* that she decided against accepting my offer. After all, no public announcement has ever been made."

"Only a madman would believe that," St. Leger said. An unholy gleam sparked in the man's eyes, his face mottled and contorted with barely suppressed rage. "Marry my sister or I'll sue for breach of the marriage contract."

James felt anger surging within his chest. Nobody threatened him. St. Leger had every right to be upset, but the man was behaving unreasonably.

"What purpose will that serve?" he asked. "Valentina will suffer by it."

"The only legitimate reasons for breach of contract are physical infirmity and immoral behavior," St. Leger told him. "Valentina has neither of those problems."

"Reggie, perhaps you misunderstood me," James said with a smile that did not quite reach his eyes. "I am proposing a financial settlement. I will pay all your debts incurred up to yesterday and add five thousand pounds to that. I will also give Valentina another five thousand pounds to ease her emotional pain."

St. Leger stared at him without saying a word. James couldn't decide if the man was angry at the offer or surprised by the large amount.

"Give over, Reggie," he said. "It's a generous offer."

"I accept it."

"Send me a list of your creditors," James said, turning to leave.

"This American must be something special," St. Leger remarked.

"Lily is an Original," James told him. Then he walked out the door, relieved to be rid of the St. Leger family.

Dressed completely in black like Lucifer himself, James walked into White's Gentleman's Club and felt the eyes drawn to him as he crossed the carpeted room to the notorious Betting Book. After reading several entries, he picked up the quill and made an entry that was bound to disappoint more than a few men in attendance.

With that done, James crossed the chamber and joined Adam, who was already seated at a table. He gestured to a servant to bring his usual whiskey.

"You certainly know how to draw a crowd," Adam said, smiling.

James glanced toward the Betting Book. Several men were reading his entry, and a small crowd was beginning to form around them.

"How did it go with St. Leger?" Adam asked.

James waited for the servant to place his whiskey on the table and leave. "Reggie was reasonable after I offered him a small fortune."

"You missed your cousin by fifteen minutes," Adam said.

"Sloane is in London?" James said in surprise.

Adam nodded. "He left to escort Valentina to the opera."

"Sloane and Valentina?" James was even more surprised by that bit of information.

"He escorted her to several affairs while you were away," Adam said with a shrug. "Want to go to the opera and watch them?"

James grinned at the idea. "I am grateful to be rid of her."

"What about Lily?"

"I bought her the necklace that matches the betrothal ring," James said. "How are the plans for the ball progressing?"

"My uncle has taken charge of that," Adam said. "The invitations will be sent tomorrow, and no one would dare refuse an invitation from the Duke of Kingston."

"God's balls, here comes St. Leger," James said.

The Earl of Bovingdon approached their table. With him were two men James did not recognize. Both men were well built. One had hair as black as his own, while the other had sandy brown hair. St. Leger nodded at Adam and then turned to James.

"Would you care to join us?" James asked out of politeness.

"I am on my way home," St. Leger refused him. He gestured to his two companions, saying, "Your grace, may I present Mr. Hampstead and Mr. Hawkins."

"I am pleased to meet you," Mr. Hampstead said.

"As am I," added Mr. Hawkins, offering his hand.

James knew they were Americans as soon as they spoke. "Americans trapped in England by the war?"

"In a manner of speaking," Hampstead said.

"We were interested in investments, but the hostilities caught us off guard," Hawkins told him.

"What can I do for you, Reggie?" James asked, turning to him.

"I wanted to let you know that I harbor no ill will toward you," the earl said.

"You've been very understanding," James said, a dry tone to his voice. "You'll send that list to me in the morning?"

St. Leger inclined his head. "Good evening to you."

Once the earl had departed, James lifted his glass of whiskey and took a healthy swig. "The thought of him being my brother-in-law gives me the hives."

Adam nodded. "The man's an incorrigible gambler. You would have supported him for the rest of his life."

"I got away cheaply," James agreed.

Two hours later, James and Adam headed for the door located on one side of the bay windows. Outside, thick yellow fog greeted them like an old friend, and the street seemed eerie with only the glow from the gaslights.

"I'll be returning to Kinross Park tomorrow morning," James said.

"That's a wise move," Adam said with a smile. "Training Lily could be unhealthy for your mother and aunts."

Drawing their attention, a lone horseman galloped down St. James Street. The rider halted his horse abruptly, raised a pistol, and aimed at them.

Adam dove behind one of the carriages and took James down with him. They heard the pistol fire just as they hit the ground, and then came the sound of the horse galloping away.

Waiting coachmen shouted in alarm. Several gentlemen from White's came running outside.

Adam stood and offered his hand, asking, "Who wants you dead?"

"I was going to ask you the same thing," James said with a grin.

"Both of us are fine," Adam announced, turning to the spectators. "Please return inside and continue your evening."

The crowd dissipated slowly.

"Someone wants you dead," James said once they were alone again.

"You are the man who abducted an American girl and forced her to England," Adam reminded him.

"Who would benefit from my death?" James said, becoming serious. "The answer to that question is Sloane."

"Sloane?" Adam echoed, disbelief etched across his features. "You can't be suspicious of your own cousin."

"Sloane accompanied my brother to his death," James said. "Tonight he arrived unexpectedly from Kinross Park, and someone took a shot at me."

"Sloane has everything he could ever want," Adam argued.

"Except the title," James reminded him. "If I die without an heir, Sloane would become the fifteenth Duke of Kinross."

"I suppose keeping a close watch on him wouldn't hurt," Adam agreed. "Kinross Park is the safest place for you at the moment. I'll see you in less than two weeks and promise that Lily's come-out ball will be everything a young woman could want."

James smiled at his friend. "Until then."

"When you enter a drawing room, look for the mistress of the house and speak to her first," instructed the dowager.

"Wear a smile, and never rush into the room head-first," Lady Donna told her.

"Anything that detracts from society's pleasure is in poor taste," Lady Nora added, and winked at her.

Great guardian angel, Lily thought, these old ladies were tormenting her with their rules. They'd even ordered her to wear her most formal gown, which wasn't very formal at all.

"Ah, here is Mr. Watkins," Lady Donna greeted the dancing master they'd hired for the occasion. "Mr. Watkins will teach you the steps for every dance."

"I was unable to learn the pianoforte," Lily reminded them.

"Dancing is much easier than the pianoforte," the dowager told her.

"Not for everyone," Lady Nora warned.

Mr. Watkins looked like a lizard. He was tall and thin and had the largest hooked nose Lily had ever seen.

"Our dearest Lily needs some instruction," the dowager was saying.

"Tess, the girl needs a lot of instruction," Lady Donna corrected her sister.

Lily snapped her head around to stare at the older woman.

"No offense intended, darling," Lady Donna

drawled, seating herself at the piano. "I only want Mr. Watkins to know what he's up against."

"Be quiet," Lady Nora ordered her sister.

Mr. Watkins stepped closer. His cologne was overpowering.

Lily sneezed and her stomach lurched. She gulped her nausea back and sneezed again.

"You cannot dance and sneeze at the same time," Mr. Watkins said in a haughty tone of voice.

"I beg your pardon," Lily said, and crossed her fingers behind her back.

"I forgive you," the man said. "Now then, the quadrille is a lively dance and the opening number of every ball. These days couples merely walk through the figures, which is a shame. The five figures are *le pantalon, l'ete, la poule, la pastourelle,* and the *finale.*" He demonstrated each of the figures as he spoke.

Lily watched him carefully but knew she'd never master the dance in ten years. This fiasco called a come-out ball would take place in ten days.

"Walk with me through the figures," Mr. Watkins said, offering her his hand.

Reluctantly, Lily accepted his hand and began *le pantalon.* When she tripped over her own feet, she had the sudden wish that her remarkable memory extended to movements as well as words on a page.

"No, no, no," Mr. Watkins chided her. "Once more, please."

Lily tried again and again and again.

"This is impossible," Mr. Watkins complained, turning to the others. "She is completely inept."

"Try something with fewer steps, like the waltz," the dowager suggested.

"Yes, your grace." With a look of contempt etched

across his face, Mr. Watkins turned to Lily. "The waltz is danced in three-quarter time, a whirling motion in step, slide, step." He held up three fingers in front of her face. "Only three movements to remember— step, slide, step. Can you remember that?"

Lily felt like slashing the man's face with her dagger. Too bad the duke had confiscated it on the trip across the Atlantic.

There were other ways of hurting this conceited buffoon, Lily decided. She could torment him the same way he was tormenting her.

"I've forgotten your question," Lily said, wearing her sweetest expression.

Mt. Watkins's face reddened with exasperated anger. "Can you remember step, slide, step?"

"I can try," she said brightly.

That seemed to mollify the man. "We will stand exactly opposite each other. Upright, please," Mr. Watkins instructed. "I will place my hand in the center of your back and steer you around the ballroom. Are you ready?"

"Yes, Mr. Watkins."

Watkins stepped to the right. Lily slid to the left.

"Try again, please."

Watkins stepped to the right. Lily slid to the left.

"You are doing it wrong," Mr. Watkins told her, his voice rising with his frustration.

"I am sliding, stepping, sliding," Lily said, feigning innocence.

"Step, slide, step!" Watkins screamed.

"What is going on here?" demanded a voice from the doorway.

Lady Donna stopped playing. Watkins and Lily

turned toward the voice. James was marching across the ballroom toward them.

"Your grace, teaching her to dance is an impossible task," Watkins complained. "She is utterly inept."

James glanced at his aunt and ordered, "Play the waltz."

The music began.

"Will you dance with me, my lady?" James asked, taking her hand in his.

"I would love to dance with you, your grace," Lily answered with a smile. "Unfortunately, my seven left feet make me beyond hope."

"Trust me." James pulled her close and placed his hand in the center of her back. Lily placed her left hand on his arm and gave him her right hand to hold.

"Relax and follow my lead," James told her.

Together, James and Lily swirled around the ballroom. He danced with the practiced ease of a man who had waltzed a thousand times. Feeling comfortable in his arms, Lily followed his lead and danced as though they had waltzed together for years. Only the man and the music existed for Lily. The others faded away.

"You dance divinely," James said. "You were tormenting poor Mr. Watkins."

"He tormented me first," Lily told him.

James laughed out loud. "Small talk is required while dancing, lest people believe you dislike your partner."

"For example?"

"I missed you," James told her.

Lily blushed and missed a step, which made him smile.

"Would you care to go picnicking?" he asked.

"I would love it," she answered.

The music ended, but James refused to relinquish her hand. He folded her arm in his and crossed the ballroom to the others, who were smiling. Instead of stopping to speak, James led Lily past them.

"Watkins, you're fired," James called over his shoulder. In the corridor outside the ballroom, he paused and said, "Change your outfit while I order us a basket."

"What about Michael?" Lily asked, thinking to bring her brother along for safety's sake.

"I passed Duncan and Michael on their way to go fishing," James told her.

Danger lay in being alone with him. Lily didn't know if she was strong enough to resist his advances.

"I promise not to seduce you," he said.

"That wasn't what I was thinking," she lied.

"Run along," James said, his smile telling her that he didn't believe her lie. "I'll meet you downstairs."

Thirty minutes later Lily walked down the stairs to the grand foyer. She'd changed into a white muslin morning dress with a scooped neck and short, puffy sleeves.

James was already waiting for her. He smiled in greeting when she appeared and, grabbing the covered wicker food basket, led her outside.

Lily paused, closed her eyes, and breathed deeply of the hay-scented breeze. The summer afternoon was warm, and the buzz of cicadas sang in her ears.

Lily opened her eyes. The duke was watching at her.

"I never knew a woman who enjoyed a summer's day like you obviously do," he said.

"That is because you've only known Englishwomen,"

she told him. "I wish I could smell the ocean. I've never been away from it for any length of time."

"This way, sweetness," James said, taking her hand in his. He led her down a path into the woodland. "The River Ver circles the outer perimeter of my enchanted forest. It isn't far."

The narrow path forced Lily to walk closer to the duke than she would have liked. She inhaled deeply of his scent, mountain heather, and suffered a twinge of regret that their whole relationship was a pretense for the benefit of his aging mother.

Mysterious little gardens and pools were scattered at infrequent intervals, and their sudden appearances delighted Lily. If this were her home, she would pass her days exploring each and every one of these wonderful surprises.

The woodland opened onto a river peacefully ambling on its way to wherever. Lily walked to the river's edge. Smooth stones bordered the shallows, and the water appeared crisply clean.

"Would you care for a swim?" James asked, standing behind her.

Lily turned around and smiled. "I prefer swimming in the grand fountain."

They walked back to the grass where James had placed the blanket. Lily sat down and opened it.

Cook had prepared a light luncheon. There were cucumber sandwiches, egg and anchovy sandwiches, fresh strawberries, lemon cookies, and lemonade.

"Today marks the anniversary of Lady Godiva's ride through Coventry," James told her.

"Today is the seventh of July," Lily informed him. "Lady Godiva rode through Coventry on the tenth day of July."

"How do you know that?" he asked.

"I read it somewhere."

"Tell me how this memory of yours works."

Lily thought for a moment and then said, "I'm not sure how to explain it."

James ran a finger down her arm, sending a shiver through her body. "Try to explain, sweetness," he coaxed.

"I suppose I recall the way the book looked," she said. "I see the page in my mind's eye like a painting. . . . your grace, I—"

"Call me James."

"James, I must speak to you on a matter of importance," Lily said.

"I refuse to send you home."

"It isn't that."

"Speak, then."

"Please do not force me into the come-out ball," she pleaded. "I will only disgrace both of us."

"Lily, I have faith in your abilities," he said.

That surprised her. "You do?"

James nodded and gestured for her to slide closer. When she did, he put his arm around her shoulder and said, "You are far more genteel than any lady of the ton. Those young misses are sharks swimming around the eligible bachelors, hoping to catch one in their jaws."

Lily smiled at his analogy. She knew he was merely being encouraging.

She turned her head to look at him. His lips were only a breath away. "Those misses know all the rules," she said.

"Don't worry about the rules," James told her. "I never pay attention to them."

His face inched closer as he spoke those words. And then his mouth covered hers.

Lily savored the feeling of his warm lips pressed against hers and hadn't the strength or the heart to push him away. Instead, she entwined her arms around his neck and returned his kiss with equal ardor.

Ever so gently, James pushed her down onto the blanket. His face loomed above hers for one brief moment, and then he captured her lips in a passionate kiss.

"So, this is the Original?"

James whirled around, and Lily bolted up.

With her hands on her hips, a beautiful blonde with the face of an angel stood there. The blond hair and the angel's face combined with the nasty tone of voice reminded Lily of Hortensia MacDugal.

"What are you doing here, Valentina?" James demanded, rising from the blanket to confront her.

The reluctant valentine, Lily realized.

"I spoke with Reggie last night and wanted to see this Original for myself," Valentina answered. She turned on Lily and screamed, "You've stolen another woman's fiancé, harlot."

Lily stared in surprise at her. *The duke had lied to her.* She cast him an accusing look and returned her attention to the furious woman.

"Do you know how I knew where to find you?" Valentina said. "James takes all his fiancées on a romantic picnic to this spot."

Lily felt humiliated. The duke had duped her again. Her heart sank to her stomach, and a wave of nausea rolled over her.

"That's enough, Val," James said sternly.

Unexpectedly, Duncan and Michael appeared and hurried toward them. "We heard the shouting and wondered what was happening," the duke's man was saying.

"Don't yell at my sister," Michael shouted, pointing a finger at the blonde.

His shouting caused a dribble of drool to roll from the corner of his lips down his chin. He reached up and wiped his mouth on his sleeve.

Valentina looked the boy up and down. Lily could see in her expression that she instantly recognized the boy's impairment.

Valentina burst out laughing and turned to James, saying, "Oh, this is rich."

"Cause trouble for me and I'll ruin you," he threatened.

Valentina cast him a deadly look. She glanced at Lily and then her brother. With a snide smile spread across her face, the blonde stalked off in a huff.

James turned and offered Lily his hand. She pushed it away and sent Duncan a pointed look.

"Come on," the Scotsman said. "Your sister wants some privacy."

"Brother?"

Michael turned around.

"Thank you for defending me," Lily said, a soft smile touching her lips.

"You can count on me," Michael said, his chest puffed out with pride. "We'll always be together." Then he followed Duncan onto the woodland path.

Lily looked at the duke and lost her smile. Without taking her gaze from his, she rose from the blanket and, in a voice filled with contempt, said, "You lied to me."

"Give over, Lily," he said, sounding weary.

"I won't give over," Lily snapped. "I will never trust you again."

"I didn't realize you trusted me at all," James countered. "Did you actually think I would tell you my personal business?"

" 'Time unfolds what plaited cunning hides,' " Lily quoted Shakespeare. She turned away and headed for the path leading through the woodland.

"The Winter's Tale," James called after her.

"Act Four, Scene Five, line five-ninety-five," Lily shouted over her shoulder. And then she disappeared into the woodland.

Thirteen

I am carrying the duke's child, Lily told herself, struggling against nausea. *Queasiness without menstruation can mean nothing else.*

Leaning her head back against the chair, Lily sat in front of the open window and hoped the cool, predawn breeze would help to quell her nausea. She closed her eyes and prayed to be wrong but could no longer deny her condition. There was no other plausible explanation.

Lily hadn't spoken to the duke in two days. She couldn't understand why that should upset his mother and aunts. If his mother could have chosen a bride for him, it certainly wouldn't have been her—a colonial wharf rat from Boston.

Marrying Bradley Howell was completely out of the question. No man would father another's illegitimate seed.

Lily slid her hand to her belly and wondered what she should do. The child was guiltless, and she felt sorry for him. Or her.

Lily knew one thing for certain; she was going to keep quiet about this. There was no telling what the duke would do if he discovered her condition.

Pray that the war ends soon, Lily told herself. Then

she could go home and have her child. She would love the babe in spite of the fact that his father was a conniving liar.

And then another, more alarming thought popped into her mind. What if her child was born with the same impairment as her brother? She loved Michael and had kept that long-ago promise to her mother, but what would she do if her own child suffered the same malady?

Lily raised her hand to her head. The queasiness had passed, but a pounding in her head had replaced it. What she needed to make her feel better was a Shakespearean tragedy. Other people's problems would help her forget her own. She would take *The Complete Works of William Shakespeare* from the Long Library as soon as she'd eaten breakfast.

Lily went down to breakfast after James left for his morning ride. His mother and aunts usually had their morning meals in their own chambers. There was little chance of seeing them.

"Good morning, Mr. Pennick," Lily greeted the majordomo, pleased to see the empty dining room.

"Good morning, my lady," the man replied.

Lily crossed the room to the sideboard. Serving herself, she placed a scone and a pat of butter on a plate.

Noticing how meager her breakfast appeared, Lily decided her baby needed something more nutritious. She piled a small mountain of eggs and ham onto her plate and then grabbed the *Times* to read while she ate.

With mutiny in her heart, Lily plopped down in the duke's chair at the head of the forty-foot table. She opened the *Times* and began to read.

Only a few minutes had passed when Lily caught a

movement near the door. She glanced up and saw the duke, dressed in his riding clothes, crossing the room to the sideboard.

James cut an imposing figure in his tight-fitting breeches, and Lily felt a twinge of regret. Perhaps if they'd been born under different circumstances—

Lily gave herself a mental shake. Thinking about what could have been in another time and place was extreme folly.

"I knew today was inauspicious," she muttered.

James turned around, sipped his coffee, and then said, "I beg your pardon?"

"I said today was inauspicious," Lily repeated, raising her voice. "At least inauspicious according to the Alexandrian calendar."

"How do you know about the Alexandrian calendar?" James asked, a smile flirting with the corners of his lips.

"I read about it," she informed him.

"For a poor tavern keep's daughter, you have had a rather diverse selection of reading materials," he remarked.

"My fiancé owns an extensive library," Lily told him, her tone haughty.

"Darling, *I* am your fiancé," James said with an infuriating smile.

"Must you torment me with your constant reminders?" Lily asked. She dropped her gaze to the newspaper, but every fiber of her being was alive with his presence.

"Am I to assume by that mountain of food that your appetite has grown since yesterday?" James asked.

Lily didn't bother to look at him. "Assume what

you want," she said, feigning a nonchalance she didn't feel.

Silence greeted her remark.

Lily kept her gaze fixed on the newspaper but didn't see a word. She wondered what he was doing but refused to give him the satisfaction of looking up.

And then a disturbing thought popped into her mind. If the duke noticed a change in her eating habits, would he suspect that she was with child?

Lily worried her bottom lip with her teeth. She hoped that she and Michael would be in Boston before her pregnancy became noticeable. Perhaps Michael and she could contrive a visit to the American embassy and seek refuge there. If only they could lose Duncan.

"Lily?"

Startled by his voice beside her, Lily gasped audibly. "Yes?"

"You are sitting in my chair."

Lily raised her sapphire gaze to his. The duke stood beside her with a plate of ham and eggs in his hand. She glanced down the length of the forty-foot table and then returned her gaze to his.

"Take another."

"I want to sit at the head of the table," James told her.

"There is another one," Lily said, pointing to the other end of the table.

"If I sit there," James argued, a pleasant expression on his face, "I won't be able to speak to you."

"I have no wish to speak to you," Lily told him.

James said nothing. He stood there and stared at her.

Lily stared back.

Finally, in exasperation, Lily rose from her chair and lifted her plate and the paper off the table. She turned away and marched down the length of the table.

Halfway to her destination, Pennick appeared at her side. "Please, let me carry that for you."

"I am no cripple," she snapped. "I'll carry it myself."

"As you wish." The majordomo started to turn away.

"Mr. Pennick, I apologize for my rudeness," Lily said.

"There's no need for apologies," Pennick said.

"You never apologize to me," James called.

"You should be apologizing to me for ruining my life," she countered.

Lily seated herself at the opposite end of the table. She set her plate and newspaper down and then resumed reading.

"Lily?"

"What now?"

"I want my newspaper."

"You'll need to wait," she told him.

"I always read the *Times* with breakfast," he complained.

Lily set her fork down on her plate. She picked up the *Times*, rolled the paper, and tucked the edges inside. Then she tossed it the length of the table. The *Times* landed in his plate.

A horrified giggle bubbled up in her throat.

James lifted the paper out of his plate and set it aside. "How long are you going to keep this up?" he asked, his black gaze pinning her to her chair.

Lily lifted her nose into the air. "I have no wish for intercourse with liars."

"You did on board my ship," James reminded her, giving her an infuriating smile.

Lily felt her cheeks heat with her embarrassment. She glanced at Pennick, who stood near the sideboard and pretended deafness. She knew better by now. The man was probably consigning every word to memory.

"Your grace, 'assume a virtue if you have it not,' " Lily said, quoting Shakespeare.

James cocked a dark brow at her. " 'Forbear to judge, for we are sinners all,' " he said, also quoting Shakespeare.

Lily stared at him. No matter what, she couldn't seem to win against him. With all the dignity she could muster, Lily rose from the table and marched out of the dining room.

Pleading a headache, Lily avoided the duke for the remainder of the day. She even managed to miss the infernal waltz practice, the dowager and her sisters having given up on her learning the quadrille. They'd concocted a scheme to have the duke deliver her to the ball after the quadrille had been danced.

Lily knew that she needed to avoid James as much as possible to keep him from suspecting her condition. Early the following morning, she watched from her window as James left on his daily ride.

Lily hurried downstairs to the dining room as soon as he'd vanished from sight. She wanted to eat before the duke returned. She planned to disappear into her chamber for the rest of the morning.

Beyond that, Lily had no idea what to do. She couldn't pass the remainder of the war dodging the duke by staying in her bedchamber.

Morning was aging toward noon when Lily heard

a knock on the door. She rose from her chair and crossed the chamber to open it.

"Pennick," she said, surprised to see the major-domo.

"His grace requests your presence in the library."

Lily cocked an ebony brow at him. "And if I choose not to grant his request?"

"I don't believe that was an option," Pennick drawled and then smiled.

"Tell him I'll be along shortly."

"Yes, my lady."

Lily changed into one of her high-waisted gowns and then sat down in her chair. She waited thirty minutes before leaving the chamber.

Reaching the door of the library, Lily paused to steel herself against him. She vowed never to forget that the duke was an incorrigible liar who had betrothed himself to two women at the same time.

Ready for battle, Lily squared her shoulders with determination and marched into the library. The duke looked up when she entered, and Lily fixed her gaze on him as she walked the long length of the library.

"How are you feeling?" James asked, leaning back in his chair when she stood in front of his desk.

His question caught her off guard. "I am better," she said.

"I hope I wasn't the cause of your headache," he said.

"Don't flatter yourself," Lily replied, forcing herself to smile to soften her words. "You aren't important enough to give me a headache.

"I am relieved to be guiltless. Please sit down."

"I'll stand."

James inclined his head. "I have been thinking that Michael will be much happier if he remains at Kinross Park when we go to London."

Lily felt angry panic welling up inside her. She leaned forward and placed the palms of her hands on his desk.

"I refuse to be separated from my brother," she said, looking him straight in the eye. "If Michael doesn't go to London, I don't go to London."

"For God's sake, Lily, you are entirely too protective of the boy," James countered. "Michael needs breathing space without his sister always looking after him."

"I need Michael as much as he needs me," Lily said. In a soft voice, she added, "The hour you try to separate us will be your last."

"He'll want to bring that pig," James complained.

"In that case, there will be two pigs in London."

Intending to leave, Lily spun away so quickly that dizziness overwhelmed her. She steadied herself against the desk and walked back the length of the library toward the door.

"Waltzing begins at two," James called. "Don't be late."

Lily pretended deafness and marched out the door. She managed to gain her chamber without another bout of dizziness.

Sitting in the chair in front of the darkened hearth, Lily reached down and lifted *The Complete Works of William Shakespeare* off the floor. She slid the palm of her hand across the book's leather cover and wondered why she even bothered to read him any more. She already knew every word he'd ever written.

Lily leaned her head back against the chair. The last thing she needed was the threat of being separated from her brother. Worrying about what the duke would do when he discovered her condition was plenty.

Two o'clock came and went. Lily was beginning to think she had successfully avoided waltzing practice again. Then she heard the pounding on her door.

"Have you come to visit me?" she asked when she saw her brother. "I'll tell you the story about Michael the Archangel."

Michael shook his head. "Duke is waiting for you in the ballroom."

"Tell him I have a headache."

"No lying, Sister."

"Michael, there are good lies and bad lies," Lily explained. "A bad lie almost always hurts someone's feelings, but a good lie prevents someone from having his feelings hurt. I don't wish to dance with the duke, but I don't want to hurt his feelings."

Michael gave her a skeptical look, as if he didn't know whether to believe her. "I'll tell Duke."

Alone again, Lily wondered how many maladies she could conjure in order to avoid the duke. Would he believe she suffered from a headache two days in a row? Perhaps she should have said a stomachache.

"What did he say?" Lily called when she heard the door open.

"He said she's going to practice the waltz even if it kills her," James answered.

Lily nearly toppled out of her chair. She stood up to face him, but he towered over her.

"What a hypocritical little witch you are," James said. "You denigrate my behavior because I lied about a previous betrothal and then teach your brother that some lies are good. My mother and aunts have made you welcome here, and now you plan on repaying their graciousness by embarrassing them."

Lily knew he was right, yet she couldn't bring herself to admit it. "Why couldn't you have left me alone? Why did you need to abduct me and ruin my life?"

"Be thankful I left you with a life, ruined or not, instead of killing you as I had planned," he said.

"No man will marry me now," Lily told him. She walked past him to the door. "I hope you are satisfied."

"Lady, you are betrothed to me," James said, following her out. "For God's sake, smile when you see my mother and aunts."

Lady Donna sat at the piano, ready to play, while the dowager and Lady Nora sat nearby to watch the practice. Lily smiled at them as winsomely as she could.

"How relieved we are to see you feeling better," Lady Donna called. "I'll pray you don't relapse, darling."

Lily smiled again and inclined her head to acknowledge the woman's kindness.

"I'm certain she only suffered a slight case of nerves," the dowager said.

"Or anger," Lady Nora piped up.

Lily snapped her head around to look at the woman.

"I have the Sight," Lady Nora reminded her. To the dowager, she added, "Perhaps our dear James gave her a headache."

"I would not doubt it," the dowager replied. "My son has certainly given me several headaches."

Lily smiled at that remark. James ignored her smile and his mother.

"Wear this," Lady Donna called, holding a fan out to her. "All the ladies of the ton use fans."

"Thank you," Lily said, taking the fan. Approximately a foot long, the wood-and-paper fan had been handpainted in jewel tones and depicted an operatic scene.

James and Lily stood opposite each other. When the music began, he drew her into his arms, and she went willingly.

Feeling the music, Lily relaxed in his arms. They swirled around and around the ballroom as if they had danced a thousand times.

A distressed feeling like the pitch and roll of a ship began in the bottom of her stomach. The uncomfortable feeling grew more intense with each of her swirling motions.

Lily feared disgracing herself. She knew she had to get away.

Panicking, Lily yanked herself out of the duke's arms and dashed for the door. She heard him and the others calling her name but kept running.

The sickness grabbed her outside the ballroom door. She doubled over with spasms of dry gagging.

"You should have told me you felt ill," James said in a concerned voice, putting his arms around her to hold her steady.

With the spasms ended, Lily leaned against him to steady herself. She looked up at him through sapphire eyes that mirrored her misery and said, "I-I missed lunch today and need to lie down."

"Why didn't you eat lunch?" he asked.

"I wanted to avoid you," she answered.

James snapped his brows together. "Why?"

"I am tired of losing in our battle of wits," Lily admitted.

That brought a smile to his face. "I thought I was the one losing," he told her. "I'll take you upstairs and order you a bowl of soup."

With his arms around her, James helped Lily up the stairs. His kindness made her feel guilty. She had castigated him for lying about Valentina and now she was lying to him about his own child.

"I'll be sure to eat before we practice the waltz tomorrow," Lily said, giving him a wan smile before disappearing inside her chamber.

A routine began to form over the following days. The morning sickness struck first but disappeared once she'd eaten a slice of bread. At lunch the dowager grilled her about society's rules, and then came waltzing practice.

Lily napped in the afternoons, her tiredness seeming to be a side effect of her condition. Once she'd even fallen asleep while reading in the library. Thankfully, the duke hadn't been present.

Dressed in a white high-waisted dress, Lily walked downstairs to the grand foyer. She'd pulled her hair away from her face and woven it into one thick braid, which made her appear more like a milkmaid than a duke's fiancé.

Lily left the foyer behind and walked out into the sunlight. She headed straight for the path that led through the woodland to the river.

The day was warm, with a dry breeze. Birdsong, buzzing cicadas, and the sweet smell of hay filled the air.

Lily smiled to herself when she saw the lady's-slipper orchids blooming within the woodland. Here and there she spied the yellow flowers of Saint John's-wort and the lavender spikes of vervain.

Only the salty smell of the ocean would have made her feel better.

And then the woodland path opened onto the River Ver. Both Duncan and Michael turned around when she appeared.

"Good morning," Lily called. "Michael, I want to speak with you."

Michael ran to her and threw his arms around her, saying, "I love you, Lily."

"And I love you," she told him.

Lily picked up a stone and skimmed it across the river. In an instant, her brother picked up a stone and imitated her.

"You're scaring the fish," Duncan called.

"Sorry," she said.

"Sorry," her brother said.

"Michael, I need to know if you want to come to London with me in a few days," Lily said.

"What do you want?" Michael asked, looking intently at her.

"I want you with me," Lily said, hugging him close.

"Can Princess come, too?"

"Yes."

Lily kissed the top of his head and turned to go. She stopped short when she saw the duke standing there.

"Did you think I was running away?" she asked.

James shrugged.

"Michael and Princess will be accompanying us to London," Lily told him. She looked at her brother, asking, "Do you want to walk back with us or fish with Duncan?"

Michael paused to wipe his chin on the sleeve of his shirt. "Fish with Duncan."

James and Lily walked in silence into the woodland. When the path narrowed, James gestured for her to walk in front of him.

"The life of a British aristocrat must agree with you," he said. "You appear to have filled out a bit since I met you."

Lily nearly swooned at his remark and was grateful he couldn't see her expression. "That observation is ungentlemanly," she said, recovering herself.

"I meant it as a compliment," he said.

"In that case, thank you."

Though he tried several times to engage her in conversation, Lily was quiet for the remainder of the walk home. Disturbing thoughts slammed into her mind, each one worse than its predecessor.

How long would it be before her pregnancy showed? What would the duke do when he learned that she was carrying his child? After all, their betrothal was merely a pretense.

Lily touched her *alpha* and *omega* cross and prayed for divine guidance. Apparently, her mother had been wrong all those long years ago. There would be no first and last love for her, only the child. And Michael.

A coach was wending its way up the drive as James and Lily emerged from the woodland. Lily worried that it would be another of the duke's paramours.

The coach halted. Adam St. Aubyn stepped out, and Sloane Armstrong was behind him.

Lily smiled and waved. She glanced at James and saw him staring in his cousin's direction. There was no welcoming smile on his face. She wondered briefly what the problem was, but let the thought drift away. She had her own more pressing problems.

"My uncle asked me to tell your mother about the preparations for the ball," Adam was saying.

James looked at his cousin and said, "I'm amazed you haven't brought Valentina."

"Give over, James," Sloane said, a good-natured smile on his face. "I escorted Val to the opera because I felt sorry for her. Since then she's taken a fancy to a pair of wealthy Americans."

"Americans?" Lily echoed, instantly alert.

"Mr. Hampstead and Mr. Hawkins are new friends of Reggie St. Leger's," Sloane said. "I heard they come from your part of the world."

"Boston?"

"New York, I think," Sloane said with a shrug. He turned to James and said, "I am relieved you suffered no ill effects from your recent experience outside White's. Be assured, I will guard your back at all times."

"With the same efficiency you used to guard my brother?" James countered.

An awkward silence descended upon them. Lily could have kicked the duke for being so cruel.

"Did you know that today is Saint Swithin's Day?" Lily asked in a poor effort to lighten the mood. "The fair weather today means we'll enjoy fair weather for the next forty days."

Sloane laughed. "How does an American know about an English saint?"

"Lily is a wealth of useless information," James said, cutting into the conversation. "She remembers everything but cannot judge what is important. I'm surprised the Americans chose to use her services."

Another uncomfortable silence descended upon them. Without a word, James walked into the mansion, and the others followed behind him.

The dowager, Lady Donna, and Lady Nora were in the drawing room. After Pennick had served refreshments, the dowager said, "Now, tell us about the arrangements Kingston has made."

"My uncle did some research and concluded that July twenty-first would be the best day for the ball," Adam told her. "Supper will be catered from Gunters, and only the best champagne will be served. He's already hired the best musicians money can buy. No one has sent regrets, so we can expect a crush."

"Society is curious about this American being sponsored by two dukes," Sloane added.

Lily felt her heart sinking to her stomach. She didn't want these people ogling her. Sweet lamb of God, she still felt unsure of which eating utensil was correct.

"Lily was unable to learn the quadrille, so James will contrive to escort her to the ball after that has been danced," Lady Donna told him.

"Our dearest Lily waltzes marvelously well—" Lady Nora began.

"—as long as she remembers to eat first," Lady Donna finished.

"What happens when she doesn't eat?" Sloane asked.

"The swirling makes her ill," the dowager answered.

Lily blushed with embarrassment. She glanced at James, but his attention was fixed on his cousin. He wore the fiercest scowl she'd ever seen.

"You will dine and pass the night with us?" the dowager asked.

"Actually, both Sloane and I have pressing business in London," Adam said.

"Then let us solicit you to be waltz partners while you are here," Lady Donna said. "Lily should experience the difference in men's dancing. Not all men are James, you know."

"Waltzing exclusively with James could become a tad boring," Adam replied, and then smiled at his friend.

"You'll need to do without Adam," James told them. "I have business to discuss with him."

Sloane smiled at Lily and said, "I would be honored to waltz with so lovely a lady."

"It's settled, then," the dowager said, rising from her chair. "Sloane will partner Lily while James confers with Adam."

Sloane hurried to escort the dowager to the ballroom. The others followed behind them.

Lady Donna sat at the piano, and Sloane and Lily faced each other. Lily prayed she wouldn't get sick from the swirling.

"Where is your fan?" the dowager asked.

"I left it in the library," Lily answered. "Give me two minutes."

Lily left the ballroom and hurried down the corridor. She was about to enter the library when she heard the duke's voice from within, and then the marquess spoke. What they said kept her rooted to the floor.

"I'd bet my fortune that Sloane had nothing to do with it," Adam was saying.

"Would you bet my life?" James countered. "My cousin was in Boston when my brother was killed and in London when that assassin shot at me. He is the only one with a motive for wanting me dead—namely, my title and all that goes with it."

Lily trembled at his words. Great guardian angel, someone had tried to kill the father of her child.

She couldn't believe Sloane was the culprit, though. He was much too charming, and the kindness in his heart shone from his eyes. But she could be wrong. Her remarkable memory didn't mean she was a good judge of character.

Her stomach lurched, as if the child protested his father's near assassination. Silently, she backed away from the door and walked down the corridor to the ballroom.

Lily knew one thing for sure: She wasn't in the mood for waltzing, but she pasted a smile onto her face and stepped inside the ballroom.

Fourteen

"Great guardian angel, give me the strength to go through with this," Lily whispered, touching her *alpha* and *omega* cross. She looked out her bedchamber window on the third floor of the Armstrong mansion on Upper Brook Street.

London wasn't what she'd expected. The streets were narrow, dirty, and crowded; the odor of horse manure permeated the air. Outside the window, a yellowish fog hung like an unhealthy shroud over the city.

"His grace said to hurry," said Peggy, entering the chamber on the run. "It's past eight already."

Lily turned away from the window. "Tell his grace I'll be down in a few minutes."

"Yes, my lady." Peggy hurried out of the room.

Lily crossed the room to inspect her appearance in the cheval mirror. Casting a critical eye over her image, she concluded that she'd never looked better. She felt like a princess on her way to a ball.

Her high-waisted gown in pale petal pink silk had been fashioned with a low-cut neckline and short melon sleeves. She wore sandals of white kid and carried white elbow-length gloves.

Under the direction of the dowager and her sisters,

Peggy had dressed Lily's ebony hair in an upswept, formal coiffeur. Diamond hairpins, on loan from the dowager, sparkled like stars in the night sky.

The only thing Lily recognized about herself was the *alpha* and *omega* cross. She held her left hand up in front of herself, stared at her diamond ring, and wished her betrothal wasn't a sham.

Lily sighed. As long as she was wishing, she might as well wish her mother alive and her brother a normal child.

Hearing the door open, Lily said, "Peggy, tell his grace I have the headache and can't go."

"Coward."

Slowly, Lily turned toward the voice. James stood inside the doorway. He looked magnificent in his formal attire of black trousers, jacket, and waistcoat, accompanied by a white shirt and tie.

Lily ached with longing at the sight of his perfection. "I don't think—"

"Sweetness, don't think," James interrupted. "I promise your fear is unfounded."

James crossed the chamber until he stood only inches away. He reached out with one hand and tilted her chin up so he could gaze into her sapphire eyes.

"Have I told you today how lovely you are?" he asked.

"You have never told me that," she said.

"That thought has lived in the suburbs of my mind every day since I met you."

His flattery was outrageous. Lily smiled at his euphemism for abducting her.

"That's my girl."

"I can't go through with this," she told him.

"Don't be silly," James said gently. "If someone intimidates you, picture in your mind the sight of him or her wearing only underdrawers."

"I'm not sure I'd want to do that," Lily said with a rueful smile.

"I was as shy as you once."

"I don't believe that."

"Are you implying that I am prevaricating?" he asked.

"A lie is a lie, James, no matter what fancy word you use to describe it," she said.

"It was one of your good lies," James teased her, and then reached into his jacket pocket to produce a velvet-covered box. "I have a gift for you."

Lily dropped her mouth open in surprise when he lifted the lid. On a bed of midnight velvet lay the most exquisite necklace, a perfect match for her betrothal ring. A yellow and white diamond pendant hung from a platinum and diamond chain adorned with several floral diamond stations.

"I can't accept this," Lily said, lifting her sapphire gaze to his.

James snapped his brows together. "Why not?"

"The necklace is priceless," she tried to explain. "I don't deserve—"

James placed one long finger across her lips in a gesture for silence. "The necklace pales beside your beauty," he said. "You deserve much more than this for putting up with me and my family."

Lily felt weak. The duke was behaving so differently. She could almost believe that he cared for her. Or was that his plan?

"I can make you love me just like that . . ." His words echoed in her mind.

"Well?"

"I'll wear it for tonight," Lily relented. "You may ask for its return whenever you wish."

"We are in agreement, my lady. Turn around."

Lily showed him her back. James fastened the necklace into place, his fingertips lingering on her bare shoulders a moment longer than necessary.

Turning to face him, Lily touched the diamond pendant almost reverently, the same way she touched her betrothal ring when no one was watching. Out of habit, she raised her hand to the *alpha* and *omega* cross.

Tonight she would play the princess, and the duke would be her prince. The memory of this special night would need to last for the rest of her life.

"Are you ready, sweetness?" James asked, taking her hand in his.

Lily inclined her head. "Yes, your grace."

They rode in near silence to the Grosvenor Square mansion of the Duke of Kingston, Adam St. Aubyn's uncle. Lily knew that James was trying to calm her by speaking of inconsequential matters, but Lily felt too nervous for conversation. Her stomach was a tight knot of apprehension, and she hoped her unborn child would behave appropriately on such an important night.

"Good evening, your grace," the majordomo greeted them at the door.

"Good evening, Higgins," James said. "What are you doing here? Are you still in St. Aubyn's employ, or have you defected to his uncle?"

"The marquess enlisted me to greet guests at the door while Baxter announced them upstairs," the man answered.

"I hope the marquess is paying for your time," James joked.

"I would prefer announcing the arrivals upstairs," Higgins said. "Five hundred guests are crowded into that ballroom."

"I'll have a word with the marquess and convince him to host his own ball," James replied.

"Thank you, your grace," the majordomo said, a smile appearing on his face. "That would be the answer to my prayers."

James escorted Lily to the stairs that led to the second floor, where the ballroom was located. As they walked down the corridor, James nodded at several gentlemen who were milling about. Uncomfortably, Lily felt their eyes on her.

"Stop trembling," James whispered. "There's nothing to fear."

And then they reached the entrance to the ballroom.

"Good evening, your grace," the Duke of Kingston's majordomo greeted them.

"Good evening, Baxter. I see that you have the plum assignment tonight," James said.

"Much to the chagrin of Mr. Higgins," Baxter said with a smile. The man turned toward the ballroom and announced, "His grace, the Duke of Kinross, and Mistress Hawthorne."

Lily stepped back a pace as a sea of faces turned to stare in their direction. Only the duke's hand on her back kept her from fleeing.

In the next instant, Adam St. Aubyn appeared at their side. With him was an older gentleman who, Lily assumed, was the Duke of Kingston.

"Uncle Charles, may I present Lily Hawthorne?"

Adam made the introduction. "Lily, meet my uncle, the Duke of Kingston."

"I am pleased to meet you, your grace," Lily said with a smile. She offered him her hand, adding, "I am also grateful for your hosting this ball."

"Child, you are even more beautiful than James described you," the duke said, raising her hand to his lips.

Lily cast James a sidelong glance. She couldn't imagine him describing her as anything but a wharf rat.

"Shall we enter the fray and meet your admirers?" James asked, inclining his head toward the mob of aristocrats.

"Wait one moment," the Duke of Kingston said. "I have an announcement to make." The Duke of Kingston turned to the crowd and said, "Your attention, please. I am happy to announce the betrothal of the Duke of Kinross and Mistress Hawthorne. You may extend your best wishes in the receiving line at the bottom of the ballroom."

The mob of aristocrats appeared shocked. And then Adam clapped his hands in approval. Others followed his lead.

Lily blushed when James raised her hand to his lips. Glancing at the crush of people, she noted the distinctly unhappy expressions on the faces of many young ladies.

"Forgive my presumption," the Duke of Kingston apologized. "Your mother asked me to make the happy announcement."

"Don't give it a second thought, Charles," James said. "Betrothals were made for announcing."

The ladies of the ton wore a rainbow of colors and

styles, depending on their ages. The men dressed alike, in black formal attire.

At the top of the ballroom, farthest from the entrance, stood the four-piece orchestra, consisting of a cornet, a piano, a violin, and a cello. The musicians began playing again at a nod from the Duke of Kingston.

Lily stood in the receiving line between James and the Duke of Kingston. Adam St. Aubyn stood on the other side of James. The dowager and her two sisters sat in chairs to the right of the Duke of Kingston, while Sloane stood just behind them, ready to assist in any way.

"Charles mistakenly invited the St. Legers," Lily heard Adam whisper to James. "I'm sorry."

"Don't worry about it," James replied. "I'm positive there will be no problem."

Lily wasn't so certain. She recalled the look on Valentina's face when she saw Michael and didn't know what she would do if Valentina became insulting. Lily only knew that her temper was short where her brother was concerned.

"A suite of rooms adjacent to the ballroom are open for refreshments," James said, leaning close to her. "There is also a card room and a ladies' rest area. Supper will be served on the ground level after the fifteenth dance."

"Yes, I know," Lily said. "Your mother and aunts are very thorough."

And then the reception line started toward them. Lily trembled, but the duke's hand at her back precluded her running away.

"Remember, our guests are only wearing their undergarments," James whispered.

His teasing reminder helped relax Lily. She gave him a wobbly smile and began to welcome their guests as graciously as a young queen acknowledging her subjects. No one would ever suspect that she was a wharf rat from Boston's waterfront.

"Lily, may I present Baron and Baroness Barrows?" James said.

Lily pasted a smile on her face. "How do you do?"

"Lily, please meet the Earl of Keswick," James said when the next person stood in front of them.

"A pleasure to meet you, my lord," she said, still smiling.

"Your graces, please meet my fiancée, Lily Hawthorne," James said when the next couple stood in front of them. "Lily, meet the Duke and Duchess of Avon."

"I am honored to meet you, your graces," Lily said to them.

"You are doing excellently," James whispered.

"As I said, your mother and aunts are very thorough," Lily whispered back.

"That bad, huh?"

"Worse."

James laughed and then greeted a heavyset young matron. "Lady Ripley, how nice that you could help us celebrate our betrothal. Lily, please meet Lady Ripley."

Lily thought the woman looked pregnant but was uncertain so she said, "How radiant you look, Lady Ripley."

"And so do you, Mistress Hawthorne," the woman replied.

James turned to Lily when the woman had moved

on. "I am truly impressed, sweetness. Something vague always leaves room for interpretation."

So it went for five hundred guests. Lily grew weary from standing in one place for so long a time, and her face was beginning to ache from the unaccustomed smiling.

"Do not panic," James whispered as the end of the line drew closer. "Valentina and Reggie St. Leger are almost upon us."

And then the Earl of Bovingdon and his sister stood in front of them. Reggie St. Leger bowed over her hand.

"Now I understand why his grace called you an Original," Reggie St. Leger told her.

Lily didn't know if she'd just been insulted or complimented. "Thank you," she said, an uncertain note to her voice.

"How is that adorable brother of yours?" Valentina asked, catching her off guard.

"Healthy," Lily said pointedly, looking the other girl straight in the eye.

Reggie St. Leger gestured to the two men standing on the other side of his sister. "Your grace, you do remember meeting my companions at White's?"

"You are the Americans," James said, offering his hand to first one and then the other. "Mr. Hampstead and Mr. Hawkins."

Shock rendered Lily speechless when she turned to greet Mr. Hampstead and Mr. Hawkins. She nearly swooned at the sight of Bradley Howell and her brother Seth standing in front of her. The two of them were staring intensely, their gazes warning her to silence.

Great guardian angel, what were they doing in England? Had they discovered her and Michael missing and come to rescue them? That couldn't be correct. How would they have known where to find them?

"Is anything wrong?" James asked, putting his arm around her waist and drawing her against the side of his body.

"I am surprised to meet Americans in England during this conflict," Lily lied, hoping she sounded credible.

"How do you come to be in England, Mistress Hawthorne?" Bradley asked.

"Yours must be an interesting tale," Seth added.

"My younger brother and I are visiting friends," she told them.

Seth looked as if he wanted to strangle her. "How nice that you had a traveling companion in your younger brother."

"I would be honored if you would save one of your dances for a fellow American," Bradley said before moving on.

Lily nodded. "I would be pleased to save you a dance, Mr. Hampstead."

"Seth, darling," Valentina said, "I have someone I want you to meet."

Seth, darling? Lily wondered in surprise, staring after her brother and her fiancé as they walked away with the St. Legers.

"Who are those men?" James asked.

Lily rounded on him, an expression of innocence on her face. "I don't know what you mean."

"You know those two from somewhere," James said in a low voice, his look telling her that he didn't believe her for a single minute. "Are they spies?"

"I've never seen them before," Lily insisted, her

voice rising, fearing she'd cause their deaths if he
didn't believe her.

"Mistress Hawthorne, you are a poor liar," James
replied, a hard edge to his voice.

Lily felt like weeping. She'd wanted tonight to be
more perfect than a fairy tale. She was supposed to
be the princess and the duke her prince. Now his anger had ruined the evening, and she felt guilty about
lying.

"Perhaps Lily is merely surprised to meet Americans
in England," the Duke of Kingston intervened.

Lily sent the duke a grateful look.

The older man held out his hand, asking, "May I
have your first waltz?"

"I would be honored," Lily said, placing her hand
in his. She would have agreed to dance with the devil
himself in order to get away from James.

The Duke of Kingston waltzed with the agility of a
younger man, and they swirled around and around
the ballroom. Trying to catch a glimpse of Seth or
Bradley, Lily scanned the great chamber. Bradley was
speaking with Reggie St. Leger and watching her. Seth
was dancing with Valentina.

"James is correct," the Duke of Kingston said with
a smile. "You are an incompetent liar."

Lily opened her mouth to protest, but the duke
said, "You needn't defend yourself to me, but I fear
James is jealous."

"Your grace, I find that exceedingly difficult to believe," Lily said, smiling at the idea. "His mother
forced us to become betrothed."

The Duke of Kingston chuckled. "How refreshing
inexperience is. Do you really believe that James is

the type of man who could be forced to do something he didn't want to do?"

Lily had no answer for that. When the music ended, the duke returned her to James.

Taking her hand in his, James led her onto the dance floor, and Lily went willingly into his embrace. The man and the music intoxicated her senses as they swirled around and around the room.

"Making conversation while dancing is customary," James said flatly. "If not, people will believe we are not in accord."

"If you stopped scowling at me, your grace," Lily said tartly, "I could relax and speak without fearing to say the wrong thing."

His lips twitched into a grudging smile.

"That is so much better," she drawled.

Lily glanced at the dowager and her sisters. The three ladies were beaming with pride. They certainly seemed to have pulled off the hoax of the year.

Lily suffered a twinge of regret that this whole scene was engineered solely for his mother's benefit. Now that she'd seen Bradley Howell, Lily was positive that she could never marry him. She loved the Duke of Kinross and would pay dearly for her folly. Only what were Seth and—

"A shilling for your thoughts," James said, yanking her back to reality.

Lily had no intention of mentioning the Americans. Instead, she said, "Your mother and aunts look so happy tonight. I feel guilty about this pretense because they'll be crushed when I return to Boston. I have grown fond of them."

James gave her a curious look but said nothing.

Adam St. Aubyn claimed her for the third dance.

After him came Sloane, Reggie St. Leger, and three aristocrats she'd met in the receiving line.

When James left her side to fetch his mother and aunts a cold drink, Bradley Howell appeared for his dance. He led her onto the dance floor and drew her into his arms. Though the music was still intoxicating, Lily knew she didn't feel the same now as she had when she danced with James.

"Smile and pretend we are making small talk," Bradley said.

Lily smiled instantly. "I never realized how wonderfully you danced."

"You would have known if you had married me the first time I asked," he told her.

Lily said nothing. He was correct; all her problems stemmed from what she'd done. Blaming anyone else was impossible.

When they reached the far side of the room, away from the duke's relatives, Lily and Bradley walked off the dance floor. Seth was waiting there to speak to them.

"What are you doing in England?" Seth demanded, sounding as domineering as the duke.

"The Duke of Kinross believed the Gilded Lily was a man and abducted me," Lily told them, speaking quickly lest they be interrupted. "He plans to keep me prisoner for the duration of the war. This whole betrothal business is merely a pretense to appease his mother."

"Has he touched you?" Bradley asked.

"Michael has been with me the whole time," Lily said, evading his question. Lying was becoming easier by the minute.

"Where is Michael?" Seth asked.

Lily looked into her older brother's eyes for the first time. She realized he knew she was avoiding Bradley's question. She never could hide anything from him; he always seemed to know when she was lying.

"Michael is safe at the Armstrong mansion," Lily told them. "I've never seen him so happy in my life."

"Happy?" the two men echoed simultaneously.

Lily nodded. "No one in England makes fun of him."

"You are leaving with us now," Bradley announced, reaching out to grab her elbow. "We'll pick Michael up along the way."

"I cannot leave England yet," Lily insisted, shrugging out of his grasp.

"Why not?"

Because I love the duke, Lily thought, but said, "The duke's mother and aunts have been kind. To leave now would humiliate them."

"I cannot believe you are saying this," Bradley said, sounding exasperated.

"Let's not do anything rash," Seth told his friend. "Our cover will be blown if we whisk Lily away now, and we'll never learn what we want. Lily can help us."

"Have you lost your wits?"

"My sister is in no danger," Seth argued.

Only my heart is breaking, Lily thought. Most men would not consider that an injury.

"The dowager is chaperoning them," Seth reasoned. "To do anything else would create a scandal."

"How can I help?" Lily asked, eager for a reason to stay with the duke.

"Spy on Kinross for us," her brother told her.

"I—I . . . What are you looking for?" she asked,

reluctant to spy on the man she loved. He would never forgive her if he discovered what she was doing.

"We want evidence that he murdered his brother," Seth said.

"What?" Lily asked, shocked by his accusation.

"The previous duke was killed while on a peace mission to America," Bradley explained. "We believe your duke conspired to kill his brother and blame the death on American subterfuge."

"We need the proof to document it to the Crown," Seth added.

"James did *not* murder his own brother," Lily defended him. "He believed the Gilded Lily caused his brother's death, which was the reason for my abduction. Only he didn't know the Gilded Lily was a woman."

"You are defending a cold-blooded murderer," Bradley said, his anger apparent in his voice.

"Lily, you have it in your power to prove us wrong," Seth coaxed her. "Keep your eyes open, listen to conversations, read whatever of his private papers you can manage without placing yourself in danger."

Lily sighed. "Very well, I'll do it," she agreed.

"We'll contact you soon," Seth told her. "Watch out for Michael."

"Be careful," Bradley said softly.

"Comparing sweet memories of the homeland?" James interrupted, his smile not reaching his eyes. "I've been searching for you, Lily. He held out his hand, saying, "The next waltz belongs to me."

James led her onto the dance floor and drew her none too gently into his arms. "I want to know what you and the Americans were whispering about," he demanded.

"We were discussing the war," Lily told him.

"Spare me your lies," James snapped. "Were you asking them to help you escape?"

"Would I leave my brother behind?" Lily cried.

Apparently her words held the ring of truth. James relaxed his grip on her, "Keep your voice down; people are watching." Then he added, "I want to know what is between you and those Americans, and I will learn the truth."

"I have had enough," Lily said, starting to pull out of his arms.

"Do *not* walk off this dance floor or it will be the sorriest day of your life," James whispered harshly, tightening his grip on her.

"That would be impossible, your grace," Lily said but kept dancing. "The day I met you already claims that distinction."

James dropped the subject of the Americans, but Lily knew he was barely controlling his temper. His lips were a tight line of anger.

"If you refuse to speak to me," Lily reminded him, "people will believe we are not in accord."

James smiled. "I could throttle you."

The disparity between his words and his expression made Lily laugh, which brought another scowl to his face. Lily felt miserable, and anxiety made her stomach churn.

In spite of that, Lily kept her head held high and a smile pasted on her face. She refused to spare one glance in Seth's and Bradley's direction lest she give them away.

Lily managed to get through supper without giving in to her misery. The dowager and her sisters had worked so hard to make her and this event successful. She hadn't the heart to disappoint them.

Finally, Lily escaped to the ladies' rest area. The other ladies fell silent when she walked in, and Valentina made a hasty exit. Lily felt certain the blonde had been gossiping about her.

Within three minutes the room had cleared of all the ladies except one young matron. She was especially lovely with her blond hair and violet eyes.

"Mistress Hawthorne, best wishes on your betrothal," the woman said, approaching her.

Lily searched her expression but could find no sarcasm. "Thank you, Lady——?"

"Isabelle Saint-Germain," the woman said, offering her hand. "My husband is the Duke of Avon."

"My apologies, your grace," Lily said, accepting her hand.

"There's no need for formalities," Isabelle said. "My husband's title does not impress me, and I have grown tired of people calling me *your grace.*"

Lily smiled at that. Here was a pocket of fresh air in the midst of a heavy fog of shallowness.

"Valentina St. Leger is a jealous scandalmonger," Isabelle warned. "Beware of her."

"I hardly know her," Lily said. "I assume she was gossiping about me?"

Isabelle shrugged.

"Do not concern yourself with her," Lily said. "I can bear her jealous spite."

"She was speaking of you only indirectly," Isabelle said.

Lily realized that Valentina had spoken of Michael. "I would like to know what she said."

Isabelle remained silent for a moment. "I suppose

you have the right to know," she said finally. "Valentina said the Duke of Kinross would get no proper heir on you because your brother . . ." She broke off, seeming unable to finish.

"What about my brother?" Lily asked.

Isabelle lowered her voice, saying, "Valentina said your brother is a drooling idiot."

"Thank you, your grace," Lily said. "I appreciate your candor and hope that we will meet again."

"I hope so, too."

Turning away without another word, Lily left the ladies' rest area. She paused inside the ballroom entrance, scanned the chamber for Valentina, and spotted her with Seth near the bottom of the room.

Ignoring the greetings of people she passed, Lily marched purposefully across the ballroom until she stood in front of the other woman. Seth and Valentina turned to face her when she appeared.

"I told you never to mention my brother's name," Lily said.

"Has Isabelle Saint-Germain been telling tales?" Valentina said, shaking her head in disgust. "That one has been known to speak to herself. I swear, she—"

"You are a damned, cowardly liar and unfit to call yourself a lady," Lily interrupted, raising her voice, heedless of the gazes turning in their direction. "If you even say my brother's name again, you will regret the day you were born."

Valentina burst out laughing. "What could an uncouth social climber like you possibly do to me?"

"Simply this." Without warning, Lily slapped her hard. Caught off guard, the blonde staggered back. Only Seth's quick reflexes saved her from falling.

The onlookers gasped collectively.

"You struck me," Valentina shrieked.

"I'll do worse than that if—" Someone grabbed Lily's arm and whirled her away, effectively silencing whatever she would have said.

"Congratulations. You have created a scandal," James said, pulling her toward the door.

"I don't give a fig about your scandals," Lily told him. From the corner of her eye, she saw the Duchess of Avon silently applauding her and smiled at the woman, which elicited a chuckle from the Duke of Avon.

James said nothing, only forced her toward the door. Passing his mother and aunts, he said, "Tell Sloane to escort you home."

"Sloane left when we went down to supper," the dowager told him.

"I'll send the carriage back for you."

James and Lily stepped outside the Duke of Kingston's town house into a moonless night. Heavy fog swirled around them like a voluminous cloak, appearing eerie in the soft glow from the gas lamps.

Seeing his coach parked on the opposite side of the street, James gestured his man to bring it around. "I hope you are satisfied with the scandal you've created."

Self-righteous anger welled up in Lily. "That blond witch was telling everyone that my brother is a drooling idiot," she said. "I will not let anyone malign Michael. Why, he's closer to God than the Pope."

"You could have—"

"If a man maligned the Armstrong family, you would call him out and shoot him," Lily interrupted. "I only slapped the girl but, I fear, not hard enough to knock some sense into her."

"Ladies do *not* slap other ladies," James snapped.

"I am a wharf rat. Remember?" Lily shot back. "I only wish you hadn't confiscated my dagger."

Suddenly a coach materialized out of nowhere and careened down Grosvenor Street. As it neared the Kingston mansion, its driver altered his course slightly and aimed his coach directly at them.

James grabbed Lily and leaped away from the street. They toppled backward onto the mansion's stairs just as the coach reached them and, without stopping, veered away and disappeared down the street.

Several coachmen ran to their aid. James rose without their assistance and knelt beside Lily, asking, "Are you injured?"

The shock of almost dying beneath the wheels of a carriage had sickened her. Much to her mortification, she gagged dryly for a few seconds and then calmed herself by taking several deep breaths.

"I can get up now," she said in a whisper.

Ignoring her words, James lifted her into his arms. He carried her the short distance to his coach.

Safe inside, James refused to relinquish her, but kept her on his lap and folded within his embrace. "You'll be fine," he whispered in a soothing voice.

"That man tried to kill us," she said, her voice hushed in horror.

"It was merely a freakish accident," he said. "The driver lost control of his horses."

"How can you believe that when someone already tried to shoot you?" Lily asked.

"Have you been eavesdropping?" James asked, his expression grim.

"I accidentally overheard part of your conversation with Adam," Lily admitted.

"I don't appreciate being spied upon," James said, his voice cold.

"I wasn't spying," Lily insisted angrily. She lifted herself off his lap and onto the leather seat.

Spy. The word crashed into Lily with the impact of an avalanche. Seth and Bradley wanted her to spy on the duke. Though she felt uncomfortable, Lily knew she would do it to prove him innocent of his brother's murder.

Fifteen

Michael.

Lily bolted up in her bed and looked around. From the dimness in her chamber, she knew that dawn was at least an hour away. Then she knew what had awakened her; she'd forgotten to warn her brother about Seth and Bradley being in England.

The best time to speak with her brother would be now, when the household slept. James would be suspicious if he caught her whispering to her brother. She didn't want to think about what he would do if he overheard her warning her brother.

Lily slid out of bed and grabbed her white silk robe. She padded on bare feet across the carpeted floor.

Opening the door a crack, Lily peered outside but knew everyone would be sleeping. She slipped out the door, closed it behind her, and walked quickly to her brother's chamber at the end of the corridor.

Great guardian angel, Lily sent up a silent prayer, *thank you for having the duke decide that Michael need not be guarded at night any more.*

Lily stepped inside her brother's chamber and closed the door. Then she crossed to the bed, pausing there to study him in sleep. A soft smile touched her lips when she spied Princess snuggled against his side.

Her mother had been correct all those long years ago. Perpetually innocent, Michael was a special gift from God.

Crouching down beside the bed, Lily leaned close to her brother's ear and reached to cover his mouth in the event that she frightened him.

"Michael," she whispered, nudging him gently.

The boy opened his eyes. "Lily?"

Princess awakened, lifted her head, and gave a tiny snort of greeting. Then she lay back on the bed.

"Brother, it's very important that you listen carefully to me," Lily said. "Can you do that?"

"I'm not stupid," Michael told her.

"I know that," she said with a smile. "Seth and Bradley are in England. I saw them tonight."

"Are we going home now?" His expression registered disappointment.

Lily shook her head, and his expression cleared. "Seth and Bradley are on a mission, so no one can know who they are," she told him. "If anyone learns their identity, they'll be hanged as spies. Do you understand?"

Michael nodded.

"If you see Seth and Bradley, pretend you don't know who they are," Lily said. "Can you do it?"

"I can do it," Michael said with a drowsy smile. "Sister, will you tell me the story?"

Lily sat on the edge of the bed. She traced a finger down his cheek and whispered, "War broke out in heaven. Michael the Archangel, the bravest warrior and fiercest of all the angels, fought Lucifer. He threw that black serpent and his followers out . . ."

Watching her brother's eyes close in sleep, Lily hoped he would remember her instructions in the morning. Perhaps she could contrive to find him without Duncan in attendance.

Lily rose from her perch on the bed and patted the piglet, which snorted in pleasure. Then she retraced her steps to the door, being careful to close it behind her.

"Oh," Lily gasped in surprise when she slammed into the duke's unyielding chest. "What are you doing?" she demanded, her heart pounding with unexpected fright.

"I'll ask the questions," James said grimly. He looked tired, as if he hadn't slept. "Are you plotting an escape?"

Lily shook her head.

"What is so important that you needed to visit your brother in the night?"

"I was checking on him," Lily told his chest, afraid to look in those black eyes of his.

"You have never checked on him," James said. "Why is this night different from the others?"

"Michael had someone sleeping in his room at Kinross Park," Lily answered. "I find your suspicions offensive." At that, she brushed past him and marched down the corridor.

" 'O serpent's heart, hid with an angelic face,' " James quoted Shakespeare as he followed her down the corridor to his own chamber.

" 'Flow'ring face,' " Lily said when she reached her bedchamber door. "If you must quote Shakespeare, quote the man correctly."

Lily opened the door but paused to see him watching her. She gave him a look of contempt and then slammed the door behind herself.

One second later the door burst open, and James

stood there, towering over her. "Never slam a door in my face again," he warned, his voice low. "Do you understand?"

Frightened, Lily nodded but couldn't find her voice. Satisfied, James walked out of her chamber.

Autocratic bully, Lily thought, closing the door without making a sound.

She hurried back to her bed, but sleep eluded her. The duke's fearsome scowl kept surfacing in her mind's eye. How could she bring herself to spy on him? Could Seth and Bradley be correct about James killing his brother? No, that couldn't be. A scowl did not prove the man was a murderer.

Tonight was supposed to have been one perfect evening she could cherish always. Instead, it had become a nightmare.

Life was one complication after another. She had just become accustomed to being the duke's prisoner when she realized her pregnancy. Now Seth and Bradley had surfaced in London. The thought of Bradley and the anguish he must be suffering tormented her.

Morning was a feeble old man when Lily emerged from her chamber the next day. She had delayed going to breakfast in order to avoid James and, in the process, made herself ill. A roll eaten in her chamber had quelled her queasiness.

Lily felt no remorse for slapping Valentina, but she'd ruined the evening for the dowager and her sisters. Now she had the sorry task of apologizing to them.

Lily walked directly to the drawing room, where she knew they would be at this hour. All three women looked up from their conversation when she walked into the room.

"Good morning, darling," Lady Donna called, smiling. "How are you feeling today?"

"The child feels guilty for creating a scene," Lady Nora informed her sister. "How do you think she feels?"

Lily stared in surprise at the duke's aunt.

"Nora has the Sight," the dowager said, "but guilt is etched across your pretty features."

Lily blushed. "May I speak with you?"

The dowager nodded. "Sit down."

"I am sorry for ruining your evening," Lily told the blue and gold Aubusson carpet. "I hope your social reputations will soon recover from this disaster."

The three women laughed, which surprised Lily. Confused, she looked at each one in turn.

"That is much better," the dowager said. "Always look people in the eye when you speak to them."

"I predicted your debut would be wildly successful," Lady Nora said. "We haven't had this much fun in decades."

"Pennick has been collecting a mountain of calling cards all morning," Lady Donna told her. "The man is positively in his glory."

Lily felt confused. "But I thought—"

"No one expected you to behave like a proper Englishwoman," Lady Donna said.

"Thank you, I think," Lily said dryly but felt vastly relieved. This was one less thing the duke could lecture her about.

"All of London is captivated by your American forthrightness," Lady Donna gushed.

"You have been declared an Original," Lady Nora added.

"After your performance last night, familial loyalty will be back in fashion," the dowager predicted.

Lily looked from one woman to the next. She couldn't credit what she was hearing. If true, these gently reared ladies had pulled off the hoax of the century. Imagine, London society admiring a wharf rat from Boston's docks.

"Slapping Valentina St. Leger is what most ladies would love to do," Lady Donna told her.

Lily perked up at the praise, but the image of the duke's scowl popped into her mind. "Is his grace still upset with me?"

"I believe James is furious," Lady Donna said. She chuckled throatily. "The poor boy is jealous and does not like the feeling."

"Jealous?" Lily echoed in surprise.

"Oh, this is so delicious," Lady Donna gushed. "Among your many admirers leaving their calling cards have been dozens of gentlemen."

"They're hoping your betrothal won't end in marriage," Lady Nora added.

"However, we have decided you must practice your pianoforte for one hour each day if you want to remain in our good graces," the dowager told her.

"We're going to forget about the quadrille," Lady Donna said. "Nora is of the opinion that you'll never master it."

The dowager stood, saying, "We are going out to pay a few calls."

"And bask in the sunlight of your success," Lady Donna said.

"Do not accept visits from anyone while we are out," Lady Nora instructed.

"Pennick will take care of your callers," the dowager said. "He knows what to do."

Lady Donna clapped her hands together in excitement. "Your admirers were beside themselves with disappointment because they could not pay homage to such an Original."

"You may accept a visit from the Duchess of Avon," Lady Nora told her.

"I doubt a duchess would stoop to call upon me," Lily said with a rueful smile.

"What a delightful little skeptic you are," Lady Nora said with a smile.

Lady Donna nodded. "A perfect match for our James."

"We shall be expecting to listen to your pianoforte when we return," the dowager said, turning to go.

Perhaps last evening hadn't been a disaster after all, Lily thought when the women left the room. The duke might be in a more agreeable mood than he was during the night.

Leaning back in her chair, Lily dropped her hands to her stomach. What would her baby be like? Would he be healthy? She didn't care if the babe was a boy or a girl, if only the babe was healthy and normal. She loved her brother more than life itself and planned never to break her long-ago promise to her mother, but her difficult life would be easier if her babe was born without any impairment.

Pregnancy and her lack of sleep the previous night had wearied her. Lily rested her head against the chair, closed her eyes, and fell into a deep sleep.

"My lady?" The voice penetrated her mind.

Lily opened her eyes and saw the majordomo standing there. "Yes, Mr. Pennick?"

"I apologize for disturbing you, but you have a visitor," Pennick said. "The Duke of Avon has a business meeting with his grace, and the Duchess of Avon accompanied him in the hope of calling on you."

That surprised Lily. Lady Nora had been correct about the Duchess of Avon paying her a visit.

"Shall I tell her grace you are indisposed?" the man asked.

"Bring her to the drawing room and then serve us tea," Lily instructed.

"Very good." The majordomo turned to leave.

Lily wondered if Bradley or Seth had stopped by to see her. "Mr. Pennick," she called. "Bring me the calling cards that people have left."

"I'm sorry," he said, turning around. A smile flirted with the corners of his lips when he added, "His grace seemed unhappy with the small mountain of calling cards and confiscated them."

Lily smiled inwardly. Perhaps the duke *was* jealous. She hoped so.

Lily stood when the Duchess of Avon walked into the drawing room. She dropped a curtsey and said, "I am honored by your visit, your grace. Please, sit down."

"I liked you better last night," the Duchess of Avon said, her violet eyes sparkling with amusement.

"I beg your pardon?"

"Do not curtsey to me or call me *your grace*," the duchess said. "Call me Isabelle, and I'll call you Lily."

Lily decided she liked the other woman. "Very well, Isabelle," she said.

"I wanted to tell you how much I admired your

actions of last night," Isabelle told her. "When John mentioned that he had an appointment with James, I begged to accompany him. I do hope we can be friends."

"I would like to be friends," Lily replied. "However, I will be returning to America once the war ends."

The duchess looked disappointed at the news. "I thought you and James were betrothed."

Lily dropped her gaze to the carpet. She felt as though she could trust this young woman who seemed as unconventional as she. And yet—

"Is it true that you speak to yourself?" Lily asked in a poor attempt to change the subject. "I apologize for my forwardness."

Isabelle smiled at her as if she guessed her insecurities. "Most people believe I talk to myself," she answered honestly. "I was actually talking to someone they couldn't see—my guardian angel."

These British were an odd lot of people, Lily thought. "You speak as if that is in the past," she remarked, encouraged by the other woman's candor. "Aren't guardian angels with us for life?"

"Our guardian angels are with us for longer than we live on earth," Isabelle told her. "Since my marriage to John, my guardian angel stays in the shadows of my life and contents herself to watch over me instead of communicating. Do you think I am insane?"

"I think you are luckier than I am," Lily answered with a smile. "I wish my own guardian angel would step forward to help me with my problems."

"Perhaps I can help until she decides to step out of the shadows," Isabelle said. "I promise I am very discreet."

Lily studied the blonde for a long moment. Had

Isabelle Saint-Germain been sent to her by her own guardian angel?

Mr. Pennick walked into the drawing room, carrying the porcelain Worcester tea service on a silver tray. He placed the tray on the table and poured tea into two cups.

"Thank you, Mr. Pennick," Lily said, dismissing the man. As soon as the majordomo left the room, she lowered her voice and told the other woman, "My betrothal to James is merely a pretense for his mother's benefit."

Isabelle looked surprised. "Both of you must be great actors. You appeared very much in love last night."

"I am a Boston wharf rat known as the Gilded Lily," Lily confessed, dropping her gaze to the carpet lest she see contempt in the other woman's expression. She'd never had a real friend before and didn't want to lose this one, but she couldn't have her under false pretenses.

The duchess fell silent. Summoning her courage, Lily raised her gaze and found the other woman staring blankly at her.

"I do not understand," Isabelle said.

"I am no lady," Lily confessed, wringing her hands in her lap. "My father owns a tavern on Boston's waterfront."

"Being a lady comes from the heart, not where you were born or bred," Isabelle said. "What is a Gilded Lily?"

"Gilded Lily was my code name," Lily told her, encouraged by the other woman's sentiment. "You see, I have a remarkable gift of remembering exactly what—

ever I read." She smiled ruefully, adding, "If you like, I could recite the Bible to you."

"Which testament?" Isabelle asked, a smile in her voice.

"Both."

Isabelle burst out laughing.

"My government made use of my talent to pass secret messages to agents," Lily continued. "His grace believed I caused his brother's death and so abducted me and my younger brother in order to keep me out of the war. When his mother discovered what he'd done, she insisted we become betrothed."

"James doesn't seem like the kind of man who could be forced into anything," Isabelle remarked. Then she said, "What a wonderful adventure."

"Adventures aren't as exciting as you may think," Lily told her. "They don't end whenever you want."

"How can I help you?" Isabelle asked.

"My older brother and fiancé—"

Isabelle burst out laughing. "You have a fiancé in addition to James?"

Lily shrugged. "Do not forget that James had Valentina."

"I meant no insult."

"None taken."

Lily decided against telling Isabelle about Bradley and Seth's suspicions concerning James's brother's death. "Seth and Bradley, who also work for my government, surfaced in London last night at my come-out ball. I need a way to get messages to them or to set up a meeting. I'm afraid that James doesn't trust me."

"I can send them messages and make arrangements

for us to ride in the park," Isabelle offered. "How about tomorrow for a carriage ride in the park?"

"That would be wonderful if James will allow it," Lily answered.

Isabelle smiled. "I can handle his grace."

"Could you also contrive to get me a small dagger to strap onto my leg?" Lily asked. "James confiscated mine."

"You want a dagger to wear on your leg?" the other woman echoed, looking shocked.

Lily nodded. "I always carry a dagger for protection and feel vulnerable without it."

"I will try, if you promise not to use it on anyone," Isabelle said.

"I promise the dagger is for protection only."

"I play the flute," Isabelle said, changing the subject. "Do you have any hobbies?"

"Caring for my younger brother is my only hobby," Lily told her.

"No, Princess. Give me my cookie."

Both Lily and Isabelle looked toward the doorway. Princess raced into the drawing room with Michael in pursuit. The albino piglet held a large cookie in her mouth.

Lily scooped up the piglet, held her on her lap, and sent the other woman an apologetic look. "This pretty girl is Princess, my brother's pet." She put her arm around her brother and pulled him close, saying, "And this is my brother, Michael." She looked at her brother and said, "Meet my new friend, the Duchess—"

"Are you Lady Godiva?" Michael interrupted.

Isabelle laughed. "I am Isabelle Saint-Germain. How do you know about Lady Godiva?"

"Duncan told me the story."

"Who is Duncan?"

"Duncan is Duke's friend," Michael told her. "Lady Godiva has long blond hair like you and is very pretty. She helped the people."

"Duncan is correct," Isabelle said. "I consider your mistake a compliment."

"My birthday is Saint Michael's Day," he bragged. "Lily named me in honor of the Archangel. Do you know what he did?"

Isabelle shook her head.

"He threw Lucifer out of heaven."

"I'm positive that you are as fierce a warrior as he was," Isabelle said.

Michael puffed out his chest with pride and said, "I like you."

"I like you, too," Isabelle said with a smile.

Watching their interchange, Lily felt infinitely relieved. Isabelle Saint-Germain had no fear of her brother's impairment. In fact, the duchess seemed sincerely to like Michael, and Lily admired her even more for that.

Tears welled up in Lily's eyes, and she felt her heart swell with unexpected joy mingled with sadness. For the first time in her life she had found a real friend in Isabelle Saint-Germain. Too bad Michael and she would be returning to Boston when the war ended.

While Lily was befriending the Duchess of Avon, James sat in his office at the far end of the corridor. With him were Adam St. Aubyn and John Saint-Germain, the Duke of Avon.

"Now that our business is concluded, could either of you advise me about how to silence the scandal

Lily created last night?" James asked. "I suppose breeding does tell."

Adam St. Aubyn burst out laughing.

"Better you than me," John Saint-Germain said with a smile. "I've had my own troubles with Isabelle." He glanced at Adam, adding, "Only a man who isn't married would laugh at Armstrong."

"You are being too harsh on Lily," Adam said. "Slapping Valentina is no great scandal."

"Every woman in that room has wanted to slap Valentina St. Leger at one time or another," John remarked.

"None of them actually acted on the impulse," James said.

"My wife bears some of the guilt," John admitted. "Isabelle spoke with Lily in the ladies' area and incited the action."

"Give over, James," Adam said. "Society will soon forget about the incident."

"I agree with St. Aubyn," John said. "You know, people once believed that my wife talked to herself."

"I never heard that," Adam said, a surprised expression on his face.

"Neither did I," James said, the hint of a smile on his face.

"Liars," John said, laughing. "Isabelle had conversations with her guardian angel who, I assure you, was as real as both of you. I saw her myself."

James hooted with laughter, and Adam joined him.

"Insanity is *not* contagious," John told them.

James relaxed back in his chair. "I wonder if women ever think, especially American women."

"Women don't think," John told him "They feel."

Adam grinned. "The women who think are ruthless, despicable creatures."

"God did not create women to think," John said. "He intended them to shop, to gossip, and to bear children." Then he pointed a finger at both of them and threatened, "If you repeat my words to Isabelle, I'll ruin you both financially."

James and Adam laughed.

"Imagine what the world would be like if women ran governments and businesses," James said, feigning a shudder.

"That is a frightening thought," John agreed.

Adam became serious. "What frightens me more is the second attempt on your life."

"*Second* attempt?" John echoed.

James was grim-faced. "Someone took a shot at me a few weeks ago."

"Bloody Christ, do you have any suspicions?" John asked.

James knew who it was but had no proof. He said one word that stunned the Duke of Avon. "Sloane."

"Your own cousin?"

"I don't believe Sloane would do that," Adam said, defending the younger man.

"Sloane is the one person who would benefit by my death," James argued. "Even bastards have ambitions."

"What do you mean?" John asked.

"His father was my grandfather's bastard," James told him. "Sloane was entitled to nothing. My father, my brother, and I always included him in our family and fortune. The Armstrong family charter even allows him to inherit the title if I die without issue."

"You can't prove Sloane wants you dead," Adam

said. "What if it's some other person, a business enemy perhaps?"

"Sloane was with my brother when he was killed," James said, turning to the Duke of Avon for support. "He has no reasonable alibi for the two attempts on my life."

"Sloane does look guilty, but appearances can be deceptive," John said. "Jumping to conclusions could get you killed."

There was a knock on the door, and the majordomo walked into the office. "Excuse me, your grace," Pennick said. "The Earl of Bovingdon requests an interview."

This is all I need, James thought. St. Leger was looking for financial compensation for his sister being slapped.

"Send him away," he instructed his man.

"Your grace, I hurried here as quickly as I could," Reggie St. Leger said, barging into the office.

John nodded at Pennick to leave and turned to St. Leger. "What do you want, Reggie?" he asked. "I will not compensate you for Lily slapping Valentina."

"I don't want your money," St. Leger said, his expression hurt. "I hurried here as soon as I heard about your near-fatal accident last night."

"That was no accident," Adam spoke up. "Someone tried to kill him."

St. Leger looked shocked. "Who would do such a thing? Can I be of service in any way?"

The last thing he needed was Reggie St. Leger dogging his every step. James forced himself to smile politely, saying, "I thank you for your concern but can handle the situation myself. Was there another reason for your visit?"

St. Leger smiled ingratiatingly.

Here it comes, James thought.

"This may not be the best time," St. Leger hedged.

"Please, speak freely," James said. *And then get the hell out of my house,* he thought.

"I would like to propose a match between my sister and your cousin," St. Leger said.

That surprised James. "Valentina and Sloane? Reggie, you never fail to amaze me."

"Sloane has been escorting Valentina around town," St. Leger said. "Besides, I do not approve of that American. Seth Hawkins is not what he appears to be. You might want to investigate those Americans."

James was instantly alert. "Why do you say that?"

St. Leger shrugged. "I have a feeling, nothing more."

"I'll speak to Sloane about your proposal," James said with a smile of dismissal. "It is past time my cousin thought about taking a wife."

"Thank you, your grace." St. Leger turned to Adam and John before leaving and said, "Good day to both of you."

No sooner had the door closed behind St. Leger than the three men looked at each other and burst into laughter. James shook his head with disbelief and wondered if Valentina knew what her brother was proposing.

"I must be leaving," the Duke of Avon said, rising from his chair.

Adam St. Aubyn stood when he did. "I'll leave with you."

James escorted them downstairs. Reaching the foyer, he instructed his majordomo, "Pennick, ask her grace to join us here." He turned to his friends, asking, "Will I see you tonight at White's?"

"I'll be there," Adam said.

The Duke of Avon shrugged. "That depends on my wife's plans."

James and Adam looked at each other and laughed.

Pennick returned a few minutes later. With him were Isabelle Saint-Germain and Michael, carrying Princess.

Isabelle smiled at Adam and turned to James. "I have invited Lily for a carriage ride in the park for tomorrow. Is that acceptable?"

Caught off guard, James hesitated for a fraction of a minute. He didn't want to let Lily out of his sight but couldn't very well refuse a simple request from the Duchess of Avon.

"That sounds delightful," he said. "I'm sure the outing will do Lily a world of good."

Isabelle folded her hand inside the crook of her husband's arm. She smiled at him and asked, "Are you ready, your grace?"

Apparently, the Duchess of Avon was one woman who did a lot of thinking, James decided when his guests had gone. She'd played the game well and won a day out for Lily. He wasn't fooled by that sweet smile of hers.

"Where is your sister?" James asked, turning to the boy.

"Lily went to her chamber," Michael told him. "Princess stole my cookie. I need another one."

James paused at the foyer table to see if anyone else had left calling cards for Lily. He heard a knock on the door and turned around when Pennick allowed entrance to the American, Bradley Hampstead.

I've got him now, James thought. He called, "Michael, come here."

Michael retraced his steps across the foyer. James glanced at the American and knew from the man's expression that he and the boy were acquainted.

James put his arm around Michael and pointed to Hampstead, asking, "Do you know that man?"

Michael stared at Hampstead for a long moment. "No," he answered, shaking his head.

The boy is lying. Lily warned him last night. That was the reason for her visiting him in the middle of the night.

"Are you certain?" James asked.

"Is he Robin Hood?"

"No."

"King George?"

"Go get your cookie," James said. He turned to the American, asking, "What can I do for you, Mr. Hampstead?"

"I wish to speak with Mistress Hawthorne," he said.

"Lily isn't receiving visitors today," James told him, and was satisfied when he detected a disappointed expression on the man's face. "Would you care to leave your card?"

"Thank you, your grace." Bradley passed him his calling card and left without another word.

James tore the card up and handed the pieces to Pennick. Slowly and deliberately, he walked toward the stairs.

His patience was depleted. Now he was going to get the truth about the Americans out of Lily. He was also going to give her a stinging lecture about how rude she was for allowing Pennick to escort the Duchess of Avon to the foyer when she should have done it herself.

Steeling himself against her beauty and wiles, James started up the stairs. Behind him, he heard the sounds of his mother and his aunts returning home but ignored them.

James knocked on Lily's bedchamber door. He heard her muffled "Go away" but ignored it.

Opening the door, James walked boldly inside. He stopped short at the sight that greeted him. Lily knelt in front of the commode and gagged dryly.

James was beside her in an instant. He put his arm around her and supported her until her spasms ended. Then he lifted her into his arms and gingerly placed her on the bed.

"I am sending for my physician," James announced. "I want no arguments."

He started to leave but stopped short halfway across the chamber as an outrageous idea struck him.

Slowly, James turned around and walked back to the bed. He stared with dawning horror at her and then said, "God's balls, you're pregnant."

Sixteen

"Those who feed grow full, your grace."

Lily sighed in defeated misery. The truth about her condition lay between them. What happened now depended upon him.

Opening her eyes, Lily sat up slowly lest the queasiness return. She leaned back against the headboard and raised her gaze. His expression on her was blacker than the devil's and colder than the north wind in winter. He had developed an angry twitch in the muscle in his right cheek.

Anger? How dare the duke be angry with her for being pregnant? Had he forgotten that he'd abducted and seduced her? He was the culprit, not she.

"I neither expect nor want anything from you," Lily told him, too proud to let him see her pain. "I can handle this situation if only you send me home."

"Has the sickness passed?" James asked, banishing all emotion from his expression except for the twitching cheek muscle.

Lily inclined her head. "For the moment."

"When were you planning to tell me?" he asked.

"I was hoping the war would end before that became necessary," Lily answered honestly, staring him straight in the eye.

His lips tightened into a white line. The twitching in his cheek increased.

"Come with me to the drawing room," James said in a stern voice.

Lily had no intention of telling his mother and his aunts about her condition. She hadn't the emotional strength to face them yet and opened her mouth to refuse.

"Do as I say," he snapped.

Autocratic to the end, Lily thought.

Fearing the queasiness would return, Lily slid off the bed slowly. She paused a moment to smooth her skirt but stopped when she realized her hands were shaking. Shifting her gaze to his, she knew he'd seen her trembling hands and could have kicked herself. One should never show fear or weakness in front of an enemy. She'd learned that a long time ago on Boston's docks.

Together, James and Lily left her chamber and walked down the third-floor corridor to the stairs. The drawing room was located on the second floor.

"What are you going to do?" Lily asked, stealing a sidelong peek at him.

James did not answer. The angry twitch had spread to the muscle in his left cheek.

The dowager and her sisters were sitting on the settees in front of the summer-darkened hearth. Pennick was just serving them tea.

"Bring us two more cups," the dowager instructed the majordomo when she saw them enter.

"Yes, your grace."

"Forget the cups, Pennick," James ordered as they passed the man.

"As you wish, your grace."

"Hello, my darlings," Lady Donna called. "We've just returned from basking in the glow of our dear Lily's social success."

"Be quiet," Lady Nora told her sister. "Something momentous is about to happen."

James gestured Lily to sit on the settee beside his mother. Lily sat down, but mutiny shone from her sapphire eyes. She would have insisted on standing just to be perverse but didn't want to argue in front of the others.

Standing in front of the hearth, James looked at his mother and said, "Prepare a wedding for the first day of August."

Shocked into silence, the three sisters stared at him as if he'd suddenly grown another nose. No one was more stunned than Lily.

How dare he assume that she would marry him. She wanted to be asked, to be wooed, to be loved.

"I won't marry you," Lily announced.

"Why? It's mine, isn't it?" James asked, fixing his black gaze on her. "Or could it belong to that American fiancé of yours? Someone else, perhaps?"

Lily flinched as if she'd been slapped. Tears welled up in her eyes, but she struggled valiantly to hold them back.

"Lily has two fiancés?" Lady Donna asked in confusion.

"I want to know what is happening," the dowager demanded, her gaze on her son.

"Tess, do be patient," Lady Nora told the dowager. "They are taking the long way around."

"I want the truth," James said, his gaze on Lily, ignoring his relatives.

"The truth is, I was a morsel for a duke," Lily said in a quavering voice, and stood to leave.

"Sit down," he ordered.

"I refuse to listen to your insults," she cried. "I want to go home."

At that, Lily burst into tears and ran out of the drawing room. James caught her just outside the door and whirled her around. She tried to break free of his grasp on her arm, but he pulled her into his arms and kept her prisoner against his body.

"You have been brave for a long time," James said, holding her close. "Let it all out now."

His unexpected kindness was her undoing.

Lily buried her face against his chest and sobbed as if she would never stop. She wept for herself, for her baby, and for a lifetime of worry about her brother.

James handed her his handkerchief when her wracking sobs subsided and then ceased. Lily looked up at him through glistening sapphire eyes that mirrored her misery.

"I want to go upstairs now," she told him, her weariness evident.

James shook his head. Taking her hand in his, he led her back to the settee in the drawing room.

Lily fixed her gaze on the carpet. She didn't want to see the disapproving expressions on the ladies' faces.

"About that wedding . . ." James said.

"No one can plan a wedding in two weeks," the dowager told him.

"Lily carries the Armstrong heir," James announced. "I want no gossip attached to my son's name. Either prepare a wedding for the first day of August or I'll elope."

"Do *not* threaten me, James," the dowager said, sounding as autocratic as her son.

Lily looked first at the dowager and then at her sisters. She saw no disapproving expressions. In fact, the ladies appeared to be taking this scandalous news in stride.

"I told you so," Lady Nora said with a smile.

"Oh, pish. Even a blind man could see Jamie was hot for her," Lady Donna replied. "An abducted bride—how utterly romantic."

"Kingston will help us," the dowager said, standing. "Let's pay him a visit." She turned to Lily and asked, "Did James force himself on you?"

"No," Lily answered, her face heating with a blush.

"Did you entice my son with the idea of marrying a duke?" the dowager asked.

"Certainly not."

That seemed to satisfy the dowager. She left the drawing room without another word, and her sisters followed behind her.

The thought of living her life as an unwanted wife sickened Lily. She wanted love and acceptance but knew she would be denied those things if she married the duke and remained in England.

"This is madness," Lily told him. "You don't want to marry me any more than I want to marry you."

"The Armstrong heir will be born on the correct side of the blanket," James told her.

"You don't love me," she argued.

"Love has nothing to do with marriage," he said flatly, and headed for the door.

I need love, Lily thought, too proud to beg for something that could never be.

"How will your mother feel when she learns her daughter-in-law is the Gilded Lily?" she asked in a final attempt to save herself from a life of misery.

"My mother knows the truth about you," James called over his shoulder and disappeared out the door.

Depleted of energy, Lily plopped down on the settee. She leaned back and closed her eyes.

How could the dowager even look at her? How could she so easily accept the Gilded Lily? When the dowager looked at her, did she see a murderer?

Lily sighed. She would never understand these people, nor could she face a lifetime of living like a stranger among them. She refused to be held hostage in England. All she wanted was to go home and deliver her baby in peace. Sweet lamb of God, even Hortensia MacDugal would be a welcome sight.

James is going to marry you, Lily told herself. *What more do you want?*

I want his love, she answered her own question. *Living without love is too high a price to pay.*

Lily dropped her hands to her belly as another, more disturbing thought stepped out of the corner of her mind. What would James do if she delivered an impaired child? Yes, he liked her brother, but Michael was not his son.

"Excuse me, my lady," Pennick said, walking into the drawing room. He handed her a package, saying, "From the Duchess of Avon."

Lily smiled in spite of her misery. She knew what the package contained. Thanks be to her guardian angel for sending her Isabelle Saint-Germain.

"Mr. Pennick, would you send my brother to me?" Lily asked.

"Yes, my lady."

Michael dashed into the room five minutes later. He threw his arms around her and said, "I love you, Lily."

"I love you more," she told him. "Look what Isabelle sent me."

Lily opened the package to reveal a small dagger with a four-inch blade accompanied by a black leather sheath and a garter to strap it to her leg. She held the dagger up for his inspection.

"Do you want to learn how to use it?" she asked. Even an impaired boy should have a means of self-defense.

Michael gave her a lopsided grin and plopped down on the carpet. He pulled his left boot off to reveal his own last-resort dagger strapped to his leg.

Lily stared in surprise at it. "Where did you—?"

"Duncan taught me." Michael puffed out his chest with pride, adding, "Duncan said a man should always be pre-pre . . . ready."

"The Scotsman is correct."

Lily patted the settee, and Michael sat down beside her. She put her arm around him and said, "Duke and I will be married soon because I am going to have his baby. That means you will be an uncle."

"Holy hell, does that mean we aren't going home?" Michael asked.

"Remember what I said about vulgar language," she scolded him.

Michael pretended deafness. "Lily, I asked Saint Michael and God to keep us in merry olde England,

and He answered my prayer. Are we having a boy or a girl?"

"I don't know," she answered. "I only want a healthy baby."

"I want a girl," Michael told her. "Just like you . . ."

Love is madness, Lily decided, crossing her bedchamber to inspect herself in the cheval mirror.

Hoping to attract the duke, Lily had taken special pains with her appearance that evening. She wore a high-waisted, azure blue silk gown with a scooped neck and melon sleeves. Peggy had brushed her hair back and knotted it at the nape of her neck.

Lily stared at herself in the mirror. Catching her attention, the diamond engagement ring sparkled in the mirror's reflection, and she held up her hand to stare at it.

If only the ring represented the duke's love for her. She touched her *alpha* and *omega* cross. If only there was a first and last love for her.

Nothing could prevent this wedding or make the love she felt disappear. She had no wish to live in a loveless marriage. Her only chance for happiness was to make James love her.

That was easier said than done, Lily thought. Starting tonight, she would smile at him and assume a pleasant demeanor.

And if that failed? Fortunately, Lady Donna knew everything about men. She would seek that lady's advice.

What if the duke could not love a wharf rat? Lily frowned at the thought. If the duke couldn't love her, she would make do. Her brother would live happily where people seemed to accept him, and she would have her own baby's love. That was more than some people had.

Lily left her chamber and walked down the stairs to the first floor. Entering the dining room, she stopped short in surprise. The room was empty except for Pennick and a footman.

"Good evening, my lady," Pennick said in greeting, pulling out the chair at the head of the table. "I believe you will enjoy tonight's fare."

"Where is everyone?" Lily asked, sitting down.

"Her grace and the ladies are dining with the Duke of Kingston," the majordomo answered.

"And his grace?"

"His grace has gone out for the evening," he told her. "I believe he mentioned something about his gentleman's club."

"I see."

Though she felt abandoned, Lily forced herself to smile. Her appetite had vanished, but she knew she needed to eat for her baby's sake.

Pennick dismissed the footman and served her himself. There were roasted chicken with mushroom stuffing, bread sauce, roasted potatoes, and parsnips. She declined the soup, the salad, and the dessert.

Lily ate slowly. She didn't want the servants to know how hurt she felt. Eating and bolting would only make them pity her. She felt pathetic enough without anyone pitying her.

"English bastard," she muttered to herself when she left the dining room an hour later. Only an Englishman would insist on a wedding and then abandon his affianced bride to eat a lonely dinner.

Lily paused when she reached the second floor. Perhaps the duke's abandonment was fortuitous. This

would be the perfect opportunity to search his office
for papers regarding his brother's death.

To that end, Lily walked down the second-floor corridor to the duke's office. She paused inside the doorway and smiled. She could feel his presence in the
room.

When she sat in his chair, Lily glided the palm of
her hand across the top of his oak desk. Her heart
ached with longing for his love.

Giving herself a mental shake, Lily took a deep,
calming breath and opened the first drawer. She studied the position of its contents in order to replace
them in exactly the same way.

And then Lily began to read the documents and
letters from his attorneys and clerks and ships' cap-
tains. No luck there. She started on the second drawer.

An hour later Lily rose from the desk and left the
office. She had found nothing regarding his brother's
death but didn't know if she should feel relieved or
not. Nothing had exonerated him either.

Wandering down the corridor to the library, Lily
wondered if Jane Austen had written anything else besides *Pride and Prejudice.* Real life had few happy endings, and she liked romantic stories where everything
ended happily.

Lily browsed the bookcases but could find no
other Jane Austen novel. Deciding the *Bible* would
put her to sleep, she reached for the Holy Book and
noticed the title beside it. *The History of the Armstrong
Family.*

Knowing her baby's ancestors would be a good
thing, Lily thought. She grabbed the thick volume and
returned to her chamber.

After changing into her robe, Lily sat in the chair

near the hearth and lit the candle on the side table. She would begin with James's generation and read her way back through the ages.

"Sweet lamb of God," Lily exclaimed softly after reading the first five pages. She knew who killed his brother and tried to assassinate James. Sloane Armstrong had to be the guilty party. Why couldn't anyone but James see that?

The eleventh Duke of Kinross, James's grandfather, had sired Sloane's father. Even bastards had ambitions, and those ambitions extended to their children. Sloane had decided to eliminate anyone who blocked his way to the Armstrong title and fortune.

Oh, how she wished James hadn't gone to his club. On the other hand, she couldn't accuse Sloane without more tangible proof. She would tell Seth and Bradley, and they would investigate.

Lily snapped the book shut and climbed into bed. She slipped her hand to her belly and prayed that her baby was in no danger from Sloane.

Awakening the next morning, Lily slid out of bed and hurried across the chamber to look out the window. She smiled with pleasure at the sight of the blue sky and sunshine, a perfect day for a carriage ride in the park.

Lily completed her morning ablutions and dressed in a pale yellow morning gown with long, full sleeves. She wove her hair into one thick braid and rolled it into a knot at the nape of her neck. Practicing her smile for the duke wasted another five minutes, and then she left the chamber.

"Good morning," Lily called, breezing into the dining room, a smile pasted onto her lips.

"Good morning," James said without looking up from the papers he was reading.

Walking toward the sideboard, Lily kept her gaze on him and wondered what was so interesting that he couldn't look up to see her smile. She nodded at the majordomo and placed a spoonful of scrambled eggs, a slice of ham, a scone, and two pats of butter on her plate.

Lily took the seat beside James, who sat at the head of the table. She glanced at the pile of papers, business documents.

"Did you enjoy yourself last night?" she asked, trying to engage him in conversation.

James looked up and stared at her blankly.

"At your gentleman's club," she said, pleased by the chance to smile at him. Her practicing hadn't gone to waste after all.

"I had quite an enjoyable evening," he answered, and returned his attention to the papers.

Though their conversation wasn't progressing as she had planned, Lily tried again. "I borrowed *The History of the Armstrong Family* from the library. I hope you don't mind."

"Not in the least," he replied without looking up.

"I was searching for another Jane Austen novel," she told him. "Has she written anything else?"

No answer.

"I am so excited by the prospect of a carriage ride," Lily said, irritated at being ignored. "Isabelle thought we should ride to Scotland and see several points of interest."

When the majordomo chuckled out loud, James looked up from his papers. He shifted his gaze from his retainer to her, asking, "What did you say?"

"Are you having a problem with your ears?" Lily asked in a voice laced with sarcasm. "Shall I send for your physician?"

"Goddamn it," James snapped. "You can see that I am busy." He passed her the *Times* and ordered, "Sit over there and read this while you eat."

Lily felt her cheeks heating with an embarrassed blush. Now he'd reprimanded her in front of the servants, the same servants who had witnessed her humiliation the previous evening and considered her a pathetic creature.

So much for civilized pleasantries, she thought.

Rising from her chair, Lily gestured to Pennick to remain where he was. She lifted her plate and the newspaper and walked the length of the forty-foot table to sit at the opposite end.

"You needn't have gone to the far end of the table," James said, watching her.

"You read your papers," she said, gesturing toward them with a wave of her hand. "And I'll read mine."

Lily snatched up the *Times* and began to read. A society gossip column on the second page caught her attention.

The reporter had seen the dashing Duke of Kinross in the company of the beautiful flame-haired actress who was the momentary rage of London. The duke and his actress had their heads close together over an intimate dinner for two at an exclusive eating establishment. The reporter wondered if the Duke of Kinross was beginning to tire of American forthrightness, which was decidedly overrated and decidedly tedious.

Lily lost her appetite. She lifted her napkin off her lap and placed it on the table. Glancing at James, she suddenly realized that he wore his evening attire without the cravat and the jacket. Slowly and deliberately, she rose from her chair and retraced her steps to the door.

"I guess you did enjoy yourself last night," Lily said, passing his chair on the way out.

"What do you mean?" James asked, looking up when she spoke.

"You and your flame-haired actress were enjoying your intimate dinner for two while your pregnant bride-to-be dined alone," Lily informed him. "I hope you're satisfied that the servants now consider me pathetic."

"Your condition makes you emotional," James said, rising from his chair. "God's balls, Lily—"

"Enough!" Glorious in her fury, Lily pointed an accusing finger at him. "Temper your tone and vocabulary when you address me, you—you philandering *bastard.*"

"English son-of-a-bitch," she muttered, climbing the stairs to the third floor. Now she would need to compose herself before Isabelle arrived for their carriage ride.

Struggling against the tears threatening to spill, Lily stopped when she reached her bedchamber door. Would James now forbid her to go for the carriage ride? Well, if he did, she would walk out the door anyway. What could he do if she disobeyed? Abduct her and steal her virginity? Humiliate her in front of other people? He'd already done those things.

Apparently, smiles and pleasantries weren't enough to get his attention, she decided. What she needed was advice on how to make him love her.

Turning away from her bedchamber, Lily walked

down the corridor and knocked lightly on Lady Donna's door. Hearing the lady call out, she stepped inside the chamber and saw Lady Donna and Lady Nora breakfasting together.

"I told you Lily needed to speak to us this morning," Lady Nora said.

Lady Donna rolled her eyes heavenward. "Darling, join us," she called, beckoning her. "Sit there on the chair."

"I need your advice," Lily said without preamble, sitting on the appointed chair. "Please tell me how to win James's love."

"I can handle this problem," Lady Nora said.

"*I'll* handle it," Lady Donna said. "Lily knocked on *my* door."

"Yes, but she knew I would be breakfasting with you," Lady Nora countered. "Lily, dear, have you considered that James already loves you?"

"He doesn't behave like a man in love," Lily replied. "Do you see him falling in love with me in the future?"

"Sometimes surprises are better than knowing," Lady Nora told her.

"I have never heard worse advice," Lady Donna announced. "Listen to me, Lily. Men prefer challenges. They want objects that are hard won or desired by other men."

"Are you advising me to make him jealous?" Lily asked, her head beginning to throb. "How can I make him jealous if I never leave this house?"

"James has a kind heart," Lady Nora interjected. "Women would run through fire to capture such a heart."

"How fascinating," Lady Donna drawled, her voice

oozing sarcasm. "I thought all the ladies wanted his money and his title." She turned to Lily. "Cupid kills some with arrows and others with traps, which—"

"She's already trapped him with her pregnancy," Lady Nora reminded her sister. "Listen to me, Lily: Get a dragon's blood plant, wrap it in paper, throw it into a fire, and whisper a prayer while you do this. I guarantee James will positively pant for you. Of course, making him cockle bread is another option."

"Lily doesn't need an aphrodisiac," Lady Donna argued. "She wants to win his heart, not his pizzle. She's already tasted—Oh, dear, what a poor choice of words."

Lily felt her cheeks grow hot with a blush. Coming here had been a mistake. Lady Donna and Lady Nora were delightful women but couldn't give her an answer. Maybe nobody could help her.

A knock on the door drew their attention. "Come in, Pennick," Lady Nora called, and smiled when the door opened to reveal the majordomo.

"The Duchess of Avon awaits you in the foyer," Pennick told Lily.

"Thank you." Lily rose from her seat, saying, "And I thank both of you for your advice."

Clutching her shawl and *The History of the Armstrong Family*, Lily hurried downstairs to the foyer. "I'm sorry to have kept you waiting," she called to her new friend.

"What is that you're carrying?" Isabelle Saint-Germain asked.

"I'll explain after we've gone," she answered.

"Have a wonderful outing," Pennick said, opening the door for them.

"Thank you," the two women said at the same time. They looked at each other and laughed.

"Lily, there you are." The duke's voice sounded behind them. "I want to speak with you."

Lily turned around and saw James crossing the foyer toward them. Was he going to rescind his permission for her carriage ride?

"Good morning, Isabelle," he greeted the duchess. "Would you mind if I stole Lily away for five minutes?"

Isabelle inclined her head. "Not in the least."

"*I* would mind," Lily informed him, narrowing her sapphire gaze on him. "Whatever you wish to discuss can keep until I return." Without waiting for his protest, Lily walked out the door.

"I suspect you read that piece in the *Times*," Isabelle said when they were seated in her carriage. "You and his grace are not in accord?"

Lily cast her new friend a sidelong smile and drawled in a perfect imitation of Lady Donna, "Darling, his grace is an autocratic arse."

Seventeen

Isabelle burst out laughing. "I like you more and more, Lily Hawthorne."

"And I like you, Isabelle Saint-Germain," Lily said with a smile. "By the way, how well do you drive this thing?"

"We'll soon find out," Isabelle teased her.

Lily could hardly believe she was riding around London in her friend's carriage, her first real taste of freedom since the middle of May. She smiled with the sheer joy of it, especially since the young woman beside her was the only friend she'd ever had. Perhaps the problem hadn't been hers, but the people of Boston's docks. Hope for the future began to swell within her breast.

Summer wore its most serene expression that morning. The sky was a blanket of blue dotted with a few fair-weather clouds. The sun's rays were warm, and in the distance appeared the greenery of Hyde Park.

"Don't feel too badly about James and that actress," Isabelle was saying. "He'll drop her once you've married."

Lily had doubts about that. James and she were not on good terms. She supposed he still looked at her and saw a murderer, albeit indirectly. He would never love her unless he thought of her as a woman—not an American, not the Gilded Lily, not his prisoner.

"My husband's former mistress appeared at our wedding reception and abandoned their daughter there in front of several hundred guests," Isabelle told her. "Now, that is scandal on a grand scale."

Her story surprised Lily. From the outside, Isabelle Saint-Germain seemed to enjoy a perfect life.

"What happened?" Lily asked.

"John wanted to return her to her mother, but I couldn't send her back to the woman who had abandoned her," Isabelle said. "I can't begin to tell you the arguments we had about it. Of course, I prevailed in the end, and we adopted her. Afterwards, we produced our own—twins, a boy and a girl. I love my adopted daughter as much as I do my own."

"Oh, I love happy endings," Lily replied.

"One day soon you will enjoy your own happy ending," Isabelle predicted. "I can feel it."

"Do you have the Sight like Lady Nora?" Lily teased her.

Isabelle laughed, and Lily joined in her merriment. Sharing a jest with a friend was such pleasure, and she would cherish this moment for a long time.

Bewitching fragrances filled the air when they entered Hyde Park. Against a background of lush greenery, the gardens inside the park presented breathtaking contrasts and harmonies. Bold primary colors—red, yellow, blue—added drama to the flower beds, while softer pastel shades harmonized with the lighter foliage.

"William the Third ordered three hundred lamps hung from the trees along *route de roi*, the road upon which we are riding," Isabelle informed her. "Rotten Row became the first road lit at night in the whole country because the king wanted to deter highwaymen."

"What is that water?" Lily asked, pointing in the distance.

"The Serpentine." Isabelle looked at her and added, "We could go boating on it."

"I had enough of boating on my trip across the Atlantic," Lily said, a rueful smile on her face.

"I'll drive by Buckingham Palace and Westminster Abbey after we meet your brother," Isabelle said. "Both aren't too far from here."

"I'd like that." On impulse, Lily touched her arm. "I'm so glad we met," she whispered when Isabelle looked at her. "I never had a friend before."

Lily worried her bottom lip with her teeth as soon as those words slipped out. She sounded pathetic and wouldn't blame the duchess if she changed her mind about being friends.

"I never had a real friend either," Isabelle admitted, patting her arm. "My parents died when I was young, and my stepmother never considered me one of hers. My stepsisters never wanted anything to do with me."

"You had your guardian angel," Lily reminded her.

Isabelle smiled. "I love Giselle—that is her name— but she did cause problems. People thought I was half-mad."

"How did you meet your husband?"

"John became my guardian when my brother Miles went abroad on business," Isabelle answered. "We fell in love and lived happily ever after."

Lily laughed. "Your life sounds like a fairy tale."

"Here comes your brother and your fiancé—I mean, his friend," Isabelle whispered, halting the carriage.

Lily shifted her gaze, her heart aching at the worry she saw etched across Bradley's features. If only she had accepted his marriage proposal, she wouldn't be in this position. Her life would have sounded like a fairy tale, too.

"I'd like to wring your neck," Seth said, drawing her attention.

Lily laughed. "I'm happy to see you again, Brother." She shifted her gaze to Bradley and said softly, "I'm pleased to see you again, too."

With his sandy brown hair and warm brown eyes, Bradley Howell was still one of the handsomest men she'd ever seen, but Lily knew she couldn't marry him. He wasn't the Duke of Kinross. If only she had never met James, she could have been happy with Bradley. Regret for what might have been welled up inside her.

"You can speak openly in front of Isabelle," Lily said, turning to her brother.

"We told you to retire the Gilded Lily," Seth said.

"James would have discovered my identity and abducted me anyway," Lily defended herself.

"James?" Bradley echoed, his gaze on her. "I still don't like the idea of you remaining in that house with the duke."

Guilt coiled itself around Lily's heart. Bradley loved her and worried for her safety. She had repaid him by carrying another's man's child. Though reluctant to cause more pain, Lily knew she needed to tell him and her brother the truth of her condition.

"His grace would never hurt Lily," Isabelle assured them. "James Armstrong is a man of integrity."

Lily squirmed on the seat. Bradley hadn't taken his gaze off her, and its intensity made her uncomfortable.

"Englishmen have no integrity," Bradley told the duchess. He sounded bitter, which made Lily feel even worse.

"Englishmen have as much integrity as Americans," Isabelle replied. "I know because I married a man of integrity."

"We are wasting time," Lily said. She passed the book to her brother, saying, "I know who murdered the previous duke. Read page five of this, *The History of the Armstrong Family*. Sloane Armstrong's father was the illegitimate issue of James's grandfather. Even bastards and their children have ambitions."

Beside her, Isabelle laughed. "Sloane Armstrong is one of the kindest, most affable men I've ever met."

"Appearances can be deceptive, your grace," Seth said.

"Sloane accompanied the previous duke to Boston, where he met his end," Lily argued. "Furthermore, Sloane has no good alibi for the times of the two attempts on James's life."

"Kinross could have staged those in order to divert suspicion," Bradley said.

Lily snapped her gaze to him. "James would never do that."

"Are you defending the villain?" Bradley asked, his anger apparent in his voice. "The man abducted you and Michael."

"Why do you insist James is guilty of murder?" Lily countered, her own voice rising with anger. "Or do you *want* him to be guilty?"

"Lower your voices," Seth said. "You'll draw attention to us. We'll investigate this Sloane possibility. How is Michael?"

"Michael has never been happier," Lily said, her gaze on Bradley, challenging him to refute her words.

"We'll be in touch," Seth said, beginning to turn his horse away.

"Don't go," Lily said before she lost her courage. "I need to tell you something important."

Both Seth and Bradley looked at her expectantly. She glanced at Isabelle, who was also watching her.

Lily took a deep breath, and then her words came rushing out. "James and I will be married on the first day of August."

"The mission ends now," Bradley said, looking at her brother for support. "I refuse to allow this. Kinross cannot prevent us from taking Lily and Michael home."

Seth seemed calmer about the wedding complication. "We are close to the truth," her brother argued. "Lily can have the marriage annulled."

"Are you mad?" Bradley shot back. He fixed his gaze on Lily, asking, "What is the rush? No one has a two-week betrothal."

"They do if the bride-to-be is already pregnant," Lily said in a small voice, her gaze fixed on her hands, folded in her lap.

"Oh, my," Isabelle said.

"I'll kill him," Seth growled.

"I asked if he'd touched you," Bradley reminded her, drawing her attention. "You lied to me."

Lily felt his pain. Her heart broke at the unspeakable hurt etched across his face.

"Did he force himself on you?" Bradley asked.

Lily looked him straight in the eye and said, "No."

"You and Michael are coming with us today," Seth told her. "Your grace, if you would follow us back to the Armstrong mansion?"

"I won't go," Lily cried, tears welling up in her eyes. "The damage has been done. I want my child to carry his father's name."

"Don't cry," Seth said. "You'll get us hanged."

"Here come the St. Legers," Isabelle whispered.

"Pass me the book so I can return it to the library," Lily said to her brother. She hid the book on the seat beside her.

"Good morning, Mr. Hawkins," Valentina called. "Good morning, Mr. Hampstead." She nodded at Isabelle and ignored Lily.

"Good morning, your grace," Reggie greeted the duchess. He looked at Lily, asking, "How do you like Hyde Park?"

"I've never seen a more beautiful spot," Lily replied, forcing herself to smile. "Hyde Park is an earthy paradise."

"I'm pleased you like it," Reggie said, and then turned to Bradley. "Mr. Hampstead, I've just remembered a business appointment I have. Would you consider escorting Valentina home for me?"

"Mr. Hawkins and I would be honored to escort the lady home," Bradley replied.

"Thank you." St. Leger nodded at Seth and then rode away.

Lily was flabbergasted when her brother turned to the blond witch and asked with a charming smile, "Lady Valentina, would you care to ride with me before I escort you home?"

"I would love to ride with you, Mr. Hawkins," Valentina answered, blushing as if on cue.

"Good day, your grace," Seth said to the duchess. "Mistress Hawthorne." He looked at Bradley. "Are you coming, Mr. Hampstead?"

Bradley looked at her. "We will speak again soon." At that, he reined his horse away to follow Seth and Valentina.

Teardrops rolled down Lily's cheeks as she watched Bradley ride away. How could she enjoy any happiness knowing how much she'd hurt him?

"I understand how difficult that was for you," Isabelle said, reaching out to touch her arm.

"I have loved Bradley from childhood. We would have already been married, but—"

"What happened?" Isabelle prodded her.

"I refused his first offer because I feared delivering a child like Michael," Lily admitted. "The war intervened after that."

"Don't worry about your baby," Isabelle said. "He or she will be fine. Do you still love Bradley?"

"I love James," Lily admitted. *There;* she'd said it openly for the first time, which made her love official. And yet—whatever happiness she won would always be tempered by Bradley's pain.

"I'll understand if you don't want to continue our friendship," Lily said.

"Don't be silly," Isabelle replied. "I'm only sorry I can't be more of a help to you. How about that short tour before I bring you home?"

Lily managed a smile. "Thank you, Isabelle. I would love a tour of London."

While Lily was touring London with Isabelle, James sat in his office at the Armstrong mansion. He tried to concentrate on the ledgers sitting on his desk, but concern for Lily interfered. Who would she meet on her carriage ride? Isabelle Saint-Germain would not help her escape, would she? No, that was absurd. Lily would never leave Michael behind.

James determined to put her out of his mind but knew he hadn't the focus for numbers at the moment. He would read those shipping bids again and decide which of them to accept.

Opening the bottom drawer of his desk, James lifted the stack of bids and counted them. *Nine bids.* There should have been ten.

James opened the drawer above it and rifled through the papers. He checked the drawer above that. *No tenth bid.*

Before turning his attention to the drawers on the left, James opened the top middle drawer and pulled out several papers. Sitting on top of the pile was the tenth bid. He always kept pending bids and contracts in the bottom drawer. How did the bid get from the right bottom drawer to the top middle one?

A knock on the door drew his attention. He looked up to see Pennick entering.

"The Earl of Bovingdon requests an interview," the majordomo informed him. "He said it was a matter of some urgency."

James rolled his eyes. "Interrupt us in ten minutes," he instructed his man.

"Yes, your grace."

The Earl of Bovingdon walked into the office a moment later. "Good morning, your grace," St. Leger greeted him.

"Reggie, I haven't had the chance to speak with Sloane about a match with Valentina," James told him. "I've been busy planning my wedding to Lily, but I promise to broach the subject with him at the first opportunity."

"Accept my congratulations, your grace," St. Leger said with an ingratiating smile. "I know you will do your best, but I haven't come about that."

James cocked a dark brow at the man and forced himself to smile. "What can I do for you?"

"I have come to do something for you, your grace," St. Leger replied. "Valentina and I were riding in Hyde Park this morning when we chanced to meet your lovely fiancée and the Duchess of Avon." Losing his smile, the earl fell silent, as if debating whether or not to continue.

"And?" James prodded him.

"I hesitate to tell tales, your grace, but this matter could be of some importance," St. Leger continued. "I spied Mistress Hawthorne exchanging some sort of document with those two Americans, Hampstead and Hawkins. When I approached the carriage, Mistress Hawthorne hid it on the seat beside her."

"I'm certain my fiancée's actions are innocuous," James lied with a smile. "Though I do thank you for bringing this matter to my attention."

"What are friends for?" St. Leger returned.

"You and Valentina will be attending my wedding on the first of August?" James asked, wondering if he had misjudged the other man. "My wedding reception would be the perfect atmosphere for Valentina and Sloane to pass some time together."

"I am honored that you would include us," St. Leger said.

"How about a drink, Reggie?" James asked, feeling expansive. After all, the earl had given him informa-

tion that could explain how the documents in his desk
had been moved.

St. Leger's ingratiating smile widened just as Pennick returned, saying, "Your grace, I am sorry to interrupt, but this just arrived for you." The majordomo
passed him a missive.

James unsealed the missive and pretended to read
the blank paper. "I'm sorry you can't stay for that
drink, Reggie," he said. "I must attend to an urgent
business matter. Join me for a drink tonight at White's.
Pennick, escort the earl out and send Lily to me when
she returns."

"Yes, your grace."

"Good day, your grace," St. Leger said, and followed the majordomo out.

The bitch is spying on me, James thought as soon as
he was alone. That meant the two Americans were
spies, but he could make no accusations without
proof.

Why would the Americans be interested in him?
James wondered. Except for holding his ancestral seat
in the House of Lords, he had nothing to do with
the government. In fact, he'd been opposed to the
war.

James returned the ten shipping bids to the bottom
drawer and locked the desk. In spite of the early hour,
he poured himself a dram of whiskey and then waited.
All his questions would soon be answered.

An hour passed. And then another.

Where the bloody hell was she? James wondered,
debating whether he should go looking for her.

"Enter," he growled, hearing a knock on the door.
He shot to his feet when she walked in.

Lily paused inside the doorway. "You wanted to see me?"

Trying to keep her off guard, James smiled warmly and gestured to the chair in front of his desk. "Please, sit down." He sat when she did.

"How are you feeling today?" he asked.

"Well, thank you."

She looks worried, James thought. "How was your carriage ride?"

"I had a wonderful time," Lily answered, relaxing enough to smile. "Isabelle took me on a short tour of London afterwards."

"I could have done that," he said.

She lost her smile. "You could have done it, but you never offered."

"After we're married, I'll take you on the long tour of London," James promised, ignoring her criticism. "I have good news. The Duke of Kingston has accepted my invitation to give you away at our wedding."

"I want Michael to walk me down the aisle," Lily said.

"The Duke of Kingston is an important peer of this realm," James explained. "His walking you down the aisle will gain you instant acceptance into the ton."

"I don't give a fig about that," Lily told him. "Loyalty to my brother takes precedence over the ton's acceptance."

James studied her for a long moment. He knew her well enough to recognize the battle etched across her delicate features and tried another strategy. "You may not care about the ton's acceptance, but you should also think of our son's future."

Lily stared at him in silence, as if mulling that over

in her mind. "Very well; Michael will be my witness," she said finally.

"Why not ask the Duchess of Avon?" James countered. "Nothing can be gained by putting Michael on display."

It was the wrong thing to say. James knew that as soon as he saw the affronted, mulish expression on her face.

"Does Michael embarrass you?" Lily asked, her gaze narrowing on him. "What will you do if our baby suffers from the same malady? Lock him in the attic?"

Did she fear delivering an impaired child? James wondered. After passing most of her young life guarding her brother, he supposed that would seem a real possibility to her.

"Michael's malady does not embarrass me," James told her. "I have every confidence that our own child will be perfect in every way. In the unlikely event that he isn't, I will love him anyway."

She thought he was lying. James could see the disbelief shining at him from those disarming sapphire eyes of hers. Her expression was as easy to read as an open book.

"If Michael isn't my witness, I will stand at the altar and tell the world that you abducted me," Lily announced.

James inclined his head. He admired her loyalty to her brother and would have applauded her pluck if she hadn't been thwarting his wishes.

"Michael will be your witness because I like him, not because you are threatening me," James relented, and then he smiled.

When she appeared to relax, James said, "You

searched my desk last night. What were you hoping to find?"

Lily paled by several shades. "I don't know what you mean," she said, shifting her gaze to the window.

James spoke slowly, as if trying to explain something to an idiot. "I mean that you sneaked into this room, sat at my desk, opened the drawer, and—"

"I did *not* search your desk," Lily interrupted, bolting out of the chair.

James knew she was lying. He'd caught her off guard and she'd faltered in surprise. That first response had been honest.

Relaxing back in his chair, James said in a conversational tone of voice, "You rendezvoused with Hawkins and Hampstead in Hyde Park. Are they spies?"

"Why do you want to marry a woman whom you obviously do not trust?" Lily asked, looking him straight in the eye.

Because I love you, James thought. Then he said, "My son shouldn't suffer because his mother is an untrustworthy wharf rat."

She flinched as if he'd struck her. Guilty remorse for his words swelled in his chest. After all, she was carrying his child. Being kind to her would cost nothing. And yet, she had been spying on him and passing information to the enemy.

"Believe me, I regret abducting you," James told her. He wanted his heart and his well-ordered life back.

"You cannot possibly regret it more than I do," Lily said with quiet dignity, and then headed for the door.

"I forbid you to leave this house until our wedding day," James called.

Lily whirled around and walked back to his desk. Her sapphire eyes gleamed with barely suppressed anger.

"*I* forbid *you* to leave this house until we are married," Lily ordered, pointing her finger at him. "*No more actresses.*" And then she marched out of his office and slammed the door behind her.

James burst out laughing. His bride-to-be was more entertaining than any player in Drury Lane. If only she hadn't been consorting with the enemy.

"Autocratic arse," Lily muttered to herself as she climbed the stairs to her third-floor chamber. In the span of ten minutes, he'd managed to ruin what had been an enjoyable morning in the company of her first friend.

Lily slammed the door of her bedchamber and, gaining perverse satisfaction, dragged a chair across the room to prop against the door connecting her chamber to his. When the duke reconciled himself to the fact that she would go anywhere she pleased, she would remove the chair.

After tossing her cloak on the settee in front of the hearth, Lily lay down on her bed. Her head was beginning to throb from the conflicting thoughts swirling around inside her.

How had James known she'd spoken with Seth and Bradley? Was she being watched? They would need to be more careful lest they find themselves on the wrong end of the hangman's noose.

How could she possibly gain James's love when he didn't trust her? Should she tell him the truth about Seth and Bradley and what they were investigating? No, she'd given her word to remain silent.

And then Lily thought about Michael. How proud he would be to participate in her wedding.

Lily didn't believe James for one minute when he insisted that Michael's impairment was not an embarrassment to him. And if she delivered a child with her brother's malady? She had no doubt that James would lock the baby away.

Pleading tiredness because of her condition, Lily remained in her chamber the rest of the day. She had no idea if James would go out with his actress that evening and couldn't bear the piteous looks from the dowager and her sisters if he did.

The following morning dawned overcast and with a fine mist, but Lily's disposition was sunny. Today she would proclaim her independence by leaving the house without permission. She could hardly wait to see the ducal reaction to that.

Determined that no one would stop her, Lily marched downstairs early in the afternoon. She'd slung her hooded cloak across one arm so that anyone who saw her would know she was going out.

Pennick stood like a sentinel near the front door. His face remained expressionless as she crossed the foyer to the door and donned her cloak.

"Where is his grace?" Lily asked.

"His grace is meeting in his office with Lord St. Aubyn," the majordomo told her. "May I be of service to you?"

"If his grace wants to know my whereabouts, inform him that I am visiting the Duchess of Avon," Lily said. "If he doesn't ask, do not offer the information."

"I understand, my lady."

Lily paused before leaving. "Pennick, may I ask you a question?"

"Certainly."

"Did his grace go out last night?" Lily asked, feeling the heat from her blush.

"His grace dined with his mother and aunts," the majordomo told her. "Afterwards, he retired to his office."

Lily's smile could have lit the whole mansion. "Thank you, Mr. Pennick."

Stepping outside, Lily pulled the hood of her cloak up to protect herself from the mist and started walking west on Upper Brook Street. She stopped when she reached the intersection with Park Lane. She didn't know where Isabelle lived, only that it was someplace on Park Lane.

Feeling like a fool, Lily retraced her steps down Upper Brook Street. Her independence day had been a failure. She would be home before James even realized she was gone.

"Lily!"

She turned toward the voice. Bradley was standing there.

"You shouldn't be here," Lily said. "His grace is suspicious."

"I must speak with you privately," Bradley told her.

Lily thought a moment. "Come with me," she said, leading him down an alley that led to the mansion's rear garden. Sitting on a stone bench, she looked up at him expectantly.

"I'm sorry for the way I behaved yesterday," Bradley said, sitting down beside her. He took her hand in his, saying, "I still love you, Lily, and want you for my wife."

Lily felt like weeping. It was too late for them, but she couldn't bring herself to say the words.

"You don't need to decide right away," Bradley continued. "We can tell people that we married abroad, and I promise to raise your child as if he were my own."

Tears welled up in her eyes. "Oh, Bradley—"

"What are you doing on my property?"

At the sound of the duke's voice, Lily released Bradley's hand. Both of them rose from the bench and faced James. Adam St. Aubyn stood beside him.

"I was walking to Isabelle's when I chanced to meet Mr. Hampstead," Lily tried to explain.

"I can speak for myself," Bradley said, sounding irritated. "I stopped to exchange pleasantries with a fellow Bostonian."

Her gaze fixed on James. Lily knew he didn't believe either one of them. She held her breath, waiting for him to respond.

"You may leave now," James said.

Bradley inclined his head. Lily could have throttled him when he raised her hand to his lips and said, "Good day to you, Mistress Hawthorne."

"I want him investigated," James said to his friend. "Hampstead and Hawkins are not what they seem."

"My uncle has connections in the war office," Adam replied. "He can help us with this."

Lily started toward the door, but James grabbed her arm and whirled her around, demanding, "What were you doing outside? I forbade you to—"

"Futter yourself." Lily shrugged out of his grasp and, feeling his gaze on her, walked back to the mansion.

Lily kept walking until she reached her chamber and locked the door. Then she burst into tears for what was, what could have been, and what would never be—a first and last love for her. *Alpha* and *omega*.

Eighteen

They didn't speak for nine days.

Lily remained in seclusion at the Armstrong mansion.

James passed no evenings at home.

Today is my wedding day, Lily thought, standing at her window to gaze at a spectacularly sunny day after a week of drizzle. She could hardly believe she would soon be married, particularly to an English duke.

Disturbing thoughts swirled around inside her. Was James going to ignore her for the rest of her life? She'd hardly seen him for the past nine days. She hadn't even read about him in the *Times,* so she didn't know if he'd passed his evenings with that actress.

What was happening with Seth and Bradley? Neither had bothered to send her a note or even a message by way of Isabelle.

Lily gave herself a mental shake. She needed to focus on her baby and her marriage. Those were now the most important things in her life, in addition to Michael.

"Here we are," the dowager called, entering Lily's bedchamber. Lady Donna and Lady Nora followed behind her.

"You'll make a beautiful bride," Lady Donna said.

She chuckled throatily and added, "James won't want to wait to get you between the sheets."

"His grace prefers flame-haired actresses," Lily said.

"James will be faithful once he's taken his vows," the dowager told her.

"Spending time with that actress doesn't mean he's been unfaithful," Lady Nora said, covering the cheval mirror with a sheet.

"What are you doing?" Lily asked.

"A bride must not look at herself while wearing her bridal outfit," Lady Nora told her. "It's unlucky. Promise me you won't peek."

Lily smiled. "I promise."

Her wedding gown had been created in ivory silk and lace. Its bodice had a *V* neckline and long, flowing sleeves. The gown was simple, which suited Lily. The dowager and her sisters would have preferred a more elaborate gown, but two weeks' preparation precluded that.

Lily had brushed her ebony hair back and let it cascade to her waist, and the dowager helped her don the ivory lace veil. The only jewelry she wore were her *alpha* and *omega* cross and her diamond betrothal ring.

The dowager and her sisters walked around and around her, inspecting her from every angle, being certain that she looked perfect. Lily was beginning to feel like a maypole.

"Darling, watch what James does, not what he says," Lady Donna said, pausing in her inspection. "Remember, there's more to marriage than four naked legs in bed."

Lily blushed.

"Honor your vows of obedience to James but never allow him to control you," the dowager said.

Lily nodded.

"Drive gently over life's stones," Lady Nora advised, grasping her hand. "Love begets love, and James will be unable to hide his away forever."

Lily smiled. She liked the lady's sentiment, even if it was nonsense.

"The Duke of Kingston awaits us downstairs," the dowager said, handing her a bouquet of orange blossoms.

"Where is Michael?" Lily asked, her anxiety rising.

"Michael became fidgety," the dowager told her. "James and Adam took him along when they left for the church."

"I've just remembered something important," Lady Nora said, her expression worried. "Do you have something old?"

"Yes." Lily touched her *alpha* and *omega* cross.

"How about something new?" the lady asked.

Lily pointed to her betrothal ring.

"Something borrowed and something blue?"

"My garter is blue," Lily told her. "I'll tell you later what I borrowed. Will you trust me until then?"

Lady Nora smiled with relief. "Of course, my dear."

Accompanied by the dowager and her sisters, Lily walked downstairs to the foyer. The Duke of Kingston smiled with approval when he saw her and stepped forward to kiss her hand.

"My dear, you make me wish to be thirty years younger," he told her, escorting her to the ducal coach.

"Surely, you aren't that old," Lily replied.

"I feel young again when I look at you," he said. "James is a lucky man, indeed."

"I wish he thought so."

The Duke of Kingston gave her a curious look. "However you met, James is completely enamored of you."

Lily smiled but made no reply. *Let the duke believe what he would.* She knew better. James hadn't even spoken to her in nine days.

A short time later, Lily stood in a tiny candlelit chamber off the nave of Saint Mark's Church. With a trembling hand, she smoothed an imaginary wrinkle from the skirt of her silk gown.

"Why are there crowds of people milling about in the street?" Lily asked, trying to calm herself with mundane conversation.

"The people came to see a duke marry," the Duke of Kingston told her.

"I didn't know James was such an important man."

"Your unimpressed attitude is probably what attracted James," the duke said. "And your beauty, of course."

"I thought my poor choice of careers attracted him," she replied, making the duke smile. "Where is Michael? He should be here."

"James decided that Michael should wait with him at the altar," the Duke of Kingston told her. "He didn't want to put the boy on display."

That dissembling bastard tricked me, Lily thought.

"Believe me, my dear, James was only thinking of the boy," the duke said, escorting her out of the chamber.

Leaving the nave, Lily and the Duke of Kingston positioned themselves at the end of the long aisle.

Hundreds of candles lit the church, casting eerie shadows on its walls, stained-glass windows, and ornate sculptures.

The organist began playing. The wedding guests rose from the pews, and a sea of faces turned to watch her.

Ignoring them, Lily gazed the long length of the aisle to where James stood with Michael, Adam, and the Archbishop of London. Bouquets of white lilies, purple violets, and blue forget-me-nots decorated the altar.

Lily nodded at the Duke of Kingston and looped her hand into the crook of his arm, indicating her readiness. They'd only taken two steps forward when she hesitated, her complexion paling. Seth and Bradley stood in the last row of pews.

Lily didn't know what to do. Could she walk past Bradley to marry James?

"Is anything wrong?" the duke asked.

"No, your grace." Lily gave the older man a wobbly smile and began walking.

Almost there, she thought when they reached the midpoint of the aisle. She kept her gaze fixed on James, magnificent in his midnight blue formal attire.

When she reached the altar, James held his hand out, and Lily placed her hand in his. She looked into his dark eyes, hoping to see some sign of love.

James smiled warmly, and Lily wondered if their marriage could work in spite of the odds against it. Together, they walked into the sanctuary.

The Archbishop of London was staring at Michael. Apparently, he had just realized that her impaired brother would witness the marriage of a duke.

"Your grace, this boy cannot witness your marriage," the archbishop whispered. "I cannot—"

"Monseigneur, please look down at my leg," Lily said, before James spoke. When he did, she lifted the front of her wedding gown to reveal the dagger strapped to her leg.

The Archbishop of London stared in horror at the blade. Then he shifted his gaze to James for an explanation.

"Monseigneur, I apologize for my bride's behavior, but the lady cannot control herself," James whispered. "She's American."

James lifted her hand to his lips. "My bride is so far from home and desperately wants her brother to witness her marriage. Humoring my bride would certainly be worth your while."

The archbishop inclined his head, granting permission for the boy to witness the ceremony. The duke's meaning wasn't lost on Lily. James had offered the Archbishop of London a bribe, and the holy man had accepted it.

Thankfully, the wedding ceremony lasted fifteen minutes. Lily's heart warmed when James lifted her veil and kissed her. Perhaps destiny *had* brought them together . . .

And then Lily noticed that Adam and Michael had left the church by a side entrance instead of walking down the aisle in front of the wedding guests. "You tricked me," she said in an accusing voice.

"Did you want Michael to witness your marriage or did you want to flaunt his impediment in front of three hundred wedding guests?" James asked. "Smile, or our guests will think we are not in accord."

"I don't care what these people think."

"But I *do* care, especially when my mother and aunts are watching."

Lily smiled brightly. "Very well. We will discuss this later."

"I have no doubt of that," he replied, also smiling, and then lifted her hand to his lips.

Lily wondered if his gesture of affection was genuine or part of a role he was playing for the benefit of their guests. Her husband was an enigma, his thoughts and moods unpredictable.

Great guardian angel, what have I done? Lily questioned her own sanity as they walked down the aisle. She'd married a man she scarcely knew and must live with him for the next forty years or so.

Lily glanced at the last pew as she passed it. It was empty, Seth and Bradley having already left the church.

The Duke of Kingston hosted a champagne breakfast for three hundred. Upon arriving at his mansion, Lily stood between James and the duke in the receiving line.

Lily felt like a fraud as she greeted their guests. She wasn't the same as these English aristocrats and didn't belong with them. But, where did she belong? Certainly not on Boston's wharves after living with the Duke of Kinross for more than two months.

"Where is Michael?" Lily asked in growing anxiety when they sat down to eat. "I haven't seen him yet."

"Keep smiling," James whispered close to her ear, putting his arm around her, "or I'll make you wish you had."

"I asked you a question," Lily said, smiling at him with adoration etched across her features. "I expect an answer."

"Michael is at Armstrong Mansion," James told her, planting a kiss on her lips. "Duncan took him directly home from the church."

Lily lost her smile. "How dare you—"

James yanked her into his arms, and his lips covered hers in a slow kiss. The warmth of his mouth and his scent of mountain heather conspired against her, and Lily returned his kiss in kind. Only the smothered chuckles erupting from the wedding guests broke them apart.

"Keep smiling. I promise we'll discuss everything later," James whispered against her lips. "That includes the dagger strapped to your leg."

"I understand completely," Lily said, reaching up to caress his cheek in a loving gesture.

"As I've said before, you would be a spectacular success at Drury Lane," James said.

"I don't have red hair," she replied. "Keep smiling, your grace."

Adam St. Aubyn rose from his chair and lifted his crystal champagne flute. He waited until the guests quieted and then spoke.

"I have the distinct honor of toasting my oldest friend and his beautiful bride," Adam began. "I thought long and hard but could find no suitable words to express my wishes for their happiness until I happened upon a proverb. *Married in August's heat and drowse, Lover and friend your chosen spouse.*'"

Adam turned to the newlyweds and lifted his champagne flute high, saying, "May you enjoy a long, happy life together. To his grace, the Duke of Kinross, and her grace, the Duchess of Kinross."

"Here, here," called someone in the hall.

James rose from his chair and shook his friend's

hand. "All of you know me very well, but my bride remains a mystery to you," James said, turning to the wedding guests. "I married Lily because of her beauty, her intelligence, and—most of all—for her keen sense of loyalty and honor. To my bride, the Duchess of Kinross."

He never mentioned loving me, Lily thought, smiling at her husband. She hoped he valued the qualities she possessed. For today, she would pretend he'd spoken sincerely.

After two hours of continuous smiling, Lily and James sat inside his coach for the short ride home. Neither of them smiled. She glanced sidelong at him, admiring his strong profile, and said, "I would like to know—"

"We will discuss that later," he interrupted her.

Lily clamped her lips together. Her husband wasn't behaving as if he believed the wonderful things he'd said about her. Was this how the next forty years would be?

James helped her alight from the carriage, and side by side, they climbed the front stairs. The door opened just as they reached it.

"Best wishes, your graces," Pennick greeted them with an uncharacteristic smile.

"Thank you," James said.

Lily smiled at the majordomo and started forward, but James scooped her into his arms and carried her inside. Setting her down on her feet, he said, "Aunt Nora ordered me to carry you across the threshold for good luck." He turned to the majordomo, asking, "Are there any messages?"

"One." Pennick passed him a sealed parchment.

Lily didn't know what to do now that she was his

wife and his duchess. She assumed she would have duties but didn't know what.

Ignoring her, James opened the missive and began reading.

"What am I supposed to do now?" Lily asked, losing patience.

James looked at her blankly and then answered, "Do whatever you wish." Without another word, he walked away.

"Thank you for the lovely wedding," Lily called after him. There was no mistaking the anger in her voice. Muttering unintelligible curses, she marched up the stairs to her chamber to discard her wedding gown and burn it in order to end this sham of a wedding day. Then she would deposit the ashes on top of his desk.

Her courage failed her.

Lily couldn't bring herself to destroy the only wedding gown she would ever wear. Hopefully, a day would come when she and James could look back at their wedding and laugh about their foolish behavior.

Dressed for seduction, Lily left her chamber that evening and walked downstairs to the dining room. She'd chosen to wear a Circassian wrapper in ivory silk, a form-fitting gown shaped exactly like a night chemise. It sported a narrow flounce trim and an ivory brocaded ribbon at the waist. The bodice was a low-cut V, and the lace front was shaped to her bosom.

Lily was uncertain whether her husband would even join her for dinner. Though it hurt to admit it, she wouldn't be surprised if he passed his wedding night with that actress.

When she walked into the dining room, Lily paused in the doorway. James stood near the sideboard and spoke with Pennick. The dowager and her sisters were absent.

"Good evening, your grace," she said, starting across the room toward him.

James turned around at the sound of her voice. His expression registered surprise when he dropped his eyes to her gown. His intense gaze pleased her immensely.

Watch what James does, not what he says. Lily recalled Lady Donna's advice. From the expression on her husband's face, Lily knew he wouldn't be seeing his actress that night.

"I'm surprised to see you here," Lily said conversationally. "I thought you might have other plans."

"On my wedding night?" James replied. "Surely I am not so crass as to leave my bride unattended on this special night?"

"I can't help the way my mind works," Lily said. "I'm American."

James escorted her to the chair beside his at the head of the table. He gestured to Pennick, who began to serve them a light supper of tomato soup, a vegetable medley, baked haddock, and a simple garden salad.

"Where are her grace and Ladies Donna and Nora?" Lily asked.

"My mother and aunts have retired to Kinross Park," James said, and then winked at her. "They wanted to give the newlyweds a few weeks of privacy."

"I see." Lily felt herself blushing and peeked at him from beneath the fringe of her ebony lashes.

"How do you ladies do that?" he asked with an amused smile.

"Do what?"

"Blush at precisely the right moment."

"What a cynical remark," she said. "I cannot speak for all women, but I have no control over my blushing."

"I have known several ladies who could blush or weep as needed," James told her.

"I'm sure you have," Lily drawled, irritated that he would speak of other women on their wedding night. "I want to know why you did not allow my brother to walk down the aisle or attend the reception."

"I was protecting Michael," James told her. "Most people will accept his impediment if they become acquainted with him slowly."

"You are lying," Lily said.

"You are overreacting," James countered. "Where your brother is concerned, you are too sensitive and ready to think the worst of others."

"I have many years of experience in seeing the worst others have to offer," she told him. "I also know when someone is lying to me."

"I don't care what you believe," James replied. His dark gaze narrowed on her when he asked, "What possessed you to wear a dagger to church?"

"The dagger was something borrowed," she answered. "The blade did work a miracle."

"My bribe worked the miracle," he corrected her. "Where did you get the dagger?"

"The Duchess of Avon."

"Are you now infecting others with your bad habits?"

"Bad habits?" Lily echoed in surprised anger. "Whatever happened is your fault, not mine. You wanted to marry me. I only wanted to go home."

"I did not want to marry you," James told her. "I wanted my son to carry my name."

Lily felt as if he'd kicked her in the stomach. She leaned back against the chair. Her head swam dizzyingly with humiliation and loss, and her heart ached with the awareness that the wedding had been a sham.

"Are you ill?"

He sounded concerned, but Lily knew better. She refused to answer or even to look at him.

"Excuse me, your grace," Lily said, rising unsteadily to her feet. Without another word, she walked slowly toward the door.

"Congratulations, your grace," she heard the majordomo say. "You have just lost the best thing that ever walked into your life."

"When I want your opinion, Pennick, I'll—"

Lily climbed the stairs to the second-floor library and took down her old friend, *The Complete Works of William Shakespeare*. She would need a friend in the coming days and weeks and years, but defeat and weariness precluded visiting with Shakespeare that night. All she wanted was to climb into bed and sleep forever.

Sitting on the edge of her bed, Lily stared at her wedding ring, a simple band of gold with a scrolled design. She slipped it off her finger and studied it in the candlelight. Too bad their vows meant nothing to her husband.

Lily looked inside the band to see if he had, at least, inscribed their wedding date. There was no date, only the words *A vila mon coeur gardi li mo.*

Why would he inscribe her wedding band in a language she couldn't read? To show her how ignorant a wharf rat she was? What did those words mean? Most likely, his sentiment was "I did not want to marry you."

Lily heard a rattling noise as if from a great distance away. She opened her eyes and realized she'd fallen asleep.

"Lily?" James called, and knocked on the door connecting their chambers. "Are you there?"

Rising from the bed, Lily padded on bare feet across the room. "I'm here," she answered.

"What's wrong with this door?"

"I've blocked it with a chair."

"Open it."

"No."

Did the arrogant bastard actually believe she would allow him entrance to her bed? Did her husband think he could humiliate and hurt her and she would welcome him with open arms?

All was silent for several minutes. Lily turned to walk back to bed when she heard the doorknob rattling and then knocking on the door leading to the corridor.

"Open the door," James ordered.

Lily smiled with satisfaction at the door. "Now, your grace, I have *my* revenge."

God's balls, James thought, staring at the closed door. She was denying him on their wedding night? He wasn't about to take no for an answer, nor would he stand in the corridor and plead for admittance into his bride's bed.

James returned to his chamber to consider his options. Yes, he wanted her. Yes, he loved her. No, he would never profess his love. Even pregnant, she hadn't wanted to marry him.

He'd be damned if he passed his wedding night

alone in his chamber. He would need to apologize for his hurtful words, but how could he apologize if he couldn't get into the room?

And then an outrageous idea spurred James into action. He dropped his black silk bedrobe and dressed in his pants, shirt, and boots.

James found Pennick in the kitchen. With the flick of his wrist, he sent the surprised servants scurrying out of the room.

"Get me a ladder," James ordered his man.

"A ladder?" Pennick echoed in baffled surprise. "Why?"

"I want the ladder propped beneath Lily's bed-chamber window," James explained.

"Are you encouraging her to leave?" the major-domo asked, his tone hostile.

"You have served the Armstrongs for many years, so I will answer your impertinent question this one time only," James replied. "I need a ladder in order to climb into her window. It's an American wedding-night custom."

"Oh." The majordomo's expression cleared.

Twenty minutes later, Duncan and Pennick propped the ladder against the mansion. The Scotsman grinned and gestured to James.

"Once I'm inside, put the ladder away," he instructed them. "I don't want any uninvited guests."

James began climbing the ladder. He whispered a prayer of thanks that the season was summer and she slept with her window open.

James peered inside the window. Lily slept with her back turned toward him.

Once inside, James leaned out the window and gestured to his men. Keeping his gaze on his wife, he pulled off his boots. Next came his shirt and then his breeches.

James walked across the chamber and lay down beside her. He kissed her ear and whispered, "Awaken, my sleeping beauty."

Lily rolled over and looked up at him. Even by candlelight, he could read the drowsy confusion in her sapphire eyes. "How did you get in here?" she asked.

"I climbed through the window," he answered "This is our one and only wedding night. Don't send me away."

"Stay," she whispered.

James dipped his head, his lips covering hers in a soul-stealing kiss that mirrored his long-denied need for her. Leaving her lips, he planted dozens of feathery-light kisses across her cheeks, her temples, her eyelids, and the bridge of her nose.

"My beautiful wife," he whispered against her ear, and heard her sigh.

James removed her sheer white nightgown and, with his tongue, traced the column of her neck down to nibble on her breasts, their nipples enlarged and darkened by pregnancy. Hearing her sharp intake of breath, he suckled upon one breast and then the other until she moaned with desire.

James slid his lips lower to her navel and the inside of her thighs, gently tormenting her with his licking and nipping, kissing every inch of her flesh. Pressing his face against the valley between her thighs, he caressed her dewy pearl with his tongue. Christ, she was so incredibly soft . . . and wet . . . and hot.

Clutching his shoulders, Lily was moaning and grinding her hips against him. She cried out in plea-

sure and melted against his tongue, surrendering herself to him completely.

"I want you inside me," she murmured.

James needed no second invitation. He knelt at her
feet and raised her legs to place them around his
neck. Ever so gently, James pushed himself forward
inside her and then withdrew slowly.

James moaned at the exquisite sensation they were
creating, and his thrusts quickened with his excitement. Lily met each of his thrusts with her grinding
hips.

Groaning and shuddering, James spilled his seed as
Lily clenched him tightly and cried out. He held her
close until her spasms of pleasure lessened and then
ceased.

James kissed her as if he would never let her go.
He lay down beside her and pulled her into the circle
of his embrace.

When she looked up at him, James smiled into her
disarming sapphire eyes. For tonight, he would pretend their marriage was loving. Tomorrow would be
soon enough to face their problems.

"How do you feel?" he asked.

"Jolly good."

James laughed and leaned down to kiss her. He
glided the palm of his hand down to her swollen
breasts, pausing to touch her *alpha* and *omega* cross.
His touch made her sigh.

"Carrying my seed has darkened your nipples,"
James said, one of his fingers tracing a circle around
each nipple. Then, "Are you blushing?" He dropped
a kiss on her forehead and said, "I'll be right back."

Without regard for his nakedness, James rose from
the bed and crossed the chamber. He smiled in her

direction when he dragged the chair away from the connecting door. Grabbing a leather-covered box off his bedside table, James returned to Lily, who had pulled the coverlet up to shield her nakedness.

James sat down beside her and handed her the box, saying, "A wedding gift, your grace."

Lily smiled shyly and opened the lid. Inside the box lay a white diamond bracelet with radiant-cut yellow diamond floral designs.

"The bracelet matches my betrothal ring and necklace," Lily said, leaning close to plant a kiss on his cheek. "It's beautiful, but I wish you wouldn't waste your money."

"You are worth every shilling I spent," James told her, putting his arm around her shoulders and pulling her against the side of his body.

"I'm worth much more than you paid for this bracelet," Lily said with a smile. "Spending *any* money on jewels is a waste of money."

James burst out laughing. "Do you know how many hundreds of English gentlemen would love to hear those words slip from their own wives' mouths?"

"Even if I could have left Armstrong mansion to go shopping, I had no money," Lily said, becoming serious. "I have no wedding gift for you."

James kissed her temple and slid his hand down to her lap to caress her belly. "Darling, your wedding gift will arrive later."

Tilting up her chin, James gazed into her shining, sapphire eyes. And then he kissed her, pouring all his love into that single, stirring kiss.

Nineteen

My husband cares about me.

That was Lily's first thought when she awakened the next morning. James didn't love her yet, but he cared enough to scale the walls and climb through her window like a hero in a romantic tale.

Lily yawned and stretched. She had awakened briefly when James left her for his work, but he had kissed her and told her to go back to sleep. On the one hand, she wanted to close her eyes and replay everything that had transpired from the time her husband had climbed through her bedroom window, but she also wanted to see him and verify in her mind that the previous evening hadn't been a pleasant dream.

Sitting up, Lily saw a note on the bedside table. She read: *Report to my office at noon. We have business to discuss.*

Lily stared at the note in disappointment. She had hoped it would be something romantic, but she supposed a profession of love from her husband would take time.

"Love begets love, and James will be unable to hide his love away forever." Recalling Lady Nora's words made

Lily feel better. Perhaps she wouldn't need Shakespeare's company.

At two minutes before noon, Lily walked down one flight of stairs to her husband's office. He stood when she entered.

With a smile of greeting on his face, James gestured for her to sit in the chair in front of his desk. He sat when she did.

"How do you feel?" James asked. His question was innocuous, but the intimate tone in his voice suggested something more.

"Jolly good," Lily answered, echoing her words of the previous evening, her heart aching with love for him. If only he could love her.

"Thank you for the most wonderful evening of my life," James said in a husky voice. "I've been sitting here all morning picturing in my mind how you looked and felt in my arms last night. I love how pregnancy has darkened your nipples."

Lily felt herself blushing.

"I knew I could make you blush," James said. "Your whole body flushes a rosy pink when we make love."

Lily felt hot, her blush deepening into a vibrant scarlet.

"Let's get down to business," James said. He opened the top right drawer of his desk and withdrew a stack of notes. After counting out a thousand pounds, he returned the extra notes to his desk and pushed the thousand pounds across the top of his desk toward her.

Lily stared blankly at the small pile of notes in front of her. She lifted her gaze to his and said, "I don't understand."

"Our betrothal contract stipulated that I would give you a thousand pounds each month," James told her.

Lily couldn't credit what she was hearing. After the wonderfully romantic night they had shared, her husband had insulted her as no other man had ever done.

"I am not for sale," Lily told him, her anger apparent in her voice.

"This money is not payment for services rendered," James explained, a smile in his voice. "A thousand pounds is pin money, an allowance."

Lily smiled with relief. He hadn't been insulting her at all. "I don't need it," she said.

James burst out laughing. "Sweetness, last night you told me not to buy jewels, and this morning you don't want an allowance?"

Lily nodded. "That is correct."

"What do you want?"

Your love, she thought, but said, "Do I need this money to put a roof over my head or food in my stomach?"

"No."

"Will you pay for any clothing I need?" she asked.

"Yes."

"Will you pay for anything our baby needs?" she asked.

"Yes, of course."

"Then why do I need this money?" she asked.

"Every British lady receives an allowance," James explained. "I want you to be the same as the other ladies."

I'll never be the same as the other ladies, Lily thought in dismay. If he wanted a wife who was the same as the others, he should have married one of them and sent her home.

"A thousand pounds is a lot of money," Lily said. "What if I lose it?"

"You will need to wait until the first of the month for your next allowance," James told her. "You won't get more from me. You'll need to learn how to manage your money."

"What if I refuse to take it?" she asked.

"Darling, this isn't the way things are done," James answered. "If the other ladies learn that you don't receive an allowance, they will speak badly of me to their husbands, and their husbands will think ill of me. I will become the topic of gossip in London."

"I wouldn't want that to happen." Lily reached out, lifted half the bills on the desk, and put them into her pocket. "I'll tell every lady I meet that you give me a thousand pounds for an allowance. However, I want to take only five hundred pounds and invest the other five hundred in your shipping business. Is that possible?"

"I could do that for you," he said. "Shall we get on—"

"I'm not finished yet," Lily interrupted.

James grinned. "Please, continue."

"Do you compute profits and losses monthly or quarterly?" she asked.

"Quarterly," he answered. "How do you know about computing profits and losses?"

"I love reading."

"I thought your preference was Shakespeare and Austen," James said.

"I didn't say I enjoyed reading about mathematics and finances," Lily replied. "I read so quickly that finding new, interesting material is not always possible."

"Where did you manage to find books about finances?" James asked, smiling.

"My former fiancé has an extensive library," she answered.

James lost his smile.

Noting the change in his expression, Lily hurried to get off the subject of her former fiancé. "Each quarter when you compute my share of the profits, I want you to reinvest half and give me the other half."

"What will you do with your profits?" he asked.

"Give it to the less fortunate," she answered.

Her husband looked surprised. "You are going to give money away?"

"I prefer to think of it as investing in another's future," Lily told him. "You did say I could do whatever I wanted with this money."

"And if there is a loss?" James asked, his expression mirroring his amusement.

Lily smiled sweetly. "I have faith in your abilities."

James inclined his head. "Thank you."

"You are welcome."

"I have another item to discuss with you," James said, losing his amused expression.

Lily watched him open the top drawer of his desk and remove two envelopes. He placed both down on his desk in front of her chair.

"Read these," he said.

With a sense of foreboding, Lily leaned forward. The envelopes were addressed to her but had been opened. The handwriting was Bradley's, and she hoped to deflect whatever James planned by taking the offensive.

"You opened letters addressed to me?" Lily said, and there was no mistaking her anger.

James nodded.

"Being a duke doesn't give you the authority to read other people's letters," she told him.

"You are not other people," James said. "You are my wife."

"I really must protest—"

"Open the damned envelopes and read the messages," James ordered in a voice that brooked no disobedience. "The one on the left arrived yesterday. The other arrived this morning."

Lily didn't want to read them. She stared at the envelopes and wondered how she could explain them away. Hopefully, Bradley hadn't written anything that would get Seth and himself hanged.

"Read them," James ordered again.

Lily lifted the first envelope off the desk. Her heart sank to her stomach when she read Bradley's note from the previous day.

It's not too late to escape before you marry the duke. We are staying at the Bedford Lodge in Kensington.

Lily stared at the note. She didn't know what to do. If she explained that Bradley was her former fiancé, Seth and he could be hanged as spies. All she had ever wanted was love for herself and a safe haven for Michael.

"Read the other," James said curtly, his voice cutting into her thoughts.

Lily lifted the second envelope off his desk. She opened it slowly, fearing what it would say. This one was even worse than the first.

You have done your duty. Your child has his father's name. You can escape with a clear conscience.

Lily stared in defeat at the note in her lap. How could she ever explain this without endangering her brother and Bradley? She understood that Bradley was in pain, but his notes had ruined whatever chance she'd had to win her husband's love. Perhaps she should have told Bradley that she loved James—

"What do you have to say?" James asked.

"Nothing."

"Damn it, look at me when I speak to you," James ordered, slamming his hand on the desk.

Lily snapped her sapphire gaze to his. She could have wept when she saw the coldness in his expression.

"You have been planning an escape," James said.

"No, I—"

"Don't bother lying," he interrupted. "The truth is written in those notes."

Lily wished she could tell him the truth. She knew she would never enjoy happiness if she jeopardized the lives of Seth and Bradley.

"Mr. Hampstead sounds like a man in love," James said, his black gaze fixed on her. "Are you having an affair with him?"

"How can you ask that?" Lily cried, insulted by the suggestion. "I never met him until my come-out ball, and I have been supervised in this house every moment of every day except for my carriage ride with Isabelle."

James appeared to relax a bit. He sat back in his chair and stared at her, as if mulling something over in his mind.

"If you like, have me guarded until the Americans leave England," Lily said, trying to make amends. "I won't mind in the least."

"You obviously want to go home," James said after

a few minutes. "I'll return you to Boston once the child is delivered. My son will remain with me."

Stunned speechless, Lily could only stare in horror at him. Tears welled up in her eyes, and her hands began to tremble.

"I won't leave my baby," she said finally.

"You have no choice," James told her. "I'm sending you home after the baby is delivered. No court will deny me a divorce."

"I won't go," Lily cried, bolting out of the chair. "I won't leave my baby." Sobbing, she ran out of his office.

"Lily!" James started to go after her but stopped at the door. She wouldn't listen to his apology now.

What had he done? Jealousy had made him cruel, and his chest ached with guilty remorse.

She was planning to escape with his son, James told himself. Wasn't she? What other explanation could there be for those notes. If there had been another explanation, she would have defended herself. Perhaps he should have let the notes reach her and watched what she did.

James poured himself a whiskey, sat down at his desk, and downed the drink in one gulp. Strange; he had never indulged in spirits before noon until he met his wife.

Leaning back in his chair, James propped his feet up on the desk and closed his eyes. What was he going to do about Lily? He loved her and couldn't let her go. If only she'd had an explanation for those notes.

The door crashed open, and James opened his eyes. Dragging something heavy in each hand, Michael marched across his office and halted when he reached the desk. With two hands, the boy lifted a sword and tossed it at James, who leaped out of his chair. The sword was old but still capable of maiming or killing a man.

"Fight like a man," Michael ordered, lifting the second sword.

James struggled to keep from laughing. "Where did you get these?"

"The wall."

"I thought we were friends," James asked. "Why do you want to fight me?"

"You made my sister cry," Michael answered. The boy pointed at the sword lying on the desk and ordered, "Pick it up."

"I made Lily cry?" James asked.

Michael nodded and again pointed at the sword.

"And you want revenge?"

"What's that?"

"Revenge is hitting back," James told him.

"That's what I want," Michael said.

"I was angry and said some bad things to Lily," James admitted.

"You shouldn't have done that, Duke," Michael said.

"If I apologize to her, can we be friends again?"

Michael paused for a long moment.

"I have a secret I can share with you," James coaxed the boy. "If I promise to apologize and tell you the secret, can we be friends?"

Michael nodded.

"Do you promise not to tell Lily my secret?"

"I promise."

"The secret is that I love Lily," James told the boy. "She can never know because she doesn't love me."

"Yes, she does."

"Did Lily tell you that?"

"No."

"Do you still want to fight?"

"I'll put this back," Michael said, reaching for the sword on the desk.

"I'll do that later," James said. "Leave your sword here, too."

"Apologize to Lily or die," Michael warned, and then left the office.

James sat down and smiled as the door closed behind him. Lily was correct: Michael could make God smile.

James heard a knock, and then the door opened. With a smile of greeting, Sloane walked across the office, saying, "You wanted to see me?"

James nodded. "There is a matter I want to discuss with you," he said, gesturing to the chair in front of the desk.

Sloane sat down and, with his gaze on the swords, asked, "Who are you fighting?"

"Michael dragged those in here and challenged me to a duel," James said, smiling.

"And?"

"I persuaded him that we were friends."

James stared at his cousin for a moment. Sloane seemed so affable, it was difficult to believe his greed had made him a murderer. Still, his cousin was the only person in the world who had a motive for killing him.

"Reggie St. Leger has proposed a possible match between you and Valentina," James told him.

Sloane burst out laughing. "You must be insane even to mention it to me."

"Don't give me an answer now," James said. "Take a few days to consider the proposition."

"I don't need to con—"

"Think about it."

"I don't love Valentina," Sloane said.

"Many husbands do not love their wives," James reminded him.

"You do."

James let that remark slide by. He wasn't about to admit to loving Lily to his cousin and then be humiliated when she left him. He wanted no man's pity.

"I can make the deal very sweet for you," James said.

Sloane looked insulted. "I'm not for sale."

His cousin sounded exactly like his wife, James thought. "Take a couple of weeks to think it over," he said. "You can do that for me, can't you?"

"Of course, but I guarantee my answer won't change."

James inclined his head and lied, "If you will excuse me, I have another appointment." He wanted to spend as little time as possible with the man who had murdered his brother.

Thirty minutes after Sloane left, Pennick walked into his office and said, "The Earl of Bovingdon requests an interview."

"Send him in," James instructed his man.

"Shall I interrupt in ten minutes?" Pennick asked.

"That won't be necessary."

When Reggie St. Leger walked into his office a moment later, he wore his usual ingratiating smile. "Good afternoon, your grace," he said.

"Good to see you, Reggie," James said, and gestured to a chair. "Sit down."

"Your grace, I thoroughly enjoyed your wedding and was so impressed by your toast to your wife," St. Leger said. "I can only hope that someday I will feel the same way about a special woman."

"I'm certain you will." James cleared his throat and said, "I've just had an interview with my cousin and broached the subject of his marriage to Valentina."

"And?"

"Sloane seemed very interested," James lied. "However, he gave me no final answer."

"I see."

"My cousin's major concern was with what Valentina wanted," James elaborated on his lie. "You did say the American had been escorting her around town."

"The American is a novelty," St. Leger told him. "My sister has enough common sense to marry an Englishman although, at times, she doesn't show it."

"One of Valentina's charms is hiding that common sense of hers," James replied.

"I understand that congratulations are in order," St. Leger said, changing the subject.

His remark baffled James. "What do you mean?"

"Congratulations on your impending fatherhood," St. Leger said.

"How do you know about that?" James asked, the other man's knowledge surprising him.

St. Leger shrugged. "Bets are being waged at White's on whether the babe is a boy or a girl."

"I suppose nobody in this town has secrets," James remarked, uncomfortable with others knowing what should have been a secret. He didn't like his personal business a topic for the gossips.

"Pardon my impertinence, your grace," St. Leger

said with a smile, "but I had a thought that might interest you."

James arched a dark brow at him. "Speak freely, Reggie."

"I wondered if it's wise for your wife to remain in London," St. Leger said. "The man who tried to assassinate you could turn his attention to her."

"I hadn't considered that," James said. Lily would be safer with his mother and his aunts at Kinross Park, which would also take her out of the American's path.

"I am leaving for Bovingdon later and could escort her grace to Kinross Park," St. Leger offered.

James stared at him for a moment and then rose from his desk to cross the office to the bell-pull. Pennick appeared a few minutes later.

"Your grace?"

"Ask her grace to come to my office," James said. "Tell her it's important."

When Lily appeared, James cringed inwardly. Her beautiful sapphire eyes were swollen and red-rimmed, and she looked hopeless, as if she'd lost her last friend in the world.

"Your grace, I hope you are well," St. Leger said, rising from his chair.

Lily ignored him.

"I am sending you and Michael to Kinross Park," James told her.

"Why?" Lily asked, a stricken look on her face.

"I'm sending you for your own safety," James explained, feeling guilty for threatening her. "Whoever tried to assassinate me could decide to target you. You'll be safe with my mother and aunts."

Lily nodded.

James felt relieved. At least he hadn't needed to fight with her about this.

"When do we leave?" she asked.

"Today. Pack an overnight bag and I'll send the rest of your belongings tomorrow," James said. "Can you be ready in an hour?"

"Yes."

James stared at her for a long moment. She seemed so listless and defeated. He could have kicked himself for threatening to take their baby away. Somehow he would make it up to her.

"The Earl of Bovingdon has agreed to escort you and Michael," James told her.

"Unless you would prefer that Sloane accompany you," St. Leger said.

"No, I prefer you."

She spoke so quickly that James wondered if his wife also had doubts about his cousin. Once she was safely ensconced at Kinross Park, he would finally confront Sloane.

"Give me an hour to pack a bag and get my coach," St. Leger said.

"You'll take my coach and a few outriders," James told him.

"It's safer to take my coach and no outriders," St. Leger replied. "No one will suspect that the Duchess of Kinross is riding in my coach to Kinross Park."

"Lily, what do you think?" James asked, trying to include her in the decision.

"The earl's coach will be best," she answered, "but he must bring it around to the alley so that no one sees us leave."

James nodded. It sounded reasonable to him.

"Michael and I will be ready," Lily said, and then left the office.

James escorted St. Leger to the foyer. Pennick was closing the door on a courier.

"This just arrived for you," Pennick said, holding the envelope out to him.

"For me or her grace?"

"For you."

James opened the envelope and read the message from Adam St. Aubyn. *Come to White's as soon as possible. Urgent.*

Two hours later, after sending Lily on her way to Kinross Park, James walked into White's Gentlemen's Club. The hour was early, the club almost deserted.

"What kept you so long?" Adam asked, meeting him at the door. "Saint-Germain and I were beginning to wonder if you would show."

"I sent Lily to Kinross Park," James answered, walking with his friend to their usual chairs.

James stared in surprise at the men seated with John Saint-Germain, Hampstead and Hawkins. He turned a cold eye on Hampstead, who'd written those notes to his wife.

"I have gathered everyone here because Isabelle was unable to keep silent," John Saint-Germain said with a smile. "She worried for all involved in this situation."

"Thank God for that," Adam St. Aubyn said.

James had no idea what his friends were talking about. The only situation here was that Hampstead was trying to steal his wife.

"These American are *not* spies," Saint-Germain told James. "Their government sent them here to investigate you. The Americans believe you murdered Hugh."

"Investigate me?" James echoed in surprised anger. With his hands clenched into fists, he bolted out of the chair and stared down at Hampstead, saying, "First you try to steal my wife and now you accuse me of murdering my own brother. Let's settle this outside."

John Saint-Germain and Adam St. Aubyn started to laugh. Even the American, Seth Hawkins, grinned, as if he was privy to a joke that James knew nothing about.

The only man not smiling was Bradley Hampstead. The American started to rise to meet the challenge, but Hawkins grabbed his arm in a gesture to remain seated.

"Sit down, James," Adam said, still smiling. "You should know who they are before you call them out."

John Saint-Germain chuckled and gestured to Hawkins, saying, "Meet Seth Hawthorne, your brother-in-law."

James studied Seth and then offered his hand, saying, "You do have the look of my wife."

"Lily has the look of me," Seth corrected him, shaking his hand.

"Meet Bradley Howell, your wife's former fiancé," Adam said, gesturing to Hampstead.

James looked from Seth to Bradley. He couldn't credit what he was hearing; then all of Lily's subterfuge made sense. She hadn't told him the truth because she feared her brother would hang as a spy. She'd had no explanation for Hampstead's notes for the same reason.

"Stay away from my wife," James warned Bradley. "That includes sending her notes."

Bradley Howell looked as if he wanted to strangle him. "Lily belonged to me long before you sailed into her life," the man said.

"Lily belongs to me now," James told him. "In fact, she's carrying my child." When neither American seemed surprised, James knew that Lily had sent them a message.

"Divorce and adoption will remedy that problem," Bradley countered.

Intent on beating the American senseless, James lunged for him, but Adam leaped up and pulled him back. "Settle your differences later," Adam said. "We need to catch a killer, or you will soon be dead by the same hand."

"My cousin killed Hugh and tried to assassinate me," James said, sitting down again.

When the last word slipped from his lips, James spied his cousin walking through the door. Sloane wore a smile of greeting as he crossed the room to the small group.

"Pennick told me you were here," Sloane said, dragging a chair closer to sit down with them.

"We need to speak to you," John Saint-Germain said.

"My cousin isn't stupid," James told the other man. "He'll never admit to it."

"Admit what?" Sloane asked, a confused expression on his face.

"Admit you killed Hugh and tried to assassinate me," James told him.

Sloane burst out laughing. "You must be joking. Was your intended revenge marrying me off to Valentina?"

"Mistress St. Leger is returning with me to Boston," Seth announced.

All of the men turned to stare at him as if he'd grown another head. Only Bradley Howell wasn't surprised.

"Val doesn't know my plans for her," Seth said, grinning broadly. "I have decided to imitate the Duke of Kinross and steal a bride."

"I'll loan you one of my ships," James told him.

"Let us return to a more serious matter," John Saint-Germain said.

"Sloane, do you deny that you killed Hugh and tried to assassinate James?" Adam asked.

"You're serious?" Sloane turned to James, his expression a mixture of anger and hurt. "How could you think that of me?"

"If you aren't guilty, I apologize," James said coldly.

"You don't sound sorry," Sloane replied.

"I'll be convinced of your innocence when we catch the villain," James told him.

"So, who wants you dead?" Seth asked. "Excepting Bradley, of course."

"The question is who benefits by his death," John Saint-Germain said.

"Sloane inherits everything if I die without an heir," James said.

"Refresh my memory," Sloane said. "When did the attempts on your life occur?"

"The first one was when I returned to London to cry off my engagement to Valentina," James answered. "The second was after Lily's come-out ball."

"That's the night your betrothal to Lily was announced," Sloane said.

James nodded.

"I would never have believed him capable of it," Sloane said. "Don't you see who would benefit from your death?"

"No, I don't," James said.

"While Hugh and I were in Boston, Reggie St. Leger pushed for your betrothal to Valentina because he knew Hugh would never return," Sloane explained.

"Now I understand," Adam said to Sloane. "When James cried off his betrothal to Valentina, Reggie tried to have him assassinated because he wanted his sister to marry you, the next in line for the Armstrong fortune."

"This is absurd," James told them. "Reggie isn't capable of killing a flea."

"He doesn't need to kill anyone if he hires someone else to do it for him," John Saint-Germain said. "He squandered his own fortune and needed yours to support his gambling."

"God's balls," James exclaimed, bolting out of his chair. "Reggie is escorting Lily to Kinross Park." He raced for the door and, scrambling to their feet, the other men followed him on the run.

Twenty

Her husband wanted to be rid of her.

Lily tried to keep that thought at bay, but her worries seeped through her defenses. She focused on the world outside the coach in an effort to erase the disturbing thoughts from her mind.

The late afternoon sun was casting long shadows across the road. Along the edges of lush, green woodland appeared the first of the goldenrods, splashes of deep yellow hinting at autumn's glory. Purple asters and chicory harmonized with the deep pink bull thistle and the pale pink marjoram.

Lily couldn't help comparing nature's serenity with her own inner turmoil. Would she ever find peace of mind for herself and a safe haven for Michael?

"I cannot believe I am escorting a pig to St. Albans," the Earl of Bovingdon said, breaking into her thoughts.

"I beg your pardon?" Lily said.

St. Leger pointed at Michael, sitting beside her. "That pig should be cooked, not pampered."

"Princess is my pet," Michael told him, and then wiped his chin on the sleeve of his shirt.

St. Leger turned away, as if he couldn't bear to look

at her brother. He seemed to fix his gaze on the passing scenery.

Lily studied the earl from beneath the fringe of her lashes. He was blond like his sister, but what was beautiful on the woman became insipid on the man.

"Why does this coach catch every bump in the road?" Lily complained.

"I cannot afford to buy the best on the market like his grace," St. Leger told her, and then smiled. "All that is about to change, though."

"How so?"

"I have excellent prospects."

"We've been riding for more than an hour," Lily said. "The bumps are making me queasy. I want to stop to stretch my legs."

St. Leger glanced out the window. "Verulamium Woods is just ahead. We'll stop there."

Ten minutes later, St. Leger banged on the coach's roof and shouted to stop. The driver reined the horses to a stop at the side of the road.

St. Leger disembarked first. Then he turned to assist Lily and Michael.

"A river lies beyond that cluster of trees, your grace," St. Leger said with an ingratiating smile. "Would you care to walk there?"

Lily nodded and started toward the trees. She didn't like the sniveling Earl of Bovingdon and wished he would disappear. If the earl had been a dog, he would have flopped belly up on the ground and groveled before her title.

The water looked crisp, clean, and oh-so-inviting. Crouching down at the river's edge, Lily cupped water into her hands and patted it on her face. The coolness of the water revived and refreshed her.

Standing, Lily turned around and was surprised to find the earl only a few inches away. "What are you—"

St. Leger reached up to grab her throat, but Lily kneed his groin. While he doubled over in pain, she ran toward the cluster of trees. If only she could get to the road.

Glancing over her shoulder to see him chasing her, Lily tripped and fell. She saved her baby by breaking the fall with her hands.

"Michael," she cried as the earl reached her.

St. Leger fell to his knees to straddle her body. He grabbed her throat and began to squeeze.

Lily pummeled his face with her fists, but he wouldn't let her go. She couldn't breath and felt herself weakening.

St. Leger screamed suddenly and fell to one side, his hand clutching his neck. A small trickle of blood seeped from a wound.

Michael stood there, his last-resort dagger in his hand. He knelt beside the earl and pointed the tip of his blade against the man's jugular vein.

"Move and die," Michael threatened.

"The brat cut me," St. Leger howled, but he refrained from moving.

Still wheezing and gasping for breath, Lily pushed herself up to a sitting position. She drew her own dagger and pointed it at the earl's face.

"Brother, thank you for saving my life," Lily said hoarsely. "You are truly a hero."

"You are welcome, Sister," Michael said, grinning with pride. "What do we do now?"

"Let's cut off his nose and feed it to Princess," Lily said.

"That won't be necessary," said a voice from behind them.

Keeping her dagger aimed at the earl's throat, Lily glanced toward the voice. James stood there, and a wave of relief washed through her. Sloane, Adam St. Aubyn, and John Saint-Germain stood behind him. Seth and Bradley were there, too.

Adam St. Aubyn and John Saint-Germain rushed forward and forced St. Leger onto his stomach. Adam tied the earl's hands behind his back, and John yanked him up to a sitting position.

With a smile on her face, Lily turned to her husband. Bradley Howell stood there to help her up and pulled her protectively against his body. "Are you injured?" he asked.

Lily shook her head. "Michael saved my life," she said, her voice still raspy.

"Good job, Brother," Seth said, putting his arm around him.

Michael beamed with pride. "I'm a hero."

Lily wondered why her husband was ignoring her. She turned in Bradley's embrace to watch him and Sloane confront the earl.

"We know your game," Sloane was saying.

"I don't know what you mean," St. Leger said.

"Admit your crimes, Reggie," James said.

"I have nothing to say," St. Leger replied.

"I'll take care of this," Michael said. Before anyone could stop him, the boy dropped to his knees beside the earl and pointed the dagger at the man's cheek.

"Tell the truth," Michael threatened. "Or else . . ."

St. Leger said nothing.

Michael scratched the earl's cheek with the tip of his dagger, drawing blood.

"Call the brat off," St. Leger cried.

"Start talking, Reggie," James ordered.

"Did you hire an assassin to kill Hugh?" Sloane asked.

"Hugh brought that on himself," St. Leger answered. "He wasn't interested in marrying Valentina."

"And you tried to assassinate me?" James asked.

"You shouldn't have broken your betrothal to Valentina," St. Leger told him.

"How were you planning to explain Lily's death?" James asked.

"She was going to fall into the river and drown," St. Leger answered. "The brat was going to drown trying to save her."

"Reggie, you'll hang for this," John Saint-Germain told him.

"You killed my brother and nearly killed my wife," James snarled, grabbing him by the throat. "I ought to beat you to death right here and save the courts a hanging."

"Hanging is too good for him, and dragging him through the courts could become messy," Adam spoke up. "I have a better idea."

"What is it?" James asked.

"We'll give Reggie to Captain Roberts to use as one of his seamen," Adam answered. "When Roberts is returning to England, he will transfer Reggie to one of your ships leaving port."

"I like it," John Saint-Germain said. "Reggie will enjoy a life of hard labor at sea."

"I won't go," St. Leger told them. "I'll shout your crime to the world."

"I don't think so," Sloane said. He removed his cravat and gagged the earl.

"Let's do it," James agreed with the others.

James turned around and walked toward Lily. She would have thrown herself into his arms, but Bradley kept a tight grip on her.

"I know you lied to protect your brother," James said. "I would have done the same. Please forgive me for threatening you."

"In your position, I would have believed the worst of me, too," Lily replied. She stared into his dark gaze trying to find a spark of love.

Before she could say more, Bradley intruded on the moment. "I still love you, Lily," he said, refusing to release her from his embrace. "I will marry you even with another man's child."

Lily looked into his eyes and saw love and hope shining in them. She turned to James, whose expression remained shuttered, and waited for him to say something.

"Do what you want," James said, and left her there.

Lily watched him walk away, a lump of raw emotion sticking in her throat, making speech impossible. He didn't love her and was willing to let her go, even if he had to relinquish his own child.

Lily wanted to throw herself down and weep forever but managed to keep her tears at bay. She would weep in private. Allowing others to see her pain wouldn't change her situation. Her husband was sending her back to the Boston wharves where she belonged.

Four hours later, Lily sat in her chamber at the Bedford Lodge in Kensington. Michael had gone to supper with Seth and Bradley, but she'd begged off as being too tired. Seth had brought her a tray, which she'd promptly given to Princess, now curled up at the foot of the bed.

Would James ever want to see their child? she wondered, her thoughts in a devastated turmoil. Would he divorce her as soon as possible? Which of those young ladies she'd met would he marry once he was free of her?

Leaving England would be best, Lily told herself. She could never be happy with a husband who didn't love her, and she wouldn't want him to stay with her because of the baby.

With tears streaming down her face, Lily fingered her *alpha* and *omega* cross. There would be no first and last love for her. She had never realized how painful love could be.

"Lock it," Lily said in a choked whisper, hearing the door open. She heard her brother walking across the chamber, looked up at him, and smiled sadly.

"Why are you crying?" Michael asked.

Lily patted the edge of the bed beside her. When he sat down, she put her arm around his shoulders and said, "I love Duke, but he doesn't love me."

"Duke loves you," Michael said. "He told me yesterday."

"Duke loves me?" Lily echoed in surprise.

"He told me to keep the secret," Michael said. "Holy hell, I'm in trouble now."

"Do you want to stay in England?" Lily asked, feeling as if a heavy weight had been lifted off her heart.

Michael nodded. "I like merry olde England."

Lily strapped her dagger to her leg. Then she pulled on her boots and grabbed her cloak.

"Do you still have your dagger?" she asked.

"Heroes are always prepared," Michael said, slapping the side of his boot, which hid the blade.

"We'll sneak down the servants' stairs," Lily told him, scooping Princess into her arms. "Tomorrow Duke will tell Seth that we're staying in England." She paused and stared into her brother's sapphire eyes, so much like her own. "Are you certain about wanting to stay with me?"

"Sister, we'll always stay together," Michael said, touching her arm.

"I don't know how I could live without you," Lily told him, tears welling up in her eyes.

"Why are you crying now?" he asked.

"I'm crying because you make me happy."

Michael gave her a wholly disgusted look and said, "Girls are stupid."

Lily smiled. "Follow me."

"Wait! We need to fix the bed so Seth will think we're sleeping," Michael said.

Lily watched him in amused amazement. Michael pulled the bed's coverlet back and positioned the pillows lengthwise. Then he pulled the coverlet up, covering the pillows completely. The bed looked as if two people were sleeping hidden beneath the coverlet.

Carrying Princess in the crook of her left arm, Lily put a finger across her lips in a gesture for silence. She opened the door, peered outside into the deserted corridor, and led the way toward the servants' stairs at the rear of the building.

"Excuse us," Lily called to the cook and his staff when the narrow stairway ended in the kitchen.

"Just passing through," Michael called, and followed his sister out the door to the back alley.

Lily and Michael walked the length of Kensington Road until they reached Park Lane. From there, they turned right onto Upper Brook Street.

An hour after leaving Bedford Lodge, Lily and Michael stood in front of the Armstrong mansion. Lily suffered one awful moment of doubt and then rushed up the stairs to knock on the door before her courage failed her.

"Welcome home, your grace," Pennick greeted her, and stepped back to allow her entrance.

"Michael and I are staying in England," Lily told him. "Where is his grace?"

"I believe his grace had urgent business at the docks," Pennick answered.

"Don't tell his grace I'm here," Lily instructed the majordomo. "I want to surprise him."

"As you wish, your grace."

Lily walked up the stairs behind her brother and handed him Princess when they reached the third floor. After being certain he went directly to his chamber, Lily walked into her husband's bedchamber and undressed down to her chemise. Then she sat down to wait.

An hour passed.

Lily felt herself dozing off. She opened the window to let the cool night air into the room and then returned to the chair.

When she heard the door opening, Lily sat up in alertness. What would James say when he discovered her there? What should she say to him?

And then Lily knew. She reached down and drew her dagger from its sheath, lying on top of the pile of her clothing.

James walked into the chamber. He undressed without bothering to light a candle, leaving a trail of clothing from the door to the open window.

Standing behind him, Lily touched the tip of her dagger to the back of his neck. "Don't move or I'll skewer you like a sausage on a stick," she threatened in a whisper, echoing the words she'd spoken at their first meeting.

"What do you want?" James asked, his weariness apparent in his voice.

He sounds tired, Lily thought, her heart breaking at the pain she heard in his voice. What fools they'd been, each too proud to speak of love.

"Well, Lily?"

He didn't sound as if he loved her, but she would try anyway. What could he do but send her back to Bedford Lodge?

"I want you to love me as much as I love you," Lily told him, and tossed the dagger on the floor.

With a groan of relief, James whirled around and yanked her into his arms, crushing her against his body. He lowered his head, his lips capturing hers in a demanding, soul-stealing kiss.

"I love you," James told her, holding her against his body as if he would never let her go. "I have loved you from the first moment I saw you."

Lily felt as if she'd finally come home. She'd found that special place of refuge for herself and her brother.

She rested her cheek against the solidness of his chest, and he rested his chin on the crown of her head. They stood as one for a long time.

"*Alpha* and *omega,*" Lily whispered, touching the gold cross he wore. "You are my first, my last, my only love."

James tilted her chin up and covered her mouth with his own. He poured all his love into that kiss. It melted into another. And then another . . .

Kinross Park, February 1814

"I am so relieved that Sarah Michael is a normal, healthy baby," Lily said, her sapphire gaze fixed on the infant suckling upon her nipple.

"Sarah Michael?" James echoed, perching on the edge of the bed beside her.

"Would you mind terribly if I named her for my mother?" Lily asked, casting him a flirtatious look.

James smiled. "Your mother's name was Michael?"

"My mother's name was Sarah," Lily answered, moving her daughter to her right arm to offer her the other nipple. "Michael is in honor of my brother."

"Look at the way her little mouth moves," James said, his gaze on his daughter. "Sarah Michael loves sucking on your nipples almost as much as I do."

"Thank you, darling," Lily said, leaning close to plant a kiss on his cheek.

"Are you ready for company?" James asked when they heard the knock on the door.

"Yes," Lily answered, disengaging her daughter's mouth from her nipple and covering her breast.

"Enter," James called.

The door opened. Michael, the dowager, and Ladies Donna and Nora walked into the chamber and surrounded the bed.

"Where is Princess?" Lily asked her brother.

"I will not allow that pig near my granddaughter," the dowager announced.

"I see a bright future for her," Lady Nora said.

"What a beautiful girl," Lady Donna gushed. "She'll be a real heartbreaker."

"What do you think, Brother?" Lily asked.

"I think she's wrinkled," Michael blurted out, making everyone laugh.

"The wrinkles will smooth out," James assured him.

"We've named her Sarah Michael," Lily told her brother. "If you hadn't saved my life, Sarah Michael wouldn't be here."

"Where would she be?" Michael whispered, making everyone smile.

"Sarah Michael would be with us and our mother in heaven," Lily answered. "When she's old enough to understand, will you tell her the story of Michael the Archangel?"

Michael beamed with pride. "I'll tell her the story every day."

"I believe it's time we allowed the proud parents some privacy with their new daughter," the dowager announced.

Lady Nora slipped her arm through Michael's and escorted him out. Lady Donna followed behind them, calling over her shoulder, "Tess, are you coming with us?"

"I'll be with you in a moment," the dowager answered. She turned a stern gaze on James, saying, "I want to see a grandson before I die."

"We'll start working on that as soon as possible," James promised.

"See that you do."

Alone again, Lily and James sat in silence for a time and watched the amazing sight of their daughter sleeping. James reached inside his jacket and produced an envelope.

"This arrived from Boston yesterday," he told her.

"What a surprise," Lily drawled, looking at the letter from her brother. "You haven't opened it."

"Touché, darling."

"Read it to me," Lily said, passing it back to him.

James opened the letter, read it, and put it aside. "Seth says that Valentina is finally starting to settle into her new life as the wife of a tavern owner. At least, they're not fighting as frequently."

Lily laughed. "I cannot imagine Valentina living on the Boston docks."

"Your brother had news of your former fiancé," James added. "Bradley Howell married Hortensia MacDugal."

"Poor Bradley," Lily said. "If I had known what leaving him would do—" She kissed her husband's cheek and then finished, "I would have stayed with you in England anyway."

"Thank you, darling." James leaned close and nuzzled her neck.

"There's a question I've been wanting to ask you for a long time," Lily said.

"What is it?"

"If you loved me so much, why were you willing to let me return to Boston?" she asked.

"I thought you loved Bradley Howell," James answered. "If you had bothered to look inside your wedding band at the inscription, you would have known I loved you."

"I did read the inscription, but it's not English."

"*A vila mon coeur li mo* is French," James told her. "It means *Here is my heart, guard it well.*"

"Kiss me," Lily whispered.

Being careful not to jostle their daughter, James

drew Lily closer against his body and tilted her chin up. He lowered his head, his lips claiming hers in a kiss as passionate as his love for her.

"How does it feel to tame a duke's heart?" he asked.

"Jolly good."

ABOUT THE AUTHOR

Patricia Grasso lives in Massachusetts. She is the author of nine historical romances and is currently working on her tenth, which will be published by Zebra Books in July 2002. Pat loves hearing from readers, and you may write her c/o Zebra Books. Please include a self-addressed stamped envelope if you wish a response.

Put a Little Romance in Your Life With
Constance O'Day-Flannery

Discover the Romances of
Hannah Howell

Put a Little Romance in Your Life With
Betina Krahn